John
Peter
Andrew
James
Philip
Matthew and six other disciples.
But of all the twelve, John was the one
Jesus loved best, the beloved disciple,
the apostle of love and peace. He was
born a son of thunder, full of fire and
storm, but Jesus' transforming touch
made him the eagle of the church.
This is his story—

JOHN
Son of Thunder

Ellen Gunderson Traylor

LIVING BOOKS

Tyndale House Publishers, Inc.

Wheaton, Illinois

Second printing, Living Books edition, August 1981

Library of Congress Catalog Card Number 77-93755
ISBN 0-8423-1902-6, paper,
0-8423-1903-4 Living Books edition
Copyright © 1979 by Ellen Gunderson Traylor
All rights reserved
Printed in the United States of America

To my own
BELOVED JOHN
my husband
without whose unfailing
love and encouragement
not one page would have
been written.

WE KNOW HIM AS THE ONE JESUS LOVED, THE
BELOVED DISCIPLE, THE APOSTLE OF LOVE
AND PEACE. BUT HE WAS BORN A SON OF
THUNDER, FULL OF FIRE AND STORM, AND
WAS HARNESSED TO BE THE EAGLE OF THE
CHURCH.

CONTENTS

Beloved, let us love one another: for love is of God; and every one that loveth is born of God, and knoweth God. He that loveth not, knoweth not God; for God is love.

1 John 4:7,8

A Note to the Reader

This is the second work of biblical fiction I have written. The first, *Song of Abraham,* was well received, and for this I am humbly grateful. However, I feel that the practice of creating fiction based on the lives and times of biblical characters may, for some, seem of no spiritual value, or may even be judged as taking unnecessary liberties with God's Word.

Writing historical fiction (whether based on stories from the Bible or on the pages of secular history) is a creative adventure. It should allow the author the same creative joys experienced by writers of purely fanciful literature. However, the very nature of historical novels binds their authors in some measure to the confines of facts. And it is at this point that pure imagination must bow to reality.

Even more limiting is the *biblical* historical novel. Especially if an author reveres the Scriptures, as I do, he will not want in any way to contradict them. He will, in fact, want them to be the foundation on which his plot is based, and the source of any spiritual truths he hopes to illuminate.

It is only after this base has been established, that the Christian author should allow his imagination to have creative expression.

But this is not to say that everything in the work is meaningless except for that which is purely scriptural. I contend that there is much of value in "sanctified imagination." Almost everyone who reads Scripture pictures in his own mind settings and characters left vague for us by the biblical writers. We cannot help it. We filter anything we read, biblical or secular, through our own experiences, and relate to people we have not met and stories we have not lived by comparing them with our own acquaintances and personal histories. If we have never in any way experienced a part of what we read, or ever met such characters, we benefit by "imagining" what they must have felt and endured, what life must have been like for them.

And in this there is nothing wrong. Our imaginations are God-given, just as are our eyes. We should thank the Creator for our sense of "inner vision," and if we allow it to be God-directed, it will serve us most beneficially. I believe God uses the yielded biblical fiction writer to aid the reader's imagination, to shed upon it new light and understanding.

A writer's years of research and prayerful consideration can help to fill in the gaps in the biblical narrative for the reader who has no time, background, or inclination toward deep study or contemplation. Mistakes are made, and new archaeological and historical data is often found, but if the characters are delineated, if the truths of God's Word are brought into sharper focus, the author has served his purpose.

It is true that none of us can know with certainty what Abraham was like, what John, or Peter or Paul were like, until we meet them in eternity. But my recommendation is that the reader study the portions of the Bible on which a novel is based, preferably beforehand. Then I ask that he judge the author's work critically and sympathetically. If nothing else, he will have given consideration to God's Word.

In regard to my work, I will receive suggestions graciously and gratefully, giving a list of sources and answering questions on request.

The credit for a work of this magnitude cannot justly go to the author alone. Therefore, I wish to acknowledge the encouragement of Dr. Victor Oliver early in the project, and the dedicated contributions of my editors, Virginia Muir and Isabel Erickson, as well as my research consultant, Dr. Walter Elwell.

If *John, Son of Thunder* blesses even one reader, if it serves to draw him closer to Christ, I shall be forever thankful.

Ellen Traylor
Spokane, Wash.

I

THE VOICE IN THE WILDERNESS

He said, I am the voice of one crying in the wilderness, Make straight the way of the Lord.
JOHN 1:23

Chapter 1

Hot blasts of desert wind scoured the yellow earth. Under a vaporless sky, the terrain lay barren and desolate. Somewhere far to the east, and at a higher elevation, lay the beauty of ancient Gilead with its legendary oaks and herds of cattle, its fertile hills and crowning forests. But this was Bethabara, the house of the shallow crossing at the Jordan. And this was the wilderness.

The muddy and meager river, which for all its ignominy had played such a vital role in the history of the region, flowed through banks of marl and jungle undergrowth at a surprising rate. To the west of the Jordan lay the gentle slopes of Galilee and Samaria. But to the east, the hills of Decapolis, which ascended abruptly two thousand feet to a great tableland, held the scorching winds within the valley.

Despite abundant vegetation, the ford was extremely sparse in its support of human life. It was a place for jackals, wild beasts, and empty, whistling breezes. It tasted of the very essence of loneliness, this vacuous tract of land. The Gentiles had labeled it "solitude."

Today, however, the solitude had been invaded. A female hyena stood erect and motionless, her great ears pricked to the sound of a human voice. Her pups turned quickly and scurried in a cloud of rubble and dust to the shelter of a nearby cave. She, waiting in curiosity, held her ground until she saw the form of a man, and then hesitantly left her bloody carrion to join her little ones, the shabby fur of her back raised in an obstinate show of fear.

Fearsome indeed was the spectacle. The hyena had seen a man

before, in the shepherd hills. She had been frightened then, but not so much as now. The oncoming creature was alien by virtue of his humanity, but his wild appearance especially confused the dog of the desert and sent one wracking tremor through her lean body.

The man was clothed in the heavy, hairy skins of animals, and these were bound close to his body by a broad waistband of leather. Bulky leggings of the same material served as bindings about his feet and calves, and were strapped in criss-cross fashion up to his knees.

His beard was full and dark, and his hair, which in accordance with his Nazarite vow had never felt the cut of a razor, flowed to his midback and was restrained only by another leather strap.

If the appearance of the man was awesome, however, his tempestuous voice, which now echoed through the gorge, was more so. He approached the ford from the region of a deep-cut wadi in the eastern bank. It seemed he came down from nowhere, for no city lay within miles of this place, and certainly not from his point of descent. As he walked he lifted rough, calloused hands to his sun-browned face and called in echoing stanzas toward the hills, words strange for this environment: "Repent! Repent! For the kingdom of heaven is at hand!"

The dog slunk nervously into the shadows of the cave, her pups cowering close to her as she lay down with a baffled whimper. She rested her head on her paws and listened from an obscure corner to what were to her the unintelligible reverberations of the voice.

The great, rough-hewn intruder now walked onto the sandy, damp slope of the river, and looked high above him to the searing sun. Then he plodded knee deep into the water and cried again, "Repent! For the kingdom of heaven is at hand. I am the voice of one crying in the wilderness, 'Prepare the way of the Lord!' "

Now the man trudged up the western bank and with seemingly effortless strides ascended into the low hills of that vicinity. Repeatedly he shouted his command. But to whom? It was conceivable that there were shepherds in this district, but highly improbable. There was water sufficient for the herds among the hills this summer, and surely no need to descend into the parched river valley where the heat might soar to 130 degrees.

Still the strange figure called toward the wadis, the rocks, and the vales, "Repent! Prepare the way of the Lord!"

If the dog could have understood the sounds which echoed through her boneyard, she might have wondered *who* should "repent" and "prepare," but her sole thought was that a threatening personality had invaded her domain. As the insistent reverberations continued into evening, ceasing only with the rising moon, she determined to leave her valley. And so she did.

Someone had heard. It had been unlikely, but it had happened. A young shepherd in search of a stray ewe had wandered near the region of Bethabara, and his ear had caught the strains of the Nazarite's command.

Though fearful, he had scrambled over a remote bluff to glimpse the source of the cries. He had not fully comprehended the implications of the words, but he had seen enough of the desert dweller to send him rushing back to camp.

That had been enough. The news was out and would spread like fire in dry grass.

The first few days after the discovery, handfuls of shepherds crept from the hills to view the stranger. For some time tales had been told of a peculiar itinerant from the Dead Sea region, who, beginning in the wilderness of Judea, had tramped all up and down the Jordan Valley, heralding judgment and retribution. Could this be the man?

So compelling was his message, so unusual his appearance, that within a week Palestinians as far away as Jerusalem, nearly fifty miles southeast of Bethabara, had been alerted. Now that he seemed to have settled in one spot, great streams of the inquisitive and the devout merged daily from every sector of the land, to hear him preach. Galileans, Judeans, Samarians, Pereans, and those of Decapolis poured like waves into the arid vale.

When the notorious wild man emerged each morning from some fold of the dry hills, he was met with increasingly large numbers who had come to hear his message. No doubt diverse motives drew them, but the Nazarite did not purpose to meet all their interests. He performed no miracles. He heralded no oratory in support of Judaism or against Rome. His message did not tickle the ears of the scribes with fresh interpretations of the Law and Scriptures.

He may have entertained mere spectators and scoffers with his ritual, for his call was to baptism by immersion in the muddy Jordan, gaining for himself the title of "The Baptist." Peculiar indeed was the sight of hundreds going down into those legendary waters. But his message was the greatest attraction, and it had created a stir of wonder which ran the length and breadth of Palestine. For there had been no prophet in Israel for four hundred years.

This day, once more, the sun seared the vault of blue above Bethabara, causing drops of sweat to glisten on the faces of those gathered there. The highway from Galilee to Judea ran along the ridge to the east of the Jordan. Nearly three thousand people had followed it out of their towns and villages, and had descended from the road into the region of the ford in anticipation of the Baptist's coming. As they sat along the bank, their jostling, eager mood was tempered by awe and suspense.

Most sat on the dry yellow hillside, straining their vision in the direction of the western bank, speaking only in whispers among themselves. Some huddled in close-knit groups as if fearful, and others dwelled solitary in the midst of the crowd, in moods of contemplation. A few rimmed the far edges, standing aloof from the others. By their dress they were recognized as the religious hierarchy, here out of Pharisaical curiosity or in response to some order to observe and report.

As usual, small armed bands of Roman guards were in attendance, their superiors feeling it imperative to monitor any sizable gathering within these provinces. There were frequent rumors of insurrections in Palestine.

There would be no insurrection today, however. Attention would be too firmly fixed on the preacher. A wave of muted whispers passed through the congregation now, for word had it he had been seen approaching from the solitude.

Here he came, his stride purposeful and steady, his gaze fixed intently on the crowd even while he was some distance away. He reached the Jordan, and only a moment's silence preceded his entering the water. Then, without preliminaries, he raised his arms, and in a voice as vehement as a trumpet, he began his familiar cry.

"Repent!"

It echoed down the gorge.

"Repent!"

It rang through the hills.

Indeed, it seemed to many present that he must be a prophet, for his demand sent a shiver of response through their bodies, and they sat awestruck in anticipation of his next words.

Scanning the crowd, he drew the brief reference to himself which had become well known to his most frequent hearers. "I am the voice of one crying in the wilderness, 'Prepare the way of the Lord! Make his paths straight!' "

The words were familiar, not only because he often repeated

them, but because they had been penned centuries before by the hand of another Hebrew prophet, Isaiah, and had been memorized, along with the rest of Scripture, by every Jewish lad for centuries.

They were beautiful and mysterious words, seeming to hint at some future event, and, as always, a murmur of fascination coursed through the crowd.

Could this be the Messiah, the long-awaited Redeemer who would rescue Israel from all its troubles? Many wondered. The prophets had spoken repeatedly in old times of the future appearance of such a man. But could this be he? It had been such a long time since any hope had been felt in the land that many had forgotten such a promise had been made. And this man seemed so strange a figure to fulfill those ancient dreams.

The Baptist was silent now. Scanning the jagged horizon, he drew the crowd's attention to the terrain.

"Every valley shall be exalted," he cried, "and every mountain and hill shall be brought low!"

The volume of his voice fairly shook the ground it spoke of. Then, as silence descended once more, the crowd considered still other familiar words of Isaiah.

"The crooked shall be made straight," he continued, "and the rough places plain!"

The crowd sat riveted, watching as the Baptist drew near the east bank of the river. Many knew what his next words would be, for the passage he quoted was ingrained in their memories, but he was giving them time to consider the weight of the matter. A thrill of anticipation held them silent as they listened to the words in their minds before hearing them. When at last the Baptist raised his eyes to the sky, his voice casting the majestic phrase heavenward, it was a reinforcing echo of their thoughts:

"And the glory of the Lord shall be revealed and all flesh shall see it together!"

The words were brief and simple, but what a volume of meaning they contained; what a storehouse of hope! The spirits of many gathered there rose and swelled with their impact.

At this point, the Baptist left off speaking and stood silent, his head bowed, and the echoes of his last words fading away in the canyons. As he waited, several of those near the front of the congregation moved reverently forward, and one or two entered the water before him. He looked at them intently . . . solemnly. "Repent, and be baptized for the remission of sins," he said fervently. Taking them one by one, he placed his hands on their heads and gazed heavenward. Then he held each penitent firmly in his strong arms, lowering him backward into the warm water, and raising him to the hope of a new purpose.

Now others came, first in small clusters, and then in wave upon wave, until the Baptist was surrounded. He would spend the next several hours thus, until his powerful arms ached with the ordeal, and until he turned away at last, with the dusk, to his solitude.

Only a few remained in the desert after his departure. Some pitched modest tents or spread pallets, planning to stay more than a day. For the most part the crowd dispersed at evening but others would trek to Bethabara the next day.

A cluster of black birds swooped gently across the horizon and the musk-rose of evening gave way to the deepening shades of night. Twilight settled over the red hills, bringing a hush. A few streams of lantern light were all that would add to the graying light of the sky until the moon shone full above.

A slight echoing clop of soldiers' horses and the muted shuffle of dust-raising travelers were all the noises to be heard. The few remaining parties were strangely still, many sitting in their tent doors or on their bed rolls under the slowly appearing stars, looking across the silent Jordan. Perhaps in their minds they yet heard the haunting voice of the prophet. Perhaps their lives had found a new hope, a new dream. For whatever reason, they would be here again tomorrow.

Up the Jordan some way, one figure sat solitary on the sloping brow of a lonely rise. He had come early in the morning and had watched the day's activities some distance from the general gathering. When the Baptist had finally exited with the fading daylight, this individual had paced him along the west side of the river until the holy man had been lost to sight in the east.

And now the figure studied the river. His young face betrayed questioning awe as he dwelled privately on what he had witnessed here. He sat thus for hours until at last, with the rising of the moon, he gazed toward the site where he had last glimpsed the Nazarite, then slowly stood, gathered his robes about him, and reluctantly turned to leave.

Chapter 2

The wind blew a dry leaf across the empty marble pavement. A hollow whistle of cold autumn air swept between two columns and brought with it several other remnants of the passing season, swirling and tossing them together as they met.

Winter would be settling over Jerusalem within a few weeks and soon the now silent Temple on the rise would be lit with the myriad lights of Hanukkah, the joyous and boisterous Festival of Dedication.

It had been about two hundred years since Judas Maccabeus had led a successful series of guerrilla attacks on the Syrian rule which had for so long held Palestine in its sway. The victor had regained for his kinsmen their right of worship, and had rescued the Temple of Jehovah from the indignity of pagan defilement. Two centuries had dulled the memory, but Hanukkah served to revive it once each year.

Tonight the same young man who had so curiously watched the Baptist weeks before stood alone within the solitude of the cloisters and gazed soberly above him. His eyes scanned the ornamented gables of the Temple area and followed the graceful lines of the columns down to the expansive porch. As they did so he shivered with the reverence he always felt upon visiting this holy place. But this evening he dwelt not so much on what he could see as on what he could not see.

Was it possible that a statue to Zeus had once stood here? That unclean beasts had been offered on Gentile altars within this sanctuary?

Virtually unaware of the cold that penetrated his light cloak, he only instinctively drew his robes close about him and squinted his dark blue eyes against an unexpectedly icy blast of wind.

Yes, it was possible. Not only possible, but true. The man bristled with revulsion, and took a few hesitating steps out of the shadows. As he surveyed his surroundings, he attempted to piece together the bits of history attached to each building, each passageway, as he had heard them recounted since childhood.

He need not remind himself that this was not the first Temple to stand on this sacred spot. Since King David had first dreamed of the original, and his son Solomon had built it, about a thousand years before, the Holy Mount had seen a history of pillaging, stripping, pollution, and destruction. The great House of the Lord had been forced to bow to Egypt, Syria, Assyria, and Babylon.

The resilience and determination of the Jewish people had seen the holy place cleansed, repaired, and rededicated. But only rarely during the long history of the nation had it been at peace with the world. There was always the intruder, the invader, the hostile horde without the gates, ever waiting, it seemed, for the opportune moment to take the land from the people or the people from the land.

The young man walked to the edge of the porch from which vantage point he could survey the streets below. The wind blew his hair back from his face, exposing genuinely Jewish features, though not so pronounced as they might be, as his sun-bleached hair and blue eyes indicated he had been touched by some Greek ancestry. But he was Jewish, nonetheless. His complexion was deep, though due not so much to his lineage as to his occupation. Sun and sea air had given him a look of age and experience beyond his nineteen years, and this added to the intent aspect he bore tonight.

Below him the marketplaces were relatively calm. The merchants' booths had been taken inside, and, with the exception of a small group of Roman soldiers who passed beneath his gaze, most of the city-dwellers had left the streets.

At the sight of the troops, the young Jew stiffened. His hands formed involuntary fists and his knees locked in place. He followed the soldiers silently with his eyes, measuring their pace and scornfully studying their proud bearing. How he despised them, the ever-present symbols of yet another crushing power to be served by his people.

Hatred and an unspoken desire for vengeance welled within him. Almost unconsciously he raised one clenched hand and struck the railing in front of him.

"Animals!" he whispered.

As the soldiers passed from view the young man grew increasingly restless. How much longer would the council be in session? he wondered. In his mind he visualized them inside the nearby chambers, his father and the many leading Pharisees and Sadducees from throughout Judea and Galilee, congregated intensely about the high priest and his officials. He wished he had gone in with them now, but he could imagine it, anyway. Caiaphas would be alternately sitting and standing, strutting and speaking. The story of the wild man of Jordan would have been told and retold, analyzed and debated fifty times by now, and by as many voices.

On the pavement behind him the young man heard the hollow echo of rapid footfalls, and he turned about, knowing who it would be.

"John," a voice called. "How goes it?"

"Still inside," the young Jew replied cryptically.

"How long?"

"Hours." He turned again to the rail. His older brother, James, stood quiet beside him, but then inquired, "What do you think will come of it all?"

John fidgeted with a fold of his robe, shrugged his shoulders as if unconcerned, and then answered sardonically, "They will have his neck."

James smiled cautiously, savoring the note of disdain which had colored his brother's response, but then he added quickly, "Don't be too hasty. You can be sure they'll think this one over long and well. The Baptist is quite popular."

John smirked. "Like Isaiah, and Jeremiah?"

The elder grimaced and then nodded approvingly. "I see your point," he said, considering the legendary deaths of those ancient martyrs. "But why are you so ready to defend him? You have never heard him."

John was glad for the night which hid the color now rising to his cheeks. He could not tell his brother the truth. "I have heard enough of the message he brings," he covered quickly. "'Repent!' I have no quarrel with him. There are those who need to hear such a command."

James was silent.

At last voices were heard coming from the direction of the council chambers and the brothers turned to meet the men who now emerged from the session. James went forward eagerly to greet his father, but John remained a few paces behind.

"Well, father, tell us about it," prompted the elder.

Zebedee wore an obvious look of self-satisfaction mixed with a hint of secretiveness, but the brothers knew the news would not be long in spilling forth. The old Pharisee bade several lengthy farewells to other members of the council, bowing low and making obscure references to some future meeting date; then he joined his sons.

They were descending the last row of broad steps to the street when at last, after several long benedictions on leaving the hallowed grounds, Zebedee said, "We will know soon enough."

James and John glanced at one another, James with the glint of a knowing smile, John with eyes which feigned indifference.

Nothing was said again until they had passed several buildings and were turning toward the hostlery. "We have given the fanaticism until spring to calm itself. If it has not begun to dwindle by that time, we will approach the Baptist and question him."

James looked at his younger brother, who finally gave him a small nod, conceding that the elder had been right. The Baptist's popularity had tempered the usually hasty verdicts of the council. The Pharisees and Sadducees would think on this long and well.

The six-day journey from Jerusalem back to their native town of Capernaum wearied the three men, but when they arrived there was no time for rest. Zebedee's fishing fleet had brought in quite a haul while he had been gone, and so a great multitude of fish needed to be dried, and nets needed mending.

The next day John sat cross-legged near the cold, slapping water of the shoreline. A heavy rope net lay across his legs, and spread far to his right along the damp sand. Mechanically, he wound a line of coarse twine up and down between the broken webs of the hemp, his calloused but nimble fingers making intricate knots where it seemed most expedient.

For some moments he studied the gray-green water, the glowering near-winter sky. A blustering sea wind was buffeting the peaks of waves far out from land, dashing white, foamy spray high into the air. He was glad the boats would not be going out tonight.

But such thoughts only superficially impressed his consciousness. He was thinking of the Baptist.

He had still not told his father or his elder brother of his venture to Bethabara the past summer because he knew it would merely create strife. It was not fear of them that had led him to withhold the story, but deference to family unity, a unity which, due to

John's own nature, had been shaken countless times in the past.

There were degrees of Pharisaism, from that of the novice, to the informed liberal, to the "Chasid Shoteh," or "silly pietist." Zebedee's vocation as a fishing tycoon occasionally brought him in touch with the "unclean things" of the sea, and did not allow him to be continually arrayed in the traditional garb; therefore, though he skirted these issues by means of priestly indulgences and personal rationale, he could not be one of the very strictest order. Beyond this single impediment, however, he was a Pharisee of the strongest tradition. He looked with the most obstinate suspicion on any new or unfamiliar development within the realm of theological interest. He feared the Baptist, however much he might attempt to cloak his trepidation. Should he learn of John's involvement, he would be outraged.

And though John longed to tell his brother, for whom he had great affection and admiration, James had been afforded what John considered the dubious privilege of rabbinical training. As the firstborn, he had received the more formal, the higher education, though John's schooling had by no means been neglected. The father's wealth had provided substantially for both. But James, due to his particular studies, leaned more toward Zebedee's traditional zeal than the younger. And so John restrained his eagerness to share this episode with him.

Stories of the Baptist, brought back by pilgrims to his vale, had stirred John from the outset. Some responsive chord in his naturally rebellious young heart had been touched upon his first hearing of the man who wore camel's skins, who ate nothing but locusts and wild honey, who led a singular, nonconforming existence in the wilds of Decapolis. And an insatiable curiosity had driven him to seek, unbeknown to his father, a glimpse of the one whom so many called "the new Isaiah," and "the new Elijah."

Growing up in the culture of Judaism, John had acquired as his heroes the ancient figures of the race. His first tastes of battle had been with Abraham and Gideon, Joshua and David—his first glimpses of obstinate manhood in Moses, Daniel, and Elijah.

Having fewer responsibilities to occupy his time than had befallen his elder brother, John had spent much of his childhood in the realm of imagination. A hundred times he had lived and relived the adventures of those he read about. His keen mind and finely exercised sense of fantasy had drawn the boys of the neighborhood to him in a close following, as they attempted, childlike, to play the roles of their heroes.

But John's reveries were not confined to the pages of Scripture, or even to the fragments of Greek epics which he surreptitiously—and most disobediently—smuggled into his room. As he had grown, his insight had grown. It was no longer the wars and adventures of literature which attracted him, but the light they shed on human nature, and the questions they posed on the purpose of life. An insatiable desire for answers, which sometimes verged on cynicism, now characterized him.

His mother, Salome, who was as devoted to John as John to his struggles, took great pride in his leanings. His contemporaries admired him; some of his teachers resented him. His brother found his inclinations curious. But his father was disturbed by them.

As a Pharisee, Zebedee was among the intelligentsia of his day, and so his son's desire for knowledge did not offend him. He sensed, however, that John had not confined himself to the study of Jewish Law and Scripture, and throughout the years this had been the source of much contention. But what disturbed Zebedee even more than his son's dabbling in Greek thought were the questions which the boy had posed about Holy Writ itself. For along with John's keen mind had been born a tendency to rebellion, which in one of lesser ability might have taken the form of mere churlishness. In John this element was often explosive in its manifestation, his questioning frequently so sharp, so baffling, that Zebedee and others in authority were at a loss to correct him.

As an adolescent, his strong will had won him great popularity with his peers. But with some maturing, he had learned that not every difference of opinion should be aired in confrontation. Nowadays he was rarely a rebel for the sake of rebellion. As with the story of his visit to Bethabara, and his feelings about Zebedee's hatred of the Baptist, he held his tongue in the interests of family peace, mostly out of consideration for Salome, who was easily pained by dissension in the home.

But how he longed to share with someone what he had seen!

Today, as he sat silent, watching the lapping water, he relived the moments at the Jordan. In his mind he could see him, the "second Isaiah." Absently, John wound the hemp through the nets, dwelling in a realm far removed from that of the fishing fleet.

Mingling with the rhythmic slapping of the water against the shore, his thoughts swayed to the cadences of the Nazarite's voice as it echoed in his memory: "Repent! For the kingdom of heaven is at hand! Every valley shall be exalted, every hill brought low . . . I am the voice of one crying in the wilderness . . . crying in the wilderness. . . ."

"John!" another voice interrupted his reveries.

The young fisherman jolted upright, looking straight into the heavily bearded face of his closest friend.

"Simon—I am sorry. . . ."

"I've called your name three times while walking this way," the other greeted jovially. "You must have been miles away!"

John grinned. "Yes, I suppose I was."

"Do we go out tonight?" Simon queried, drawing his bulky shoulders down into a huddle against the wind.

"No. It's too rough out there. Better wait until it dies down. Probably tomorrow."

It was not simply the rugged weather which would keep the men off the water tonight, but the nature of the sea itself. This might have seemed a minor wind on other bodies of water, but the Sea of Galilee was known for its sudden and inexplicably violent squalls, which could overwash and capsize the largest of local vessels without warning, and especially under just such conditions as these.

The same could happen in the calmest seasons, so the men of Capernaum and other ports had learned to live with the risk, out of necessity. But there was no reason to force the odds when experience told them this was the most likely time for such freak occurrences.

John looked again at his nets and his large friend squatted beside him. Both worked at the mending in silence, until, no longer capable of restraint, Simon insisted, "Where are your thoughts, my friend? The only time I act as you are, I am in love!"

John's face broke into a broad grin and the two men roared with laughter.

"No, I am not in love, Simon," John smiled. "Not today, anyway."

Simon was about to tease John, feigning surprise that John's thoughts should be on a woman. For the young son of Zebedee had always sworn he had little use for such matters. Oh, certainly, he appreciated a pretty face and form, but, he had always insisted, women could wait. There were "greater" things to pursue. Simon would have alluded to such things—but noting John's once-again-somber mood, he thought better of it.

"What then?" was all he asked.

Simon, whose father owned a junior share in Zebedee's fishing business, lived in the less prosperous port neighborhood of Capernaum, known as Bethsaida, the fishermen's quarter. He had, nonetheless, been John's closest ally since their earliest days of youthful adventure. And in many ways the love of risk was still present in them both. John knew his friend would find his story appealing.

"I was thinking of the Baptist."

The larger hands ceased their labors, and Simon studied his companion carefully. "I have heard much of him," he said in a burst of interest.

John fell silent again, and Simon nudged him anxiously. "So, go on, John! What of the Baptist?"

The young Jew looked up and down the beach cautiously, and then leaned forward in an attitude of great secrecy. "What would you say, Simon, if I told you I had gone out to hear him?"

Simon's eyes grew large and round. "I would wrap you in this net and toss you into the sea!" he roared with pleasure.

John laughed aloud. "Why, Simon?"

"Because you did not take me with you!" Another resounding laugh followed this, but then the big fisherman looked rather skeptically at his friend. "When did you do this? You have not left Capernaum for months, except to go to Jerusalem with your father."

John leaned toward him. "It was last summer when James and Zebedee and the rest of you were out for several days. Do you remember I did not go with you? I said I had other business."

Simon scratched his head, and then, recalling the incident, nodded slowly. "Ah, yes! I thought that was strange at the time." But then, his voice mellowing, he drew close to John and asked, "Tell me about him. Is he everything they say he is?"

John's eyes took on that faraway look again, and he answered, "More, Simon. Much more. . . ."

Chapter 3

Zebedee warmed himself before the winter fire. The red flames cast a moody glow upon his face as he stooped before them, feeding several twigs of kindling onto the flashing, greedy tongues.

It was winter now, the twenty-ninth day of Kislev, and five days into the eight days of Hanukkah. But the family would not go to Jerusalem this year. Though their wealth allowed them to own a second house in the sacred city, where they usually spent the holidays, the journey was a major undertaking for a man of Zebedee's age, and the recent trip to the "City of Peace" for the council with Caiaphas had been enough for this season. Unless another session of the Sanhedrin was called, demanding more than the one-third quorum normally needed, Zebedee would remain in Capernaum.

Zebedee straightened his stiff legs and leaned back into the large wood and leather armchair beside the hearth. The old man appeared to be relaxed, but his brown, weathered face told a different story. The firelight emphasized the crevices of his brow, the product of toil and windy exposure at sea. Tonight they were deepened by his thoughts.

Across the room numerous candles set in nine-pronged holders lit the ornately latticed windows and lined the magnificent stone walls. To degrees varying with the wealth of the inhabitants, each house in Capernaum, and indeed in all Jewish centers, displayed such illumination, for Hanukkah was the Festival of Lights, the commemoration of the rededication of Jerusalem's Temple.

From the street could be discerned the sound of dancing and singing as numerous merrymakers wound their way through the village. Throughout Palestine, this was one of the happiest times of the year.

Zebedee's house was among the most brilliantly lit in Capernaum. Each of his many servants, hired laborers, and slaves was afforded a menorah of his own, and these, added to those of the immediate family, provided enough light to brighten even most remote corners of the villa, from the roof to the gallery to the inner court.

Behind the facade of gaiety, however, Zebedee's home was not so festive.

"You think of the boy?" Salome asked softly as she observed Zebedee's contemplative mood.

No answer was forthcoming, but there was no need for it. What else would hold his eyes riveted to the flames for such long hours? The only sounds interrupting the extended silences of the couple were the crackling of the kindling, the spitting of pitch here and there on the firelogs, and the muted shuffling of servants in the dining room as they cleared the low tables of festive leftovers.

Salome drew a footstool near her husband's cedar-framed chair and sat quietly studying his countenance.

"It is cold even in this room tonight," she said, drawing the broad, blue-edged hem of his garment over her own feet. Sighing at his continued silence, she leaned her head on his arm and fingered the leather strap of the phylactery bound there, the trademark of his sect.

The glow of the embers softened her face, accentuating a youthfulness that belied her age. Though Salome was much younger than her husband, not unusual in their culture, she was in mid-life. But as Zebedee watched her, he reflected—not for the first time—upon how kindly the years had treated her.

Salome did not see Zebedee's admiring gaze, but if she had she would have read something of his need for her. He was not one to reveal this overtly. He was too proud. So, when she looked his way again, he stared once more into the flames.

"Do not harbor such ill feelings toward him, husband," she pleaded. "You know his nature. What he did should not surprise you."

She was picking her words carefully. It was a sore subject to deal with, but she knew it must be done. The past week had been spent in tense uneasiness by servants and family alike.

This was not the first time she had attempted intervention in a father-son quarrel, but this debate was worse than others. Only a few days before Hanukkah, Zebedee had stormed into the house, furious because of what he had overheard in the village.

"That I should have to hear such shameful news from strangers—indeed from that . . . that wild man's very devotees! John—is it true—did you indeed go out to Bethabara to mingle with the Baptist's rabble?" John had turned away without a word and no civil conversation had passed between them since that hour.

Salome knew she must be her most skillful as intermediary this time, or the chasm between her husband and her youngest would never be bridged.

"Of course I know his nature!" Zebedee responded at last. "Indeed, I do!" He had now risen from his chair and crossed the room rigidly.

"But what is it, exactly, that disturbs you about this Baptist? Have you explained your feelings to John?" she asked.

"Repeatedly! Need I express the same to you?" His tone was one of rising anger, and Salome drew back, but then, regathering

her courage, she said discreetly, "Please, my lord, do explain. I
am an unlearned and foolish woman. I do not understand how
the Baptist's teachings contradict your own."

"He does not teach the Law, woman! He asks us all to repent,
and yet he does not teach the oracles of God which we have taught
for centuries! What need have *we* to repent? It is he who should
learn from us!" Zebedee's words raged with his conviction. He
spoke, of course, of the Baptist's open attacks on the Pharisees
and other religious leaders who had come out to hear him.

"It does sound strange, husband," Salome mused. "Then what
is his teaching?"

"I wish I knew!" Zebedee thundered. "It is certainly not ours.
He preaches some new form of 'righteousness.' And whatever it is,
you may be certain it is heretical. What could a wild man add to the
traditions and contemplations of the elders which would not be
heresy?"

Salome was baffled by her husband's seeming logic. She, too,
wondered what new teaching could be more strictly legal than that
of the Jewish hierarchy.

"And yet the people go to hear him in droves. . . ."

"He tickles their ears, woman. You know the kind of ignorant
riff-raff that goes out there!"

A wounded look crossed Salome's face at this remark. "You
speak of your son. . . ."

Zebedee hesitated a moment. He hadn't consciously meant to
draw that parallel, yet, when confronted with his own hastiness,
he stubbornly maintained the statement. "Truly," he continued,
"it is no comfort to realize it. But, it is a confirmation. . . ."

"A confirmation of what?" The voice was John's. Zebedee
wheeled about to face his youngest, who had come silently to the
chamber door.

"Please!" cried Salome. "No more of this, now!" And running
to John she pleaded brokenly, "No more, son. Let it pass!"

But John's ears burned with what he had heard, and his
impetuosity drove him to demand the answer he already knew.

"No, mother, what did he mean, a 'confirmation'?" he retorted
acidly.

"Have we not heard this all before?" Salome cried, placing her
hands over her ears. In utter frustration she then ran from the
room, hot tears coursing down her cheeks.

The servants had wisely departed at the outset of this new
episode, leaving John and Zebedee to face each other alone across

the cold, silent parlor. This was the first time it would be so. Always before, during the recent debate, there had been another family member present: Salome, or James, or both. Now they would deal with the issue without hindrance.

Zebedee's temperament was not so fiery as John's, and yet neither was he a gentle man. His feelings were deep and firmly established, and came forth in torrents of opinion when he felt occasion required it. John's pulse sped as he watched his father pace the floor, as he waited for the venomous reproach he knew would be forthcoming.

"A confirmation, boy, of all I have known to be true since you entered young manhood; indeed since before that!"

"And what is it you have known?" John baited him.

Zebedee's fists tightened and his eyes glared in hot contempt of his son's past delinquencies and of the taboos which he had broken.

"That you have denied the traditions of the elders!" he asserted. "That you have trampled underfoot the admonitions of the venerable," he shouted, "and have toyed with forbidden fruits!" Then, pointing a menacing finger in John's face, he gathered all his reserves and cried, "That you have denied the law of your father!"

John stood silent. Yes, he had heard it all before. Somehow the thrill of confrontation had goaded him to hear it again, but now he tired of its repetition.

"You color me as if I were a drunkard and a sluggard!" he smirked. "As for the law of my father, you speak of it as if it were the Law of God!"

Zebedee's eyes flashed indignantly. "Is it not, John?"

The son's anger cooled somewhat at that rebuttal. It was true the Scriptures were adamant in their warnings against dishonoring the edicts of one's father. And Zebedee, being a Pharisee, was especially careful to remain scrupulously close to Moses' Law in everything he required of his children. To be a member of the Sanhedrin, Supreme Court of Judaism, required moral uprightness, experience in the lower courts, judgeship in one's native town, and general leadership and representation of the people.

Though this touched John with uneasy awe, it also stirred the chords of rebellion more deeply than anything else might. For he loved God, as well as he could with his concept of him, but that concept was rooted in his concept of his father, as any son's might be. And his love for his father was so intermingled with fear and resentment that he kicked as viciously against the God he represented, as he did against Zebedee himself.

All John knew of God was a contradictory dichotomy. He believed, as he had been taught, that Jehovah was a God of love and retribution. These two qualities were not in themselves antithetical. John knew philosophically that love cannot be true unless tempered with true justice, which might sometimes require punitive action on the part of the Lover.

Yet it seemed to John that God was not totally just, for he required super-human scrupulousness in his followers, and returned punishment more often than mercy for the breaking of his impossible laws. At least to John it seemed so, for thus had his upbringing conditioned his views.

It was not his nature to let his fears of God cow him; not outwardly, at any rate. To all appearances John was a rebel, not one to follow unquestioningly what he could not completely accept intellectually. But his zealous self-assertion was frequently a front to hide deep-seated insecurity. Way down inside himself there was a thriving tangle of confusion. He could not hate his father's God. If he could have, he might not have struggled with his doubts as he did.

He loved Jehovah. He could not wipe out the reverence he felt for him. Yet when he wondered at this seeming contradiction in himself he realized it sprang from the fact that he did not fully accept Zebedee's picture of the Lord. He could not love that picture. Somehow, it had never set right with him.

His fists clenched tensely, John stood by the window, peering out on the winter street. The sound of the dancing had ceased, but the merry lights of the neighborhood seemed out of place this evening. To his right, upon a gilded sconce, sat his own menorah, the one he had lit with its ninth master candle each night of Hanukkah since he was a child. Near it stood James', a bit more elaborate, as it belonged to the firstborn. A tingle of sentiment nudged at his heart as he fleetingly recalled the warmer holidays of times past. But quickly he repressed the memory.

His throat was dry and tight. Stinging tears rose to his eyes and threatened to overflow, but John scorned womanish weakness. He was a man, not a boy. He quickly replaced the desire to plead for understanding with the desire to seek revenge.

Steeling himself, John continued to peer out the window, concentrating only on his next words, not on the large flakes of snow which drifted to the street.

"Father," he began slowly, deliberately, "this Law of which you speak—is it the same Law which allowed Judah Bar Micah to watch a woman crushed by stampeding oxen rather than pull her to safety, because your Pharisaic tradition taught he should not touch a woman?"

Zebedee's hands drew into tight, angular knots at the memory, and as John turned about he saw he had hit on a delicate point.

"And father, is it the same Law which delayed Master Bar Simeon from reaching to save the young boy who could not swim? It is said he let him drown as he attempted to untie the phylactery from his own arm before plunging into the water."

Zebedee could bear no more. "Enough!" he cried. "You approach blasphemy!"

John feigned innocence. "How is that, father?"

"'God's ways are not our ways,' say the Scriptures. 'Lean not unto your own understanding'!"

John's voice was bitter. "It is God's way, then, to see a boy die for the sake of a dry phylactery?"

"Apparently it was, in this case . . ." Zebedee stammered. "His ways are higher than our ways . . ." But these words rang hollow even in Zebedee's ears. It seemed he clutched at straws.

"Oh, father!" John flung his arms wide and turned away, shaking his head in exasperation.

Zebedee remained silent until his son was ready to hear him again. And this time he chose his words more carefully. "You have dealt in emotional examples, son. They are not typical."

"They may be extreme, but they are typical!" John interrupted. "Typical of the monster you call 'God'!"

"Blasphemy, John!"

"Blasphemy? You yourself said the incidents were not typical. Is that your way of saying the elders made the wrong decisions in these events?"

"No!" Zebedee responded fervently. And then, drawing back a little he repeated more indefinitely, "No. . . ."

John saw a chink in his father's armor. It appeared the old man was weakening. But there was fight left in him. Zebedee was a man of intelligence and deep thought. His Pharisaism had been well established by what he believed to be the soundest logic. It was not a casual tradition, but a system of life toughened by years of study and contemplation. To him it was reasonable.

After several moments of silence during which John basked in his supposed triumph, Zebedee crossed the room with a renewed steadiness which somewhat surprised his son. As he came, he spoke softly, slowly. "Son," his voice was almost tender, "will you listen?"

John did not respond, but only eyed his father warily.

"You know that the traditions of the elders are not based on emotion. It is true that often God's ways are inscrutable. But insofar as he gives us insight into his will, the traditions are based on logic."

John stiffened. "Example, father! How do you explain the drowning boy?"

"All right, son. Let me give you a lesson in logic." Zebedee stared straight into John's eyes, making the younger man flinch inwardly. "Follow my thoughts closely," he began, and then pacing the room back and forth, emphasizing each point with angular gestures, he said, "Will you concede that the name of God is to be honored?"

John was hesitant, but saw no reason to deny this. "Yes, of course I will."

"Then, son, will you also concede that the words bound within a phylactery include the name of the Lord at least twenty-three times?"

What met John's ears was incredible, though it should not have been. He was aware of the Pharisees' system of reasoning. But he could scarcely believe what his father was leading up to.

"Do you mean to say that it would have dishonored the name of the Lord to dip a phylactery into the sea, because God's name is written upon the contents?" John asked in astonishment.

"Indeed!" said Zebedee.

"You cannot mean it, father!"

"Is it not logical, son?"

"It is logical that his name would be honored by just such an act of rescue!" John shouted.

Zebedee bristled. "The Law is unclear on that point, John. It says nowhere in Scripture that the name of Jehovah should be obliterated for the sake of anything, including a life. What is clear is that it is to be honored—and it is honored by being bound about our foreheads and our arms, as the Law says; written on our doorposts, as the Law says. When the Law is clear on one point and unclear on another we must follow the clearest route!"

John snatched up his cloak now, which lay where he had carelessly tossed it upon first entering the room. "What is clear to you, is not clear to me," he declared, striding toward the doorway.

"Then you have not studied Scripture, John," Zebedee stopped him. "Your love of God has been weak and fruitless!"

"Oh, it would be most convenient for you if I claimed I had rejected your God, wouldn't it, father? You would like to hear me say, 'You are right. I do not love Jehovah.' That would clear you of all difficulty in dealing with me. But you know it is not true," John asserted. "I *do* love God, but perhaps not the God you love!"

"Who then? Some myth from your contraband Gentile classics?"

"No, father, they are even more ludicrous than your own!"

"Who then?"

"Jehovah—a different Jehovah than the one you know."

Zebedee could no longer restrain his son's hasty flight for the door.

"Where do you go, John?" he cried in anger and bewilderment.

"I go to seek him. . . ."

"The Baptist?"

"Jehovah!"

Chapter 4

The way out to Bethabara was not so easy this time. Not only was the weather a hindrance, with its biting wind and occasional knives of sleet, but there was a storm raging in John's soul.

It was not a light thing to leave the bulk of one's upbringing and education in one moment of decision. It was true that this was the culmination of years of misunderstanding between his father and himself. But that did not make it easier to cope with voluntary estrangement.

It was even more difficult when he considered how unsure he was of his destination. What did he *really* know of the Baptist? He had heard him only once. Did he actually hold a different truth than Zebedee espoused? And what if he did? Would it be any more right? John knew only what he did *not* believe, not what he *ought* to believe. He knew only that if God were the God of his father he could not serve him. Yet a nagging fear persisted: what if Zebedee were right? What if Jehovah were as he pictured him?

To purposely leave one's father was one thing; to purposely

leave one's God quite another. A shudder went through his body as he contemplated this, and he tried quickly to suppress it.

"Consider the Baptist," he told himself, as he skirted the last town on the verge of the wilderness. "Remember his words. They were different from any you've heard before. *He* was different. Remember . . . remember. . . ."

Though he had traveled fifteen miles on foot since leaving Capernaum, as he stood within sight of the vast, empty expanse, the last city of Galilee behind him, it was only such thoughts which persuaded him to go on. To turn back would mean he could accept Zebedee's law. "Impossible!" he whispered. There was only one alternative open to him.

The storm drenched his garment. Night would be descending soon. John turned his young, weather-browned face to the sky, and let the cold rain pour through his gold-streaked hair and over his sturdy shoulders.

Memories of the hundreds who had allowed the Jordan to cover them as they rested in the arms of the Baptist filled his mind. A smile lit his wet face and a sense of freedom flooded him.

He tramped confidently toward Bethabara.

There was another day of strenuous travel before John reached the site of the Jordan. The flat hills which, months before, had been ringed with thousands of eager Palestinians awaiting the preacher were now silent and empty.

It would be a rare Jew who would leave his homefires during Hanukkah, and especially in this weather. Even the Baptist did not draw crowds to this spot now. For the past few weeks only handfuls had made the pilgrimage, and no one stayed more than an afternoon. Due to the seasonal depth and swiftness of the water, there were no baptisms and the preacher was heard from across the barrier of the Jordan.

Come the drier season, the crowds would be larger than ever, but all things considered, it was a miracle anyone made the journey during the winter; so much the more evidence of John's desperation in leaving home.

Upon reaching this place, the young Jew scrambled for the shelter of a rocky overhang and awaited some reprieve from the storm. A merciless rain pelted against the surface of the river, stirring the waters into a torrent of mud and foam.

What a dreary place! John wondered why the Baptist had chosen such desolation as the site of his preaching.

Crowding his way beneath the overhang as far as he could, John sat down on the damp, sandy floor and rested. He pushed his streaming hair back from his forehead, wringing the water from it with the pressure of his hand. The cold residue trickled down his back, beneath his cloak, and his skin rose in goose flesh.

Removing his outer garment, he held it before him and wrung it tightly in a long coil, until it hung limp and wrinkled when he shook it out. Then he removed his soggy sandals, slapping them sharply against the rock wall.

Hunger gnawed at him, but as he considered the bread and cheese in his satchel, the storm began to abate. He could not take time to eat. There was no way of knowing how long the rain would let up, and he must do his best to find the Baptist before nightfall.

Stepping from the shelter, John now strained his vision across the water and far to his right where the Baptist was known to disappear after each day's preaching. A new thought struck him. If he were to find the Baptist before dark, he would have to cross the river. There was another route to the west bank, via the Scythopolis highway, but he would likely end up spending a freezing night without shelter, if he did not reach his destination now.

But cross the river? At this time of year? John walked onto the sandy beach where just months before droves of men and women had come to be baptized. How was this feat to be accomplished?

Locating what he determined to be the least risky area, John stripped himself and rolled his clothing into a neat bundle. Mercifully, the wind had died down, but he was still numbed by the cold, and alarmingly weak from hunger. Only the trade to which he was accustomed could have toughened him to this fierce exposure.

Using his sash, he tied his bundle of food and clothing to his shoulders with a fisherman's knot, and proceeded to wade ankle deep into the rapids.

What a sight he made, hesitating there, naked and quivering. A fresh knife of wind cut at his flesh, and tears of agony forced their way to his eyes, but he bit his tongue and held them back. Possibly the water would be warmer than the wind, he consoled himself. At knee-depth, the rapids nearly pulled his feet from under him, but he steeled himself against them tenaciously as he had learned so well to do when his father's boat was overwashed by Galilean waves.

He knew that momentarily he would lose contact with the rocky bottom which now cut and gouged the soles of his feet, but he gripped it as long as possible despite the pain. At first the water

had seemed warmer than the air, but presently it ripped at him
with freezing fingers and at times he could feel nothing as it swept
ferociously past his reddened limbs.

Still he kept the far shore in sight. He was halfway there when
the bundle about his shoulders loosened, pulling him under.
Gasping for air, he removed it and held the loose end of his sash
tightly. He would leave the bundle to the mercy of the river as he
concentrated on his crossing.

He could no longer touch bottom. The waves buoyed him up too
high. Stretching his calloused hands before him, he swam as best
he could against the current. But it swept him like a frozen leaf far
from his destination.

It seemed he fought a stone wall. Strength nearly failed him, but
somehow the bottom ascended again and he found his knees
scraping the sharp rocks. With a final heave of desperation, he
grasped for a thick root protruding from the bank, and pulled
himself to shore.

Blood trickled from his legs and feet. He could not move for
several moments, though icy air penetrated his wet frame like the
honed edge of a flint blade. But as he lay upon the frigid sand, he
gave a wracking sigh of accomplishment.

The rain was beginning again. His food had been ruined, but his
clothing had been spared, and after he at last wrapped his cold,
water-soaked garments about him, he dragged himself up the
western bank.

After some slow progress, he could make out several large caves
in the hills ahead. The Nazarite must be somewhere up there, he
reasoned.

John lifted a rasping voice to the gray sky and called, "Baptist!" The name echoed up the hollow. "Baptist!" But there was
no response. Continuing along the bank he neared the vicinity of
the caves, and forcing his aching legs up an incline, he reached
the mouth of one cavern. Peering into the deep, musty recesses,
he cried hoarsely, "Baptist!" The sound bounced from wall to
wall, returning with the scramble of a small rockslide. The noise
sent a chill down his back. It occurred to him that wild animals
undoubtedly kept house in these hollows, and as he proceeded up
the way he looked about him cautiously.

Cave after cave yielded no human response. Night was coming
on quickly and new fears smote him. What if he had come here for
nothing? What if the Baptist would not be found? What if he had
ceased his preaching and gone back into his previous solitude?

Trembling with fatigue which rivaled the life-force, John at last sat down and struggled with his emptiness. For the first time in years, large tears coursed down his cheeks, though he fought them. But as he raised his damp face from his arms, something caught his eye and he quickly turned to the left.

Yes! There it was! Through the fog he could make out the glimmer of a fire. It appeared to be glowing inside a distant cave.

Summoning strength John did not know was left to him, he got to his feet and stumbled toward the light. His legs fairly collapsed before he reached the prophet's camp, but as he drew near he cried once more, "Baptist!"

He inched his way up the slope to the cave's mouth. It was likely he had not been heard, for the rain was very loud as it struck the stone floor before the cavern. Creeping hesitantly toward the opening, John peered in. Yes, there he was—the Baptist!—reclining before the fire.

For some seconds John watched as the rugged preacher prodded the kindling with a long staff.

He was as he remembered him, and now a fresh sense of awe filled the young Jew. How dare he approach him? How could he explain himself? For the first time since reaching Bethabara, visions of turning back crossed the doorway of his mind. "Ludicrous!" he whispered. "He is only a man . . . as I am . . ." he tried vainly to assure himself. At last he poked his head hesitantly into the opening.

"Sir?" It was barely more than a croak.

The Baptist jumped to his feet and stood rigid, his legs spread wide and his heavy crude staff grasped horizontally before him. Apparently he was not sure he had heard anything, for he stood thus several seconds, peering past the flames toward the opening.

John drew back but finally stepped into full view, his legs shaking with exhaustion and trepidation. The Baptist stood his ground, eyeing the disheveled newcomer doubtfully. John must not have appeared much of a threat, for at last the preacher lowered his staff and called to him demandingly.

"What is it you want, stranger?"

"Sir, I have come a long way to see you." John tried to control his trembling.

Still eyeing his night visitor curiously, the Baptist responded, "Come in, then. Warm yourself."

John entered the cave, the absurdity of his own appearance now dawning upon him. He wrapped his blood-stained coat about him to hide his scrapes and cuts from the preacher's view.

"Sit here," the Baptist said, noting the embarrassed silence of his young guest. The fire was a blessing immeasurable, and John sat as close to it as possible, holding his hands directly over the flames.

Questions flooded the Baptist's mind as to who this might be and why he had come at such apparent personal risk. But he attempted to give aid where it was so obviously needed, maintaining all the while a cautious reserve.

"Take off those damp clothes," he said, handing John several warm skins in which to wrap himself. John complied gratefully, then voraciously downed the strange meal of hot wild honey which was offered next.

Another span of awkward silence ensued. As John finished the offering he could not look his patron in the face, feeling increasingly abashed by his naive intrusion upon the man.

The Baptist had his own thoughts. As he studied the visitor's young face in the firelight, he was keenly aware of the insecurity evidenced there. The preacher leaned more casually now against the cave wall, and crossed his arms. As he surveyed the young man silently, the hint of a smile softened his countenance. John had leaned so far into the warmth of the fire, it appeared at any moment the skins would go up in flames.

"Careful! You'll set yourself afire," the Baptist warned.

John caught his note of compassionate humor, and it gave him courage. Supposing the preacher would want some explanation, he began, as strength returned, "I am from Capernaum. I heard you once last summer, and had to come again. . . . My father is a Pharisee and . . ." one bit of information chased another in rapid succession. "My brother is a rabbi; I have many questions; I crossed the river . . ." he continued, but realizing that this must be obvious, he fought for other words.

"Enough for now," the Baptist interjected, laughing. "You will tell me more with time. What is your name?"

Color rose to the young intruder's face. Hadn't he even introduced himself?

"I am called 'John,'" he stammered.

New interest lit the Baptist's face, and his mouth broke into a wide, handsome smile. "That is my name, as well!"

Something of a kinship between the men was born at that instant.

John the Baptist reached for John Bar Zebedee's hand and they greeted each other with a warmth that defied the winter chill.

Chapter 5

It was late the next morning when John woke to find himself alone in the cave. The fire was burning low where the Baptist had apparently kept it fueled throughout the night.

John sat up stiffly and looked about him, the events of the preceding day a shadowy mirage in his memory. It took him some moments to get his bearings, to recall where he was, and why. Every muscle in his body ached from the ordeal he had put them through, and once again howling hunger gnawed at his strength.

He found himself seated on a bed of skins like those in which he had been wrapped, but he could barely recall what had transpired since he had sat beside the fire and introduced himself to the rugged preacher. Apparently they had talked but little before retiring, and John had fallen into the deepest slumber of his life.

Even now he felt he could sleep through the day, but judging by the hazy, gray light outside the cave, he knew it must be near noon by now. He could not recollect ever having slept this late before, and an embarrassed scowl clouded his face.

"What must he think of me?" John wondered. But then a more sobering thought: the Baptist was gone.

John stood, wincing at the dull throb of protest in his legs. He crossed the cave, and peered outside. The Jordan did not look so ominous in the daylight, despite the depth of its murky-brown torrent. And though the sky was still iron-heavy with clouds, the rain had ceased.

Still, as he cast his eyes in all directions, he saw no sign of the preacher.

Returning to the fire, he found a gourd of dressed-out meat. He knew the Baptist could not have much use for it, if the tales were true that he ate only the roots and nectar of the earth. John sighed with relief. If the preacher had cared enough to prepare this food for him, he had surely not left permanently.

But the sense of John's imposition struck him afresh. His presence must surely be stifling to the Baptist's way of life. He had probably left the cave site for the first time in days just because of John.

"I will leave before tonight," he promised himself. "I was a fool to come here!"

As he stamped this resolution firmly upon his mind, he picked up the gourd and skewered several chunks of meat onto the end of a pointed stick. Fresh and bloody, they slid easily down the stripped prong. John put away his Jewish scruples as he contemplated this fare. Hunger was more overpowering than tradition.

He drew a large stone near the fire and rested the crude instrument against it, the meat dangling just above the flames. These he fed with a new supply of fuel, and then rose to clothe himself in his own apparel, now dry from night-long exposure to the heat.

He was feeling nearly human again. Strength returned more surely with each bite. It was not until he had finished the food that he allowed himself to question what animal's flesh he had eaten.

He put the thought from him, however, as a queasiness touched his orthodox stomach. "It met my needs," he rationalized. "That is all that matters."

It was nearly sunset. John saw no reason to stay longer. As the hours had passed, it had become increasingly apparent that he had been mistaken. The Baptist would not return.

Looking apprehensively at the river, he began his descent from the cave's mouth. This time, rather than cross the river, he would take the long way home, via Scythopolis.

A mixture of feelings was his: fear of the wintry journey home, shame as he pictured his father's face upon his return, but more painful yet, self-hate and the foolishness of his venture here.

Anger welled within him. He kicked viciously at the stones beneath his feet and glared at every jog in the path, his heart pounding in dull thunderclaps of resentment. Though he had felt himself an intruder, he turned on the one who had been the subject of his hopes.

"The Baptist! A man of God! Ha!" he grumbled. "What does he care for me or my confusion?"

Here the brooding young rebel stopped short. Standing before him in the middle of the path was the Baptist, holding his staff erect at his side.

John was a tall man, and good-sized for his age. But the preacher cowed him with a force more than physical. There was something in his rugged bearing which made John feel very small, and he lowered his eyes to the ground.

"I see you are leaving," said the Baptist at long last. "And where will you go?"

John was used to making quick retorts, and nearly blurted out, "What is it to you where I go or what I do?" But he was awed by this man. Indeed he sensed that he was holy—a prophet, a minister of God. On second thought, the desire to make such a reply was gone. Why should he be angry now? Had the Baptist not returned after all?

John stammered his confession. "Sir, I have nowhere to go."

"You were turned homeward," the Baptist said knowingly.

John looked up at him in silence, and the preacher reached forth a large, strong hand, placing it on his shoulder. The Baptist's dark gaze softened, and his ruddy visage betrayed genuine tenderness for his would-be disciple. "You were seeking something when you came here, boy. Will you find it elsewhere?" he asked. "You were running from the wrong answers. Will you find the right ones anywhere but here? Will you seek for God in some other corner of the world? And will you find him there?"

A chill ran up the young Jew's spine. While the words laid bare the dilemma of his soul, they seemed more than questions. They seemed glimpses of truth, visions of hope, as if doorways to their own answers.

Instinctively, unaccountably, he sensed he could not leave.

The last phrase rang repeatedly in his mind, "Will you seek for God in some other corner of the world? And will you find him there . . . find him there . . . find him there . . . ?"

John was humbled. "Sir, I shall not find him elsewhere."

Chapter 6

John learned quickly that his new master's disappearances were part of his life-style. Many were the hours the disciple spent alone in the cave or by the river awaiting the

Baptist's return. Occasionally the preacher ventured into the remoteness of his solitude for days at a stretch, and during these periods John was left to occupy himself in whatever way he saw fit. He came to understand that the strength of the Baptist's ministry lay in hours of meditation, and though he could only guess as to the express nature of that activity, he never again took offense at being left alone.

The months of winter passed slowly in this way. At times John grew restless, but he did not feel his days at Bethabara were meaningless. The hours he *was* afforded in the Nazarite's company were too filled with new discoveries and rich treasures to allow self-pity.

It had been clear in his mind why he had left home, what he could not believe in. It had been unclear just what he sought. He had felt instinctively that the Baptist had answers for him, and day by day he gained assurance that this hope was well founded.

The very night of John's decision to remain here, the preacher had told him that if he desired to be his student, he must follow in the rite of baptism. This had not been difficult for John to accept. He had known his master's call to repentance, and though he had been chilled by the Jordan only the day before, he welcomed the privilege of stepping once more into the muddy waters for a righteous cause.

The day after, the Baptist had taken the preliminary steps in discipling him. But John had not expected the ironic and painful manner in which he would do so.

Following the evening repast, during which the Nazarite had maintained his vegetarian role, and John had dined on roast fish, the preacher began to draw him out.

Propping his great legs upon a rock and resting his head back against his hands, he studied his young admirer for some seconds. The bulky leggings which normally encompassed his rock-like calves he had untied and allowed to flap open to steam away the perspiration and river-spray accumulated from the day's walk.

This holy man was surely not like the hierarchy of orthodox Judaism, John smiled to himself. He could imagine his father's face had he seen this earthy champion of an untitled cause, pacing before the people and quoting the hallowed phrases of the prophets as if they did not belong only within the whited walls of the synagogues. He could imagine his father's friends had he brought home this hairy itinerant with such an introduction as, "Meet my new master, the Rabbi John of Bethabara."

His face stretched into an involuntary grin, as he tried to envision the Nazarite cleanly groomed, short-haired, piously robed and adorned with the phylacteries of a Pharisee.

"You are feeling better now," the Baptist commented.

John jolted into sobriety, hoping the preacher had not read his thoughts. "Yes, sir. My strength is nearly back to normal."

"Do you often muse to yourself so openly?" the other queried.

John blushed, knowing the Baptist had indeed read more than he had hoped in his expression.

"Sir . . . I was only thinking of my father . . ." he hedged.

"I thought you were on poor terms with your father. But just now you smiled in good humor."

"Yes, sir. I guess I did. I was only . . . well, making comparisons."

"Him with me?"

"Yes, sir . . ." John answered, astonished at the preacher's perception.

"And what did you conclude?"

John would have chafed under this examination if he had not sensed the good nature which prompted it.

"Sir," he grinned, "there is *no* comparison."

The Baptist drew his legs up to his chin and gazed into the fire. "He is a Pharisee?"

"Yes."

"Of strict tradition?"

"Yes—how did you guess?"

"You might have tolerated his ways longer had he been more liberal."

"I think not, sir." John warmed to the subject. "I can see nothing to merit toleration in the teachings of the order!" Perhaps because his thoughts on the subject had never been welcomed at home, he feared a reprimand for this statement. But he then recalled the Baptist's reputation for criticism of the Pharisees.

The preacher continued to stare into the flames, his mind absorbed in thoughts far deeper than John's superficial fears.

"What teachings do you espouse?" asked the preacher.

John's face reddened somewhat, but the flames hid the color. He did not know just how open he might be with the Baptist. And yet the tone of the question assured him that the preacher was not laying a trap.

"You know the teachings of the rabbis?" replied John, floundering for a way to approach the topic.

"Indeed," said the Baptist.

"Many of them are noble."

"Yes. Do you follow one of their schools?"

"No, sir . . ."

The Baptist looked at him quizzically but did not prod him. John went on.

"And the Essenes?"

"Yes; do you admire them?"

"In a sense—"

"But you do not follow them?"

"No, sir."

"Nor the Pharisees?"

"No, sir."

"Nor the Sadducees?"

"No . . ."

The Baptist shifted his position. "You play games with me!" he laughed.

John reveled in this response. For once in his life it seemed he had found a mind which would not take offense at his arguments.

"Not really games, sir. If my answers confuse you, you catch a glimpse of my mind, for I am confused." To acknowledge this required courage, for never had John made such a confession. But threat seemed no part of the Baptist's manner. "I can only tell you what I believe by reciting the list of philosophies in which I do not believe," John continued. "And it seems there is nothing left. I have studied them all. None satisfies me. I know of none other to pursue."

The preacher leaned forward, intrigued. "You take this very seriously, I can see. Most men would not find the lack of a creed of great importance. They would merely shrug their shoulders cynically, and deny the existence of any truth at all."

"I am familiar with the Cynics. They revolt me," answered John. "But I have come close to their conclusions many times," he said, his forehead knit with sincerity. "I cannot, however, take the lack of a creed lightly. Something drives me on. I guess I am stubborn."

"You are a seeker," said the Baptist.

"You flatter me." John smiled, taking pleasure in what he considered a great compliment. The designation tickled his ego, for such he had always liked to consider himself. Therefore, the preacher's next words were leveling.

"No, I do not flatter you, John. It is good to be a seeker—but only if you find."

The correction was gentle, but unexpected, and John was stunned by its validity.

"I see your point." John's mouth twitched in an uncomfortable grin. "But if I cannot find, shall I cease to seek?"

The Baptist sensed the hint of belligerence with which this question was forwarded. He looked insistently at his young disciple. "Have you become convinced that there is no alternative to the routes you have pursued?"

"Almost," John nodded sadly.

"Almost?"

"Yes, sir."

"You feel there is still hope, then?"

John thought a moment. "I do, sir."

"And where does it lie?"

The young Jew's heart sped at the question. He could not conceal the admiration which rose in his hero-seeking soul as he considered the prophet before him.

"Why, sir, I hope it lies here!"

John expected a pious benediction upon his testimony of devotion. That would have been the way of most rabbis. And John would not have been offended, for he truly believed in the Baptist. What followed, then, came as yet another blow, and another lesson in the character of his new teacher.

The Baptist said nothing at all but walked to the mouth of the cave and peered soberly toward the starry night sky. The rain clouds had dispersed and the moon lit his face in a silhouette of awe and contemplation. He stood thus for several long moments, until John began to wonder at the severity which etched his rugged countenance.

His words, when at last they did come, struck the listener's heart like spears of ice. "Do not seek answers from me, John," the preacher spoke in heavy tones of warning. "I am but a man, as any other man."

John looked wide-eyed at his master, struggling inwardly against this pronouncement. Once before he had attempted to convince himself that the preacher was "only a man." He had not succeeded then, nor could he believe it now.

"I am no philosopher, John." The Baptist was still speaking. "I am no miracle-worker. I bring no new ideology for your contemplation." Turning to the bewildered young man, the Baptist demanded in strident tones, "Tell me, boy, what did you expect of me? Who did you think I was?"

John sat in the dark shadow of the man who now nearly filled the doorway with his broad frame. He could not read the Baptist's face, for the preacher's back was to the moon and the embers burned low within the hollow of the cave. He could imagine the fire of his expression, though, for he had witnessed the Nazarite's passion at the Jordan months before.

In John's confusion, however, he could not discern the source of his master's agitation. Did he truly mean what he said? Why this sudden shift in the tenor and direction of the evening?

John's mind reeled. Who *did* he think the Baptist was? What answers *had* he expected? He tried to formulate a credible response, but had none. And why had the Baptist put him on the defensive? With no warning, it seemed, this gentle conversation had turned into personal rebuke.

"You ask me this?" he stammered. "You ask questions of *me*, who has come to learn of *you*?"

The Baptist's silence answered in the affirmative, and John looked at him wildly. "If you need answers of *me*, I will tell you who you are!" he cried, his voice picking up sudden volume. "You are a pitiable hermit, unable to cope with human society, living a lie to the misleading of thousands!"

Silence filled the cave. John scarcely believed such words had escaped his own mouth. He might have spoken to his father that way, but *never* the prophet.

As the words still hung in the air, self-hatred rose to replace his bitterness. But pride kept him from retracting a single syllable.

Instead, he stood to his feet and was about to force his way past the mighty man before him, when one strong hand reached out to restrain him.

In vain, John tried to wrench his arm free, then stood his ground, staring miserably into the now visible face of the Baptist. He did not encounter, as he had expected, a look of anger or self-defense. Instead, it seemed the preacher had read deep into his soul and understood his confusion beyond natural capacity.

"You respond with the fire of lightning, John," he said gently. "Your soul roars with thunder at the least provocation."

John avoided the eyes which bored through him so easily. The analogy was true. His temperament *was* fiery, and did not cool easily. Belligerence welled up in him with little warning. His propensity for retaliation had caused him much pain in his life, but pride would not let him deal with it. Shamed by his own behavior, he stared at the ground as the preacher spoke again.

"I have not meant to bring a rift between us," he went on. "But if you are a true seeker, John, you must not be afraid of questions.

The truth does not come easily. You must not be afraid of blind corners or streets which seem to lead nowhere. Will you allow me to pose one more question for you?"

This time John listened without retort.

The Baptist still held him in an iron grip. "What I told you is true, John. I am a man, like any other. You should not seek answers from me, more than from anyone else. But, will you consider this? What was it that held you at the Jordan that day, long ago? What was it in the words of Isaiah that brought you back again?"

John studied the river and tried to remember. But his mind was so riddled with conflict he could not revive the memory.

"Go now, if you will," the Baptist was saying next. "Return home, if you must, or fly to the capitals of men's minds, to Alexandria or Athens. But try to remember, John. Try to remember the words."

The grip now loosened, and John sighed deeply. He did not know where he would go, but he must be alone.

Chapter 7

That night John slept but little. The cave he had chosen for shelter provided no warmth, only a break from the winter wind.

In his restlessness, however, he had time to contemplate the Baptist's questions. He had never really forgotten the message he had heard months before. He had only failed to call it up in the moment of conflict during which the preacher had asked for it.

Now it rang with the clarity of a great bell in his mind. The words of Isaiah repeated themselves again and again in his memory as he huddled in the solitude of the cave.

"I am the voice of one crying in the wilderness . . . prepare the way of the Lord! Repent, for the kingdom of heaven is at hand. Make straight in the desert a highway for our God!"

The hours passed in black silence as John mulled over the prophecy. It had held such promise, such hope for him. But what did it mean?

It was well past midnight when the young Jew finally drifted into a troubled and anxious sleep. When he awoke a few hours later the words still marched relentlessly, like soldiers, through the corridors of his mind.

As he emerged from the cave the sun was breaking majestically over the sheer ridge to the east. The sovereign yellow ball sent shafts like arrows to the earth and John shaded his eyes against them.

Glints of brilliant gold bounced from hillside to hillside. The whole earth seemed filled with it. "Every valley shall be exalted . . ." the message came again. "The rough places shall be made plain . . . and all flesh shall see it together . . ."

"What shall it see?" John whispered. "O Lord God Jehovah, what shall it see?" he pleaded, raising his arms toward the vault of blue above.

He left the hill and walked down toward the river. Kneeling beside the rushing swell he plunged his hands deep into the rapids and brought the cold water to his face. After a night with little sleep he was somewhat refreshed by this and stood again, studying the swollen Jordan. Again it came to him what he had witnessed months before. As clearly as if he stood before him, he could see the Baptist knee-deep in the water, and he could hear his voice as if for the first time.

"Prepare the way of the Lord, make straight in the desert a highway for our God!"

Suddenly John jolted into the present. This was the answer! This was what the whole earth would see together!

Surely the clarion call referred to some visitation of God. Scripture was full of warnings—warnings of judgment and retribution. But as John dwelled on the phrases he could not feel that they were words to fear. They rang like bells of jubilee. They seemed to call for celebration, not for cowardice.

"Every valley shall be exalted—the rough places shall be made plain. . . ."

John felt he stood on the edge of a great discovery, that some moment of revelation was about to be his, unlike anything he had before experienced. Yet still he groped blindly for an understanding of the passages.

"God, make the rough places plain!" he cried. "What is it you wish me to see? If there be any truth on earth, teach me, for you hold it in your hand."

He sat silently on the shore, feeling very much alone. The wave of anticipation passed, leaving him empty and desolate. But then gently, the stanzas repeated themselves, this time slowly, softly, like a cool hand of soothing.

"Prepare the way of the Lord . . . make straight in the desert a highway for our God." A shudder went through the young man huddled beside the river. The refrain drew pictures for him nearly too awesome to consider. Still they were beautiful pictures, delightful to the mind's eye. When he allowed himself, he could almost see God walking, coming toward him down a wilderness road.

"Impossible!" he shrugged. But the impression returned insistently.

"The words are symbolic!" he argued aloud, as if in a classroom debate. "They are not to be taken literally!"

But then he recalled the stories he had read as a child: stories of Enoch, who walked with God; of Abraham, who spoke and ate with him; of Moses, whose face shone like sunlight after having seen the Lord.

"It cannot be." John persisted, remembering the Baptist's injunction to study the words. "And yet, this is all the master preaches. He insists I am not to follow him, and yet his words cry for commitment, for dedication to—someone."

John paced the bank, anxiously, in keen anticipation. "If I am not to follow him, whom am I to follow?"

Hearing footsteps behind him, he wheeled about. The Baptist had come to search him out, and now eyed him expectantly. "Is there truth, boy?" he asked, his voice deep with compassion.

"Sir, I believe there is. . . ."

"And have you found it?"

John turned back and gazed across the river. "Sir, I have never believed in visions . . . I do not believe I had a vision . . . but . . ."

"What did you see?" the Baptist smiled.

"I could almost see . . . God . . . walking . . ." John stammered.

A look of triumph crossed the Baptist's face, and John could not help reveling in it.

"Can it be, sir?" A thrill went through him. "Can God walk with man?"

"We shall see," the Baptist assured him.

"All flesh shall see it together?"

The Baptist smiled broadly, and placed an arm about his disciple.

The rough places were becoming plain.

Chapter 8

There were many who wondered if the Baptist might be the long-awaited Messiah, the one prophesied from time immemorial, the one expected to set Israel free from the oppression of its enemies. John himself had pondered the same question often.

But the insight he had received by the river, the mental picture of God walking, had strengthened the instruction that John should take his eyes off the Baptist; that the future would unfold greater things than he had to offer.

Still, as John lived with his teacher, he could not help but be caught up in admiration for him.

The disciple was a bundle of contradictions, for though he was willful, headstrong, belligerent when challenged, he was also a seeker, as the Baptist had described him. And that propensity for searching, that longing for answers, had left him ripe for discipleship to any man who could truly win him.

Once won, John would be the most loyal and unshakable of followers. Rebellion would give way to zealous adoration, and the energy before spent in promoting his own will would be transferred to a crusader's enchantment with his master.

The Baptist had won him, though he had never set out to do this. The seeds had been planted months before when John had first heard him at Bethabara, and after the primary struggles, they had taken firm root and blossomed easily. In the months which followed, John's devotion grew so strong that the Baptist himself would find it difficult to transplant.

The preacher rarely discussed his own life. What John came to know about his background was based on bits and pieces, but even an incomplete chronicle of the Baptist's past made a fascinating tale.

The prophet's father was Zechariah, a priest, well respected and very righteous. The priest and his wife had grown old together, childless. When at last a son was given them, he was dedicated to the Lord's work, and in adolescence, having taken the vows of a Nazarite, he had gone to dwell alone in the desert, awaiting the time of service to God.

He must have lived in this manner some fifteen years, for John judged him to be about thirty. His contact with humanity had been severely limited in all that time, until he began his preaching ministry.

John was amazed by the Baptist's intellect. As the son of a priest, he had undoubtedly received a good formal education as a youth, but that could not explain his keen insights into a world with which he'd had but little contact for nearly two decades.

His knowledge of Scripture baffled the disciple, for it was based on memory, the preacher having no scrolls or parchments to study. Yet his ability to call up the words of the Law and the Prophets was seemingly effortless.

There was much more to learn about the Baptist's history, but some things he withheld, knowing John was not ready for them:

Meanwhile the weeks went by quickly as they awaited the warming of spring and the recommencement of the prophet's preaching. The two men spoke together of many things.

"My father says you preach a new form of righteousness," John began one day, after the Baptist had returned from the hills.

"Righteousness does not come in various forms, boy."

John smiled. "True, sir, but you do not preach the Law."

The Baptist sighed and paused in thought. "I do not deny the Law, John. The Law of God is perfect, but man is not. For all your father's legalism, is he perfect?"

"He keeps the Law, sir."

"Does he? Is his heart humble? Is he contrite in spirit? Does he prefer mercy to sacrifice?"

John did not answer. His silence spoke for him.

The Baptist looked compassionately at his friend, realizing that he still did not understand.

"Who, then, can be perfect, sir? What is the point of religion? We all fail in so many things."

The master drew near the young disciple, studying him across the flames of the cave's fire. "Exactly, boy. What do you think I preach?"

"But what is the point of preaching to sinners that they are sinners? It is hopeless cruelty."

"Did you feel hopeless when you heard the message last summer?"

John reflected. "No, sir. I was full of expectation."

"And so you should be."

The song of a desert bird woke John. It was only slightly past dawn, yet when he looked toward the pallet where the Baptist usually slept, he saw that the master had risen even earlier.

The young disciple dressed hastily, eager to catch up to the preacher. Pehaps he would allow John to accompany him into his solitude today.

Proceeding up the river in the usual direction of the Baptist's ventures, he stooped to take a drink and wash his face with the icy water of a small, trapped pool. As he did so, his reflection showed the marks which months of wilderness living had left upon him. His golden hair and beard had grown too long for his liking, and his unkempt, tattered clothing evidenced the lack of luxury to which he had become accustomed. He laughed audibly at his ragged appearance. The day was too glorious to allow self-pity. As he dipped his hands into the water, the pathetic image was obliterated, and he drank heartily of Jordan's sweet brew.

The sun massaged his back with warm fingers, and as he knelt on the sandy beach, wiping his mouth with his sleeve, he noticed small green shoots which had pushed their way up from the desert floor.

Spring had come! Even the jungle growth of Bethabara's lonely banks reveled in new life.

A sense of excitement nudged John. It would not be long until the crowds came again, until he would hear his master in his finest element once more.

As his memory constructed for the hundredth time the message he had first heard in this very valley, the words became suddenly audible.

"Repent! For the kingdom of heaven is at hand!"

Every fiber of John's being was instantly awakened. That had been more than his imagination. He wheeled about, facing downriver, and listened with tense anticipation.

Soon it came again. "I am the voice of one crying in the wilderness . . ."

With a jubilant shout, John was off, racing like lightning back toward the shallows.

Coming in view of Bethabara, John stopped short, scarcely able to believe the scene before him. Thousands of people ranged the hillsides east of the river, and many more could be seen joining them, streams of humanity merging from all sectors of Palestine.

John had not expected the crowds to be arriving already. What intuition had told the Baptist to arise and prepare on this given day?

John was alone on the far side of the river, and he felt conspicuous and awkward, so he secluded himself beneath a rocky overhang and sat down to watch the proceedings with eagerness.

Surveying the crowd from this vantage point, John was astounded to see the diversity of those gathered here. Various modes of dress and appearance revealed that many had traveled from the most distant parts of Jewry. They must have begun their journeys days before.

Again, of course, there were the ever-present Roman troops. However, to John's amazement and private disgust, even a handful of tax-collectors had joined the congregation. That the Baptist would tolerate them perplexed John greatly, but he put away such thoughts for the present.

The disciple now turned his eyes toward his master. The prophet stood in the river, his sturdy legs braced against the swollen current. His waistlong hair and magnificent beard were as wild as the skins he bound about him, and his head was lowered in silent meditation.

How John longed to be like him! Not in appearance, perhaps, for he could never compare on that scale. But in spirit, yes! Perhaps he would one day assimilate enough of the preacher's courage and soul to approach him on that plane.

"But look at me!" he scowled. "Hiding away in a corner for fear of being noticed. A long way to go before I'm like my master!"

John's introspection was cut short. A shuffling at the rear of the crowd indicated that a party of some importance had joined the throng.

Anxiously he sought to identify the source of the agitation. Yes, there they were, at the very back of the gathering: the Pharisees. He held his breath as he named them, for fear his father might be among them. To his relief, he was not, though these men were close friends of Zebedee. They were many in number and they were among the most elite corps from both the southern and northern provinces.

Clearly, they had been commissioned to come here. They had probably met at Jerusalem before beginning their journey.

That this was not a pleasure outing for them was proven by the fact that they had been joined by a group of their fiercest theological rivals, the Sadducees, another of Palestine's most influential sects. The High Priest had cleverly chosen to send the two opposing parties in hope of gaining the clearest possible picture of what would transpire. If the enemies agreed in their description, he would be sure of the truth.

A chill went up John's spine as he recalled the avowed plan of the council to "give the fanaticism until spring to calm itself." Zebedee had hinted at some action to be taken against the Baptist, should his popularity continue past that point.

It was apparent that the "fanaticism" had not cooled. The crowd was larger and the prophet more in demand than ever. John studied the pious ones. What plot would their superiors, Caiaphas and the priesthood, pose against the Baptist? There was no doubt it would be vicious.

The preacher had now waded across to the opposite side and paused on the bank before addressing the crowds. The Pharisees and Sadducees, huddled in exclusive conversation, eyed him like birds of prey.

"Master, be careful . . ." the disciple whispered.

The prophet scanned his spellbound audience and then his gaze settled upon the elite corps at the back.

Whispered excitement raced through the crowd. What would happen if the prophet were to challenge his adversaries face to face? Whose side should they take? The Pharisees were the spokesmen of Judaism, the very backbone of the Law. The congregation parted before the Baptist, leaving a wide opening between him and the holy men above.

Every muscle in John's body tensed. The drama was real but incredible. Dozens of the pompous self-righteous faced one lone man of God, across a space of barren desert hillside. Thousands watched a moment of climax in the life of a nation.

Not a sound was heard, save the rushing of the Jordan. Even the breathing of the onlookers was controlled as they awaited what the Baptist would say to his enemies. When at last the words came, they were reminiscent of those which he had often used when addressing the commoners who came for baptism. He had even been known to address the more humble orders of Pharisees and Sadducees who had come in good number to receive his touch. He would not alter his message to please his unrepentant enemies. In fact, his words were full of sarcasm and vengeance. Like the rumble of storm clouds, they were low at first, and terrible, picking up volume until they fairly shook the earth.

"You generation of vipers!" he roared. "Who has warned you to flee from the wrath to come?"

The crowd was dumbfounded, the holy men stunned, and wide-eyed.

"Bring forth fruits fit for repentance!" the prophet cried again, leveling penetrating eyes upon them.

The people fell back as the Baptist made his way up the path. His bearing was ominous, his tread determined.

In rebuttal to the self-defense his enemies were formulating, he continued, "And do not say to yourselves, 'We have Abraham as our father,' for I say to you . . ." and here he paused, kicking the pebbles beneath his feet, "God is able from these very stones to raise up children for Abraham!"

Silence descended. No one among the thousands dared breathe a sound. Beneath the preacher's persistent gaze, the ones who had been the subject of his rebuke lowered their heads. Not that they had been convinced of the truth; their pride could not allow that. But they had no ready word of rebuttal.

Slowly the Baptist turned and walked back toward the river. A hushed thrill marked the spectators as they glanced from the preacher to his speechless foes.

The self-righteous ones gradually lifted their heads, eyeing their conqueror and one another in anger and humiliation. After a brief interlude, their leader gave a nod of affirmation in the direction of the departing prophet. "You have wounded us . . ." he seemed to say. "You will pay." And then the group drew their robes about them and haughtily turned to leave.

The crowd could restrain itself no longer. Questions were voiced aloud, each onlooker attempting to analyze what he had witnessed.

By the time the preacher reached the river, the noise of the throng was nearly deafening, their excitement unleashed, their apprehension gone. For the first time in their generation they had seen the hierarchy of Judaism challenged and defeated. And whether for or against the Baptist's actions, they did not know how to evaluate what they had seen—what it might mean for themselves and the future.

The preacher was in the water again, looking at his bewildered people, and knowing they sought the reason for his attack on Israel's leaders.

His voice reached past the hills and met the ears of the retreating Pharisees and Sadducees, sending a shudder through them, and through all gathered about him:

"The axe is laid unto the root of the trees," he cried, the triumphant sound filling the desert like a Decapolis wind. "Every tree which does not bring forth good fruit is hewn down . . . and cast into the fire!"

Chapter 9

Even though the spring day had been warm throughout Palestine, a large fire blazed behind the hearth at the end of the council hall. This was the stone-hewn sanctum of the elders of Israel. Year around, it was winter-cold inside these massive gray walls, and the large gathering took bodily comfort in their numbers.

A buzz of masculine voices filled the hall, but Zebedee knew this would cease when he entered the room. He stood outside the chamber door as long as he dared before joining his fellow dignitaries. He dreaded the disapproval he knew was forthcoming, the questioning glances, the whispers.

Though the Sanhedrin's jurisdiction was limited by Roman law to Judea proper, its influence was over the entire Jewish nation and its representatives were of several provinces. It had taken the old Galilean, Zebedee, many years of hard work to gain a position of respect among his Judean comrades. Even yet there were those who scorned his provincial background. But he had proven himself a leader and his enemies had become less outspoken. How they would be reveling, now, in his son's departure from the faith.

When at last he could wait no longer, he placed a perspiring hand on the great door's lever and opened it. He was the last to arrive, but it was not for this reason that those closest to the entry eyed him with the anticipated curiosity.

Caiaphas and his father-in-law, Annas, sat at the far end of the chamber, well visible on their elevated platform. While Annas had been removed from the high priesthood by Roman edict, the general populace still considered his a lifetime appointment, and respected him as a high priest emeritus. Along the walls, in a semicircle of seventy-one curved chairs, would sit the Sanhedrin, supreme court of Judaism, and in front of them would be three rows of novices, here to study the Law. The court rarely met for any purpose but to try men suspected of criminal acts; but in a sense, this *was* a trial. A decision was to be made concerning the Baptist.

Many of the Pharisees and Sadducees milled about the center of the long room in noisy conversation, awaiting the commencement of the proceedings. As Zebedee had expected, however, silence fell upon them all at his appearance.

So, here he is, they began to whisper—the Pharisee whose son has turned heretic, a "Jew of Jews" whose youngest has left the truth.

Zebedee attempted to maintain a facade of pride and casual indifference to the ones about him. But he felt their scorn as surely as he would feel a knife in his back.

He knew their thoughts—they need not be voiced. They could be ravening wolves in their attack of the defenseless.

It was coming back on him now, the viciousness which he had leveled at others. But, pridefully, he shut any such thought out of his mind, divorcing himself from it, as he always did when the truth came too close.

Summoning what courage was left to him, he raised his head and faced his accusers as they gossiped among themselves. "What must it be like to lose a son to heresy?" they doubtless wondered. In the tradition of the orthodox, a "heretic," like John, was to be considered dead by his family. Only an isolated face here and there showed any pity for Zebedee's loss. But pity was as hard for this proud man to stomach as rebuke.

He gave a shudder he knew must be visible to those nearby. John *had* been lost to him, as surely as if he had died. It had taken months for this realization to impress itself upon him. At first he had flatly rejected it, believing that John could not be serious about leaving home, that he was not truly turning to heresy. He would return with the continuing winter winds.

But as the days had stretched into weeks, and the weeks to months, he had been forced to accept the worst.

Zebedee restrained the tears trembling at the corners of his old eyes. No one would ever know his feelings, least of all those around him. Stubborn pride raised an effective wall to hide them. John was dead. Let it be.

The voice of a council attendant now broke the silence. The meeting was beginning, and the room was abustle as all took their places. Annas would be generally aloof throughout the proceedings. He would not bother himself with anything less than the ultimate decision. And so he would sit in stern dignity at the head of the gathering, his wide-sleeved arms outstretched formally upon the arms of his stately chair.

Caiaphas himself was not a young man. Only a few years separated him from his father-in-law. This was not unusual in a society where fathers chose their daughters' husbands, and where men often married women much younger than themselves.

Still, even the few years' difference, the relative family positions, and the popular high priesthood of Annas called for reverence on the part of Caiaphas. So, he looked to Annas for the signal to begin.

A nod from the elder sent Caiaphas to the front of the platform, where he called loudly, "It is the purpose of this gathering to decide the treatment of one in question: one John, called 'The Baptist,' a Nazarite of the vicinity of Bethabara, beyond Jordan."

A rumble of excitement began to rise, but subsided as Caiaphas continued.

"It has been broadcast far and wide that the Baptist preaches heresy, a new form of 'righteousness,' and that he is misleading the multitudes. These are the charges. It is for us to weigh the evidence."

At this, one Pharisee stepped forward and asked to be heard. Another course of whispers and comments followed, for he was a member of the more liberal order, and was well known for his readiness to give an ear to questionable doctrines.

"Speak, Master Nicodemus . . ." Caiaphas allowed reluctantly.

Nicodemus had not always been a questioner. In his younger years he had been a strict legalist, as staunch as Zebedee. In fact, the two had at one time been great comrades. But as time had hardened Zebedee in his ways, for some reason it had mellowed Nicodemus. He was no longer so sure of his beliefs, though he was still greatly respected for his intellect and leadership.

The old gentleman approached the platform, daring to raise an inquisitive glance directly at Annas, bypassing Caiaphas. "Good sir, is it not the tradition of the Sanhedrin to allow one so charged to face his accusers?"

Annas shifted uneasily in his chair. Nicodemus' confrontation did not surprise him, though it appeared very daring to the younger men present. The challenger had known the elderly priest since they were boys, and so was not easily awed by him.

However, Annas had not achieved his high station by being slow of wit. Though he chafed under the inquiry, he was ready with an answer. "True, brother, it is the tradition. But we are not meeting for the purpose of formal trial. This is merely a gathering for discussion."

"But, sir," Nicodemus prodded, "has not Caiaphas said we are to decide the 'treatment' of the Baptist? If this is not a trial, how can we come to such a conclusion?"

"'Treatment' is not 'sentence,' Brother Nicodemus," Annas said firmly. His patience was growing short, and Nicodemus knew he must tread softly.

"Good sir," he said as reverently as possible, "to me that seems mere semantics. And so is the insistence that this is to be only a 'discussion.' "

"Shall we proceed?" Caiaphas interjected, attempting to recover his hold on the meeting and to sidestep Nicodemus' challenge.

But the elderly Jew would not be put off. "My question has not been answered," he said, maintaining his respectful but assured attitude.

Annas leaned forward, the strength of his position impressing itself upon all present. "Friend Nicodemus, we *shall* proceed. The purpose of the gathering has been defined."

Nicodemus bowed to the rank of the man above him. He had, however, scored his point. He felt confident the proceedings would bear the mark of his opinion, and so he stepped back silently into the congregation.

Caiaphas now called for witnesses and the large group of men parted to let those approach the front who had seen the Baptist. They had rallied from the blow to their pride delivered by the wild man at Bethabara only days before. They were ready to call down retribution.

The leader of the group, Master Jacob Bar Harsha, went forward. "Sirs, we are witnesses to the preaching of the Baptist, having been commissioned by yourselves to go to Bethabara."

"What do you have to report?" Caiaphas asked, expecting a detailed oration on the events at the Jordan, with a lengthy interpretation of what the commission had witnessed.

"Sirs," Master Jacob said again, straightening his old shoulders and planting his feet firmly, "this man is a plague on our people!"

Caiaphas was taken aback, as were all present. None had been prepared for the brevity and force of this pronouncement. A low murmur arose about the room, as Caiaphas looked at Annas in bewilderment.

The elder priest eyed Master Jacob sharply. "Good man, is this all you have to say?"

Master Jacob cleared his throat dramatically and took another step forward. "Sirs," he said, gesturing to the four walls, "most all of Palestine is aware of the Baptist's message. Everyone knows he calls for repentance, baptizes in the Jordan, and makes obscure references to some future divine visitation. To that report we can add little . . ." Here he paused, gathering ammunition from deep inside himself. "However," he continued, "he preaches rebellion and heresy, and we would warn all present that this man is a menace to our nation!"

The crowd had been eager for just such a judgment as this, and scattered applause punctuated their reaction.

Annas was not one to defend the Baptist. But he must keep some semblance of order here; he must see to it that at least the amenities of a proper hearing were adhered to before a conclusion could be drawn.

Under his piercing eyes, the uproar tapered to quick silence. He then scrutinized the spokesman carefully.

"Now, Master Bar Harsha," he said with a heavy tone of warning, "just how has the Baptist preached rebellion and heresy?"

The old Pharisee Bar Harsha was, like all his fellows, a lawyer. Thus far he had played his role of accuser very well. Though he had not had to defeat any opposition other than Nicodemus', he had strengthened the feelings of antagonism which already existed here against the Baptist. Like the most clever of prosecuting attorneys he had gained an emotional foothold with his opening statement. All that remained was to throw out a few well-chosen bits of evidence for the crowd to sniff at. They would go for them like starving dogs for carrion.

Having plotted his course and the predicted responses well in advance, he approached his case confidently. Stroking his beard and pacing back and forth, he began, "Gentlemen, we will all agree that the backbone of our nation and our creed is the Law." He stopped his pacing, gave his statement time to underscore itself, and then resumed. "The men gathered here are, by profession and by social recognition, the interpreters and the staunchest supporters of that Law." Here he stood still again, this time giving lengthy study to the faces before him. "Now . . . is it not true that if one wishes to destroy a nation, he must first destroy its foundation?" His voice mounted and he demanded, "How does one do this? Must he not first destroy the people's confidence in that foundation? Would a rebel not seek to destroy Israel's confidence in her Law?"

He knew the congregation agreed on that point, and so he continued. "What is the surest route to reach that end? Why, is it not to destroy the nation's confidence in those who *support* the Law?"

A tidal wave of comment followed this, as almost all those present nodded their enthusiastic approval of Master Jacob's logic.

A glint of triumph danced in his shrewd old eyes. And now he drew in the net: "Gentlemen," he appealed, feigned humility coloring his tone, "has not the Nazarite done just this? How else can we explain the brutal treatment my brethren and I received at his hands, in full view of the impressionable public?"

So this was how they had reasoned it, Nicodemus sighed. This was how they had rationalized their way out of the need to take the Baptist's rebuke to heart. The prophet was attempting to mislead the nation, to create a question as to its laws and precepts. A comforting assumption! he smirked.

Silently, he watched the mass mind at work. Despite the legal trappings of this hearing and the facade of propriety, he knew that a mob's heart beat beneath the surface as surely as it would at a gathering of street rebels. These men were as eager to overthrow the Baptist as any Jewish Zealot to overthrow Rome. They fed on the same emotion and whetted their instincts on the same fiery appeal. The Baptist had been tried and condemned before this mockery had ever begun.

Now that Master Jacob had said his piece the room was hot with blood-fever. The triumphant old Pharisee turned to the platform, and, bowing low, offered, "Your honors, I leave the conclusion to you." He then resumed his place in the crowd and awaited the obvious.

Caiaphas leaned over to Annas in intense consultation, and then, his brow furrowed, he called for order. "Gentlemen! Gentlemen!" The silence came at last. "You have heard Master Bar Harsha. Are there further comments from the witnesses?"

It seemed that everything had been said, but presently a shuffling in the crowd indicated there was more to come. Master Jacob was attempting to encourage a hesitant young Pharisee to go forward. The novice, who had not been a formal member of the commission, but who had followed with them to Bethabara, was shaking his head obstinately. At last with a sigh, he stepped up. "I am sure Master Sheva can add more to the discussion," Master Jacob appealed. "Go ahead," he prodded the shy one. "Tell them."

"Well," he paused, "I assume Master Jacob wishes me to tell what happened after the others left."

"State your case," nodded Caiaphas.

That seemed to rattle the young man. It appeared to Nicodemus that he did not at all wish to bring forward any "case," but had been put on the spot, and must deliver out of obligation, not desire. The old Jew watched him with interest.

"Well," he paused, "the day of our observation at Bethabara, I remained behind when the others left. After the Baptist had addressed us . . ."

"Rebuked us!" demanded Jacob.

". . . rebuked us . . ." the younger repeated haltingly. "After that, there were many questions from the crowd. It seemed that if the righteousness of the Pharisees and Sadducees had been questioned, surely everyone's had."

Caiaphas listened intently. "Continue," he urged.

The young Pharisee hesitated. It was apparent he was not sure he was doing the right thing, but with a nudge from Master Jacob, he went on.

"I remember that several in the crowd asked the Baptist, 'What then shall *we* do?' And he responded, 'He that has two coats, let him impart to him that has none; and he that has meat, let him do likewise.' "

As he said this, his eyes took on a faraway look. That he had been deeply impressed by the Baptist was apparent to Nicodemus and all who had any sensitivity. After a moment's silence the young man was jolted back into the present by Caiaphas' voice.

"Yes? How does this apply to the discussion at hand?"

"There is more . . . much more!" interjected Master Jacob, nervously. Gritting his teeth and eyeing Sheva sideways he whispered, "Tell them!"

Young Master Sheva heaved another sigh. "There were publicans and Roman guards present that day. They also asked the preacher what they must do to be righteous."

At this a roar of hilarity ascended from the floor and, though Caiaphas found the laughter gratifying, he called for order. "Silence!" he demanded. "Let the lad continue!"

"To the publicans the Baptist said, 'Exact no more than that which is appointed you,' and to the soldiers, 'Do violence to no man, neither accuse any falsely; and be content with your wages.' "

A brief span of silence followed. Could it be that this was all the Baptist had demanded of these servants of Rome? Had he not denounced them? Had he not taken advantage of the situation to call down disgrace on Israel's enemies? Had he subjected Palestine's leaders to public mockery and yet said nothing against Caesar's tax-collecting robbers or his bloodthirsty troops? When nothing more was added, furor spread through the crowd.

Nicodemus continued to eye the young witness. Again the novice's gaze was faraway; sadness etched his features. Had he betrayed a good and honorable man? he seemed to be wondering.

The young Pharisee could still envision the small group of publicans who had approached the waters of baptism that day at Bethabara. He could yet remember the tall, red-caped soldiers, astride their steeds, looking, for the first time, very humble as they made their way toward the preacher.

And he would never forget the Baptist's voice, ringing with rebuke as he had denounced the commission, then soft and patient as he spoke with the enemies of Zion.

But Caiaphas was speaking again. "It would appear, gentlemen, that Master Jacob and his commission have drawn a good conclusion. What man would denounce our leaders and not Rome's unless he meant to head a rebellion against Israel? We thank you, Master Sheva, for your most important bit of evidence."

At this Sheva gave a shudder, and bowed his head.

But Caiaphas did not notice. He was surveying the crowd in search of one more witness, for it was best to have three establish a verdict.

"Is Master Zebedee of Capernaum present?"

All heads turned toward the rear of the room.

"Yes, your reverence," Zebedee called weakly, his face suddenly white with fear.

The motive which drew the priest to single out Zebedee was clear only to himself. Perhaps he wished to make a public example of a heretic's father. Perhaps he hoped Zebedee might have something more to offer the council.

"Master Zebedee, it is said that your son John has become a follower of the Nazarite. . . . "

Zebedee's palms were clammy and a cold sweat dotted his forehead. "Yes, sir. Some say so."

Caiaphas scrutinized him. "You do not know?"

"No, sir. I have not seen or heard from my . . . from John, since last winter." Scenes of that sad Hanukkah flashed across his mind and he lowered his gaze.

"You accompanied the commission to Bethabara. Did you not see your son there?"

Zebedee fidgeted. "Sir, I did not go to Bethabara . . . I . . . I had urgent business in Capernaum. You gave me leave to stay home."

Caiaphas strained his memory. "Oh, yes . . . I recall."

Zebedee looked again at the floor. He hoped the high priest would not question what "urgent" business he had had. The truth was that he could not have borne such a journey. To see John with the Baptist would have killed him. He had begged out of the commission for that reason.

Perhaps Caiaphas sensed this, but he did not pursue it.

"All right, Master Zebedee, I had hoped that with your . . . special . . . attachment to the situation, you would have some definite insights."

Zebedee did not look at him. "None sir . . . I will support whatever decision the council concludes."

Chapter 10

Though the meeting of the council had been held for discussion only, it had, in fact, been a trial. Nicodemus' challenge had been well founded. The Baptist had been named guilty without a chance to defend himself.

However, Annas and Caiaphas were too cautious to call for an end to the Baptist's influence without following the etiquette of legal proceedings, at least on the surface. They could not risk the public outrage that would surely follow anything less.

It was for this reason that a final commission was sent to Bethabara.

Those included among the group were mostly Pharisees, some of whom were Levites and priests. These were to question the preacher, so that he might have the chance to face his accusers and speak for himself, thus giving the final stamp of legality to his own sentence. They realized the Baptist might not know the full purpose of their inquisition, but to them that was of little consequence.

This time, Zebedee accompanied them. He dared not refuse

Caiaphas' request again. But he was not a leader among his
brethren on this venture, as he would have been in times past.
Even if skepticism and scorn had not been written on their faces
whenever they looked at him, he could not have held his head high
in their presence. Zebedee was not the man he once had been.

As they walked, he maintained a position far to the rear of the
group. He did not shrink from conversation when it was directed
toward him, but neither did he initiate it. His mind was on what he
would find at the Jordan, how he would react should he see his son,
and how John would behave upon seeing him. For he surely *would*
see him if he was with the Baptist.

The Baptist. The thought of him stuck in the old man's mind. He
was the one to be blamed for his son's rebellion. But then Zebedee
smirked, "No, the boy would have followed *any* heretic zealot to
come along. Still . . ." Zebedee growled beneath his breath, "it
was *this* heretic who won him."

As the old Jew contemplated this, his fists drew into clenched
knots, and his stride became rigid and angry. Enveloped in the
privacy of his inner struggles he did not see one of the group draw
near him.

"Brother," the voice carried a tone of compassion, "perhaps the
lad will come home soon."

Zebedee jerked involuntarily at that remark, and looked
wide-eyed into the face of Nicodemus. But regaining a measure of
dignity he said calmly, "Of what do you speak?"

Nicodemus only smiled and Zebedee tensed under his knowing
gaze. "Sir, if you speak of my son . . . you speak of the dead," he
said bitterly, his eyes full of indignation. "I do not think of him,
nor should you!"

Zebedee sensed that Nicodemus was not convinced, but the two
walked in silence for some distance. At last, thoughtfully,
Nicodemus began again. "Let us speak of other things, then. What
do you think will become of the preacher?"

Zebedee stared at the ground. A large red ant scampered across
the road in front of him. A gleam in his eye, the old man raised a
foot, quickly crushed the helpless creature, and then covered it
with a kick of dust so that he might not come in contact with "any
dead thing," in accordance with the Pharisaical code. Grinding it
into the earth with his full weight, he looked silently up at his
inquisitor. Not a word was necessary.

It was the afternoon of the fourth day when the commission

reached the Jordan. As they left the road to venture down the desolate wilderness track, they merged with others making pilgrimage to hear the Baptist.

Zebedee became increasingly uneasy as he and his companions drew nearer Bethabara. Already the preacher's commanding call could be heard echoing to the oncoming crowds and demanding repentance.

So this was the "voice" so notorious throughout Palestine; the voice which had called his son away from home and family. Zebedee cringed.

As planned, the commission would stand on the edge of the crowd, not mingling with the unsanctified commoners. They would observe the day's proceedings until the congregation had grown to its largest size, and then, when there were as many witnesses as possible, they would approach the preacher and begin their inquisition.

Zebedee remained toward the rear of the group, unable to bring himself to look up from the ground. He could hear the Baptist's voice, and he was most eager to catch a glimpse of the legendary figure, but he trembled to think he might see John standing with him.

"O Lord Jehovah," he whispered, "have mercy. . . ."

Though the commission stood aloof from the crowd, they were occasionally jostled by those who were pouring through the vale toward the river. One particularly large family now passed close to the pious ones. The old father of the group, a small, bent man in the rags of a street vendor, bowed humbly and shamefacedly as he sought the path of least obstruction, bringing him shoulder to shoulder with Master Jacob Bar Harsha.

In the family's train was carried a stretcher bearing a crippled child, and a broad avenue was necessary for its passage. With this interruption the commission was forced to move far to one side and Zebedee was made to look up. As the family wended its awkward passage, Zebedee's eye was caught unexpectedly by a figure standing some distance away in the congregation.

The man was a young Jew, perhaps in his early thirties. A light woolen mantle covered his head, but a smooth forehead and regular features were visible beneath. From what Zebedee could determine, his hair and beard were light brown, with glints of golden auburn where the sun lit them.

His tanned skin indicated he had spent a good part of his life out of doors. He was not unusually tall, and yet he did stand head and shoulders above many of the men present. Beneath a simple peasant's cloak was a sturdy set of shoulders, and his rolled sleeves exposed rough-hewn arms apparently used to hard labor. Had Zebedee been closer he might have seen that his hands, which were clasped loosely in front of him, were large and calloused.

These terms might have described many men. Though certain physical qualities about him could be called attractive, there was nothing particularly outstanding about his appearance. Yet Zebedee found himself unable to ignore him, and some moments passed before he realized how intently he had been studying the stranger.

It was something in his bearing, in his very demeanor which had captured Zebedee. Despite the jostling, pressing crowd, he seemed to stand apart, and yet, he, like everyone else, was hemmed in on all sides, shoulder to shoulder with the masses about him. In a multitude, where every human emotion was visible, from reverential awe of the preacher to simple curiosity, from deep inquisition and confusion, to ridicule and scornful disgust, this man seemed to have thoughts unique to himself.

Something in his fair eyes, in the set of his head, suggested serenity, a special kinship with what he witnessed, as if he had insight into the proceedings denied to the people surrounding him.

Yet there was no haughtiness in his manner. Instead, he emanated confidence tempered by gentility difficult to define.

Zebedee wondered if he came here often, if he might know the Baptist personally. "Perhaps he is one of his disciples . . ." Zebedee reasoned. But at that thought, sorrow crept upon him afresh. "Does he perhaps know . . . John?"

He looked away but then found himself studying the stranger once more. What might that face contain? he wondered. "Why does he seem so detached from those about, and yet so . . . alive . . . to this spectacle?"

Zebedee was at last brought back to the reality of his own purpose here. The voice of the preacher pierced his consciousness, and as the last few arrivals took their places, the previously noisy, unsettled throng began to grow quiet.

Zebedee could put off the inevitable no longer. He must look on the Baptist, whether or not John was with him.

Finding an aisle of vision unobstructed by the multitudes, he was both relieved and disappointed that he did not see his son. But there stood the preacher, calling his song of repentance. Zebedee was astounded. He had heard much of this man. He had not, however, expected anyone this . . . unusual. He would have laughed, but something quenched that impulse.

It was not difficult to see why the Baptist attracted the masses, why some might even have been foolish enough to wonder if he were the Messiah.

But a sneer crossed the Pharisee's aged face. "Fools, indeed! Don't you see?" he thought to himself. "Why, unlikely as it might be, anyone could dress in this manner. The simplest opportunist or lunatic could parade through the water shouting the Scriptures. Do you take up with every wild man who poses as a prophet? The hills are probably full of them!"

Yet, Zebedee could not shake the eerie feeling which gripped him as he gazed on this man. There *was* something unique about him—he could not deny it.

"But, Messiah?" he laughed uneasily. "Never!"

Suddenly, Zebedee and all those present were caught by the most unexpected of messages. In answer to the question carried in the minds of thousands since his first appearance at Bethabara months before, the Baptist ceased his pleas for repentance, raised his arms and cried, "I indeed baptize you with water unto repentance! But . . ." Here he paused, allowing his next words ample room for impact, and casting his gaze deep into the crowd, ". . . but—he that comes after me is mightier than I . . . I am not even worthy to carry his shoes; he shall baptize you with the Holy Ghost and with fire! He will gather his wheat into the garner, but he will burn up the chaff with unquenchable fire!"

Mute wonder gripped the crowd, and as they considered the meaning of this new message, excitement poured over them. One "mightier" than the Baptist? He *had* spoken often of "preparing the way of the Lord," of "making straight in the desert a highway for our God . . ." Could he have meant this to be taken literally? They looked at one another, each seeking some sign of comprehension on the face of his neighbor.

Near the river, obscured from Zebedee's view, stood John. Days before, he had decided to join his master during his appearances, rather than spend the weeks observing from a distance. When the crowds came forward to be baptized he often assisted his master, at his request.

With this new development in the Baptist's message, the disciple tingled with anticipation. The strange vision he had had by the river now came to mind again. As vividly as before, he could see God, walking down a desert road.

But his reveries were interrupted by the sound of a voice behind him.

"Sir . . . do you know?" it asked.

The question had been directed toward him, and he looked about for the source. Everyone was talking. Who had spoken to *him?*

"I say, sir . . ." it came again. "Do you know?"

A small withered man, a total stranger with a pointed beard and inquisitive eyes leaned toward him through the crowd.

"Pardon me?" John said.

"You *are* his disciple, are you not? Do you know of what he speaks?"

John had no ready answer, but he was saved from embarrassment by an interruption in the crowd. Someone was coming toward the river.

It was the young Jew whom Zebedee had found so fascinating earlier. As he came, the people nearby moved aside, quieting as they watched him, until the entire throng was still, sensing that something of great import was about to happen.

Making his way slowly down the hillside, he seemed divorced from those who watched him, as if something far beyond the immediate moment and surroundings held his thoughts. Yet it was also apparent he was consciously bent on some great purpose at this present time, in this certain place—that he was keenly aware of the impact his appearance made on the congregation.

John was captivated. As the stranger drew near, he found himself moved irresistibly by the study of him. In his face was a perfect harmony of humility and strength; in his eyes, truth and understanding. Could this be the one the preacher had spoken of? The one mightier than he, who would purge the nation?

By the time the man reached the edge of the Jordan the only sound to be heard in the whole of Bethabara was the rushing of the water. Not a spectator moved for fear of disturbing the witness of what was to come. Not a word was whispered, not a breath was drawn too audibly.

The stranger stood on the bank for some seconds, in silent communion with the Baptist, who gazed upon him wonderingly. The preacher's expression spoke volumes. How he longed to cry out, "Are you the one . . . the one who was to come?" But the question went unasked, for he knew the answer.

The stranger now stepped into the cold, sweeping water, and lowered the mantle from his own head. Tears of joy welled up in the preacher's eyes and spilled down his cheeks. "I need to be baptized by you," he said bewilderedly, "and do *you* come to *me?*"

The crowd hung on these words expectantly, waiting for the stranger's response.

John stood near enough that he could clearly see the face of the mysterious visitor. Never would he forget his look. It was full of compassion such as he had never before seen, and when at last the stranger spoke, the Baptist's disciple trembled with awe and suspense.

"Allow it to be so now . . ." the man was saying, "for thus it becomes us to fulfill all righteousness."

The sound of the voice was right. It matched the stranger's appearance, unassuming and yet gripping in its authority.

Who was he?

The Baptist studied him incredulously but reverently, and then, nodding in affirmation, reached out his arms to hold him.

As John watched, his master willingly took second place in the scene he had always before so dramatically dominated. He was no less the man, but he was no longer the central figure. For the first time, one he baptized overshadowed the Baptist, and he allowed it to be so, joyfully accepting the role he had been destined to perform.

A mesmerized crowd watched as the pilgrim went through the rite of baptism. But what followed was to be far beyond their wildest anticipations.

As the man came up from the rushing waters, he looked high into the sky, and the clouds over Bethabara suddenly separated in a wide arc above him. From the heavens poured a shaft of brilliant light, almost tangible in its energy and outline, and it surrounded the very form of the stranger.

The crowd fell back in fear, cries of bewilderment and dread rising from every hill and hollow.

But this was not to be the end. Now the sky rumbled, as if with thunder. Yet it was a spring day, and there was no sign of storm. It seemed a voice pierced the heavens and traveled down the shaft which touched the stranger.

"This is my beloved Son," it came, loudly and distinctly, "in whom I am well pleased." Then it died away as it had come, with the rumble of departing thunder, and in its wake deathly silence filled the vale.

The shaft of light slowly disappeared, the clouds resumed their previous position, and the crowd looked on in wonder.

Not a soul took his eyes off the stranger as he lowered his gaze and bowed his head. Not a man, woman, or child ceased watching him as he drew up his wet robes and turned to the Baptist. The great preacher stood trembling before him, his face full of longing. But the man gave him a tender smile, and contemplated the wilderness to the south.

Hesitating only momentarily, his bearing marked with a mixture of intense inner struggle, unexplained heaviness, and strong resolution, he returned from the river and passed silently down the shore, as though driven by an unseen force. All eyes followed his determined stride, until he was lost to sight in the wilds of Jordan.

Though the Baptist would not speak another word, though there would be no more baptisms that day, it would be sunset before the crowds would disperse.

And it would be nightfall before the young disciple John would leave the riverbank.

Chapter 11

The drama at Bethabara was quickly noised far and wide throughout Palestine. No one knew precisely what to make of it all. Some said the light and the voice heralded the coming of the Messiah. Others laughed at this idea, attributing the rumor to mass delusion and hysteria. The sky, of course, had only thundered, they said, and the shaft of light was only lightning. There were even those who supposed it had been a great plot to deceive the people, that someone or some group had cleverly persuaded most of those present to enter into a conspiracy to spread this wild tale. What reason there would be for this, they were unable to speculate.

The Pharisees, for once, remained silent on the issue. They were not about to risk a statement on such a volatile subject; not yet, at least.

Master Jacob Bar Harsha and the commission felt it a most inopportune time to approach the Baptist with their inquisition. They must know, first, the meaning of what they had witnessed. They felt unsure just how to proceed now, and whether they wished to admit it or not, they were deeply fearful.

They had been just as amazed, just as awed as any commoners in the congregation. Dread of the unknown had shown in their faces just as it had in the faces of all who had witnessed the light and the voice.

When they had recovered their senses sufficiently, they discussed their next move. Considering this new development, they felt it best to return to the capital city even though they had not fulfilled their mission. Surely Annas and Caiaphas would agree with their decision, once they heard the story.

John had sat perched atop a great boulder all afternoon. His master had been gone since the previous evening, having trekked into his solitude following the pilgrim's appearance. Though John had been eager to speak with the Baptist concerning what had happened, he had been content to wait, even rather glad to be alone with his own thoughts.

Now, however, he became restless. From this vantage point above the river, he could watch for the preacher's return, and the moment he caught a glimpse he would run to meet him.

The sun was just lingering on the edge of the horizon, casting a coral glow over the desert, when John made out the figure of a man far in the distance. Strangely, he came from the direction of the shallows, rather than from the north, where the master usually ventured. It must be the Baptist, though. Who else would be coming toward the cave at this hour?

John slid down the side of the giant rock, dropped quickly to the ground, and raced to meet his teacher.

"Sir! I am so glad you are here!" he called as the distance narrowed.

Still the twilight seemed to play tricks with his eyes. The approaching form did not look like that of the Baptist.

"Since when do you call me 'sir'?" came an amused reply.

John stopped abruptly in his tracks. "Andrew?" he asked incredulously.

"The same," called the newcomer, now clearly visible to his friend.

"It can't be!" John exclaimed as they embraced each other jubilantly. "What are you doing out here?"

"One might ask the same of you," Andrew smiled.

"Of course. But I'm sure you know."

"Yes. Zebedee has told us. Why do you think I have come?"

John paused, his jovial spirit suddenly turned sullen and suspicious. Andrew was the brother of John's best friend, Simon.

They had all grown up together in Capernaum, and had all fished with Zebedee's fleet. But though John knew this slight, soft-spoken fellow very well, the mention of his father's name put him on the defensive.

"He has sent you! To persuade me to come home!" he growled.

Andrew received this like a blow. "John! You suspect me of such betrayal?"

John eyed his friend carefully and then looked away, ashamed. It seemed sometimes that he had no control over his own tongue. "Then why *did* you come?"

"Not for the reason you suggest. Besides, if Zebedee had wished to call you back, he would have done so yesterday!"

"Yesterday?" John asked. "What do you mean?"

Andrew caught his note of perplexity. "You did not know your father was here?" he stammered.

"At Bethabara?"

"Of course! I thought surely you would have seen him with the other Pharisees, on the hillside."

"I did not," John whispered, looking at the ground. A strange new sadness worked at his heart. He who had just flared with anger at the possibility of his father's asking him to return, now shrank from the fact that Zebedee had been here and not sought him out at all.

Andrew sensed his friend's disappointment, and added compassionately, "I see why your father gave me only a nod as we passed in the crowd. He had nothing to tell me of you, because you did not see each other. How his heart must have broken, to have missed you. . . ."

John's throat tightened with sentiment, but pride forced the emotion aside.

"No, Andrew. If he *had* seen me, and who is to say he did not, he would not have spoken. Something else brought him out here—not love for his son."

Sympathetic silence was the only response, but at last, John emerged from his melancholy.

"Andrew! Look at that wet cloak! Come, let's get a fire going." He smiled, embracing his friend once more, and leading him toward the cave. "The 'shallows' are not so shallow this time of year. You must dress in short skins like the Baptist to keep from getting your clothes soaked when wading across them." The memory of his initiation in the Jordan brought a twinkle to his eye and he laughed aloud.

"I don't know why the Baptist ever bothered to baptize me. I was sufficiently doused the first night I crossed that river!"

As John began the fire, Andrew removed his wet garments. At the sight of Simon's little brother disrobed, the disciple stifled the temptation to laugh. It had always been difficult to believe this small fellow was so closely related to the burly fisherman, but John remembered only too well Andrew's sensitivity to any comparison, so he resisted the urge to mention it.

"You never did answer my question, Andrew," he said instead. "What are you doing out here? Apparently you were present at the Jordan yesterday."

Though huddled near the flames, Andrew attempted to conceal his bony physique.

"I came out probably for the same reasons you first came months ago. I was curious. I had heard so much . . ." Andrew's voice tapered to a whisper, and John empathized with the awe evidenced in his tone. Recovering himself, the little fellow went on. "Since Zebedee had given us all a brief vacation during his absence from Capernaum, I decided to take advantage of the time and come out here to see the Baptist for myself."

"And what do you think?" John asked.

Andrew's eyes reflected the flames and their shadows. "What *am* I to think?" he said softly. "He is everything I had heard, and more. But . . ."

"But what?" John urged.

"But, I certainly never expected . . ." his voice trailed off again.

John knew what he was thinking. "You never expected . . . a miracle?"

Andrew straightened. "Right, John! That's what it was! Don't you agree?"

The disciple nodded solemnly.

"John, who was he?" Andrew asked urgently. "You are the Baptist's disciple. Can you tell me who the stranger was? What the sound and light were?" Forgetting his appearance, he stood, and his voice rose with excitement. "Oh, John! What is it all about? Surely you know something the rest of us do not!"

John prodded the kindling with a pointed stick and stood also. "No! I do not know who he is," he answered somewhat sharply. But then he caught himself and continued, turning to the twilight sky. "I know very little more than you, Andrew. I can only guess, like anyone else."

"At least your guess would be educated!" Andrew pleaded. "You have been closer to the preacher than anyone."

John sighed and sat down again. "Yes, I suppose that is true. And I do have my theories—though they are only that: theories," he warned.

"Yes, yes! So, go on! What do you think?"

John paused, hesitating to reveal his deepest longings. "You know that the Baptist uses the words of Isaiah whenever he speaks of some future coming of the Lord," he said.

"Yes." Andrew squatted again by the fire and leaned forward breathlessly to catch each syllable.

John fought the tingle of excitement which worked up his own spine. Not wishing Andrew to think him overly mystical, he assumed the tone of intellectualism which had always served well to cover feeling. "Expositors of the Scriptures have traditionally held that these passages refer to . . ." but here his facade broke down, and the force of wonder made him fall silent.

"To what?" Andrew prodded. "They refer to what?"

"To the . . . coming of the Messiah," John admitted at last, his voice deep with emotion.

Andrew trembled. "You think the pilgrim was the Messiah?" he whispered.

John turned an intense face toward his friend. "I wish I knew, Andrew."

His young companion was mute with awe. But John shook himself and stood again, busying his hands with the gathering of more firewood from the back of the cave. "Tell me," he called, "why did you not join me last night? Did you stay in the desert?"

"I wanted to be alone," Andrew replied, "as many probably did, after all that happened. It was a cold night. But, like a shepherd, I slept under the stars. There were campfires to be seen all over the hills."

"And when will you return home?" John asked, rejoining him with an armful of driftwood.

Andrew hesitated. "What would you say if I told you I wish, like you, to follow the Baptist? That I wish to stay?"

John was surprised, and showed it clearly. "Why, I would say 'welcome!' Welcome, indeed! Do you mean it?" he asked enthusiastically.

"Yes—if you'll have me," Andrew replied with relief.

"If I'll *have* you! Why, you'll never know how I have missed my friends!"

"I realize I have not been as close to you as Simon has."

John only laughed. "You have been like a younger brother!" he assured him. "For my part, I am glad you are here. Of course, the Baptist will have the final say. But I am certain he would welcome a new face. He must be growing tired of mine by now!"

The warmth of John's ready acceptance made shy Andrew glow with pleasure.

"Speaking of your brother," John's voice was full of memories, "why did he not come? Before I left he spoke often of doing so."

"He wanted to come, more than any of us. He has missed you, John," Andrew said gently. "Zebedee put him and James in charge of the ships. They were in need of some repairs, and he chose them to oversee that project. It has kept him very busy. He could not come."

At the new mention of his father and his brother, sorrow tore at John afresh.

Andrew studied his friend. "You think of your family?"

It was not really a question.

There was no reply.

Chapter 12

Of course the crowds still came, more thronging the Jordan than ever before. News of the miraculous baptism had brought many who would stay days at a time, in hopes the unknown pilgrim might return.

Andrew had found himself eagerly accepted when the Baptist came home, but he would not benefit from the intense comradeship John had enjoyed with the preacher over his months of discipleship. Though the crowds were great and the Baptist had a new, young follower, he remained relatively inaccessible these days.

Following each evening's baptisms, he would retire to the solitude of his cave with the two disciples, and often hours would pass with little conversation. The great preacher spent much time every night gazing out the cave door as if in expectation of someone. Or he would sit crosslegged, staring into the fire, his mind obviously far away from the present moment.

John and Andrew did not question. They knew he thought on
the stranger, that he waited hopefully for his return. But, John
especially ached for his master. He could clearly sense the
yearning of the mighty man's heart, could easily read the longing
void which filled his eyes.

Always before, the Baptist had inspired expectation in his
hearers. His preaching had rung with power and authority, a
demanding, awe-provoking spirit. He had captivated the crowds
with energy and a stormy vengeance.

But ever since the appearance of the stranger, when the great
orator himself had been so overcome with awe, things had been
different. His message had not changed, his attraction was still as
strong as ever. But the mood of his fiery soul had been tempered,
gentled, as a mighty, roaring lion suddenly quieted, appeased, and
waiting for its tamer's voice.

Something in the way he approached the people each day
seemed to say, "My labor is nearly complete. I am not sorrowful,
but longing for its fulfillment. I have seen him, and I yearn for his
return."

It would be over six weeks before the Baptist would emerge
from the privacy of his inner self. John would never forget that
day.

The master's gait, as the two young men followed him to the
shallows, bespoke his urgency. John would remember Andrew's
look as he watched the Baptist. He, too, apparently sensed that
something was about to happen.

The preacher wasted no time. While still on the western bank,
he began to call to the congregation with words he had not used
before.

Summoning all the force available to him, his eyes closed, his
head lifted toward heaven, and his massive arms flung back in
abandon, he cried, "Who has believed our report? And to whom
has the arm of the Lord been revealed?"

The echoes rang in the hills as he made his way into the water
and called, "He shall grow up before the Lord as a tender plant,
and as a root out of a dry ground! He has no form nor comeliness,
and when we shall see him there is no beauty that we should desire
him! He is despised and rejected of men. . . . " His voice was full
of feeling, occasionally breaking with the weight of it as it did now.
"A man of sorrows, and acquainted with grief. . . ." Here he
paused and looked at the ground. "And we hid, as it were, our
faces from him. He was despised . . . and we did not esteem him."

He stood thus for several seconds and then raised his great, sad eyes toward the crowd, pleading, "Surely he has borne our griefs and carried our sorrows: yet *we* did esteem him stricken . . . smitten of God, and afflicted! But!" he now waded toward the eastern bank, and confronted his hearers, gesturing emphatically, "he was wounded for *our* transgressions, he was bruised for *our* iniquities! The chastisement of *our* peace was upon him . . . and with his stripes we are *healed!*"

Tears poured down the Baptist's face as he again lifted sorrowing eyes to the congregation and spoke words which pierced their very hearts: "All of us, like sheep, have gone astray! We have turned every one to his own way . . . and the Lord has laid on *him* the iniquity of us all!"

Here his voice broke again and he had to cease speaking to recover himself. When he at last resumed, the crowd was deathly still, for he talked very softly, as if the subject were too precious to handle loudly.

"He was oppressed, and he was afflicted," he began, looking far away into the wilderness. "Yet he opened not his mouth. He was brought as a lamb to the slaughter, and as a sheep before her shearers makes no sound, so he opened not his mouth."

The tempo now increased, the volume rose, and hearts pounded. "He was taken from prison and from judgment; he was cut off out of the land of the living!"

The Baptist stopped, looking into the faces before him, as if to impress upon their minds what he was about to say more indelibly than any other words he had ever spoken. Again tears coursed unchecked down his face and he cried with indescribable heaviness, "Yet . . . it pleased the Lord to bruise him. *He* has put him to grief. He shall see the travail of his soul, and shall be satisfied. By his knowledge shall my righteous servant justify many, says the Lord, for . . . he shall bear their iniquities!"

The congregation was dumbfounded. They had never heard these words of Isaiah so plainly or so powerfully spoken. Could the Baptist be using them to refer to the stranger? Was the nameless pilgrim indeed the Messiah? And what did he mean, "He shall bear their iniquities"?

But the Baptist had come close to the shore and was calling to them again:

"Ho, everyone that thirsts!" he beckoned with his great hands. "Come to the waters, and he that has no money, come, buy and eat!

"Seek the Lord while he may be found, call upon him while he is near. Let the wicked forsake his ways and the unrighteous man his thoughts: and let him return to the Lord, and he will have mercy upon him; and to our God, for he will abundantly pardon!"

The preacher's head dropped in exhaustion and his sturdy shoulders drooped as if to say, "The message is complete. No more can be added to it."

And as he thus stood, waiting, the crowds came—droves of them, almost rushing for the Jordan, as if to hesitate would mean they were lost.

John and Andrew were called upon to assist the Baptist, but as they came forward Andrew stopped and whispered, "John, it appears we have visitors."

Making their way through the throng were the Pharisees, their heads held erect and austere, their robes drawn close to them to avoid touching the masses. Their stony looks contradicted the present mood of the people. Nothing in the Baptist's message had persuaded them to reverence the moment. And their previous hesitancy to approach him, due to the witness of the strange miraculous baptism of the stranger, no longer restrained them. Though they had never come to a satisfactory explanation of that event, Annas and Caiaphas had directed that they should waste no more time in their inquisition.

And with them was Zebedee, toward the rear of the group. When John caught a glimpse of him, his young heart pounded violently. Had his father seen him? he wondered. Surely he had. And yet, the old man only looked straight ahead, refusing to yield to the desire to gaze upon his son.

"Father, father!" John whispered to himself. "Must it forever be like this?"

At last the old Pharisee risked a glance in John's direction, and when he found that his son studied him, he trembled. How could a man feel such love for his offspring, and such contempt at the same time? His breath came sharply and, not knowing how to cope, he turned quickly away.

Tears swam in John's eyes. How he longed to run to him, to beg forgiveness. But, interpreting Zebedee's behavior as yet one more sign of rejection, his pride said, "You have nothing for which to be forgiven."

Their wounded egos shielded from imagined danger, and neither one knowing the goodwill buried deep within the other, the two obstinate men allowed one more rift to part them and turned their thoughts to the Baptist.

Why the high priests had rescheduled the commission for this particular day was unknown. But soon the crowds would see the wonder of the Almighty's timing.

The pompous ones worked their way to the Jordan until they came face to face with the preacher, and Master Jacob stared down on the man in the water with a look calculated to freeze the marrow in the prophet's bones.

The Baptist was not easily frightened, however. Motioning the disciples to turn back, he bravely faced his inquisitors alone. For some time silence was their only communication. The preacher's eyes penetrated the elder man's until his confidence seemed to waver. But Master Bar Harsha would not long be intimidated. Clearing his throat and straightening his shoulders, he demanded, "Who are you?"

A simple question, but one present in the minds of all the congregation.

The Baptist knew the Pharisees were asking more than this, however. They were really inquiring if he were the one many had rumored him to be. And so he told them not who he was, but who he was not.

"I am not the Christ. I am not the Messiah," he said, loudly and clearly.

At last he had brought it into the open. There could no longer be doubt on that issue. An undercurrent of excitement coursed through the crowd.

The Pharisees were taken aback, and looked to one another in bewilderment. They really had not expected to gain an answer to that question without a struggle. They obviously floundered now for direction. The historic moment of inquisition for which they had planned and primed themselves these many weeks was progressing much too easily. Something was wrong.

Master Bar Harsha and his followers leaned toward each other in a quick strategy meeting. Occasionally they darted sidelong glances at the Baptist, shaking and nodding their heads as they spoke, but striving to maintain their poise.

"Go ahead; ask him!" some seemed to be saying. Finally, above the murmur of the crowd, Master Jacob brought forward another question:

"Who are you, then?" he sneered. "Elijah?"

This set off a spark of laughter from those in the audience who agreed the Baptist was probably a lunatic, thinking himself the reincarnation of some ancient prophet.

But the preacher was not unnerved. Facing his accusers confidently, he simply said, "I am not."

Master Jacob had no quick reply. A nervous smile twitched at his face and he fidgeted to rally his own confidence.

"Do you think you are Jeremiah?" he laughed hollowly, following the same line of attack for want of a better one.

Again the Baptist looked at him steadily. "No."

At this point another of the Pharisees stepped foward—Nicodemus, the forceful liberal. He wished to spare whatever might be left of Master Jacob's dignity, for the sake of the commission. But he also saw no reason to assault the preacher in this manner, and so he approached the mighty man more gently:

"Tell us who you are, that we may give an answer to those who sent us," he said. His old eyes were full of wisdom, and his respectful attitude was far more effective than Master Jacob's officious way. "What do you have to say about yourself?" he asked again.

But the Baptist knew he was on trial. No matter how the questions were posed, or by whom, he knew their purpose. Responding to them, he would be fulfilling the legal requirements for a Jewish trial. He would be facing his accusers and speaking his defense. This was all the inquisitors wanted. They did not care what his answers were, as long as he gave them. The sentence had already been formulated.

So the preacher looked at Nicodemus sadly, as if to say, "You need no answer. You know who I am." But then he repeated, aloud, "I am the voice of one crying in the wilderness, 'Make straight the way of the Lord,' as said the prophet Isaiah."

Nicodemus nodded his head appreciatively and humbly, knowing he should not have expected more than this. But Master Jacob did not condone Nicodemus' attitude. His pride had been hurt and he would see to it that the Baptist paid. Reaching out and pushing his gentler associate aside, he snarled bitterly, sarcastically at the preacher: "Good sir, we know you say this of yourself. As for what it means, we are not certain. But tell us, then, *why* do you baptize if you are not the *Messiah*, nor *Elijah*, nor *Jeremiah?*"

Now, even the Baptist had his limits. For years he had lived and for months he had preached under the most impossible of conditions. He had been scorned, mocked, questioned, worshiped against his will, followed by men who expected more of him than he had to offer.

It was an irony that his young disciple had always credited his times alone to some kind of mystical meditation. What would he have thought if he had seen him hunched over in despair, wracked with sobs because of the mission for which he had given up everything? Indeed, he appeared strong, fearless, indomitable. But no one knew how fully he must rely on a force beyond himself.

He wished to cry out as he had to John months before, "I am only a man as you are! Do not try me so!" But the commissioners would not tolerate any sign of weakness.

Looking up, he saw that the people were waiting for his answer, and as he did so he caught a glimpse of the pilgrim. He had returned!

Suddenly, the Baptist's soul was lifted, his heart pounding with joy unspeakable. *This* was what had brought him thus far! *This* had been his hope, his message, his confidence, his dream.

A joyful smile lit his countenance as he gazed on the stranger, and he was renewed with courage to answer his inquisitors.

"I indeed baptize with water!" he cried, deeming it unnecessary, now, to answer their questions. "But there stands one among you, whom you know not. He it is, who coming after me, is preferred before me, whose shoelace I am not even worthy to untie. It is he who will baptize in the Holy Ghost and with fire!"

Chapter 13

John the disciple slept very little that night. He could not erase from his wakeful mind thoughts of his father, of the inquisition, and of the Baptist's response to it. But most powerfully etched upon his consciousness were memories of the pilgrim.

He tossed restlessly on his bed of skins until almost dawn. A strange combination of feelings was his. He was almost irresistibly drawn by the stranger. He sensed a great moment of change was about to be his own, a time of new discoveries. He could not name what that change would involve, what the discoveries would be. He only knew he was anxious to move on.

Yet, at the same time a terrible sadness swept through him. A great loneliness for this place . . . this time . . . for the Baptist, whom he loved so well.

"Silly," he murmured. "How can you be lonely for a man when you are in his presence, for a place when you are there?"

He sighed deeply and threw back the heavy skin which blanketed him. Tension had overheated him. He lay in a bed damp with perspiration.

Stretching himself full length on his back, he clasped his hands behind his neck and rested his weary head. Only the vague glow of moonlight lit the cave. Despite the warm season, Palestine's typically cold night, and the danger of prowling beasts, demanded a fire. He watched the crackling flames, wishing the night would end.

A movement beside him indicated that Andrew was likewise having difficulty sleeping. John grasped at the chance to converse.

"Andrew?" he whispered tentatively, fearful lest he might rouse him against his will.

"Yes?" came the welcome response.

"Have you been asleep?"

"Very little."

John did not feel so alone now. A span of silence elapsed.

"Where do you suppose the pilgrim dwells?" John spoke.

Andrew thought. "Somewhere in the wilderness, perhaps, like the Baptist."

"I wonder if he has any followers?"

"I have not seen any."

"What do you suppose he teaches?"

"*You* are asking *me?*"

"Not asking—only wondering."

Andrew smiled. "You are captivated by him."

John sat up in bed and peered toward his friend through the darkness. "Aren't you?"

Andrew's silence spoke for him.

"Anyway," John continued, "I would *never* leave the Baptist for another master!" Even as he said this, however, he wondered why it seemed necessary to make such a passionate affirmation, why the possibility of leaving would even occur to him. "Never!" he repeated.

It was Friday morning. At sunset the Sabbath would commence, and so the crowds would not be coming to Bethabara today. When the Baptist arose, John followed him to a point high above the shallows. Andrew had fallen asleep at last, and they had not wakened him.

The two men walked in silence, John reading in his master's face a nameless sadness. They had not talked alone for many days and John yearned for the Baptist's confiding voice once more.

Why did he not speak? What thoughts were they which clouded his countenance?

At last they reached the preacher's destination, a pinnacle giving a vast view of the wilderness. The mighty man spread his feet wide, and stretched his arms before him, clasping the top of his staff with his rugged hands. Looking high above, he took in the sky with a sweep of his dark eyes and then closed them with a sigh.

John knew it was not time to speak.

At last, the master surveyed the panorama below, his long, wild hair blown gently by the ascending breeze. "Boy," he said, "do you remember the day you came to me?"

His disciple smiled at the memory. "I do, indeed, sir."

"Have you been disappointed?"

"Not at all, sir!" was the quick reply.

The Baptist turned smiling eyes to him. "But, John, son of Zebedee, have you found what you came for?"

John gave thoughtful consideration to this. His answer was not hasty, but it was direct, as was his nature, and because he knew he could be honest with his master. "Sir, you have not laid bare God's nature for me. You have not answered all my questions. But, I am hopeful, as though there *are* answers . . . which is more than I felt when I came here."

The Baptist laughed warmly. "Indeed, I am not divine, John. You have made that discovery for certain." But now he sobered, and confronted John with another question. "Boy, this 'hope' of which you speak—on what is it based?"

The young disciple paused, not because he needed to formulate an answer, but because he hesitated to approach it. The awe he felt of the subject was evident when he did speak: "Master, all that has happened at Bethabara—yesterday and that other day weeks before—all of that has given me hope."

The Baptist was more pointed. "You speak of the stranger."

"Yes, sir," John stammered. And then, compelled by a desire he could no longer resist, he suddenly blurted out the question which had weighed upon him for weeks. "Master, is he the Messiah?"

The Baptist gazed across the desert. "What if I told you he was? What would you do then?"

The disciple knew what his master referred to, though the words did not reveal it. He spoke of the eventuality of John's leaving him to follow this man. And with this thought a terrible emptiness gripped the younger, much like the hollow sensation which must grip a fledgling when it first looks out from the nest in anticipation of flight.

"You ask what I would do?" John repeated.

"Yes."

John swallowed with difficulty and shook his head unconvincingly. "I do not know, sir."

The preacher studied him carefully. "You would follow him, of course."

John shuddered and drew his robes tightly to him. "No, sir! I would never leave you!"

The Baptist smiled, but his face bore the same trace of melancholy which John had noted as they trekked up the mountainside.

"Son, listen well," the master said. "When you were growing up in your father's house, did you ever believe you would flee from him?"

The disciple saw no analogy here. "No, sir. I did not. But when I left him, I was angry, bitter, searching. That is no comparison with what I feel for you!"

The Baptist placed a warm hand on his young friend's shoulder. "John, it is true that to leave your home full of questions was painful. But to leave here pursuing the answer will be a joy."

John shook his head sadly, not understanding the master's words. "You *wish* to see me go?" he whispered.

His rugged teacher placed an arm about him. "Do you not see he sorrow in my eyes at the thought of it? But a parent is joyful as well as sorrowful when his little one matures, when his child launches out to seek his own destiny." The disciple looked apprehensively, silently at his master and the great man drew him close. "You cannot grow further here, John," he said. "You have learned well, but it was only in preparation."

"Preparation. . . ." That word echoed in John's ears, reminding him of the day he had first heard the Baptist's message. "*Prepare* the way of the Lord; make straight in the desert a highway for our God."

This was the refrain which had held his thoughts the morning he had knelt by the river after a night struggling for understanding of the Baptist's words; the same stanza which had brought to mind the almost tangible picture of God walking down a wilderness road.

John looked out across the desert, his eyes blurred with tears he could no longer suppress. Must he leave his master, the one who had meant more than any father could?

As he gazed below him, he was suddenly caught by the figure of a man following a sandy pathway near Bethabara. It was the pilgrim, the stranger! John's heart sped. But as he took in the scene, he blinked his eyes incredulously. It seemed to be the dream all over again, the vision he had had that morning long ago!

"It cannot be!" he whispered. "And yet, this *is* what I saw. . . ."

The Baptist's attention had also been drawn by the figure. The stranger below now turned their way, and as he walked he looked high above to the point where they stood. It was apparent from his bearing that he had not just chanced this way today, but had come *to* them, that they might consider him in the solitude of this morning.

Pointing joyfully to the stranger, the Baptist said, with awe and wonder, "Behold! The Lamb of God, who takes away the sin of the world!"

John was stunned, speechless. Did his ears hear correctly?

The master turned to him, excitement and deep love filling his words: "Son, this is he of whom I said, 'After me there comes a man who is preferred before me . . .' " he paused and gazed upon the pilgrim again, "for he *was* before me . . . I have not known him, John, but I have been preaching and baptizing so that he might be made manifest to Israel!"

He drew the disciple close again and continued. "That day at Bethabara, when this very man came to be baptized, when the light shone upon him, I looked above, as did everyone gathered there. But I saw more than the light, John." He trembled with the memory. "I saw the Spirit, descending from heaven like a dove, and it rested upon him!"

John turned wonderingly to his master, who continued, "I did not know the pilgrim, but he who sent me to baptize with water said to me, 'Upon whom you shall see the Spirit descending, and remaining, the same is he which baptizes with the Holy Ghost!' "

The preacher paused a moment, then looked once again toward the stranger. "And I saw, and bear record that this is the Son of God."

Chapter 14

It was now Sabbath morning. The sun had not yet shown itself over the eastern ridge, and the dawn sky was still deep with the retreating shades of night. John and Andrew stood with the master silently. Only their measured breathing traced life on the soundless air.

Just one sentence had been spoken since they had awakened. When the two disciples had stirred from sleep, they had found their master standing over them. "It is time," he had said simply, tenderly. His eyes had said all the rest. John and Andrew had known then what was to come.

They had risen with the Baptist, had hesitantly but obediently packed what few belongings they possessed, and had followed the master's silent lead to this place.

Never had there been heavier hearts than theirs. John Bar Zebedee and John the Baptist felt this trial most painfully. It was a test of the preacher's sincerity of purpose all these months, and of John's intention to seek the truth.

It was only a matter of time now. The shallows flowed quietly behind them as they waited on the east side of the Jordan.

John did not take his eyes off his master. For all he knew, this would be the last time he would look on him. How he loved this man, more than his own brother! He carefully took in every detail of that beloved face, allowing its lines and features to impress themselves upon his memory.

He had often seen determination in the Baptist's aspect, but never had his chin held such a flintlike angle, or his stance such a look of rock. It seemed he resisted some tremendous pull to turn in weakness from the destiny of the moment. John knew his master did not wish to see him go.

But suddenly, as John scrutinized him, the preacher's eyes were filled with light, and the disciple need not have turned about to see the source of that transformation.

Some distance ahead, the Stranger had appeared, traveling toward civilization. John and Andrew knew it was he, though he was too far away to be seen clearly.

John's throat grew tight at the sight of this man. He was torn miserably, wishing to go with him, and wishing to stay longer with his master.

He looked longingly again at the Baptist who had now taken a step in the direction of the Pilgrim, as if he, too, wished to follow after him. But the preacher restrained himself, knowing his mission still lay in preparing the hearts of those who would come to hear his message. He turned again to his young friends. Finding no words adequate to express his feelings of loss, he pointed across the desert, directing their attention, as always, away from himself and to the one for whom he had paved the way.

"Behold the Lamb of God!" he said, softly but urgently, as if to hesitate would lose him to the task.

John obediently watched the Stranger's progress as he traveled the narrow wilderness road, and once again tears arose in his eyes. He did not question the necessity of leaving. But he turned for one last gesture of reassurance, and found himself clutching the master fervently to him, his own head buried on that sturdy shoulder for a long moment.

"Master . . . it is a hard thing . . . " he whispered.

The Baptist was silent with understanding and with his own grief. But at last he sighed deeply and said, "John, it is hard to be born, but it is a joy to find life."

The disciple raised his head now, and gazed into the Baptist's eyes, finding, mingled with sorrow, the strength he needed to step away.

As he and Andrew began their journey, they looked back only once. There stood the Baptist, tall, erect, an ensign of faith.

And ahead walked the Master of a new day.

THE WAY

All that the Father giveth me shall come to me; and him that cometh to me I will in no wise cast out.
JOHN 6:37

Chapter 1

It was late in the morning now. John and Andrew had followed at a great distance behind the Pilgrim since leaving Bethabara. When he rested, they rested; when he walked, they walked. They wondered, however, if he even knew of their presence behind him.

Their awe of the man restrained them from making themselves evident. They did not know how to approach him, what to say, or what he would say. He was alone. Apparently he had no disciples. Perhaps he wanted none.

The road along which they traveled was a lonely one on a Sabbath, and so, though they moved in the direction of civilization, they met only a handful of people as they progressed.

But the fact that they went toward the Galilee Sea, rather than Judea, surprised John. He would have expected a great rabbi to head for Jerusalem, the capital of the intelligentsia, rather than for the less-educated realms of the north. Proud though John was of his own homeland, he knew the elite of Judaism scorned its residents as backward and unversed in the Torah. And with this thought, came another interesting question. The Stranger they had been directed to follow was traveling on the Sabbath. How far he intended to go, John wondered. What did he think of the teachings of the elders who set strict limits on Sabbath journeys? That the Stranger might be a Galilean was unsettling to John; that he might be a rebel, was a delight. But, by nature, John was composed of contradictions.

Many speculations were his and Andrew's as they walked, but they said little. John led the way, grateful for his staff which might serve as more than a walking stick. Though evening was yet well distant, the fear of bandits was an ever-present consideration.

"At least we are going in the direction of home," Andrew broke the silence.

"At least?" said John.

"Well, it's a comfort. In case . . ." Here he stopped, not wishing to voice his doubts.

"In case what?" John prodded.

"Well, what if he—doesn't want us?" he explained.

John did not reply quickly. "He will want us," he said uneasily. "He has to! The master would not send us away to follow a man who would refuse us."

With this, Andrew's attitude began to shift from one of hesitancy to one of expectancy, until at last he said in excitement, "John, why don't we catch up with him? It is ridiculous to follow so far behind! We must introduce ourselves."

The road along which they traveled was dotted occasionally with rest stops. It was not until they were about to bypass him that they came face to face with the Stranger.

John stopped short in the highway, his young follower colliding with him. When Andrew saw the source of his friend's surprise, his first impulse was to duck, nervous and shy, behind John.

There beside the road sat the Pilgrim, resting upon a rock, his mantle lowered to cool his perspiring forehead, his staff lying idle beside him. Having lost sight of him as they conversed, the two followers did not know they had caught up with him as he rested.

Neither John nor Andrew could bring himself to utter any greeting. Had it been anyone else, they would have exchanged the pleasantries of the day easily and quickly, but now neither could call up a word.

The Pilgrim was not so speechless, however. He smiled openly and stood in greeting. When he spoke, the voice was as John had remembered the day of the baptism—gentle, confident, reassuring. "It seems you have been following me, friends. What do you seek?"

"Good-day, Rabbi . . ." John stammered. "Where do you dwell?"

Such a question! Why had he asked this? he wondered, as soon as he had said it. Why not, "What is your name?" or "May we walk with you?"

But the Pilgrim seemed to understand his awkwardness. Rising, he took his staff, as though to move on, and said, "Come and see."

Andrew sighed with relief, and John nudged him, whispering, "See, he did not refuse us!"

The Pilgrim caught a glimpse of their covert exchange, and a knowing smile crossed his face. "I am called Jesus, of Nazareth," he said, as they walked now together. "And you?"

An excited gleam danced in Andrew's eyes, and he leaned near John. "A fellow Galilean!" he whispered.

"Sh-h-h!" John ordered in a quick aside, embarrassed at his friend's overzealousness, and attempting to appear confident and casual before this man. Besides, he was thinking: Nazareth? Galilee was surprising enough, to say nothing of Nazareth, one of the smallest and least respected of all the province's cities. It was one thing to belong to a member of the select "Nazarite" sect, as had John the Baptist. But that title had nothing to do with the "Nazarenes," citizens of Jesus' hometown.

However, clearing his throat, he answered, "I am John Bar Zebedee of Capernaum, and this is Andrew Bar Jona of Bethsaida."

"And what are you doing on this road?"

John looked to Andrew. What should he say? At last he offered, "Sir, we have been with the Baptist at Bethabara. We are his disciples. He has sent us to you." It was a well-spoken response, and Andrew gave a nod of approval.

The Pilgrim did not question them further. He appeared to sense their uneasiness, and John felt Jesus had even read the doubt in his eyes at the announcement that he was a Nazarene. Nevertheless the Stranger said warmly, "You are welcome to stay with me this night, if you wish. I have no lodging. I will sleep by the Sea of Galilee."

It was Andrew who readily grasped the invitation.

"We are fishermen," he responded eagerly, finding courage to continue. "We will welcome just such a night!"

Chapter 2

Galilean fishing crews generally plied their trade at night. The Sea of Galilee was so clear that during the day, especially under the bright sun of spring and summer, the fish could easily see the ships overhead, and were thus surprisingly wary and difficult to catch. Night fishing was often more successful, and was therefore the preferred mode. Zebedee's fleet had temporarily left the northern ports to troll these distant waters. They had put in several long nights, but this was the Sabbath, and the warm summer air was a comfort.

Simon and James had anchored their craft in the shallows near the shore and settled themselves for a nap in the gently rocking vessel.

The lazy motion of the boat and quiet slapping of the water against its sides gradually relaxed the weary men. But more than the warmth of the late afternoon breeze caressed Simon's mind. The vision of a girl twined its way in and out of his consciousness, becoming part of his dreams when he dozed, and remaining the focus of his thoughts when he woke.

"What are you mumbling about?" came James' voice from the other end of the vessel.

Simon jerked out of half-consciousness and replied, "I must have been talking in my sleep."

James turned over disgruntledly. "You spoke of Andrew," he said.

Simon drew his knees under his chin and rested his head upon them. "So I did," he laughed. "I can just see his face now! Coming home to a houseful of women!"

James sat up, resigned to insomnia, and laughed with him. "Two women is hardly a houseful!"

"For a perennial bachelor like my brother, one woman is too many!"

"Well, take heart, Simon! You can't let Andrew worry you. You have enough to contend with, supporting a new bride *and* a mother-in-law." James could not conceal his obvious delight in the topic. "You, with a mother-in-law!" At this he roared hilariously until his companion good-naturedly splashed a handful of sea water in his face.

"Enough, James?" Simon grinned. "Now, let me sleep."

James wiped his face, chuckling, but soon Simon was speaking again. "I'm sure he won't be surprised, anyway," he said, as though needing reassurance on the topic. "He knew of my interest in Deborah when he left."

"True. But why are you so concerned for his opinion?"

Simon straightened his shoulders disdainfully. "Concerned? I am not concerned. He is but my younger brother!"

James was unconvinced, but he turned again to his pillow, and Simon settled down for more sleep.

Chapter 3

The three travelers from Bethabara would not reach the Galilee Sea, and Jesus' campsite, until late afternoon.

Many thoughts crowded John's mind. Cultural bigotry was difficult for him to shake. True, he had taken pride in the fact that Zebedee disapproved of the Baptist. The preacher had been *so* unique, criticism had not dimmed his glamor and romance, but rather enhanced it. Jesus was not a glamorous figure, however, and therefore societal biases more easily detracted from his spiritual allure.

John was torn between reverence for Jesus, due to events at Bethabara, and genuine skepticism, due to what he now knew of his background. Yet this commoner *had* been the recipient of a miraculous baptism; he had been lauded and adored by the disciple's own beloved master.

The Baptist. John sighed. He had intended him to follow Jesus. Then why did these doubts fly at him? Why was he not of simpler faith, like Andrew?

The disciple tried to put his mind to other things. There was much to learn about the Nazarene. What did he think of Caesar? Was he politically involved? What did he think of the Pharisees? He had apparently lived in the wilderness. Had he been an Essene? As the questions tumbled about in his mind, John trembled with the memory of the Baptist's words concerning this man. "Son of God . . ." His mind boggled at the thought, and reason deserted him.

Andrew doubtless struggled with questions of his own, and wondered, like John, how to inquire, where to begin. The Nazarene was not unaware of the two men's reflective mood. At last he stopped beside the road and lowered his mantle, wiping his perspiring forehead with his sleeve.

"It is a warm day. Let us rest awhile," he offered, pointing toward a small grove of palms. "You said you are fishermen by trade?"

"Yes, sir," Andrew answered.

"And you are from the northern ports?"

"Yes."

"You are hired men?"

"I am, and so is my brother Simon. John's father owns the fleet. His elder brother manages it."

"And what is your elder brother's name?" the Nazarene asked, turning to John.

"James, sir. He is a rabbi."

As soon as he had added this information he wondered why he had done so. Apparently, deep inside, he still retained pride in the knowledge that James was of that select group. Or did he think the fact would impress Jesus?

Whether or not it did, the Nazarene picked up on the topic. "Then your family is devoted to the Law?"

John sensed more than etiquette in this question, but having no idea what Jesus' thoughts on the Law might be, he hesitated to approach the subject. "Sir, they are."

To his relief, Jesus did not inquire further, but turned to Andrew. "All of you are close friends?" he asked.

"Oh, the best, sir!" Andrew smiled, proud to include himself in the group, though his age and size had, in fact, often excluded him from its fellowship.

"I should like to meet your brothers." Jesus smiled.

John and Andrew looked at one another, Andrew with obvious pleasure, John with some hesitancy. As he thought on James' predictable reaction to this enigmatic figure, Andrew responded, "Perhaps you shall, sir. We would like that."

The Stranger had begun to draw out the two fishermen. As they had been wondering about him, he had been encouraging them to speak of themselves, and had in the process begun to win their confidence. John felt freer to inquire concerning him.

"Sir, have you home and family?"

"My mother, brothers, and sisters still reside in Nazareth. My father was Joseph Bar Jacob."

"He is no longer living?" John asked thoughtfully.

"He is not."

"I am sorry, sir. . . ."

"No need to be," Jesus said softly. "That was a long time ago."

"Have you lived elsewhere?" John looked for some hope of position in his new acquaintance.

"I was born in Bethlehem of Judea," the Pilgrim replied, and John took encouragement. But then he was again cast down as Jesus reiterated, "But I was raised in Nazareth." The disciple would ask no more.

"And what is your trade, sir?" inquired Andrew.

"My father was a carpenter. I followed his profession: making furniture, most anything of wood." His voice was mellow as he thought on his years of apprenticeship and craft.

But this was yet another blow to John's sensibilities. A carpenter? One of the most menial of professions! It was true that the rabbis traditionally held manual skills in addition to pursuing the world of debate, for they taught that labor was honorable. But carpentry? He must indeed have been from a poor home. While John dwelt upon this, feeding his growing doubts, Andrew looked at it all differently.

"That is an art, sir," he said. "All John and I do is cast nets and draw in wet, smelling fish!"

John bristled. Fishing was honorable, profitable! Sometimes he did not understand Andrew's easy adaptation to extremes.

"It is a taxing vocation," Jesus replied. "But it requires great courage at times. And the sea, the air . . ." he breathed deeply, imagining himself there. "A man could easily envy you that!"

Andrew beamed, warming to him more quickly than ever. John did not know how to react, and was caught off guard, when Jesus turned to him.

"Tell me," he said, "how did you come to follow the Baptist?"

The disciple did not think it the time to speak of Zebedee. "I sought answers, sir. I was curious as to whether the Baptist might have them."

"And did he?" Jesus asked, his eyes intent on the young man.

"Sir, he had many," John answered, his brevity revealing that for him there were still many unsolved mysteries.

Jesus said nothing more for the moment, but only studied him with what John sensed to be deep compassion. The disciple turned away, the shame of his bigotry spearing his conscience. How could this Nazarene be so kind to him, when it was obvious from his own silences, his expression, that he doubted his credentials so stubbornly?

The son of Zebedee drew his cloak about him as if with a chill and looked at the ground. But his trembling was not due to the summer breeze. He felt Jesus read his very soul, and the contents of his heart and history. Once again he thought on the Baptist's words concerning him. Who was he—really?

Jesus leaned toward him. "I am certain you still have many questions, John. There will be time to speak of them all."

Evening was only two hours away when they reached the site where Jesus wished to stay, and built a small fire on the beach. Soon the moon would be shining brightly overhead, lighting the sea majestically, and local sailors would be at work once more. Sprinkled here and there were fishing boats of the nearby villages. Andrew watched them fondly, thinking of Capernaum.

"Do you suppose our ships will go out tonight?" he asked John.

"It is difficult to tell," the disciple answered, carefully surveying the horizon. "If the skies are as clear up north, they will."

The three men knelt in the sand, feeding the flames with small pieces of driftwood. Jesus was silent, but watched Andrew closely. His slight, young follower could not seem to detach himself from an interest in those boats, and at last Jesus said, "Follow your heart, friend. We will wait for you."

Immediately Andrew was on his feet, surprise and joy in his eyes. "Yes, sir," he called as he turned and ran down the beach excitedly.

John sat back in bewilderment and looked at the Nazarene. "Sir, I do not understand. What was that about?"

"You will see soon enough." Jesus smiled.

Andrew flew down the shore, his heart beating rapidly.

"Boatsman!" he called, seeing a figure some distance away, repairing a line of nets. "Boatsman! Has Zebedee's fleet from Capernaum been fishing these waters?"

The stranger looked up, frightened by being suddenly overtaken so late on the Sabbath. "Who wants to know?" he demanded, quickly turning from the work which the holy day condemned.

"A friend!" Andrew shouted, still running toward him.

When he reached the boatsman he was panting hard, and the sound of his heart pounding loudly in his ears muffled the man's answers, but he understood clearly enough.

"If you are one of the hired men, you're a bit late. That fleet has been here a week already."

"Then they *are* here!" Andrew insisted.

"Yes, man . . . they are," the bewildered sailor repeated.

"Where?"

"What?"

"Where are the ships?"

The boatsman stood, wiped the sand from his clothes, and scratched his head in contemplation.

Andrew fought the urge to shake the stranger from his slowness.

"Why, I believe they're down that way," he finally decided.

There were many boats scattered in clusters along the shore, but Andrew took him at his word.

"Thank you! Thanks so much!" Andrew exclaimed. He turned again and headed further down the beach, leaving the boatsman more confused than ever.

From fleet to fleet, Andrew ran, alert for the sign of a familiar face.

"Simon!" he cried. "Simon, are you here?"

"Quiet!" unfriendly voices rebuked him. "It is a day of rest, you know!"

"I'm looking for Simon Bar Jona of Zebedee's fleet," he explained.

"That way," the strangers motioned, eager to have him gone.

Following the direction, he soon found the desired company. His burly brother was not to be seen, but Andrew could make out the forms of men familiar to him, and his heart sped.

A dozen heads turned when he called, and celebration spread through the ranks. "Andrew, can it be you?" voices rang from the rocking boats.

"Yes—it is!" he replied.

"What are you doing here?" came the excited questions.

"I am looking for Simon. Can you tell me where he is?"

Now he was knee-deep in the water scanning the well-known ships and greeting his lifelong friends.

"Your brother is with James, yonder!" was the answer.

"Thanks!" he offered, and eagerly headed for the distant ship. Again his voice rang out, "Simon!"

At last, he discerned the massive form of his elder brother. Simon, stumbling to the stern of the boat, peered over the waist-high gunwales and strained his eyes and ears in the direction of the call. "James? Did you hear something?" he whispered.

James sat up and listened.

"There it is again," Simon said, as though speaking too loudly would stifle the sound. "Can it be?" he wondered, his eyes wide with amazement. "Andrew?" he called. "Is it you?"

"Simon?" the young sailor cried again as he neared the ship. Excitedly he plowed through the water with more strength than he thought possible, leaving a wake behind himself.

When he at last reached the boat, Simon's sturdy arms wasted no time in lifting him into the vessel and the two brothers embraced joyously.

"Andrew, you little water rat!" his sturdy brother teased. "You have whipped the sea into a froth! The fish will go back to Capernaum!"

The two laughed in abandon, and Andrew glowed with pride at his successful venture. "I have found you, brother. That is all that matters!"

"So it is!" Simon smiled. And then, "You are back to stay?" he asked eagerly, betraying his loneliness for this little fellow.

"Brother, I am here to take you with me," Andrew insisted. And then fervently he declared, "Simon, we have found the Messiah!"

Chapter 4

Herod's hellenistic capital, Tiberias, lay only a short distance north of Jesus' camp. The pagan city with its sulphur springs and Roman baths was situated for the strategic military defenses the sea and hills provided, and not for pleasantness of climate. Though Galilee was the most beautiful of Palestinian provinces, this particular area was one of its hottest regions. John was glad the sun would soon be descending below the horizon.

In times past the sea, which was about seven miles across and thirteen miles in length, had been known as Gennesaret, and was still called by that name on occasion. Gennesaret, "the gardens of the princes . . ." John smiled and stretched his legs lazily on the warm sand. He hoped Jesus would proceed up the coast highway and away from the barren Tiberias terrain. He longed for the lush vegetation, the villas and orchards which were more typical of Galilean country.

Still, there was abundance to be found even here. In the distance he spied several wild fig trees. The Rabbi lay quiet, despite the heat, in a sleep which betrayed great weariness. John would bring food for the two of them in case Jesus woke for supper.

Darting away from camp, he leaped boulders and bushes, eager for the juicy fruits. He plucked at least a dozen and tossed them into his lap, then returned to Jesus' side.

Smiling, John lay the bundle on the sand, and waited. As the Nazarene slept, the young follower studied him intently. Somehow, when they had first met, he had not noticed certain aspects of the Rabbi's appearance. It was evident that the man had recently been living under extreme conditions of exposure. His face, John noted, was wind-burned and darkly bronzed, far more so, even, than faces of fishermen who had toiled days and nights at a stretch on the open sea. The man's hands, now lying idly on the sand, were rough and red, healing in ragged lines from some kind of labor John could not imagine.

Where in the wilderness had he come from? John wondered. What nameless torments had he endured? Even the Baptist had not contended with such extremes as he had apparently survived. His physical appearance had not seemed so distressed the day John had first seen him at the Jordan. Something since then had demanded incredible endurance, unspeakable stamina. How John longed to talk with him!

To his delight the Nazarene did waken when hunger roused him. But John looked away quickly, not wishing to be caught staring.

"Sir," he said, smiling and picking up the satchel, "see, I have brought you some supper."

"Ah," Jesus sighed, sitting up and stretching his arms wide. "Good, John. I am grateful!"

"You were very weary, sir."

"Yes."

John could not resist the urge to know more about him. "Where did you spend your time after your baptism?" he asked as they devoured the tender figs.

Jesus hesitated to answer, as though the subject pained him. "I wandered into the wilderness," was the brief reply.

"I thought so, sir. But . . ."

"But what, John?"

"I only wondered . . ." John stammered.

Jesus looked at him knowingly. "You have been studying my appearance while I slept."

John turned white.

"It is all right." Jesus laughed. "I am sure I must look like a ragged cloth by now."

John smiled. How relaxed he made him feel!

"Friend, if I were to tell you of my ordeal, I doubt that you would believe me. Anyway, now is not the time. It will all be spoken of later."

Presently the Rabbi glanced up at a movement along the beach, and stood in greeting. Andrew was enthusiastically tugging at a hesitant Simon. "Brother, there he is!" He pointed.

It was obvious that Simon, though happy to be with Andrew, questioned the wisdom of following him here. But despite his denials, his younger brother did have a certain amount of influence over him. And so he followed.

"Do not grab at me, Andrew," he frowned. "I am coming . . ."

When John saw his old friend, he knew the mystery of Andrew's sudden departure up the coast, and running excitedly to meet him, he shouted, "Simon! How good to see you!"

The big fisherman's mouth fell open. "John!" he gasped.

Tearing down the shore, the two met and embraced each other fervently.

"John! My friend!" Simon roared. "You did not turn into a tumbleweed after all!"

The two laughed together heartily, and then Simon's eyes were caught by the Stranger standing ahead.

Andrew watched his brother's face, and knowing it was the opportune moment, took him by the arm and led him down the shore. "Simon, this is he of whom I spoke. Jesus, of Nazareth."

Jesus beheld him intently, and then reached out a hand of greeting.

Simon walked forward silently, and returned the strong handclasp.

John and Andrew looked at one another, the thrill of the moment fresh in the younger brother's eyes.

Simon, for once, had no words. It was the Rabbi who spoke first. Carefully surveying this hulk of a man, he smiled and said gently, "You are Simon, the son of Jona . . . But you shall be called Peter, a rock."

Chapter 5

The next day would be spent further proceeding into Galilee. The sea coast highway was a busy one. Caravans and pedestrians bypassed not only fields, vineyards, and orchards, but busy ports, potteries, smoking furnaces, and dye works. This province was the great industrial section of the land.

Tiberias' marble palace held a commanding view of the sea. Named for the Emperor Tiberius, the city had been built by the man presently in command of Galilee and Perea, Herod Antipas, son of Herod the Great. His rule was, of course, subservient to that of Rome, but he catered at every turn to Israel's greatest enemy. And his stronghold bore the mark of pagan influence in every corner and arch. Roman columns upheld his halls, as surely as Rome upheld his rule.

But despite the gilded splendor of Herod's city, immorality lay over it like a stinking mantle. And beneath it lay a graveyard. Yes—Herod's magnificent fort had been erected upon the site of ancient tombs. The thermal resort was therefore not only heathen but, according to Jewish law, "unclean," its foundations being in direct contact with the dead. For this reason, if for no other, it was to be strictly avoided by the orthodox, notwithstanding the fact that Antipas called it his own.

As the road neared the descent into this city's valley, another veered to the west, and this was the traditional route of the pious. It took them well away from the tainting influence of the metropolis. Peter, John, and Andrew looked askance as they neared this Y in the road, barely daring to let Tiberias come within their line of vision. Peter even went so far as to give the traditional spitting gesture to show his disgust for the place.

It was, therefore, of great amazement to his followers when Jesus, upon approaching the junction, stood looking over the city.

Holding back, the disciples peered at him questioningly, and John called out, "Sir, that is Tiberias! Surely you will not enter."

Jesus turned about and asked, "Why do you say this?"

"Rabbi," Peter replied, surprise marking his tone, "surely you know that this place is erected upon graves. It is against our laws to touch that which is unclean."

But Jesus continued to survey the valley, and replied, "It is not the dead who lie buried beneath this city who make it unclean, but the hearts of many who live within its gates . . ." At this he read the faces of his followers. They were entirely willing to believe pagan hearts were unclean. Was that not even more reason to refrain from entering here? His next words, however, dumb-founded them. ". . . hearts like those of men everywhere," he said, "even in Jerusalem."

John shook his head bewilderedly, wondering at the Nazarene's statement. "Then you do mean to enter?" was all he could say.

The Rabbi looked at his young follower compassionately and smiled, "Are you afraid?"

John said nothing, but kept his eyes to the ground.

"This time, for your sake, I will pass by," the Teacher said. "But only the dead need fear the dead . . ."

As they stopped to rest a few miles from Magdala, John sat apart from the others. He needed time to think. It was very difficult for him to transplant feelings of loyalty, from the Baptist, to this relative Stranger. But had that not been a problem, others intervened. He found himself in much the same predicament as when he had run from the Baptist, when the preacher had told him he was not all-knowing, that he could not, or would not answer all his questions.

The situation now was not identical, for John was not presently concerned with Jesus' answers or even whether he had any; but the fact that he was of doubtful origins plagued John as a weakness, as surely as the preacher's lack of omniscience had. Unless John resolved this lack of confidence it would hamper his respect for the Rabbi's teachings.

He thought on Jesus' compassionate response to him, just today, regarding the Tiberians. He had not understood the Nazarene's words, exactly. They had, however, rung with wisdom.

And then, he recalled the Baptist's declaration when they had stood on the hill together, watching Jesus on the wilderness road. "Behold the Lamb of God," he had said. "I saw heaven opened, and the Spirit descending upon him . . . the voice saying 'this is my beloved Son, in whom I am well pleased . . .' "

John's mind was far away, reliving that moment. But as he looked up from his reveries he found that the Nazarene, while still seated with the others, had turned about and was studying him. John trembled. Did it matter that this man was a mere Galilean, like himself? That he hailed from a poor city, or that he lacked the status of a higher trade?

John rose and walked toward him, smiling. "Master, where are we going next?"

The answer to that question was "Cana." A friend of Jesus' family was to be married there in a few days, and he wished to be present. The disciples would, of course, accompany him, and so their journey would take them further up the coast and then westward into Galilee.

As they approached the seaport town of Magdala, John noted that his friend, Simon Peter, seemed curiously uneasy. Andrew and the Master went ahead, and John called Peter to walk with him by the sea.

"Something troubles you," he opened, hoping to draw the big man out.

Simon fidgeted with his beard. His dark eyes scanned the horizon, but his thoughts were not there. "John, I cannot go far with you. I must turn back before dark. I am expected home day after tomorrow . . . "

John did not understand. "You do not mean to follow after Jesus?"

Peter's brow knit sadly. "I cannot . . . "

John was silent, not knowing what to say. "Why?" he finally asked.

"I suppose if anyone should know, you should," Simon sighed. "While you were away I . . . married."

It took some time for the reality of his friend's pronouncement to dawn upon John. Peter never had been one to closely follow the social amenities. Obviously no lengthy betrothal had preceded this union. When the disciple did finally grasp the news, a devilish gleam lit his face and a broad smile stretched his lips. "You! Simon! I cannot believe it!"

When the response was so good-natured, Peter too laughed aloud. "Yes . . . it is true, John! You may threaten me with Roman torture, but it is true!"

John continued to beam with approval, but momentarily he sobered. "Then, this means . . . "

"Right . . . " Peter frowned. "I truly cannot go with you."

"Does Andrew know of this?" John inquired sadly.

"I could not bring myself to tell him. He was so enthralled with your discovery of this man."

"Who is she, your wife?" John asked, trying to cover his own disappointment.

Peter studied the sand. A half-smile came to his face at the thought of her. "You remember Deborah?"

John thought. "The girl of Tabigha?" he said, mentally filing through the great list of women in whom Simon had expressed an interest over the years.

"Yes," Peter answered.

John congratulated him. "I knew you were a great fisherman," he teased, "but how did you accomplish such a catch?"

"She is beautiful, don't you agree!" Peter's eyes lit with renewed enthusiasm.

"Indeed," John said heartily.

Peter roared with pleasure. But then, even as he looked at his friend, he grew quiet again, and he walked away toward the lapping water, gazing upon it thoughtfully. Genuine sorrow etched his ruddy face. He had never engaged in anything beyond the routines of trade and social life. And he now felt deeply that he had missed something which the others had found. Thinking of Jesus, he said, "I envy you, John. He is . . . "

"Fascinating?"

"Yes—more than that. I cannot put words to the feeling he gives me," he answered. "I am certain you know what I am trying to say."

"I do." John smiled, his face lit with fervent admiration for the Nazarene.

A span of silence again colored Peter's mood as he gazed out to sea. John felt for him, and wishing to cheer him said, "I envy you your marriage."

"In a sense, perhaps, you do, but not very greatly," Peter sighed. He then looked ahead and his eyes fell once more on the Nazarene. He thought for some time, and then said, "I suppose it will do no harm if I accompany you at least one more day."

Chapter 6

They did not intend to stop at Magdala, but they had to at least pass through, for it was the last sea town before turning toward Cana, and the highway continued this way.

A noisy throng at the marketplace prevented their easy passage through the village. The loud bartering of the merchants and their customers was typical of any oriental street scene, as were the smells of fruits in open stalls, the wafting of bakery aromas mingling with the odors of rich spices. Here were glistening, honey-covered pastries, and raw meat hanging from hooks behind the butcher's booth. The general upheaval of the place might have led the uninitiated to think they were in a madhouse. There was a definite system to all the trade commenced here, however, and a study of the scene would soon yield an appreciation for the shrewd business tactics employed in every corner by housewife and tradesman alike.

The many peddlers dealing in dyed wool and salted fish set this suq apart as unique to Magdala. Such products were the city's specialty, and particularly the fish, cherished by buyers as far away as Rome and Spain, had brought small fortunes to many in these parts.

There was, however, another specialty in Magdala. Prostitution was almost synonymous with the name of the area. Peter, John, and Andrew, despite their orthodox upbringing, could not help but find themselves looking here and there curiously, thinking they might "accidentally" see some of the local harlots. They would recognize them easily enough. Their descriptions were common in the tales told among the rowdies of Galilee. The fishing trade was notorious for leaving its men at loose ends in seaport towns. When the hauls were good, sailors often found themselves far away from home with time on their hands, while the fish were being sold for pickling and export. And though adultery bore the death penalty, if a man wanted to find a harlot, he need not look far in Magdala.

But here and there, even in this ribald town, the local Pharisees could be seen. An incongruous addition to the setting, they walked quickly through the pressing marketplace, their heads bent down and their cloaks drawn in close, as though they were seeking to avoid the very breath of the place. Yet what a spectacle they made of themselves. How proud they were of their righteous indignation!

As John took all of this in, he watched the Master closely. What did he think of the pious radicals of Judaism, or the flashy streetwalkers who propositioned passersby from the doorways?

Studying him, John felt as he had the first day Jesus had come to the Jordan. He was a part of life, a man—and yet, even in this bustling throng, he seemed set apart. To John's surprise, he betrayed no outward signs of disgust for the women in the alleyways, but as he caught glimpses of them, only compassion marked his face.

When they had at last come well through the square, they rounded a corner to find the road leading to Cana. A distance down that road they would rest like most weary travelers under the boughs of the wayside fig trees.

While Jesus and his company were still some way from this spot, however, two other men were enjoying its shade. One of them was well known to John, having been his schoolmaster at the academy of Capernaum. They, of course, had no knowledge of Jesus, having heard of the Baptist's messages concerning a coming Judge only by way of the rumors spreading up and down Palestine.

They were, therefore, totally unprepared for the strange events which were about to transpire in their lives this day. But the conversation in which they were involved strangely suited the upcoming hours.

Philip of Bethsaida, the scholarly young teacher, rested his head on his hands and read the dirt in front of him. His closest friend, Nathanael Bar Tholomew of Cana, sat beside him, deep in contemplation. "I do not doubt your words, Philip," he was saying. "I know you have not avoided the philosophy of the Greeks."

Philip laughed. He remembered the great stir of controversy his knowledge of Gentile classics had caused among the pious of Capernaum. "Indeed!" he said. "Many are aware of that, and I have paid dearly for it in times past! I nearly lost my teaching position a few years ago when the constituency learned that I was versed in such subjects."

Nathanael smiled. "Fortunately for you, you teach in Galilee," he offered. "The Judeans would never have tolerated such dabbling."

"And they consider themselves superior to those of our province!" Philip declared bitterly. "As far as I am concerned, they excel primarily in their bigotry. We may not have the intelligentsia quartered here, but at least we see the world around us more realistically than our cloistered neighbors to the south!"

Nathanael was aware that the numerous highways which crisscrossed Galilee had brought ideas from the farthest reaches of the Mediterranean world directly onto every Galilean's doorstep. "I quite agree." He smiled sardonically, thinking of the intellectual snobbery of their Judean city-cousins. "But as the rabbis say," he mimicked their austere posturing, "'Cursed are these Galileans, who know not the Torah.'"

He and Philip together roared with pleasure at this. But then Nathanael became solemn again. "As I was saying, I do not doubt your words, Philip. But it *is* surprising that the Greeks should believe such a thing as you were telling me. It sounds so much like something out of Moses or Isaiah." Here he paused and contemplated. "What did you say the name of the philosopher was?"

"Plato."

"And again, what were his words?"

As Philip quoted the taboo teachings of that Gentile who had lived four hundred years before in Athens, his eyes took on a faraway look. "'Not until philosophers are kings or kings are philosophers, not until learning and leadership are centered in one man, will the human race be redeemed.'"

Nathanael sighed. His memory, well-trained since childhood as that of any son of Israel, was busy tracing back through the Scriptures. "'Oh that my words were now written! Oh that they were printed in a book! That they were graven with an iron pen and lead in the rock for ever! For I know that my redeemer lives, and that he shall stand at the latter day upon the earth . . .'"

"From the book of Job," Philip confirmed. "How it sounds like Plato!"

"How Plato sounds like Job!" Nathanael corrected with good-natured Jewish pride.

"True." Philip laughed. "And what about the words of Isaiah? 'For unto us a child is born, unto us a son is given . . .'"

Here Nathanael chimed in and they chanted the familiar words in unison: "And the government shall be upon his shoulder: and his name shall be called Wonderful, Counselor, The Mighty God, The Everlasting Father, The Prince of Peace." Their voices swelled with emotion as they continued, "Of the increase of his government and peace there shall be no end, upon the throne of David, and upon his kingdom, to order it, and to establish it with judgment and with justice from henceforth even for ever!" Tears of emotion and desire for the prophecy's fulfillment welled from their hearts. "The zeal of the Lord of Hosts will perform this!"

They were silent now, the moving strains of the prophet's dream echoing in their minds.

"Strange . . ." Nathanael whispered. "Surely the Greeks do not expect a Messiah!"

Philip watched the people passing on the road in front of them. "Not a Messiah, no. In fact, I doubt many of them are even aware of such teachings from their own philosophers. But, Nathanael, the Greeks are not the only Gentiles who have such writings. I have also read Ipuwer, the ancient Egyptian. Listen," he quoted from memory, "'This leader brings cooling to the flame of injustice. He is the shepherd of all men. When the herds in his pasture have gone astray and their hearts are afraid, he passes the hours in bringing them together again. He smites the evil ones and rescues the good. . . . Where is he today? Is he asleep perchance? But take comfort; when the time is ripe, he *shall* awake!'"

"Incredible!" Nathanael exclaimed.

Philip shook his head. "Not so incredible; just difficult for us to accept."

"Now *I* stand corrected." Nathanael smiled.

This discussion would have been too liberal for the ears of their countrymen, but John would have reveled in it. It was for the reason of this very attitude in Philip that John had so greatly enjoyed being under his tutorship as a boy.

Only a select few had been afforded the opportunity to hear this teacher expounding on such subjects. Though by synagogue tradition a schoolmaster was not to have favorites, Philip had found it difficult to resist favoring the keen perception he had found in John. And, as a result, they had had many private discussions together, apart from the other students.

Of course, Zebedee had sensed that John's interest in such

dubious subjects was being aroused surreptitiously. Since even Philip's name was Greek, indicating that his family had admired the great heathen Philip of Macedon, the very mention of him in Zebedee's household had been cause for strife. But there had been no true evidence of any heretical belief on his part, and the old Pharisee's heated disapproval of Philip had only driven the boy closer to him.

Nathanael looked at the teacher, his eyes wide with fervor. "Do you think we will live to see the day of the Messiah?"

"Friend;" he answered wistfully, "what Jew for generations has not asked himself that question?"

The afternoon was wearing on now. Philip had to be going, and Nathanael would return to his home in Cana. Their chance meeting on this road had been a joy to both, but they had wives and families who would worry if they did not return soon.

Each stood to leave. "We will meet again," they said, and bowing with the traditional, "Peace," they parted, Philip down the road toward Magdala and, ultimately, to Capernaum-Bethsaida, and Nathanael toward Cana.

As Philip walked, the phrases from Plato and Ipuwer kept weaving in and out of his thoughts. How he longed to know the meaning of those words! How he longed to understand how cultures so diverse from his, so pagan and so Gentile, could long for the same things as Israel!

He did not notice the group which now came toward him down the Cana road. His head was bent and his mind in a realm other than that of the dusty thoroughfare. In fact, it was not until he had gone well past the men that he realized someone had spoken to him.

Turning about absent-mindedly, he stared blankly at the group of disciples and their leader, Jesus. Such small entourages were a common sight in Israel. Everywhere young seekers found and followed teachers who might hold their interest for a day or two, perhaps longer if they were very capable in their art. He could not imagine who would have called out to him, but as he sought the answer, the supposed strangers took on familiarity.

"Simon, Andrew!" he exclaimed, recognizing his own townsfolk. "And John Bar Zebedee!" His voice mellowed with the love he felt for the young man.

The joyful reunion of teacher and pupil was marked by a fervent embrace, and John choked back the signs of sentiment which flooded over him at the sight of his old confidant.

"I'm glad you stopped me," Philip said. "I was so busy with my own thoughts I did not even look up as we passed. I would have gone my way not knowing you were here."

John smiled, but explained, "Sir, I did not see you until just now. It was not I, but the Master, who called out to you."

"The Master?" Philip asked.

"Yes," John replied, leading him to Jesus. "Philip of Bethsaida . . . this is my Master, Jesus Bar Joseph, of Nazareth."

Philip easily read the ardent pride John took in this introduction. The fact that the man was from Nazareth apparently did not detract from his worthiness, if a student like John had taken to following after him.

Philip bowed. "Peace, sir. I am glad we have met." Then straightening, and with his brow knit quizzically, he said, "Pardon me, but why did you call out to me as we passed?"

Jesus gave him a warming smile, but still he was not prepared for the Master's response. "I called out to you because I knew what was in your heart," he said. "I knew the words upon which you meditated."

Philip's face grew pale. How did he know he had been meditating? But straining for composure, he reasoned, it would be easy to guess such a thing from his preoccupied posture. And so, testing him, he asked, "And what words were those?"

"Words concerning the Messiah," Jesus answered. But then he added softly, "Words of the Gentiles."

Philip received this like a blow, but the disciples looked at one another blankly, not understanding the conversation. Only to the Bethsaida schoolmaster was it clear, and he trembled with the weight of it.

"And what was it you said to me as we passed?" he stammered, almost afraid to hear the answer.

Jesus looked at him gently. "I said, 'Follow me,' Philip. I am the one spoken of. I am the one you seek."

Philip was an intellectual. He could scarcely believe what his ears told him this moment. His head swam and his body grew damp with a strange, dewy sweat.

John reached for him and supported him until he regained himself, but even then Philip was nearly mute with wonder. Speechless, he stared at the Stranger, and then, suddenly, he turned about to leave, his face toward Cana.

"Sir," he called back anxiously, "do not go away! Wait right where you are! I will return immediately!"

Confused, John, Peter, and Andrew looked at Jesus, who walked to the side of the road and sat down to wait. They did not question him, but silently followed his lead and rested beside him.

Away up the road Philip ran with a flurry of arms and legs hardly becoming a dignified schoolmaster. "Nathanael!" he cried, nearly leveling those who impeded his hasty progress. "Nathanael!" Would he never find him? He could not have gotten far in this little while.

At last he spied him, walking in the same preoccupied manner as he himself had done earlier. Oh, what news he had for him!

"Nathanael!" he called once more, finally achieving the desired response.

At last Nathanael turned. "Philip? What are you doing here?" he asked, laughing.

The schoolmaster was winded and clutched at Nathanael's shoulder. He realized what he must look like, but he could not waste time with humor. "Oh, friend!" he panted. "We have found him!"

"Found whom?" Nathanael asked.

"We have found him, of whom Moses in the Law, and the prophets, did write! Jesus of Nazareth, the son of Joseph."

Nathanael looked at his companion as though to ask whether he had been imbibing too much wine. "Can any good thing come out of Nazareth?" he roared with hilarity.

But Philip was indeed serious; Nathanael could see that. And his laughter was quickly quelled.

The young teacher breathed deeply and said soberly, simply. "Come and see."

Nathanael followed him, and when they arrived before the Master, Jesus stood, took one look at Philip's friend, and reading the skepticism in his face, said softly, "Behold, an Israelite who is truly honest."

Nathanael blushed. Were his wariness and distrust of the Nazarene that obvious? "How do you know me?" he smiled nervously.

Jesus looked at him tenderly and explained: "Before Philip called you, when you were under the fig tree, I saw you."

Nathanael stared blankly at him, the meaning of the words taking some time to dawn upon him. He then turned to Philip, who nodded in affirmation of what he had heard. Could it be? How had this man known where he had been earlier? He had never seen him in his life!

"Rabbi . . ." he whispered, "you *are* the Son of God . . ." His hands trembled as he recalled the Scriptures he and Philip had chanted together. Tears came to his eyes, and he bowed his head. "Master, you are the King of Israel!"

Jesus stepped over to him quietly and placed his hands upon his shoulders, bidding him to look his way. Then, probing his soul he replied, "Nathanael Bar Tholomew, do you believe in me because I said unto you that I had seen you under the fig tree?"

Nathanael was silent with anticipation.

"You shall see greater things than these," Jesus said. And then he looked above to the sun-split clouds. "Truly, truly, I say to you, in the future you shall see heaven open, and the angels of God ascending and descending upon the Son of Man."

Chapter 7

John's head spun. So much had happened so quickly. How could he take it all in, and what should he make of it? It seemed Jesus had the power to sweep up followers as a woman sweeps up crumbs from a table, and yet he was so simple and unassuming.

John's world was divided into two realms when he considered this man. Often he found that he had to *remind* himself of the Baptist's words, calling him the "Son of God"; that he had to force himself to recall the day of the thunder and the voice. Other times, as when Jesus had spoken to Philip and Nathanael, he seemed almost . . . divine, and the baptism leaped before John as vividly as the hour it had happened.

Who was this fellow? he questioned once again. What charisma commanded men of such diversity to cling to him? To forsake home and occupation to be with him? Hired fishermen like Andrew and his newlywed brother, Peter; a scholar like Philip; a liberal Jew like Nathanael; and John himself—the rebellious son of a Pharisee? All of them, following him with no real understanding of who he was, what he believed, what he had to say for himself!

John dwelled long on this as they walked toward Cana. The entire group was, in fact, very silent, each disciple probably thinking similar thoughts.

Uppermost in John's mind, however, were the words Jesus had

spoken to Nathanael. Obviously he had been referring to himself. But what could he have meant, "the Son of Man"?

Hadn't Daniel, the prophet of old, spoken of "the Son of Man" coming in the clouds of heaven, and attaining "dominion, and glory, and a kingdom, that all people, nations, and languages, should serve him" everlastingly? Had not all the prophets spoken of such a man to come? Could Jesus be the one they heralded?

And how would the disciples see heaven opened and angels surrounding Jesus?

John could remember the story of Jacob's dream, a ladder ascending to heaven with angels traversing up and down upon it, in service between earth and the throne of God at its top. The memory of the miraculous baptism dawned afresh upon him, and he shuddered. Surely heaven had opened that day! Sometimes he felt his head would split with the memory, so awesome and tangible it had been!

The dichotomy of John's own personality caused him to struggle. He looked at all this skeptically, and yet his fervent desire for truth was consolidating his allegiance to the Nazarene, as it had kept him loyal to the Baptist.

It was not fanatic desire for a cause which led him to trek after Jesus. If it had been blind impulse on his part to seek a Savior, he could have been caught up with any number of self-proclaimed "messiahs" who had come and gone through the years. And the same could have been said for Peter, Andrew, Philip, and Nathanael.

But they had not been engaged in any such frantic hunt.

It was *Jesus* who had captivated them—not a dream. Though John might be called a dreamer by nature, though Andrew and Peter had longed for the Messiah, though Philip and Nathanael might have been labeled roadside philosophers, it was *Jesus* the person, *Jesus* the power, who held them—not a transient hope or a fireside vision.

How they wondered who he was!

Son of Man?

Yes—he was a man.

Son of God?

They trembled; they hoped; they followed.

Chapter 8

The Galilean night rang with the sounds of music and laughter. Ten young girls, holding torchlights high above their heads, whirled and spun their way through the streets, singing of the radiant beauty of one who rode in a litter behind them.

A proud young man wearing garlands about his neck jostled for a position near that litter, but was teasingly prevented by friends who persisted in chanting tales of his great bravery and prowess.

Somewhere along the way, Jesus and his company joined this merry processional, and as tradition dictated to anyone in the street, they began to mix with the crowd. John and the other disciples from the northern ports were strangers to the gathering, but they were quickly caught up in the joy of the occasion.

Indeed, the bride was beautiful. She had been "captured" this night by her groom, his companions, and his best friend. Upon their arrival at her home, her father had pronounced a blessing, and she was now being escorted to the groom's house where a week-long wedding feast would commence. Of course, the "capture" had been well anticipated. Her heavily embroidered garments, her jeweled veil, her many ornamented necklaces and bracelets had taken a year to prepare, but this had been her chief joy since the day the groom's father had paid bride-price for her.

The dazzling array of lanterns, the happy sounds of harness bells dangling from the necks of camels in the entourage, the clapping of hands, and the wild tossing of nuts, grain, oil, perfume, and wine, led all the way to the door of the new home. Another blessing was said and all entered.

The disciples stood along the sides of the room as the others were seated. Everyone present would take a position at the table according to his rank in the community or his relationship to the bride and groom, who sat together at the head of the room. But since Jesus and his companions were not of the immediate family, they waited to see where they should be placed.

The governor of the feast, seeing that a rabbi was present, gave a most complimentary position to the Master and his followers. Jesus took it graciously, but John could tell it would have made no difference to him where he had been seated.

Presently the festivities began.

It was common, among certain rabbis, to frown upon such excesses of merrymaking. But as John studied his Master, he could see his attitude was anything but severe. He mingled pleasantly with all about him, putting them at ease, yet still retaining that indefinable quality of uniqueness which set him apart from the crowd.

John leaned toward the Master asking, "Sir, are the bride and groom friends of yours?"

"They are distantly related to my mother."

John nodded. "It is too bad your mother could not be here."

"But she is here, John." At this, Jesus directed his attention up the room to a lovely matron who sat in happy conversation with several other women. She hardly seemed old enough to be the mother of a man in his early thirties, but this was not unusual.

John was intrigued with her face, for it appeared to carry a volume of history for one so young. Though she was involved with those about her, she frequently scanned the crowd as though in search of someone, and John wondered if she knew of the Master's arrival.

"She is a beautiful woman," he said, hoping the Nazarene would not take offense.

Jesus said nothing, but John could tell he did not disapprove of the compliment.

The family of the groom was not exceptionally wealthy, but the food was sumptuous, the evening joyous. And now the happiest of hours arrived. Rising from the table, the groom took his bride by the hand and the two walked toward the elegant canopy which served as a symbol of their union.

The best friend of the bridegroom stood before them and said to the young man, "Do you promise to please, to honor, to nourish, and to care for this woman, as is the manner of the men of Israel?"

"I do promise," he answered.

"Then you wed this woman according to the Law of Moses and of Israel."

At this, great celebration broke out, and as the parents of the couple once more blessed them, the "sons of the bride-chamber," the groom's friends, led him and his bride through the canopy and then to the head table.

The party now went wild with joy. The dancing became merrier than ever. The feast would continue well into the night, the wine would continue to flow, and the music would ring out for hours.

While it was the duty of the governor to keep any party lively, this was no task at a wedding feast. In fact, it fell to him, now, to keep order. All in all the job was a pleasant one, and indeed, an honor. The only thing he needed to insure was that the festivities were not cut short for lack of any food or beverage.

It was, therefore, much to this governor's dismay when one of the servants called him aside for a private conversation. The guests had not been aware of the governor's private fears. They were happily engaged in their celebrating. But he knew the groom's father was not an aristocrat, and he had wondered if the gentleman extended too many invitations. Could it be that the servants had run short of something?

Hoping no one would notice, he stepped down from the platform on which the head table was positioned, and walked to the pantry where the servants watched after the wine.

"What is it?" he asked, trying his best to retain a pleasant expression.

"Sir," the head-servant muttered, "the wine is gone."

The governor turned white. "Gone! You imbecile! What do you mean, 'Gone!'" His hands shook with anger and humiliation. "Can it be that you did not follow my instructions?"

The servant shrank from him. "Sir, I *did* follow your instructions!"

"One part water to four parts wine?" he rasped.

"Yes, sir. Just as you ordered."

"Oh, for the sake of Israel!" the governor groaned.

The servant stood mute, and the other wine-bearers gathered silently behind him. "What are we to do, sir?" one whispered.

The governor flashed angry eyes at them. "Are you certain you have not been . . ." and here he pantomimed the act of drinking.

This met with obstinate cries of "No, sir!" "Certainly not, sir!" and "How can you think that, sir?"

"Well," the governor said, throwing his hands in the air, "a beautiful wedding, ruined! I knew the master had overextended himself . . . Do you think he would listen to me? Six more days of celebrating, and we are already out of the main staple!''

At this, he motioned emphatically that the servants were to leave his sight, and he turned, head down, to reenter the banquet hall.

Never had he felt such shame! He peered through the curtain at the merry throng and watched the pitchers of wine being poured all about as if there were no end to the supply. When he looked at the bride and groom, so happy in their ignorance, he desired to run from the house. But he held himself erect and stepped again to the head table.

No one in the room seemed to sense his burden, but when he entered, Mary, the mother of Jesus, read the story in his face. It did not come as a surprise to her, for she knew the family well, and had been amazed at the lavish fare they had provided.

Was there anything she could do? she wondered. It would be improper to approach the governor about the matter, and it would be considered unbecoming for her to speak familiarly with any of the other men in the gathering. Who could help?

Looking about the room once again, seeming to hope against hope, her gaze fell upon Jesus. And tears of happiness welled in her eyes at her son's presence.

Excusing herself from the table, she restrained the motherly desire to run to him, but eagerly she approached Jesus, and tenderly, softly she whispered, "O my son!"

Jesus looked up at her compassionately. "I have been here all along," he said. And then with good-natured affection, he added, "You have been so busy visiting, you were blind to the fact."

Mary blinked back her tears and reached out a hand to touch the Master. Jesus took hold of it gently and whispered the answer to her unvoiced question. "I am fine, mother. All is well with me."

The lovely woman shut her eyes in gratitude, and John wondered how long it had been since she had beheld her son.

It appeared she fought the urge to embrace him. Culture was an impediment to that demonstration. But as she gazed at his wind-burned face and studied the torn and broken hands she clung to, her voice trembled. "Your face . . . your hands," she whispered. "Where have you been?" John remembered having asked the Master the same thing. Surely he had lived through something terrible in the wilderness.

But Jesus only answered, "You know where I was, mother. Don't trouble yourself."

Mary gave a half-smile, and John read in it that she understood the Master as no one else might ever understand him. She knew the story he had not yet told to anyone, and she would say no more.

Now she searched her son's face beseechingly. As was the custom in Israel when the father of a household passed away, his eldest son took command, and the mother was to reverence her son in the same way she had her husband. Therefore, it was with care that Mary approached the subject of the wine and the feast, for she had a favor to ask of Jesus.

"Son," she said softly, "they have no wine."

John listened in carefully and caught the gist of the conversation.

Jesus was silent a moment. "Woman," he said gently but firmly, "what do you want with me? The time has not come for such a thing."

Mary said nothing more, but continued to plead with him by her presence and expression.

John watched the Rabbi's face. He appeared set in his decision, and yet in his mien was a glint of flexibility. The Master seemed to soften under Mary's gaze, and almost imperceptibly he gave her a smile.

At the instant she sensed that glimmer of change, she called for the servants. "Do whatever he tells you to," she said.

Only the disciples were now aware of the strange proceedings, and as Jesus went toward the pantry, the servants wondered what he was going to do.

In the back room stood six stone waterpots. Each one, if filled to capacity, would hold about one-hundred-and-fifty gallons. Jesus drew back the curtain of the chamber and inconspicuously stepped into the narrow hall.

In a low voice, so as not to draw the attention of the guests, he commanded: "Fill the waterpots with water."

Questions flooded the minds of the attendants. But, so full of authority had been the command, that they did not hesitate to carry it out.

It would take some time for all the jars to be filled. How John longed to see what was going on behind that curtain! But he lacked the audacity to go where he had not been specifically invited, so he kept his seat.

When the waterpots were brought to the Master, he saw they were full, as he had desired, and said to the men waiting on him, "Draw out a cupful, now, and bear it to the governor of the feast."

The headservant looked at him blankly, then almost laughed, but something in Jesus' expression prevented him. Instead, he motioned his subordinates to do as the Master had asked.

The attendants ladled an ample supply of the liquid into a chalice and walked toward the door. Looking back, they were greeted by the nervous nod of the headservant, and so they departed shakily for the governor's table.

The reception was predictably gruff. "What is this?" the governor snapped, as they offered him the cup. "Do you bring me goat's milk?"

When they told him that a certain Jesus of Nazareth had asked him to taste it, he growled, "I do not know this Jesus!—of Nazareth, did you say?" His lip curled in a sneer of contempt for the city. But then his eyes brightened. Perhaps, just perhaps, there were a few wealthy Nazarenes. Could it be that this Jesus had gotten wind of the problem of the wine and had magnanimously donated from his own reserves?

Hoping against hope, he took the chalice and sipped some of the contents. The servants stood well out of his reach. But the response was not negative. Suddenly the ruler of the feast was on his feet. "Jesus of Nazareth, whoever you are," he was thinking, "you are truly a generous gentleman!"

The servants were incredulous as the governor called for the bridegroom and said ecstatically, and so that all present could hear, "Every man serves the best wine at the beginning of a feast, and when everyone is well filled, then the poorer wine. But," he smiled broadly and let the family take the praise, "you have kept the good wine until now!"

Chapter 9

John had never before seen a miracle worker. He had heard of such people. The Scripture and history of Israel were full of references to such individuals and their deeds. The incident at Cana reminded him of the story of Elijah the prophet, who had, centuries before, miraculously replenished the supply of oil and meal in a poor household.

But such a thing hardly seemed possible today. After all, no one but the servants had seen what had transpired behind the curtain of the pantry in Cana.

Nevertheless, none of the disciples could fully doubt. John was entranced by Jesus; more and more drawn to him; more and more awed by him. When the Master and his followers left Cana, it was John who walked closest to him.

Mary and her other children, James, Jude, Joseph, Simon, and Jesus' sisters, who had also been at the feast, left Cana with the company. Mary longed to be with her eldest son, and Jesus had not denied her companionship.

But as they walked, John sensed a strange coolness on the part of Jesus' brethren toward the Master. If anything, they seemed ashamed of him, certainly holding no reverence for him apart from that customarily due the head of a house. Observing their silence, their aloof postures, John wondered if they were even contemptuous of Jesus, thinking him of doubtful sanity.

All of this could have troubled John greatly. But he put it from his mind. The miracle at Cana was too fresh in his memory to allow strong skepticism toward the Nazarene.

John's eyes turned again to the Master, and to his lovely mother. Their relationship made John lonely for Salome. The two women were much alike, he acknowledged.

John sighed. The sky was clear, the air warm and balmy, reminding him of the sea, and calling up distant memories of home and childhood. Sentiment nudged him, and despite Zebedee, John found himself, for the first time in months, longing to return to Capernaum.

Jesus was not heading for Nazareth, as John had expected, but was turned toward the sea.

"Master," John asked breathlessly, "where do we go?"

Jesus seemed to sense his feelings. "I would like to see your hometown," he said.

"You mean to go to Capernaum?"

"Yes, and Bethsaida." Jesus smiled.

John turned to Peter, who had planned to leave the group at the main highway to head for home and wife. A look of excitement colored the big man's face. A heavy load had obviously been lifted from him, for he had not known how he would bring himself to part with the Master.

"Sir," Peter exclaimed, "you must dine at my house! My wife and mother-in-law would want to meet you!"

Jesus accepted with a silent nod, and Peter stood even taller than usual.

Chapter 10

John had never met Deborah, Peter's wife. He remembered her as the auburn-haired girl he had seen at a distance once or twice when Peter had pointed her out. But then, Peter was forever pointing out girls. John had paid no more than passing attention to her, noting that she was attractive, thinking her little more than a child.

He was therefore curious to see how this rough fisherman related to the delicate bride from Tabigha.

Peter's initial enthusiasm to have Jesus dine at his home seemed to dwindle somewhat as they drew nearer the Bethsaida neighborhood where he lived. Perhaps he was dubious about Deborah's reaction to a houseful of unannounced company and his overdue arrival. Doubtless, she would wonder about her husband's sudden infatuation with the Nazarene. But the determined angle of Simon's chin said he would not let a woman rule him.

The snug fishing village sat on the rim of the great lake. Peter's house was humble, but as warm in appearance as might be expected, considering that two bachelors had lived there alone until recently. The shine of the brass fittings on the doorpost attested to the new womanly touch the quarters were enjoying, and from the street John spied hand-made tapestries hanging on walls, which before had always been bare.

Peter placed a decisive hand on the door handle and stooped his tall frame to enter. "Deborah!" he called, his voice ringing with a mixture of excitement and caution.

A shuffle of eager feet brought the small woman from the back room. "Oh, Simon!" she called, her dark green eyes full of happiness. Her husband was truly home from the sea.

She ran breathlessly to hold him, but just then she spied his friends outside the door, and her impulsive desire to embrace her spouse was squelched. "Simon, who are these men?" she whispered.

Peter cleared his throat apprehensively and answered, "Guests, Deborah." But then, taking on a commanding air, he said, "Make ready, woman. They are staying here for a few days."

Custom did not require a man to explain unexpected company to his wife, nor was it imperative that he introduce them to her. Deborah was, therefore, turning toward the kitchen in silent anger and downcast resignation, when her husband called to her again. His bulky frame housed a tender heart, and he could not play the taskmaster with her for long. "Woman," he said gently, but not so much as to offend the masculine audience, "meet my companions."

Deborah turned about in surprise, and humbly advanced toward the group which had now been ushered inside. Though it went against her spunky nature to do so, she kept her eyes down, not overstepping the boundaries of propriety which culture had determined for her sex.

Peter took her from one to another of his friends, beginning with the Master. "Deborah, this is the Rabbi Jesus Bar Joseph, of Nazareth. I have been with him awhile since I left the sea. He desired to come for a visit."

Deborah bowed, not questioning the strange reason for Peter's late homecoming. "I am pleased to meet you, sir," she greeted Jesus.

"I trust our presence will be no burden to you," the Master replied.

Men did not say such things! Deborah hardly knew how to respond. "Certainly not, sir," she said, somewhat humbled. And as Peter led her away, she wondered if the Rabbi could actually have been concerned for her feelings.

Each disciple, in turn, was introduced to Peter's wife. She retained womanly restraint, but she was warming to her husband's indulgence and found herself forgiving his delayed return.

When, however, Peter brought her to Andrew, her patience was once again tested. She had never before met her brother-in-law, nor had she expected to do so for some time. The last she had been told, Andrew had been following after the strange wild man of Bethabara. Would he now be living under their roof? Undoubtedly so, she reasoned. This had always been his home.

Deborah bristled as Peter introduced her, but tried to replace her negative feelings with more constructive thoughts. How long she had wondered what he would be like! Would he approve of her? Would he be difficult to please?

Obvious surprise marked her face as she studied him. John almost laughed at her expression. Of course, she had expected a much larger man, someone like her husband.

Still she maintained a measure of poise. "I will do my best to serve you," she bowed.

Andrew read her thoughts, and blushed a little. But he appreciated her reverence for him. Though in times past he had seen Deborah from a distance, as had John, he had wondered, since hearing of the marriage, what Peter's new bride would be like. "I believe my brother has done well for himself," he said, nodding.

Deborah lifted her head and smiled.

John waited until morning to enter Capernaum. He hoped that his father would be away from the house when he arrived.

The grand home had not changed. John's heart beat quickly at the sight of it. Somehow he had always known he could not stay away forever.

Would Salome be at the hearth? That was how he always thought of her. Though she had many servants and helpers, she was the hardest worker in the villa. Her hands were always busy, though they need not have been. She had ample time to dally with the wealthy gossips of the neighborhood, but she had never found an occupation more to her liking than that of tending the home-fires.

How John longed for the sight of her!

He was now at the gate. His hand trembled as he reached for the latch. Pushing the door open silently, he peered uneasily into the entryway, and approaching the courtyard, he cast a furtive glance about the premises.

Suddenly the realization of the pain he had so often brought his mother dawned upon him afresh. He must be careful in approaching her. He must not hurt her again.

As he stood outside the main hall, the thought of his wild appearance occurred to him for the first time since the spring day he had caught a glimpse of his reflection in the pool at Bethabara. Until now, it had not seemed very important. Even at the wedding in Cana, personal looks had seemed of minor consequence. The excitement of being with Jesus the Nazarene had dominated his thinking.

But now, as he was about to see his mother, he was suddenly aware of his lack of grooming. He had bathed and had donned a set of Peter's clothes the night before, but now even that seemed insufficient. The great fisherman's cloak was cumbersome for him, and his hair was still shaggier than he liked. As a child might do, he smoothed his straying locks and straightened his baggy clothes with a sigh of resignation. Then he walked through the door.

Salome stood with a maidservant at a low table across which were draped several bolts of bright fabric. The two women were discussing the cloth, when Salome heard the sound of John's footsteps behind her.

Turning about to see who approached, she suddenly grew pale and limp, the material she had been holding slipping from her grasp. She said nothing, but slumped into the chair nearby, and the maidservant reached for her hand.

For a long time nothing was said, as mother and son studied one another. It was obvious his fears for his appearance had been for nothing. He was a beautiful sight to her eyes, and as tears began to stream down Salome's face, John knelt shakily at her feet and buried his head in her lap.

"My child," she whispered.

How he ever began to explain to his mother all he had learned in recent months would be lost to his memory forever. He had not planned his words ahead of time, and reconstructing the afternoon's conversation would be forever impossible. But he would not forget her face as he told her of the Baptist, and of Jesus the Nazarene.

Salome was loyal to Zebedee; she admired his zeal, his intellect. His form of Judaism was the only religion to which she was accustomed, or of which she knew very much. The recounting of John's days at the Jordan, of the freedom he had felt there, of the strange attachment he had for the notorious prophet and for the man of Nazareth, were difficult for her to understand. But she was fascinated with her son's stories, curious to know more.

Still, she was hesitant to pursue the topic, fearful of betraying Zebedee's opposition to all John had come to seek and follow.

Nevertheless, she could neither deny nor ignore the fiery enthusiasm her son expressed in his blossoming, though unformalized, beliefs. His devotion was contagious, his zeal most persuasive.

"Son," Salome asked softly, after nearly an hour of intense involvement with John's story, "this Jesus—you say you were present the day he was baptized?"

"Yes, mother," John asserted.

The slender Salome rose from her chair and walked to the latticed window, from which she gazed into the street. The lights of the wall torches lit her face and accented the random strands of silver hair which here and there gave evidence of her departing youth. It was apparent from her faraway look that she was attempting to envision what that baptism had really been like. "Was it as they say?" she whispered.

John stood and walked toward her. "How do they say it was?" he prodded gently.

Salome continued to stare into space. "They say there was a light . . ."

"Yes, mother. There was a light."

". . . and a voice?"

"Yes."

The disciple's mother shook her head in amazement. She could not doubt her son's words. She contemplated this for a long moment, and finding no way to question it further, she turned to him, sadness marking her countenance. "John," she pleaded, "tell me—whoever this man is, this Jesus, do you think your father would approve of him?"

John sighed, not wishing to speak of such things. But he knew he could not avoid the inevitable. "Mother," he said, walking across the room, "father was present the day of the baptism. Surely he has told you of it."

"No, John. I know he was there, for he was with the commission. But he has never discussed it with me."

John gave a resigned shrug. "I should not be surprised," he answered accusingly. "He never has faced the truth." But, then, seeing her pained expression and realizing he was betraying his resolution not to hurt her, he added quickly, "Please, let us not talk of such things just now." And returning, he took her in his arms, pressing her head to his shoulder.

"Mother," he said wistfully, "if only you could meet the Master. Your questions would lose their importance. If only you had heard the Baptist, if you had known him, if you had seen his face the day he baptized the Nazarene—you would only want to know more of Jesus . . . just more of Jesus."

Salome looked up at her son's face, and the reverence it reflected for the Master touched her soul. Still, she was hesitant to be swept up in a current which would oppose her husband. Carefully she chose her response. "Perhaps I shall meet him one day," she said.

"Meet whom?" came a familiar voice from the doorway.

John wheeled about excitedly. "James!" he shouted.

The two brothers rushed to one another, meeting in a joyful embrace. James could scarcely believe his eyes, and he revealed his delight with abandon.

"Brother! Is it really you?" he cried.

"It is!"

"And you are home to stay?"

John laughed warmly. "For a few days."

"We will see about that!" James countered, his brilliant blue eyes full of enthusiasm. "Come! Sit, brother! Tell me everything! Start at the beginning! Tell me of the Baptist, what you learned, everything! Speak of anything but leaving this place!"

John was thrilled to be once again near his elder brother. But as he began to talk with him, an even stronger emotion arose. He recalled Andrew's urgent desire to bring Simon to the Nazarene, and he was consumed with the same feeling which must have driven the slight son of Jona on his seemingly senseless errand to find the big fisherman.

As John began to relate his story to James, however, the hitherto absent member of the family entered from the courtyard.

Suddenly, John found himself on his feet, standing rigid and pale before his father. James stayed riveted to his chair, wondering apprehensively what would transpire.

Salome took a few hesitant steps toward Zebedee, as though to defend her youngest.

"Father?" John attempted a greeting.

Zebedee seemed not to hear, but his face was white and drawn and his old calloused hands quivered a little. His eyes, while fixed upon his son, seemed not to see him, and he said nothing as though fighting for the strength of some former resolution.

Salome was incredulous. "My lord . . ." she approached him, "he has come home! Your son has returned!"

But still the old Pharisee said nothing, and Salome trembled. "Please, Zebedee!" she cried.

Hearing her petition, the old Jew appeared to waver a bit, but then steeled himself coldly against her beseeching voice. Setting his chin in a stony angle, he walked toward the fireplace and sat down in his cedar armchair, calling for a goblet of wine.

A servant responded quietly, and the family observed the old man disbelievingly as he took his ease in the chair, his back turned to the little gathering. James rose to challenge him.

"Father, your son has returned!" he asserted angrily. "Can you deny your desire to hold him?"

Zebedee only gazed into the flames, his gray face frigid with resolve. "My younger son," he said deliberately, "is dead."

For one moment, cold, heavy silence filled the room. Salome eyed her husband wildly, and then turned to her sons, torn unmercifully between them. "Jehovah help me!" she demanded hoarsely. "What am I to do?"

James went to her and took her in his arms, but she wrenched free from him, not consenting to be consoled by anyone.

John considered the situation before him, the same one which had bound him since childhood. He must do the only thing he knew to do, the only thing which had ever brought him a measure of freedom from his father. He turned for the door.

Salome rushed after him, grasping his cloak and crying out, but he could not stay.

With one lingering glance, he studied her face, as though for the last time. Then, loosening her clutching, maternal hands, he held them tightly in his own and, with a sigh, released them.

Through the courtyard, through the door, and into the street, John moved. The night air was both bitter and sweet.

Chapter 11

Though it was but spring of the year, the weather was becoming very hot, especially in the more barren province of Judea. Nevertheless, the Jericho highway from Galilee to Jerusalem was crowded with travelers making the annual pilgrimage to the sacred city for the most holy of Jewish festivals, Passover.

John walked in dejected silence beside the Master. Strange, he was thinking. When he had left home the first time, to seek out the

Baptist, it had been Hanukkah. And now, once again, he was fleeing Zebedee, this time to go with Jesus, and at the season of another important holiday. Nearly a year and a half had passed since he had called the grand house in Capernaum his residence. He wondered if he would ever again have family security.

Jesus walked at a steady but leisurely pace. From Galilee it would take at least four days on foot to get to Jerusalem, and travel was especially slow through the rugged wilderness which gradually ascended to three thousand feet between Jericho and the Holy City. There was no sense in accelerating the tempo of the journey, as Passover was yet a week away, and the usual fear of robbers along this highway was at a minimum with so many pilgrims about.

"Deborah will miss you," the Master spoke to Peter.

"Yes." The big man jolted, wondering at the Nazarene's perception of his thoughts.

"It was good of her to let you come," Jesus said. "It is a hard thing for a bride."

Peter shrugged, feigning unconcern, and attempted a casual reply. "She had little choice."

The Master read through this, and he and Andrew smiled knowingly at one another. They knew it had *not* been easy for Peter to leave his wife. She had not taken kindly to his decision, and it was apparent he felt uneasy and guilty for it. But Jesus said no more.

Philip and Nathanael, who would usually be full of philosophical conversation on such a journey, were, like John, relatively quiet. Their thoughts were on what had transpired in recent months on the Cana road, and at the wedding feast.

But Jesus' attention turned to the young Jew at his side. It had become somehow natural always to find John closest to him. The Master sensed a sincerity of purpose in this young man, a depth of hunger for knowledge which drew him close to the teacher's heart.

"Tell me, John," he began, "it did not go well at home?"

John sighed. "No, sir."

"Is it hard for you to leave your family?"

"It is, sir . . . at least to leave my mother and my brother . . ."

"And your father?"

John did not answer quickly. "I left him long ago."

Jesus was silent, and then he said, "Your father has hurt you many times, hasn't he?"

The disciple watched the road absently, but the Master spoke again. "John, can you overcome the pain you feel?"

The disciple did not understand the purpose of this question, but answered, "Not easily, sir."

"True, John. And the fact is that you never will overcome it if your only purpose in leaving was to flee your father. If you have no goal beyond that, he will be a constant memory and you will feel constant pain."

John gave this some thought. "Yes, I can see that," was the sad reply.

"Does it still give you sorrow to think of the Baptist?"

"I miss him, sir. But I left him to follow you, and that makes it easier."

Jesus smiled. "Let it always be your purpose to follow me, John. Then no pain can conquer you."

The light of the Teacher's lesson brought a gleam to John's eye, and a new lift to his chin.

Chapter 12

In the distance lay the Holy City, crowded with burgeoning masses of Jewish faithfuls who had come from all parts of the Roman world to celebrate one historic day of God's mercy. Jerusalem spanned two great hills, bordered by a large gorge, the Valley Kidron. Despite the mighty towered walls which flanked the town, the winding streets, full of pilgrims and citizens, could be seen from the vantage point of the mountain road which Jesus and his followers descended.

Keeping watch over the city was the Temple, brilliant white and shining with gold ornamentation. As the sun hit it, the men shielded their eyes from its glow.

No matter how many times John had visited the House of Jehovah, he always thrilled at the sight, for this was the pinnacle of his nation's history, and the resting place of its God.

Passing through the outlying fields, the Master led his disciples from the vicinity of the Mount of Olives, through the great bronze gates of the guarded walls.

John wondered how Jesus intended to celebrate the festival. The disciple wished they might all stay in the home which his own family maintained in the city, but Zebedee would be coming soon to reside there for the holidays, and so they would not be welcome.

It was customary, however, for Jerusalem's citizens to open their spare rooms for pilgrims at this time of year. And so, they would find lodging.

Undoubtedly, the Master would venture first to the grounds of the Temple, as, traditionally, the days before the Passover were to be spent in meditation and purification.

The gate through which they passed lay to the north of the Temple compound. Today the city streets near the sacred edifice were the most congested in Jerusalem, and would continue to be so until the feast had come and gone.

Beggars seeking alms found this a profitable time. Not only was the population heavier, but hearts were religiously softer during a holy season.

Peasants from the farming districts also made the best of the festival's opportunities. Beasts of burden, laden with produce and handcrafted wares, shuffled like small mountains through the crowds, their masters seeking out the most auspicious corners in which to erect booths of trade.

The clamor, the clatter of wagon wheels, thousands of voices, the laughter and play of small children, the shouting of merchants, all mingled into one festive cacophony.

A novice might have wondered how solemn this holy season was to most Jews. There were those who saw it mainly as a time to rake in large sums of money, but for the true lovers of Jehovah, the noise, the merry atmosphere were symbolic of celebrating God's faithfulness.

On the first Passover, centuries before, when the God of Israel had smitten the firstborn of the Egyptians who held his people captive, he had provided an escape for his chosen nation. Every Jewish house where the blood of a sacrificial lamb had been sprinkled was "passed over" by the Angel of the Lord on that night, and not a child of any of those homes had been harmed.

Annually, since Moses had declared it imperative, this act of mercy had been remembered at this time. And though there were those who took advantage of the faithful, God was to be praised.

Jesus and his disciples worked their way up the street slowly. John had been watching the Master since they had neared the town. Compassion had marked the Nazarene's face upon seeing the lepers outside the walls. It had appeared he desired to reach out and touch them. To John's relief, however, he had only looked at them sadly, as if to say the time was not yet, and had walked on.

John remembered Jesus' words to Mary when she had asked him to remedy the lack of wine. "The time has not come for such a thing." What had he meant?

Now that they were in the throng, Jesus' face still bore an indefinable sadness, and John assumed he yet considered the lepers. But he seemed to study those about him, and then he raised his eyes to the mountain of the Lord's House.

The Temple itself occupied only a small portion of the mammoth grounds of the compound. Just inside the colossal stone walls which surrounded the leveled mountaintop, and encasing the entire seven-hundred-and-fifty-foot square of the grounds, were tremendous columned buildings, known as the cloisters, the greatest of which were the King's Porch and Solomon's Porch. Up from the base of these buildings, and ascending in consecutive terraced levels to the zenith of the hill, were a series of immense courts which ran, one inside the other, all the way around the dwelling of God.

And this, Herod the Great's architectural pride, sat like a cut diamond in the most splendid of settings.

Upon viewing it, Jesus did not reflect the same awe as John and the others. Undoubtedly he appreciated the glory of the structure; undoubtedly his native heart beat a bit faster upon viewing it. Surely this was Jehovah's House. But his response to the spendid sight appeared deeper than John could understand.

The Master now lowered his gaze and continued to make his way through the crowd, his steps marked with a new tempo. It would not be long before they stood inside those hallowed grounds.

A warm spring breeze found its way through the maze of Corinthian columns on the King's Porch. Jesus stood with his disciples, watching the small gatherings clustered about the sprawling structure. Here sat the thinkers of Judaism, where they and their kind might always be found, debating the Law, discussing the prophets. All sects mingled here, Levites of the priestly order, doctors of the Law, rabbis, scribes, Pharisees, Sadducees, Zealots of all sorts.

If a stranger wanted to catch the heartbeat of orthodoxy, the mind of a singular and peculiar nation, he might do it in this place. So serious the thinkers appeared, standing or reclining upon the steps, heads bent studiously, as they concentrated on the words of the current speaker or on a rebuttal.

To be seen here were the elders of the people, and the members of the leisure class. But there were also penniless, itinerant rabbis and their disciples. Jesus might have been described so, though at present he was observing rather than instructing.

Selecting one group from among the many, he walked to the edge of the company and listened intently to their conversation. It concerned a debate between a handful of Sadducees and a larger number of their rivals, the Pharisees. They discussed a point of doctrine on which they were renowned opponents: life after death. The Sadducees denied any such thing, and the Pharisees clung to it tenaciously. Each knew the Scriptures, one group quoting from Ecclesiastes upon the futility of life and the hopelessness of death—the other expounding emotionally from Job, about the certainty of immortality.

White beards shook, aged eyes flashed, tongues leveled bitter insults, and the debate went on.

John looked to the Master. What was his opinion?

Jesus was silent, his mind not so much on the topic, as on the men who debated it. He watched them for a long time, and then turned away, never having spoken, and never having been asked to speak.

In a far corner, upon a crude box, stood a shouting Zealot, denouncing Caesar; near the wall stood a self-proclaimed miracle-worker, demanding a shekel a cure; up the great aisle roamed a group of chanters singing a psalm.

A circus of ready opinion displayed itself here. It rivaled the forum at Rome, the Parthenon at Athens. Listening in, one might have wondered, Roman-like, if Truth even existed; or if it did, how it could survive the tugging, pulling and tearing it received at the hands of men.

Leaving this arena, Jesus took a seat at the top of the porch, turned his back to the cloisters, and studied the multicolored pavement at his feet. It was Philip who finally worked up the courage to approach him concerning what they had just witnessed.

"Master," he said. But Jesus did not respond. His thoughts were his alone, and he was not open to sharing them.

Philip stepped back, and the disciples waited awkwardly. Moments passed, while the sounds of the great philosophers hammered at their ears.

Jesus looked above him, at long last, surveying the great cedar roofs with a sigh. The indefinable sadness, which was so typical of him, colored his countenance once more. His gaze then traveled to the Temple and lingered there for a while.

Peter nudged John quizzically, as though to ask why the Master behaved so strangely. John silently shook his head and shrugged his shoulders.

But the Master's eyes now left the House of the Lord, and scanned the scene before him, that adjacent to the porch. At first, he did not really see what was staged ahead. It dawned upon him with merciful slowness.

This was the "lower" court of the Temple compound, first in the series of terraces which ascended to the sanctuary itself. Known as the Court of the Gentiles, it was a free gathering place for anyone. No Gentile could go beyond it, however, on penalty of death. This was spelled out clearly in Latin, Greek, and Hebrew on the partition which separated it from the higher places.

What drew the Master's attention was the use to which this court was being put. It was the precinct of the Temple marketplace, otherwise known as "the shops." For many years, ever since a period of enslavement to the Babylonians, when Jews had returned from dispersion into foreign lands, these shops had been necessary. After generations away from Israel, thousands had come home without Jewish currency, which was required to pay the annual Temple tax. Tables where moneychangers could conduct their banking business, exchanging foreign for domestic coins, had been a necessity.

In time, however, this practice had become so perverted by the greed of the bankers and their lustful profiteering that it was a disgrace to the nation.

True, there were still many Jews dwelling in foreign lands, and when they made pilgrimages to Jerusalem, they found it necessary to do business with these men. But this did not excuse the lengths to which people had gone, taking advantage of the situation. As the bankers had added profit to profit in their charge for exchanges, merchants had added other businesses to the grounds. Cattle-drivers now brought their herds of sheep, goats, and oxen into the court, selling them for sacrifices. Grocers erected booths from which they sold goods necessary to the preparation of the offerings: wine, oil, salt. Cages of turtledoves, manned by eager keepers, were sold as votive gifts.

Add to all of this, still more merchants had had the audacity to bring in wares having nothing whatsoever to do with the Temple or its service.

It had become a virtual fairgrounds. Bawling cattle, chattering birds, loud and angry bartering—none of it suited the sacred purpose of the property. It was a wholesale mockery, a profanity.

The disciples watched Jesus closely. His previous sorrow was changing to indignation and outrage. As he surveyed the grounds, he stood to his feet and began walking from stall to stall, table to table, his face bearing a look of iron and fire, his hands forming angular fists.

John and others followed at a distance, wary of his mood. Scattered onlookers may have wondered at the Stranger's defiant appearance. But the crowds were mainly preoccupied with their own affairs.

Never had John dreamed he would see Jesus look this way. Compared to the stormy Baptist, he had seemed the gentle Rabbi, the soft-spoken Teacher, generally meek in temperament, and not given to such violent emotion as now apparently raged within.

The Master stood in the middle of the marketplace, glaring ominously at the greedy exchangers seated before him. He then turned to a merchant's booth, where bolts of fabric and skeins of cord were sold. John watched speechlessly as Jesus ripped a spool of shining red rope from the counter, quickly unraveled it and began forming something which looked like a multilayered scourge.

The dispossessed merchant reached indignantly for the braid, but the Nazarene gave him one unnerving glance and he stepped back.

The cord was wound securely about the Master's hand and wrist, and a sizable whip dangled free in his grip. There was a bewildered stir in the crowd, which had begun to notice his strange behavior.

Jesus took in the scene once more, this time staring vengefully at those who stood nearby. He fingered the limp cord in his hand, and then, letting it fall to his side, began swinging it to and fro in warning, his jaw set with determination, his eyes full of flame.

At last, a deep rumble of revenge thundered from the recesses of his soul. "Out!" he cried. "Out!" And the scourge was wielded. Fury, wrath, righteous indignation—no description was adequate. The "gentle" Nazarene was godlike in his retribution.

Onlookers fell back, stumbling over one another to escape the whip. The Master was driving literally hundreds from the sacred grounds. His arms, hardened by years of manual toil, were showing their storehouse of strength. His forceful carpenter's hands, toughened by countless hours at the workbench, pushed back the crowds with ease.

Had his physical presence been less dynamic, however, his zeal alone would have stayed any opposition. He seemed the anger of Jehovah personified, the wrath of Yahweh unleashed.

Stalls of cattle and oxen, tethers of sheep and goats were his next objects of assault. With long, angry strides, he approached them, unbolting and flinging back the gates which restrained the larger animals, and loosening the ropes which secured the smaller to posts weighted on the ground. Then the scourge flew again, cracking above the heads of the baffled creatures. Away they stampeded in wild confusion, bleating and lowing in their flight.

The crowd which remained was joined by those who had been in the cloisters and elsewhere about the grounds. Curious thousands huddled around the edge of the open square, vying for a view.

There were still men seated at the banking benches, open-mouthed with awe, but fearing to leave their tills. Some of them, their eyes full of an urgency befitting their trade, hurriedly scooped money off the tables, their sweaty hands cramming it into drawstring bags. They knew they were next, and were eager to be gone when the Stranger approached their vicinity.

As Jesus turned toward the changers, his gait was purposeful and heavy, his robes whipping tempestuously.

Now *all* the moneychangers tried to gather up their treasures. Coins fell from slippery fingers, tinkling to the ground like small pleas for help.

But now he stood before them, his gaze stripping them one by one. Slowly they ceased their desperate scrounging, shrinking back into their chairs with rigid apprehension.

All but one. This man did not give up his greed so easily. The wizened old Jew was down on hands and knees, poking in the cracks of the pavement for a shekel, a bag of coins already clasped hotly under one arm.

He did not see Jesus approach, did not even realize he had been noticed, until he felt the bag being pulled from under his sleeve.

Turning his head, he saw the sandaled feet of the Nazarene, and sweat beaded afresh on his already damp brow. His gaze traveled up the person of the Master and then to his face. The old banker trembled, and seemed temporarily to forget his quest for the lost coins.

But then he saw the bag of silver in Jesus' hands, and reached for it angrily. The Master held it for a short while, then silently loosened the strings of the pouch and turned it upside down.

Coins crashed splendidly to the pavement, dashing against the stones and clashing in a metallic chorus for yards in all directions. With the last gentle spin of metal on stone, the final rolling tinkle of escaping silver, the old Jew's mouth contorted. He looked at Jesus silently, pleadingly.

But the Nazarene turned away, again wielding his scourge, pouring out the remaining contents of the open tills, and dispersing their substance about the court.

Up and down the aisles of the exchange he went, reaching his hands beneath the tables and overturning them with splintering reverberations, one after another, after another . . .

The court's marble pillars absorbed the echoes of the storm and passed its tremors around the mammoth Mountain of the Lord.

But allowing not a moment's reprieve, the Nazarene went directly to the stalls of the dove-keepers. Few of these men had remained with their wares, but gasps of fear betrayed their positions among the spectators.

Quickly Jesus' hands were on the cages, picking them up like so much straw and rattling open the flimsy doors. In a flurry of feathers and down, the birds wriggled their way to freedom and spread their wings in an arc of liberty. Up, up they circled, to the heights of the cedar roofs, where they triumphantly chortled and sang their release.

The clamor and clash of multiplied echoes continued through the hall, and was challenged at last only by the cry of the Master's voice. Flinging his arms wide and surveying the cluttered, disheveled grounds one last time, he demanded, "Take these things hence!" His head fell back, and his justification came in the tones of a victor's trumpet, "Make not my Father's house a house of merchandise!"

Chapter 13

By the day before Passover, news of the strange incident in the Temple marketplace had spread throughout Jerusalem. John stood at the window of the second-story room where they were lodging for the holidays, and peered apprehensively upon the street below. Occasionally during the past hour he had noticed passersby looking inquisitively toward the house, whispering to one another and gesturing. They knew the Master dwelled there, and they were full of the mystery he had created.

Who was he? they undoubtedly wondered. Some said he was the same Pilgrim whose strange baptism had been rumored a year before. Some said he was merely an eccentric, delusioned preacher from the Galilee hills. Whoever he was, they would keep an eye on him.

The Master had stepped downstairs to converse with those who had allowed them lodging, and the other disciples dozed on their beds in the corner. It was a hot day, and this upper room absorbed the worst of the sun's rays. John fought drowsiness himself, but all that had recently transpired kept him awake.

It could no longer be thought that Jesus was not as fiery, as dynamic as his previous master. John tingled at the recollection of the Master's voice, the lightning of his indignation. He could sit spellbound for long, silent minutes just reliving what he had witnessed, reveling in the thunder of it all, for it reflected his own personality like an echo.

And then would flash to his mind the gentility of Jesus' ways, the nearly awesome sadness which could color his face, and the long, uninterrupted periods of quiet to which he was given. Such contrasts befitted John's Lord. Such mystery, and yet such clarity. How he had grown to love him!

He did not really see the people who now passed below. He was at the window still, but his thoughts were not on the street. Everything external was somehow very insignificant.

"Master, if I might know you . . ." he whispered. "If I might only understand who you are . . ."

His young heart beat heavily, for along with the desire, came fear. What if he *were* allowed to fully know Jesus? What if he were allowed into his confidence? Would he be capable of coping with what he would find there? Would he be able to live with such knowledge as had drawn light from heaven, and a thundering voice from the skies?

John heard a soft footstep behind him. Turning, he faced the Master. There was compassion in the Lord's eyes which greatly calmed him.

"John," Jesus said tenderly, "you *shall* know me. You shall know me as no one else shall ever know me."

Chapter 14

The morning before Passover, Jesus and his disciples went again to the Temple. Philip and Nathanael had been assigned the task of selecting a sacrificial lamb, and of having it blessed by the priests and offered upon the altar. Therefore, they passed quickly ahead of the others, eager to get an early start. Thousands of other Jews on the same business would make the lines hours long.

Already, as he walked, Jesus was drawing a crowd. Strangers recognized him easily, and even those who had not been present the day of the overthrow in the Temple quickly learned his identity.

John was only a little uneasy. He knew the mood of the crowd could readily become mob-like and unruly, especially if some wanted to seek revenge against Jesus. But since the Master's words to him in the upper room, John had been full of confidence.

"My Master can manage this situation," he assured himself, setting his shoulders in a square of courage.

The Nazarene was quiet as the jostling throng followed his steps to the Temple Mount. John kept very close to him. Only as the adjacent streets brought more and more people into their wake did he begin to lose some of the self-composure in which he had been reveling.

"Master, there are so many," he whispered apprehensively.

He expected his Teacher to soothe him with some appropriate phrase, as he had the day they had passed Tiberias. But today, Jesus seemed bent only on what lay ahead.

As they entered the Court of the Gentiles, Jewish elders came from the King's Porch. John noted among them men who had been debating doctrine in the cloisters the day of the overthrow, and others who had questioned the Baptist at Bethabara. Undoubtedly they had witnessed the Lord's purge of the marketplace.

They conversed together, following Jesus with their eyes, and John feared they plotted some evil against the Nazarene. Having been thwarted in their efforts to silence the Baptist, they would naturally turn on the One whose way he had pointed.

The disciple nudged his Master, and directed his attention to the secretive group. Jesus stopped in the center of the court and the crowd fell silent.

The leading elder was a dignified man, probably in his early sixties, with a full white beard, and the robes of a most wealthy scholar. He approached the Nazarene, motioning the people to step back, the shining phylactery upon his forearm catching a brilliant flash of morning sun.

"My good sir," he addressed the Master, allowing a note of respect to mark his tone, "are you not the one who entered the marketplace on the day before yesterday?"

Jesus studied him before answering, and when he did speak, his manner was one of humility. "Sir, there are many who come and go here every day."

The audience murmured with suspense.

Angry consternation passed over the aged gentleman's face, but he covered it with a careful smile. "Are you not the one who drove out the cattle," he specified, "who poured out the bankers' money and overturned their tables?" His voice rose, and his use of detail seemed to mock the Lord's previous response. "Are you not the one who set the doves free and who then denounced the activities of this holy place?"

Jesus looked at him squarely and answered, "I am the man. And you have said the truth; this *is* a holy place."

The Pharisee gloated, assuming he was receiving some confession of wrongdoing on Jesus' part. But the Master was not finished. "This is a holy place," he reiterated, "but not all the activities carried on here are holy, any more than milk is wine because it is carried in a wineskin."

Laughter rippled through the crowd, and the elder had no retort. Nevertheless, the old man was not a novice at debate. Holding his head high he returned. "But, sir, this is the House of Jehovah. What right have you to do such things?"

Cleverly, when he could not trap Jesus with a question of motives, he would tackle his credentials. It seemed to the orthodox Jew that no one, save Jehovah, had the right to behave spectacularly in this sacred place, no matter what his purpose might be. This was God's house, and it was God's business to correct what transpired here if he did not like it; it was not the business of some homeless itinerant.

Therefore Jesus' answer was most incredible. "Even if you were to destroy this Temple," he declared, "in three days I would raise it up!"

The old man fell back in astonishment, and the crowd went wild with outrage. "Blasphemy!" they cried. "Who is he to speak so? What foolishness is this?" It had taken forty-six years to erect this building! And he would raise it up in three days?

The din was nearly deafening, and John shook with terror. The people were capable of anything in this mood. What was the Master thinking to say such a thing?

Jesus held his ground in silence and John turned to him fearfully. "Master!" he cried. "What shall we do?"

But the Nazarene searched the crowd, looking deeply into it for some particular person. Amid the continuing upheaval, he singled out a small child with a withered leg, and drew close to him.

Those nearby were hushed with anticipation, fearful of his intentions. The same hands which had sent the moneychangers' tables crashing about the court, now held the young child, and breathlessly the throng watched as the Master bent over the boy, whispering into his ear.

The lad looked at him quizzically, and then at his own wooden crutch. Hesitating only a moment, he did as the Nazarene had told him, letting the crude support fall from his side with a clatter.

He did not need it! His leg was straight!

An eerie shudder passed through the throng as the boy walked without assistance up and down the court, tears pouring down his smooth young face.

The Master made his way through the crowd, touching the infirm, the palsied, the blind, the crippled, the maimed. Cries of joy and deliverance filled the air, each miracle following some other in such rapid succession that no one could take it all in.

Then, just as the people had followed him to this place, full of antagonism and fury, they began to pursue him with cries of need and expectation.

But Jesus did not commit himself to them, because he knew their hearts.

Chapter 15

There had been no Passover like this in the history of Jerusalem. The Man from Galilee had created an excitement which would not soon be forgotten.

When the last hymn of the paschal feast had been sung, and the last candle in the upper room snuffed out, the Master retired to his bed, but the disciples would not easily be able to sleep. For some time they lay talking about what had transpired, and when at last they drifted into a form of slumber, a knock was heard at the outer door.

Peter arose, lit a candle, and stumbled foggily to answer the summons. Whoever it was, he had come up the outside stairs rather than disturb the owners of the house, and this made the men somewhat wary.

"Who is it?" Peter called.

"A friend," was the only answer, and this was given in an urgent, secretive tone.

By this time all the disciples were awake, and Jesus rose from his bed.

"Let him in," he said.

When the door was opened, the candle lit the face of an elderly man, dressed in fine, festive garments. John looked at him carefully. Something about the visitor seemed familiar. When he entered, John's heart stopped. He was a Pharisee, and now he recognized him: Nicodemus, the liberal member of the Bethabara commission. But though he was not of the strictest regimen, the disciples feared his intentions.

"I seek the Galilean," he said, uneasily.

"I am he," Jesus greeted him.

Peter began to light more lamps, but this seemed to make the old man apprehensive, and he darted several glances toward the windows. "Please," he said, "I have come at some risk. Could we have but one light?"

This request was made graciously, and with sincerity, so that the group began to wonder just why he had come.

Jesus motioned Peter to oblige the elder, and then offered the visitor a seat. "You are most welcome here," he said. "I am Jesus of Nazareth."

To John's surprise, the old Jew did not react adversely to the mention of Jesus' origins, but returned, "I am Nicodemus."

The Master's unquestioning acceptance of him seemed to put him at ease, and yet he appeared uncertain just how to explain his arrival. As he searched for a beginning, Jesus said, "You fear you were followed to this place?"

Nicodemus did not wish to offend the Rabbi, but was nevertheless frank with him. "I am certain you realize that the elders of the people are doubtful concerning you. That is why I have come through the streets at this late hour."

Jesus smiled. "To avoid being seen?"

"Sir, if my associates knew I was here, my position would be in jeopardy."

The Master nodded his appreciation. "You are a straightforward man, Nicodemus."

"It would serve no purpose to be otherwise," the old gentleman conceded. John found himself warming to the visitor, despite his own prejudice toward his sect.

Jesus looked at the Pharisee closely. "Just why have you come?"

The dim candlelight emphasized the elder's furrowed brow. John sensed that the old man was having difficulty formulating an answer to that question. He seemed to bear a heavy burden.

"Rabbi," Nicodemus began, choosing his words with scrupulous care, "we know that you are a teacher come from God . . . for no man can do these miracles that you do, except God be with him."

It must have taken courage for the Pharisee to say that—as much courage as it had taken for him to risk this visit. Yet he had not really asked what was on his heart; anyone could see that. He had only made a flattering observation.

Jesus leaned forward and looked intently at the Jewish ruler. He appeared to be reading the unspoken contents of the Pharisee's mind, the true message of his thoughts. And then, as if it were in line with the natural flow of some unheard conversation, Jesus said, "Truly, truly, I say unto you, except a man be born again, he cannot see the kingdom of God."

Nicodemus reacted with astonishment. What could Jesus mean? And why had he said this? The words burned into his soul like probing fingers of fire. The Jewish leader faltered for words, and at last, with a look of utter confusion, he stammered, "How can a man be born when he is old? Can he enter the second time into his mother's womb . . . and be born?"

The disciples were as bewildered as Nicodemus. But the Master continued to concentrate on the visitor, and with soft, compassionate tones, replied, "Truly, I say unto you, except a man be born both physically, *and* of the Spirit, he cannot enter into the kingdom of God." Giving his new pupil time to absorb what he had said, he continued, "Do you understand? That which is born of the flesh is flesh; and that which is born of the Spirit is spirit."

Nicodemus and the others, who were now as caught up in the lesson as the man who had come for it, looked at one another in consternation. Jesus stood and walked over to the window, seeking a way to illustrate his point. His eyes lit and he walked to the door, placing his hand upon the latch. Then turning to his students, the great Teacher said, "Do not be surprised because I said you must be born again." With this he opened the door. A warm breeze was gently moving the palms which lined the street, and through the narrow aperture now available it softly whistled into the room, tickling the candle flame as it passed.

"Do you see?" Jesus asked. "The wind blows wherever it wants, and you hear the sound of it, but you cannot tell where it comes from, or where it goes . . . " He then shut the door, and drew close to the men who considered his words. "So it is with everyone that is born of the Spirit."

John's heart swelled with the words, and Nicodemus' voice was full of wonder. "How can these things be?" he asked, echoing the disciple's own thoughts.

Jesus stood next to him and placed a hand upon his shoulder. His tone was warm and understanding, "Nicodemus, are you a master of Israel, and yet you do not know these things? Truly, truly, I say to you, we know what we are speaking of, and we testify to what we have seen . . . yet, you do not receive our witness."

John knew the Master did not refer to his disciples when he used the plural just now. They were too new to his teachings themselves to be "witness" to anything he was describing. Yet these words reminded him of conversations he had had with the Baptist. Could he be referring to that great prophet?

"Friend," Jesus continued sorrowfully, "if I have spoken to you of earthly things, and you believe not, how shall you believe if I tell you of heavenly things?"

Nicodemus looked at the floor, obviously ashamed, and Jesus walked again to the window. Peering out at the night sky, his gaze traveled far away, and his thoughts seemed to leave the group gathered about him. "No man has ever ascended up to heaven . . . except he who came down from heaven . . . " he said.

The Master held his position for some time, and then turned again to the men. " . . . that is the Son of Man . . . which is *in* heaven."

There was no response. Only baffled silence.

Son of Man? They had always assumed he referred to himself when using that term. But what did he mean when he spoke of his ascending up to heaven, coming down from heaven, and being in heaven?

John shook his head.

And now Jesus was giving another illustration. "Do you remember how Moses lifted up the serpent in the wilderness?"

Of course, all present remembered the story from Hebrew Scripture concerning what had happened to the Children of Israel after their miraculous escape from Egyptian bondage. Despite God's miraculous deliverance of them, they began to lose faith in his guidance when they entered the barren region across the Red Sea. Because of disbelief they were left to wander, homeless and poor, for forty years, in that hopeless country. At one point in the history of those wasted years they had been plagued by swarms of poisonous vipers, and Jehovah had told their leader, Moses, to erect, upon a pole, the image of a brass serpent. Anyone looking upon that serpent, when it was raised for all to see, would be spared the venomous death. Anyone failing to put trust in God's provision would have no protection.

"Yes, we remember," they nodded.

"As Moses lifted up the serpent in the wilderness, even so must the Son of Man be lifted up," he explained, "that whosoever believes in him should not perish, but have eternal life."

John, like all the others, was rigid with awe. But he would not be given time just now to dwell upon these strange new concepts. The Master studied his hearers intently. His old look was back, the one

with which John had become so familiar, the face of peculiar
longing and sadness to which the Master had become so
accustomed. The great Rabbi held his pupils spellbound, and then
spoke words which John would never forget, words which would
ring down through history as yet unrecorded.

*"For God so loved the world, that he gave his only begotten Son,
that whosoever believes in him should not perish, but have
everlasting life."*

The young disciple trembled. "Everlasting life?" It rang in his
ears and pounded in his mind.

"God sent not his Son into the world to condemn the world,"
Jesus continued, compassion flowing from him, "but that the
world through him might be saved."

He was now rising and crossing the room, pacing slowly back
and forth, the weight of his message too great to be borne without
movement. Tears seemed to be just beneath the surface, but the
Master kept them in restraint. "He that believes on him is not
condemned," he said in low notes, "but . . . he that believes *not* is
condemned already . . . because he has not believed in the name
of the only begotten Son of God."

The enthralled listeners followed his movements about the
room. "This is the condemnation," Jesus was saying with great
heaviness, his eyes to the floor, "that light is come into the world,
and men loved darkness rather than light, because their deeds
were evil." Again he walked to the window. "Everyone who does
evil hates the light, neither comes to the light, lest his deeds should
be reproved."

And then he turned once more to the small congregation. "But
he that does truth comes to the light, that his deeds may be made
manifest, that they are wrought in God."

The message was stamped indelibly upon the young disciple's
heart. Not all the years which lay ahead would be able to dim one
line of it, not all the trials which awaited him would be able to
rearrange its impact. It would grow in him as he grew, and it would
become clearer as his insight increased. Though he did not
comprehend it fully now, it would never leave him.

"Son of Man," hadn't the Master said? "Son of God." Could
the two be one and the same? And hadn't the Baptist called Jesus
the "Son of God"?

Chapter 16

This year the seasonal heat was exceptional, even for the region of Bethabara. And the shallows where the Baptist had previously performed his ministry were now so sluggish he had been forced to move from there to another site. There were probably other places he could have chosen, besides Aenon. Surely, to the Jews, it was a grave insult that he now carried his work into the land of the hated Samaritans.

But Aenon was abundant with water. The very name meant "the springs," and it was fertile and green, a sharp contrast to the sparse wilderness in which he had dwelt for so many years of his life.

Jesus had left Jerusalem shortly after the Passover, and had ventured, with his disciples, north into the outlying regions of Judea, not far from the borders of Samaria.

For some reason, unknown to John, the Master had taken him aside one day, suggesting that he should seek out the Baptist, to spend some time once more in his company. The Lord's expression had been urgent, and John had sensed sorrow in his bearing, as though he feared some evil were about to befall the mighty preacher.

John had parted from the Lord with mixed emotions. Following the incidents in Jerusalem, he wished to remain close to him. But if, as Jesus seemed to hint, the Baptist were in need, John would not hesitate to go.

The fact that he traveled through alien territory did not at first daunt him. He would simply ignore the stench of the Samaritan villages, the peculiar dress and speech of the inhabitants, he told himself. He would bear straight up the road for the town of Salim.

Still, this was the first time in his young life that he had actually traveled through this province. Always, except on very unusual occasions, Jews going between Galilee and Judea traveled the road to the east of the Jordan, through Perea. Thus they avoided the contamination of their enemies. John could not deny the fears which crept upon him.

The history of the provincial rivalry was long and complex. Samaria had always been notoriously idolatrous. Nearly nine hundred years before, a Jewish king named Ahab had erected a temple to Baal in this region, and over seven hundred years before, this land had been taken from the hands of the Israelites and conquered by the king of Assyria, a great empire to the east.

As exiles placed by the Assyrians began to arrive, setting up their government in the area, local Jews began to capitulate to the idea of intermarriage. The hybrid race, which resulted from unions with pagans, threatened the old beliefs.

The "Samaritans" as they came to be called, gradually shifted the focus of their worship from Jerusalem, to a newly constructed temple upon their own Mount Gerizim. And their religion consisted of an unorthodox form of Judaism, mixed with pagan elements.

John rested at the brow of a hill which overlooked a broad western slope. This might have been beautiful country to journey through, were he not so aware of its history. No Jew was welcome here, just as no Samaritan was welcome beyond its borders.

Perhaps, he thought, if they had only kept to themselves, the two nations could have gone on indifferent to one another. But such had not been the case. When some of the Jews had been allowed to return, many generations later, from their captivity in the east, to reconstruct the crumbled Jerusalem Temple, the Samaritans had offered to help them with the project. After all, they had said, they too worshiped Jehovah.

A wry smile crossed the disciple's face. If he had been there then, he would have reacted just as his ancestors did. Hybrid pagans touch the house of the Lord? Absolutely not!

When the Jews turned them away, the long history of the hatred began. Animosity had been unbounded on both sides from that day forward. Because the Samaritans were located between the northern and southern provinces of the Jews, they could not be totally avoided, but only the most meager of social and commercial relations were carried on. Samaritans were openly condemned in the Jewish synagogues. No Samaritan could bring testimony in a Jewish court. No Samaritan could ever enter the Jewish faith. He was not even eligible for eternal life, so said the Jews.

Before dawn, John rose and continued on his way. The primitive villages he passed by were pathetic. Sewage ran freely through hovel-lined streets, and all that he saw seemed to confirm the teachings he had received since childhood, and to affirm the native intolerance he felt for the sect. Samaritans were "dogs," he acknowledged.

But now his thoughts turned again to the Baptist. He had just reached Salim, and Aenon was not far. His heart beat faster. It seemed an eternity since he had seen the prophet. Not that his life had been uneventful in that time, but the loneliness he felt for his old master had never really gone away.

The countryside was becoming progressively greener and he knew the springs could not be far. Then he heard it, the old familiar voice of the preacher!

As John came over the last rise, his throat grew tight with joy. Yes—now there he was! He had not changed! And the crowds were as large as ever.

The disciple worked his way forward and came to the edge of the water. As he drew near he noticed that several other young men were scattered along the shallows, apparently ready to lend their assistance to the master. John determined that his old teacher must have attracted a new group of students, and though he knew it was childish, jealousy nudged his heart.

Perhaps, he thought, he would simply melt away into the crowd. But as he considered retreat, the master's eyes fell upon him. For a long instant the Baptist stared at his young friend, incredulous at the sight of him.

John's heart warmed with the embrace of that gaze. "Yes, master," he nodded. "It is I . . . "

The Baptist flung his arms wide, and the disciple ran to hold him.

The prophet's face glistened with tears.

At late evening they were left alone. The Baptist took his friend and walked with him apart from the others, along the spring-fed pond.

John breathed deeply, taking in the warm evening like a balm. He was at peace in the presence of his old master. The moon was brilliant and a soothing breeze rippled the nearly silent waters.

He turned to the Baptist. There was so much he wished to tell him, so many questions he had for him. Especially he longed to discuss with the prophet the conversations Jesus had had with the Pharisee, Nicodemus. The words still haunted him. How he longed to know their meaning, to have it all explained! How he wished to know if Jesus spoke of himself when he referred to the mysterious "Son of Man . . . "

"Sir, there is much to speak of," he began.

The Baptist smiled. "These months have been busy?"

"Oh, sir, you could never imagine! This Jesus of Nazareth does such wonderful things!"

"I hear he performs miracles."

"Of all sorts!"

The Baptist's eyes looked far away. "It must be wonderful to be with him," he said wistfully.

"Yes, it is . . . "

The preacher scrutinized him. "I detect hesitation in your voice."

John looked at the ground. "Not exactly, sir. I have grown to love the Master very much."

"What, then?"

"I simply have questions."

"When did I know you to be without them?" the Baptist grinned.

John nodded appreciatively, but then grew somber again.

"Tell me your questions," the Baptist urged.

John did not know where to begin. But as he formulated his thoughts, the preacher ceased walking. A group of Jewish leaders, being led by the Baptist's disciples, was approaching from the direction of Salim. Strange that they should come at this hour.

As they drew near John saw with dismay that they were many of the same Pharisees and Sadducees who had tested the preacher at Bethabara, and the Nazarene in Jerusalem. The young followers of the prophet appeared bewildered, as if having just been, themselves, subjected to some inquisition.

"Do my enemies never grow tired of this?" the Baptist muttered.

As the finely robed commissioners greeted the preacher they seemed surprisingly congenial, but John detected a trap lying behind their smiles.

"Master," the chief of the group called out, "we come from Judea with a question for you."

The Baptist nodded warily. "Why do you come at this hour?"

"Sir," the elder replied, "pardon our late arrival, but we have been journeying some hours. We were in the north of Judea and heard you were here, so we decided to come on to Aenon."

The preacher was not a little doubtful. "Gentlemen," he offered, bypassing further amenities, "it seems a strange thing that you would come through Samaria merely to pay me a visit. What do you want?"

The Pharisees had not expected a warm greeting. But the elder stroked his beard and eyed the preacher carefully.

"I have been speaking with your disciples about purification," he said. "Let them put our question to you. They are obviously as perplexed by it as we are."

The Baptist's men shuffled uneasily, hesitating. But at last they replied, "Master, you are not the only one who is baptizing. Where these men have just come from, there is another. Rabbi," they said almost apologetically, "the One who was with you beyond Jordan, to whom you have pointed, is also baptizing, and many are following him."

John was bewildered. Could they be referring to Jesus? He was not baptizing. Only his disciples were doing so. But it was true that many were seeking him and following after him. John listened breathlessly.

The Pharisees had posed an unspoken challenge. They were really saying, "Explain this, Baptist. How do you account for this?" They were hoping, of course, that the idea of competition for the people's loyalty might make the Baptist resent the newcomer's popularity. They were hoping he might say something which would set him at odds with Jesus, thus discounting not only the Nazarene's ministry, but his own years of paving the way.

But the Baptist was radiant. Answering his disciples confidently he said, "A man can receive nothing, except it be given him from heaven."

What more fitting answer? The Pharisees could not disagree with that, whatever their beliefs concerning Jesus. John wondered at his old friend's cleverness.

But more than cleverness lay behind the words. Joy filled the Baptist's voice as he continued, "You yourselves have heard me say that I am *not* the Christ, the Messiah, but that I am sent to prepare the way for him." The prophet smiled triumphantly and lifted his face to the sky. "I am like the friend of a bridegroom. The groom will have the bride, but I will be joyful with him. Therefore I rejoice at the news you bring!"

A hush came over the disciples and the inquisitors. For a long moment the master stood in silence, his head thrown back, his eyes closed. Then softly and with a tone of deep fulfillment, he spoke something which John would never forget.

"He must increase . . . but I must decrease."

The disciple struggled against that statement. "No, master!" he wished to cry. "You shall never decrease! You shall always be great—the greatest of men!"

Still the truth of the preacher's assertion was undeniable. This *was* what he had come for: to prepare the way for one greater than himself; and to then step back into the shadows of his successor's growing importance. Though it pained John to hear these words, he recognized their validity, and as he watched his friend's radiant face, he began to feel something of his joy.

But now stranger truths were spoken. Shifting the focus of attention once again from himself to the Nazarene, the Baptist was saying, "He that comes from above is above all. He that is of the earth is earthly, and speaks of the earth, but he that comes from heaven is above all!"

The trumpet-voice shook John's soul, for the message was reminiscent of the one Jesus had given Nicodemus. Had he not described the Son of Man as "ascending into heaven," coming down "from heaven," and being "in heaven"?

"What he has seen and heard, he testifies about, but no man receives his testimony," the Baptist continued. "He who does receive his testimony receives the words of God, for he speaks the words of God. There is no limit to the Spirit in his life. The Father loves the Son, and has given all things into his hand!"

Again, the very concepts Jesus had spoken to the seeking Nicodemus! It was of these things that John had longed to ask the Baptist.

He trembled as he watched the prophet's countenance. Never, in all the time he had heard him preach, had he seen him look so.

"He that believes on the Son has everlasting life," he cried, his counsel penetrating the core of John's heart like the point of a hot iron. "He that believes not the Son shall not see life . . . the wrath of God abides on him!"

Chapter 17

The caves above Aenon were chilly and damp, unlike the prophet's home at Bethabara. This was not, however, what kept John awake tonight.

It had been two weeks since the Pharisees had come to Aenon. No longer did John wonder who the "Son of Man" might be. It was apparent Jesus referred to himself when using that term. And the message was abundantly clear. According to the Baptist and the Nazarene, Jesus was "the Son of Man," "the Son of God," come down from heaven and yet still in heaven. Somehow, if one believed in him, he was assured eternal life. If one failed to put trust in him . . .

John felt almost sick. He surely did not understand these doctrines. Much less was he sure he believed them. But what he did comprehend of the message made him lightheaded.

He was glad for the dark of the cave which hid his face. The disciples of the Baptist who lodged there would not see his torment. Seeking a shield against anguish, John concentrated on his surroundings . . . on the steady drip of water from condensation on the ceiling . . . on the even snoring of the men nearby . . . on the eerie moonlight which made its way into the dark recesses.

But it was no use. Nothing abated the haunting message. No matter how unreasonable it seemed, no matter how it defied logic, he could not shake it. Within the words lay a challenge—an ultimatum. It said, "Accept me or reject me. I call for faith, not for understanding. The Son has come. What will you do with him?"

John stood up, white and cold, hounded by an echoing refrain. "He who does not believe the Son shall not see life . . . the wrath of God abides on him . . . wrath of God . . . wrath of God . . . "

"No!" John whispered. But the words did not leave him. "I have forsaken all to follow him," he reasoned. But still the message returned. "I have followed him daily!" And yet the words persisted.

By this time John was outside the cave, crazed and trembling. He had known the fear of the Lord—but never like this.

Awkwardly he stepped away from the cave, breathing deeply and attempting to regain his self-composure. "How foolish to feel this way," he laughed.

Amid his clattering thoughts he tried to get a grip on his own history. He had left home to find the Baptist—to flee his father—to find "truth." "I would be better off as a Pharisee, like Zebedee," he thought. "At least his teachings are 'logical.' " But grim humor would not spare him his torment. He continued with the memories. He had found the Baptist; the Baptist had sent him to be with Jesus; he had followed Jesus: out of obedience; out of duty; out of curiosity; out of awe and reverence and love; out of . . . desperation.

Suddenly it struck him. Nowhere in that list of reasons was faith to be found. Nowhere in his troubled search had he come to true—commitment.

John walked numbly to the site of the spring and sat upon a rock overlooking it. In the moonlight, his reflection stared back at him, pale and cold—but he did not speak to it. It was in conversation with the unseen Nazarene that he sighed, "So this is what you want of me?"

"Yes," returned the silent voice. "Whosoever believes in me shall not perish, but have life everlasting . . . "

John knew instinctively that believing, in this case, meant more than saying "yes" to an idea. It meant accepting, receiving, embracing—committing.

So, he now understood this much: that to find Jesus interesting was not enough; to be curious was not enough; to observe him and study him was not enough; to follow him about and to attempt to be like him was not enough; to give up all one's wealth for him was not enough; to claim discipleship was not enough . . .

What *was* enough was simply to believe, to accept, to receive him as Lord. He could do nothing less than this.

John sat for a long time just staring into the water. He was at the fork of two roads. He knew which ways were open to him. He hung vacantly in the limbo in indecision—cold, lifeless, worthless.

Suddenly, the pool's reflection showed the form of another man beside him. Turning about he saw that the Baptist had come. John struggled for strength to speak. "Sir? You slept well?" he asked, seeing it was nearly dawn.

The preacher did not answer him on that count. It was obvious from his bearing that he was concerned for weightier things. "You have been thinking, son?" the Baptist asked.

"Yes, sir."

"I recall that as we walked together, after you first arrived, you said you had many questions for me. We were interrupted and you have not spoken of them since."

"I understand, sir," John nodded.

"May we speak of them now?" the preacher offered.

John shook his head. "It is really not important now."

The Baptist was silent. Then, "Not important, John?"

The disciple was quick to explain. "Oh, sir, of course—it *is* important. I have many questions about your teachings—Jesus' teachings. But they can be answered some other time." Then he looked away. "I must deal with what I *do* understand."

The Baptist seemed to comprehend. "I sense you are struggling, John. You have reached a bridge and you do not know if it is safe to cross."

John smiled. "Well put, sir. That *is* how I feel."

The Baptist leaned close to him. "I believe I know your struggles. Do you recall my parting words the day you left to follow Jesus?"

How could he ever forget? He would always remember burying his head on the Baptist's shoulder that long-ago morning, and he would always remember those words. He repeated them. " 'It is a hard thing to be born . . . but it is a joy to find life.' "

The Baptist nodded in affirmation, and now John recalled Jesus speaking of such things only days before. Hadn't he said, "You must be born again"?

"Oh, sir," John whispered, "I do want that. But it *is* a hard thing."

"The hardest—and the easiest," the preacher smiled.

John opened his mouth to pursue the subject, but just as he did, the sound of trampling feet invaded the still morning.

Over the crest of the hill above Aenon came a dozen soldiers.

"Master!" John stammered. "What can they want?"

The Baptist rose, his eyes wide, but he said nothing.

The troops were armed with spears and shields, the leader

mounted on a fine steed. When they saw the prophet beside the spring, the officer called out, "We seek John, called the Baptist!"

The great prophet stood tall and answered, "You have found him."

John stood by, helpless and mute.

"You are to come with us, Baptist!" the captain shouted gruffly.

"On what charge?" the prophet demanded.

"Herod will answer that!" the commander returned, and then waved his men forward to take the preacher by force.

Herod? Why? For what cause? John could scarcely believe his eyes.

As the soldiers advanced to seize the Baptist, though he was not resisting them, John lunged forth in defense.

"Master!" he cried helplessly, but the troops thrust him down. By now the other disciples had emerged from the caves, but they also were restrained by the weapons confronting them.

"Back!" the leader commanded, "or you'll join your master."

The Baptist was led roughly away, his hands bound with rude cords. As the troops left the springs, their helpless cargo in tow, the prophet looked behind, seeking the face of his dearest friend. When his gaze met John's, tears rose in the young disciple's eyes.

"Master!" he cried again. But there would be no answer.

Chapter 18

John's flight from Aenon was full of terror. Anyone connected with the Baptist might be next in line as Herod's prey.

Seeking a hideaway in the tangle of undergrowth along the path, John found a measure of comfort, and lowered his mantle.

"Herod . . ." the very name sent a shudder through him. Such a history of insanity, cruelty, and crime was connected with that family. The man now on the throne of the Galilean and Perean tetrarchy, Herod Antipas, was a son of the notorious Herod the Great, arch-maniac of Jewish legend.

The Herodian house had always been questionable to the orthodox. As descendants of Esau, rather than of Jacob, the Herods were not full Jews. In fact, it had been Rome which had elevated them in the government of Palestine. It had been Mark Antony who had promoted Herod the Great to the kingship of the country, and it had been Augustus Caesar who had given him his crown. The Jewish people had not accepted him as their ruler until he had subjugated the Holy City by force over sixty years before.

Though the first Herod had attempted to win the Jews by engaging one thousand wagons and ten thousand workers to rebuild their glorious Temple at Jerusalem, his hypocrisy had been too evident. He had also rebuilt the temple of the Samaritans, their hated enemies. And prior to constructing a great monument to the past Jewish kings, he had tried to confiscate the riches stored in their tombs. But perhaps the greatest crime rumored of him was that he had desired to lay hands on the genealogical records stored at Jerusalem, so that he might alter or do away with those pertaining to the coming Messiah.

John rested his head on his knees and thought. How desperate that crazed ruler must have been! Such fear the prophecies of the Christ must have stirred in him!

So anxious had he been to keep his throne secure that, years before, the hopeless fiend had sent orders slaying all male infants in Bethlehem, the prophesied birthplace of the coming king. Suddenly John recalled that Jesus had been born in that city, about that time. "Lord," he whispered, "was Herod looking for you?"

At this, John sobered. Memories of Herod the Great's numerous treacheries tumbled one after the other through his mind. Like father, like son? Was it this kind of man who had hold of the Baptist? If Herod the Great had put to death his favorite of ten wives and her two brothers; if, five days before his own death, he had taken the life of one of his own sons; if with his dying breath he had ordered the execution of all Jewish noblemen in the country so that the mourning at his own funeral might be more adequate—if the father had performed all these atrocities, of what was the son capable?

Antipas' brother, Herod Archaelaus, carried the character traits of the father. One Passover he had had three thousand Jews slaughtered, and had filled the Temple with their corpses.

Now what could Antipas want with the Baptist? The disciple squirmed uneasily. He remembered that his old master had condemned Herod's private life openly during his ministry. Was it for this that the tetrarch now took hold of him?

It was widely known that Antipas had unlawfully taken as his bride Herodias, the wife of his own brother, Herod Philip. The relationship was bigamous on both sides, as Antipas and Herodias both had living spouses. And the daughter born to Herodias and her first husband was a further impediment to the legality of this match.

The entire scandal was a horror to the Jews. And yet John sensed that the Pharisees who had questioned the Baptist the night before had encouraged Herod to arrest the mighty prophet.

John drew his cloak tightly about him. He was indeed fearful, not only of Antipas' intentions, but of the alien land in which he sought sanctuary. He must be going—but where?

"To Jesus," was the natural answer. But with that came another jolt of anxiety. The Baptist had been taken by Herod. What would prevent Jesus from being arrested in the same manner? Surely the Nazarene had no fewer enemies than the Baptist, especially since his display of vengeance in the Temple. The Pharisees and doubtless the entire Sanhedrin were watching him scrupulously. Had not they questioned the Baptist the night before he was taken? Surely the Master was in similar danger. If Herod had nothing against him, there were other authority figures holding great power, who had undoubtedly been offended by his claims.

John studied the ground at his feet. "What have I gotten into?" he asked himself. "I must be a fool to choose such revolutionaries for my teachers!"

Yet, at this thought, his heart beat faster with zeal for the very men he questioned. The fact that they were condemned by the authorities made them only more attractive to the young rebel. To turn back from them now was unthinkable.

As he considered the Nazarene, remembering his strange baptism, his display of power in the Temple, the miracles he had performed, and the beauty and mystery of his words to Nicodemus, he recalled the Baptist's confession: "He must increase, but I must decrease."

In a very real way, the Baptist had already decreased. He had been physically removed from John's reach. The disciple could no longer look to him for leadership. There was now nowhere to go, but to Jesus.

As John stood, he felt again as he had the night before: as though he had come to a bridge and must decide whether or not to cross.

"Jesus, I am coming," he whispered.

Chapter 19

The seemingly momentous decision, made in the undergrowth of the Samaritan roadside, was, weeks later, little more than a hollow echo in John's memory. It was a lonely young man who, today, walked along the shore of the Galilean sea.

As he made his way up and down between the nets hung out in rows to dry in the sun, he remembered one time he had worked here at his trade. That day he had been dreaming of the Baptist as he mended the ripped hemp of the nets, and Simon had insisted he tell him all about the wild man of Bethabara.

He was calloused to illusions, now, he reasoned. The Nazarene surely had destroyed them.

He would never forget finding Jesus at Jacob's Well. John had not known that his Master had ventured into Samaria. He had expected, after leaving Aenon, to find him still in Judea. It had been a joyous surprise to him when, after skirting the village of Sychar, he had glimpsed the Nazarene seated at the city watering place, called Jacob's Well, just outside town.

But as he was still a good distance from the Master, another part of the scene had dawned upon him. Jesus was speaking alone, with a woman—something unheard of for any proper rabbi. And, she was a Samaritan woman, at that! Had all this not been enough to insult the values and hot bigotry of the disciple, the woman was obviously of ill repute, an outcast in her own society, for she had come to the well to draw water at noon, in the heat of the day, when no other women would be present. Jesus had been speaking to her when his diciples were not with him—when they were not near to see his true colors, John had reasoned. Where they were, John had not known. The Master had apparently sent them on some errand, so that he might be on his own, was John's conclusion.

As he recalled this, he experienced the same revulsion he had felt that day. He had not approached the Master. He had only watched for some time from a distance, giving his beloved Teacher time to prove him wrong. But when he had seen that Jesus engaged in lengthy conversation with the marked woman, he had turned sadly and slipped quietly away. In Magdala, John had given Jesus credit for what seemed only compassion toward the streetwalkers. What a fool I have been! he considered.

His dream was shattered. His illusion dissolved. Jesus was a man like any other, and perhaps worse than many, for he had claimed to be so much more.

John had not seen the Nazarene or any of the other disciples since that day. When all routes had been closed to him, he had returned home, to Capernaum, to Zebedee.

The breeze off the sea had always had a way of calming inner turmoils when he was a boy. Today it served no such function. John would not easily overcome the bitterness and melancholy which had found a home in his defeated heart.

When James came out to join him at the nets, the two brothers worked together in silence. The elder son of Zebedee looked with concern on John's withdrawn attitude. He had not questioned him as to why he had come home. The night John had arrived on the doorstep, James had read a volume of misery in his face. He knew that, in time, the story would come forth. He also knew his brother well enough to refrain from pressing the issue.

Still, he was full of curiosity.

"Father is proud to have you home," James finally broke the silence.

"Is he?" John was apprehensive.

"Indeed! Proud and happy."

John looked at his brother, answering sardonically. "Proud because I have licked his shoes, and happy to see me do it. He revels in my loss, for it proves some kind of victory for him."

James shook his head. "You are too hard on him, John. Father does not feel such ill will for you as you might think. He was a broken man when you were away."

"Not because he had lost a son," John warranted, "but because he thought he had lost a debate."

James sighed deeply. It would do no good to pursue the subject. How he longed to ask John about the Master, about why he had left him. News of the deeds and teachings of the man of Nazareth were spreading like wildfire up and down the land. But James would get no information from his brother.

At noon Zebedee arrived to look over the boats for the night's fishing. The old man came down the beach with uncommon vigor, his stride nearly youthful when he caught a glimpse of his two sons.

"Fine day!" he called. "It will be good fishing tonight!"

James called back to him, but John said nothing. The elder brother gave a fleeting look of consternation, but it did not faze the younger.

"Ah! Breathe that air!" Zebedee exclaimed, taking in a chest-full and extending his arms widely. "Invigorating! Don't you agree!"

"Indeed, father!" James returned.

Zebedee stood next to the nets eyeing his young prodigal. The elder son read true devotion in the old man's face as he watched John. Why must there be war between them? he wondered.

The father surveyed the nets, as if looking for a way to open the conversation. "You have done good work with these," he offered awkwardly, and perhaps too enthusiastically. Had John been more sensitive to the feelings his father attempted to express, he would have acknowledged this gesture graciously. Instead, he made only a low murmur and went on about his work, his head bent away from the old man.

James felt like slapping his younger brother. Not that he had always sided with his father. He knew only too well that the old Pharisee had brought his son's reactions upon himself. Still, John might at least try to make peace.

Zebedee's facade of lightheartedness was shaky. But in one more awkward move, he reached for his son, clapping him stiffly on the back. "Good to have you back, John," he said.

John looked up from his work and gave a sideways glance at James.

There was not much feeling in his voice, but he strained an answer. "Glad to be back."

The marketplace at Capernaum was one of the largest in Galilee, for this was a key fishing village of the northern coast. Today it was especially crowded, the fleets of commercial vessels having brought in an unusual quantity of fish.

John and James had been overseeing the preparation and sale of their haul since dawn. Now they meandered through the stalls taking the opportunity to browse for bargains.

John was a bit uneasy being here. Many of the townsfolk showed great interest in the fact that he had returned to the home port. Undoubtedly those who knew his story wondered why he had come back, and were eager to question him about Jesus. Here and there women leaned together in guarded conversation as he passed, and men of the town stared after him. He attempted to stay in James' shadow so as not to attract attention. But it seemed the entire city had come to market today, and he could not long remain anonymous.

"The news is spreading," James said in low tones. "What are you going to say when they question you?"

John looked at him sullenly. "I do not need to say anything."

James shook his head. "You are a fool," he murmured. But John walked ahead rapidly, determined to pass through the city gates and go down to the beach where he might escape the probing eyes and whispering tongues of the citizenry.

Seated at the gate were the tax officials, men of Palestine hired by Rome to collect tribute for Caesar. Capernaum was a customs station, and anyone coming into or going out of the city was subject to inquisition concerning his financial status with the government. Of course the tax collectors were among the most despised men of Israel, for, not only did they support Rome, but they were notorious for overcharging their victims and keeping the extra revenue for their own purses.

John usually passed by them without so much as a nod. His father had always kept an accurate tax account, and they would have no reason to question a son of Zebedee. Besides, John would want nothing to do with any of them, especially the man in charge today.

John had known Matthew Bar Alpheus, also called Levi, since childhood. Matthew had been a few years ahead of him in school, but when that promising young scholar had turned to this hated profession, it had been a shame to all who knew him. Since the day he had signed up as deputy to the local Roman publican, he had been an outcast among his fellow Jews. None had asked him why he had made such a move. There had been no discernible forewarning of such a change in his nature. He had simply chosen a life of sin, they reasoned.

And now, here he sat, his deep brown hair handsomely oiled, his beard impeccably groomed. He was wearing the wine-red robes and heavy pendants of a heathen. John had given him as little consideration as possible. Only when he neared his fine home in the city had Matthew ever crossed his mind, and the idea of him was so distasteful to the young Jew that he had dismissed it each time with a spit.

Normally John would have gone by the seat of customs with quick detachment, but today the scene nearby could not escape his attention. There was a pulse of excitement in the air. A large group of Roman soldiers stood beside the gate attempting to keep order over a gathering which was eagerly reporting some incident to the elders of the city.

"What is it?" James asked as he caught up with John.

"I don't know. Listen."

The Romans, members of a military garrison quartered in the city, struggled to calm the crowd. At last the ranking officer demanded the right of way and some semblance of order was established.

James and John strained to catch the essence of the news, but because of the throng, were able to make out only a few words. "Point of death . . ." they heard, and "healed!" "Master Bar Arnan . . ." "Cana . . ." "his son . . ." "servants . . ." "seventh hour!" and again, "healed!"

The two brothers looked at each other hopelessly. "We'll have to ask someone," James commented, but it was difficult to find anyone who would explain the commotion. Here and there heads shook incredulously. Those who had caught the full story conversed so excitedly with one another that it was difficult to find a clue to the mystery.

At last an elderly woman, eager to spread the tale elsewhere in town, worked her way out from the middle of the throng, rapping her cane upon the shins of obstructors.

James caught her before she got past him. "Mother," he used the common address, "do tell us what they were saying."

The small, bent matron peered up at him, her hooked nose wrinkled disconcertedly. "You heard it as well as anyone," she answered gruffly.

"Only a few words." James smiled anxiously.

At this she sighed, realizing it would serve her schedule better to speak quickly than to debate with the young man. "Master Bar Arnan . . . a nobleman of our city . . . "

"Yes, yes, we know him . . . "

Another sigh at the interruption, "his son lay sick, near death only recently—"

"Yes—"

"Well, boy, he's been healed!" she insisted. "Just yesterday

Master Bar Arnan went to Cana to seek out a rabbi, and the man healed his son then and there. . . ''

"There? They took the boy there?"

"No," he answered impatiently. "He was healed *from* there—from that distance!"

James gave his younger brother a disbelieving chuckle.

"Don't you laugh at me, boy!" the little woman shook a crooked finger in his face. "Master Bar Arnan's servants are witnesses! They got the truth from the nobleman himself! Met him on the road when he was returning from Cana, to tell him the son was better. When he asked them what time the boy began to mend, they said 'the seventh hour.' That was the same time the Rabbi had told Master Bar Arnan, 'Go your way; your son lives.' "

John, who had been listening to all of this covertly, had a sinking feeling deep within him, but said nothing. James did not see his ash-white face when the woman answered the obvious question.

"Mother, who was the rabbi?" the elder asked.

"Now, who do you suppose, boy? Jesus of Nazareth."

Chapter 20

Salome watched her younger son carefully. He had stayed home today rather than go to work for his father. He was obviously in a bad humor, for he had spoken to no one all morning.

Occasionally he rose from the chair near the fireplace and paced before the latticed window which looked out onto the street. His thoughts were apparently far away, and his knit forehead showed the great heaviness which burdened him. When more than an hour had passed in this manner, Salome placed aside the spool of yarn she had been winding and sighed deeply.

"Son, when will you tell us?"

John jolted. He had almost forgotten his mother's quiet presence in the room. "Tell you what?" he attempted casualness.

"You have been home for days now, and we have yet to know anything about the months you were gone, or what persuaded you to return." Her voice was full of mother-love and concern. Had anyone else questioned him on these points, he would have backed away quickly. With her, he could not be so abrupt. Still he could not help but remember the last time he had shared with Salome, and what had happened shortly thereafter.

"Mother," he said, "there is much I would like to say. But it would be very different from what I told you the last time I was here."

Salome nodded her head. "I am sure it would be." A warm glow came to her face. "You were so excited about this Jesus of Nazareth! You were so certain!"

"Stop, mother!" John interjected. And then, shamed by his outburst, he quickly added, "Please—say no more, mother. That is past. It is dead . . ."

The last syllable hung in the air rancidly. "Dead . . ." he repeated, a cynical tone in his voice. "Sounds familiar, doesn't it? My own father pronounced *me* 'dead' the last time I was here."

Salome started. "Oh, John, if anything is past, that is! You know how proud he is to have you home again, how he has accepted you!"

John smiled wryly. "Proud! James used that word, too."

"Because it is true."

John shrugged his shoulders and turned away. "Oh, well, that is not the issue now. Besides, I tend to agree with father's pronouncement. Perhaps I *am* dead."

Salome walked to him, recapturing his gaze. "John, you have always been full of life."

But his heart was stony. "I am dead inside. No life exists here any longer," he insisted.

Tears came to Salome's eyes. "What of the Baptist? the Nazarene?"

John squared his shoulders. "You have surely heard by now. The Baptist has been taken by Herod, and Jesus may join him there for all I care!"

Salome went back to her chair. Her care-worn face showed the years of unhappiness life had brought. If she had loved her younger son less, she would have taken his troubles more lightly. Raising him would not have afforded such heartache. Still, at the present moment, she would have preferred the old battles, the open confrontations which had been so often staged in this room. Anything would be better than seeing her son so . . . defeated.

She knew it would do no good to pursue the secrets he kept. "So, John," she asked with a resigned and hollow tone, "what do you do now? Will you stay here? Will you work as a fisherman the rest of your life? What are your plans?"

John gathered that she could think of no more miserable finale to his once-exalted dreams. "Would it be so bad for me to choose that way of life?" he asked.

Salome's heart beat heavily. She hesitated to speak further, but something brought her to it. "Son," she began, her voice breaking periodically, "I will say but these last words to you. You will accept or reject them. Then I will say no more."

John knelt down and reached for her hand, but she withheld it. "I have never said this to anyone, my son. It is never to go beyond you and me." He nodded in affirmation. "You are my younger child. It is the tradition of the people of Israel to love their firstborn above all other children. By tradition, I should love you less than James. But," here her eyes gleamed with tears, "John, I am like Rebekah of old, who loved Jacob over Esau."

A lump formed in John's throat. "Mother . . ."

"Let me continue. Even Jewish mothers break tradition. The heart is not governed by such things as men's laws. John, you were always the more perceptive, the more sensitive of my two boys. God knows I love James. But you have been the child after my own heart since you were but a tiny lad." Her face beamed with memories. "Oh, the way you used to tell tall tales! The way you used to bring such imagination to my world! The way you have always dreamed!" She looked at him, and placed a hand on his face. "Do you remember the day Zebedee caught you with the Greek parchments?" she asked, her voice a mixture of laughter and tears.

"Yes, mother," he smiled.

"And the way you used to play you were King David? Oh, the songs you wrote!"

"Yes," John nodded, repressing the memories of Zebedee's confiscation and destruction of those precious poems.

"Son," she sighed, "don't you see? To lose your dreams is to lose yourself—the most important part of yourself! If you have lost that, perhaps—perhaps you *are* dead!"

John stood stiffly and gazed down upon her. "But, surely, mother, you are not saying that I should continue to follow after a man who has proved himself unworthy!"

The beautiful woman shook her head. "Are you so sure he is unworthy, John? Oh, I do not claim to know. I only ask. But whether or not this Jesus is a good man, do not let one disillusionment kill your spirit. Son, do not become like . . . your father."

John studied her in surprise. Jewish wives did not say such

things! He was seeing a side to Salome he had never known before. Such misery she must have endured all these years, to speak so only in a moment of desperation. "Mother, is that how you see me? Am I becoming like him?"

"I hope not, son," she sighed. "Bitter, lonely old man that he is! He is so unhappy." And then, pleading, she said, "Continue to seek your answers, John. And when you find them, bring them home."

The young son of Zebedee looked compassionately upon his mother and drew her to him. He did not know just now how to respond, or even what he felt.

As they clung together in silence, a knock was heard at the door.

A servant announced the arrival of a young woman, and shortly after, in the parlor stood the red-haired Deborah, Peter's wife.

Salome had apparently met her on some occasion, for she greeted her happily. "Deborah! What brings you here?"

"Mistress," she said quietly, "I was anxious to share the good news with you . . . I have received word that my husband and his brother are coming home!"

Salome turned quickly to John, who stood now with his arms folded as if to say, "So, they have come to their senses, too."

But Deborah added, " . . . and Jesus of Nazareth will be staying at our house!"

Chapter 21

The curtain of night over the Sea of Galilee was raised slowly by dawn's foggy fingers. But it seemed to John that the darkness went too quickly.

Knowing that Peter would be returning to Capernaum today, he had wished the night might never end, that he could stay in the fishing boat forever and not return to shore. He was not eager to face the questions the brash fisherman would put to him. Nor was he eager to tell him why he had left the Master—what he had seen at Sychar. He knew the truth would be a blow to his good friend.

All too soon, however, the time came when the last net was drawn in by the hired men, and Zebedee gave the order to row the fleet ashore.

James and John worked together quickly, their cold fingers glad for the warmth of the rising sun as they hung the nets on the racks. But more than the nippy air spurred James' efforts. His coarse red hair glistened with sea spray as the sun hit it, but the sparkle in his eyes rivaled the natural liveliness of his coloring.

"Today is the day!" he said aloud.

John need not ask what he referred to. Since James had heard of Jesus' coming visit to the city, he had intended to meet him. Strange, John thought, that since he had left the Master, James' interest in the Nazarene had grown. This should not have surprised him, however. Some of the contrary nature which typified John, also characterized his brother. Though John was the more self-assertive, both sons of Zebedee reveled in challenges. The fact that the younger had taken so readily to the Baptist and to Jesus had made James leery of them. Now that John had turned from them, they were more attractive.

As the brothers sorted the catch, throwing out the trash fish and keeping the good, John worked too slowly for James' liking.

"It is nearly noon!" the elder shouted angrily. "I am leaving for the city after lunch. If this job is not completed by then, I'll leave it for you!"

John's eyes clouded. "Fine with me!"

James glowered and heaved a slimy fish into his lap with a resounding splatter. Then, wiping his hands on his cloak, he disappeared down the beach.

John bent over his work with a scowl, tossing fish from pile to pile, inwardly dreading the coming confrontation. As he stewed anxiously, the distant sound of raucous laughter came to his ears.

Looking up, he saw that James had been met by Peter and Andrew, and he turned his back quickly, hoping they would not recognize him.

"John!" came the familiar call. And Peter was running down the beach with a hulking stride. "John, you old sea hound! So you have not vanished from the face of the earth!"

The smaller fisherman looked up resignedly, but when the friendly giant reached him, stooping down with his broad, toothy smile and clapping him on the back with a meaty hand, John could not help but respond warmly. "Simon!" he laughed, preferring his original name. "Good to see you, old man!"

In no time the big fellow was seated beside him on the sand, breathing excitedly from his run. "So you find fish more attractive than the Nazarene?"

John recoiled, but lacking a better response, said, "At least it earns a living."

Peter was not entirely lacking in sensitivity. He could read the uneasiness his question had given rise to. He watched silently as John went about the business of sorting. But it would not be long before he would speak again. "John, you know you cannot keep the truth from me," he said in an unusually soft tone. And then with a chuckle, "I will make you miserable until you tell me why you did not return to our group."

The big fisherman's face showed genuine concern, but John was apprehensive. "Simon . . ."

"Call me 'Peter,' " the large man corrected.

"Peter," John faltered, disliking the taste of the Master's label, "I have simply come to realize that the life of an itinerant is not for me."

Peter was skeptical. "Since when?" he bellowed.

John knew the alibi was not convincing. If anyone had longed for adventure it had been himself. He breathed a sigh. Perhaps it would come as a relief if he did tell the truth. If Simon turned on him, he would find a way to live with that.

"I suppose it will do no good to give you anything but the unveiled facts," he said at last.

The massive man leaned back with a satisfied nod. "It will not."

"All right, if you must know—I discovered a side to Jesus which persuaded me he is a fake."

Peter's face darkened. "I am sure you did!" he said sarcastically.

"The picture is not pretty," John warned.

"It would not be half so ugly as what I am thinking of you this moment!" Peter blared, his eyes full of storm.

Still the younger looked at him confidently. "Do you want to hear me out, or don't you?" Peter's fists loosened their tight knots, and John continued. "You have asked for this. If it does not set well with you . . ."

"Go on!" the fisherman demanded.

It was not an easy thing to relate, but John managed to get through the story. The words, "Samaritan woman . . . a harlot . . ." hung rancidly on his tongue, and the sick feeling he had experienced upon seeing the Master with her swept over him afresh.

John looked at the sky, relieved that he had voiced the memory of the scene. But even as he did so, he thought of Peter. "Friend," he said, "I don't know where you and the others were that day. I assume Jesus sent you on some errand, and then concealed the secret rendezvous from you all." He shook his head and gazed sadly across the sea. "It has been no joy to tell you this."

He expected that when he got courage to look Peter in the face, he would see a defeated man. The thought pained him to the heart.

"Ha!" came the reverberating reply. Peter was rocked with mirth, and John turned to him wide-eyed, finding him with his head thrown back in abandon. "Oh, John!" he roared, slapping him on the back once more, and sending a sharp pain down his spine. "Did you really think that's what you saw at Sychar?"

John straightened with a scowl, and studied the big man bewilderedly.

"I do not care for Samaritans any more than you do," Peter continued, laughing. "But you have misjudged the Master!"

John looked at him sideways. "How?"

"Jesus went into Samaria when he had heard the Pharisees were stirred up about all the baptisms we were performing. It is true that we were not with him during the time he spoke to the woman at the well. We had gone into Sychar to buy food."

At this John gave him a nod as if to say, "I figured as much."

"When we returned, they were just finishing their conversation, and of course, we reacted just as you. We were shocked and disillusioned at what we thought we saw—our Master dealing with a Samaritan harlot behind our backs! But none of us questioned him to his face because just as we returned, our judgment was proven wrong."

John was doubtful, but nonetheless curious. "Explain, Peter."

"When we were still a little way from them, before either of them saw us, the woman turned to leave, obviously very excited about something. She even left her waterpot at the well. And she went tearing into the city calling out to all the men, 'Come see a man who told me all about myself! He knows everything I have ever done. He must be the Messiah!' "

John looked at the ground silently.

"Of course, we did not fully understand, even then, what was going on. Perhaps someday we will know the full story of their talk. But we offered the Master some of the food we had bought, and he said the strangest thing . . ."

Peter was lost in the memory, and his voice took on a faraway quality. "He said, 'I have food to eat that you do not know of.' We wondered what he meant by that. Had someone brought him food while we were gone? But then he said, 'My food is to do the will of him who sent me, and to finish his work.' "

As John listened to the Master's words, his heart filled with loneliness. How he had longed to hear such things again, things which only Jesus seemed capable of saying. Truly, since he had been gone from the Master, he *had* been empty, as Salome described him. "Dead," as he himself had said.

But his emotions were in conflict. Pride told him not to be easily taken in again. His heart told him that when he had left Jesus he had left the path of truth and life.

Peter continued. "As we listened to the Master, a great crowd of Samaritans came out from the city. I tell you, we were frightened! We had no idea what such a mob might want with a small band of Jews like ourselves. But just as they drew near, Jesus motioned to us to look at them. 'Do not say there are still four months until the harvest,' he told us. 'Behold, I say unto you, lift up your eyes, and look on the fields, for they are ripe and ready to harvest.' "

John's throat was tight. Could he have been so stupid as to try his Master without a case against him? Memories of the Pharisees and their accusations of the Baptist returned to him. But he repressed the comparison quickly.

"We stayed with the Samaritans for two days," Peter went on. "Believe me, it was not easy." He smiled. "But by the time we left, there were many who had come to believe Jesus' claims. They were calling him the Christ, and the Savior of the world!"

"Samaritans?" John was astonished. "He allows Samaritans to call him Messiah?"

Peter nodded.

John would not be so foolish as to make an issue of this, no matter how it repulsed his sensitive Jewish values. He must not be quick in his judgment of the Master again.

The big fisherman eyed him carefully. "Friend," he said, "I find some things difficult to accept, just as you do. Perhaps, if I had been in your shoes, coming upon that scene by myself and not knowing where the rest of the disciples were, I, too, would have run from it."

John smiled gratefully. "Perhaps . . ." he nodded.

"And you know I have no stomach for Samaritans!"

The two of them laughed together, but then Peter grew quiet again. "There is one more thing I must tell you. Perhaps it will help you decide what to do."

"Go ahead," John offered.

"On our way back to Capernaum, we went to Nazareth, where the Master was brought up."

"Yes—"

"On the Sabbath we went to the synagogue, and the elders asked if Jesus would do the honor of reading the Scriptures. He asked for the scroll of the book of Isaiah, the prophet, and then read, 'The Spirit of the Lord is upon me, because he has anointed me to preach the gospel to the poor; he has sent me to heal the broken-hearted, to preach deliverance to the captives, and recovering of sight to the blind, to set at liberty them that are bruised, to preach the acceptable year of the Lord.'

"John," Peter added softly, "when he was finished reading, everyone in the room was dumbfounded. And the Master looked at us all, saying, 'This day this Scripture is fulfilled.' "

Chapter 22

John was supposed to be asleep. It was James' turn to help Zebedee oversee the crew of the little ship as it navigated the deep night waters. But the restlessness of John's mind and heart would not allow him any calm.

It had been three days since Jesus and his followers had come to Capernaum. James had seen the Master and could not stop speaking of him, of his teaching and his miracles. The whole city was on fire for the Nazarene.

But John had kept his distance. His soul burned within him as he thought again and again on the news Peter had brought. He *had* misjudged the Master; of that there was no doubt. But what was left to him now? Shame and pride were a barrier to his return.

He stood again at the same point of decision he had reached at Aenon. The alternatives were very clear. He could go on living in defeated emptiness, or perhaps, if Jesus would have him, he could, again, follow after his Teacher in the robes of a disciple. He knew, though, that either route would be a mockery, unless he were fully committed to the claims of the Nazarene.

The boat rocked gently on the warm waters, and a flurry of sea birds, roused from their dozing, flapped their way into the sky overhead. As John's eyes followed them, his vision was caught by the myriad stars in the velvet black above.

"No man has ever ascended up to heaven, except he who came down from heaven; that is the Son of Man . . . which is *in* heaven."

Strange that those words should return to him now. Of all the things Jesus had said of himself, this was one of the hardest to believe.

But now it seemed the sea wind itself carried another refrain to his ears, and it blended with the swaying of the vessel. "For God so loved the world, that he gave his only begotten Son, that whosoever believes in him should not perish, but have everlasting life." Again and again it came, growing in intensity and in persistence, until John thought he would go mad. "Stop!" he whispered hoarsely, placing his hands over his ears.

The other men in the boat did not hear him. He was alone with his agony. But just as the hounding voice within his soul died away, another quieter, smaller one nudged his heart. "You must be born again, John . . . It is a hard thing to be born, but it is a joy to find life. You must be born again . . . born again . . . born again . . . He that believes on me has life everlasting . . . believe, John . . . believe . . ."

The hours of night slipped by, and as the sun came with its first hint of light far in the east, John was still struggling, like a fish as it tries to escape the net.

How he wished for solitude. "Oh, my God!" he cried internally, tears filling his eyes. He hid his face in the pillow, and pretended to be asleep. "O God, what can I say? I know the way. I cannot live with the truth unless I accept it. It will kill me inside to reject it, to turn it away." His breath came heavily, but he did not want the others, especially James and his father, to see his torment. "I am a broken man, my Lord," he sobbed quietly. "You have broken me, but I love you, God."

"Do you believe?" came the voice.

"Yes, Master, oh, yes! I *do* believe. With what little faith I have, I *do* believe, for there is no other answer!"

Suddenly, with that acknowledgment, came a peace he had never known. Somehow, the struggle was ended, and relief poured through him like cool nectar. "Jesus," he found himself saying, "will you take me back again?"

The boat had pulled into shallower waters with the dawn, and James shook his brother from his supposed sleep, telling him it was time to help with the work. Zebedee and the hired men began hauling the dragnets into the boat, and the hemp was passed about for the mending to begin. John sat up and crossed his legs, pulling a rugged skein into his lap.

Peter and Andrew had joined the fleet the night before,

determined that as long as they were in the home port, they would do what fishing they could. Their boat was moored down the beach a way, and they took the remaining hours to fish from the shore, throwing their large nets out into the shallows.

Though John busied himself with the mundane tasks of his trade, his mind still communed with the inner voice of his soul. "Lord," he was saying, "if only I knew you would have me, I would leave this boat so quickly, the sea itself would not keep me from you!"

As he acknowledged this, a strange, inexplicable feeling overcame him. The balm of peace still soothed his heart, but now, with it came a sense of longing, of hunger and restlessness. What it was that stirred him so, he could not understand. But he was unable to concentrate on the work of his hands. Distracted, unsettled, he found himself drawn to scan the shoreline, as if in pointed search for something.

Up the beach, coming from the direction of town, a distant figure entered his line of vision. Though he was too far away to be clearly identified, John's heart sped involuntarily. "My Lord?" he whispered.

The early light of day slowly brightened, bringing the oncomer into clearer sight, and John gripped the side of the boat tensely. Yes! It was the Master. He was heading this way!

Excitement flooded John's soul. His previously unexplained sense of longing and urgency came into focus, and every muscle in his body drew itself taut like a bowstring. It was all he could do to remain in the boat. "Would he want me?" the question haunted him. "Could he take me back?"

Peter and Andrew continued to work their net, tossing it again into the shallows. They were too far to hear John call out to them.

"Lord!" he thought. "Don't they know you are coming?"

But none of the fishermen, save himself, had yet seen the Master. "James," John said hoarsely, ". . . do you see him?"

"Who?"

John could only point mutely, and James looked doubtfully down the beach. "It is Jesus!" the elder cried excitedly. "What can he want so early in the morning?"

Peter and Andrew had moved closer to Zebedee's fleet. John could have alerted them, but he cared for nothing but the sight of the Master, and his eyes strained with desire.

As Jesus came near the two waders, he stopped. "Peter, Andrew! Sons of Jona!" he called, his voice filling John with great joy. The two brothers wheeled about, stunned at the unexpected presence of their Teacher. But before they could greet him, he called out words full of challenge and promise.

"Follow me, and I will make you fishers of men!"

Immediately, they dropped the net from their hands and joined the Master on the shore.

John's heart pounded, and he breathed to himself, "Could you want me also, Lord? Would you take me back?"

Jesus, Peter, and Andrew continued down the beach, nearing the boats of Zebedee. John looked excitedly at his brother and father. He saw that James, like himself, sat rigid with tension. Zebedee, also, was caught in rapt attention, but his gray eyes observed beneath a stony, furrowed brow, his stubborn old heart having put up a wall of resistance, though his awe prevented him from challenging Jesus.

The Nazarene now stood before the vessel in which the old man and his sons were stationed. John sat like a trap ready to spring.

Jesus looked from face to face in that little ship, and then—his gaze settled on its youngest member. For a long moment the Master and his disciple were fixed upon each other.

Then, holding out one hand with a beckoning gesture, turning first to the elder, then to the younger, Jesus called, "Sons of Zebedee! James. John. Follow me!"

James' breath came with a sharp jolt, and he stared incredulously at the Rabbi, then at his own brother. Hot tears coursed down John's face, and without so much as a glance away, he bolted over the side of the vessel into the Galilean water.

It seemed an endless journey to that shore. Nothing could move him quickly enough, as he first swam and then waded his way to the patient Nazarene. Behind him he could hear the sounds of James, who, too, had heeded the call, and he could feel the angry, disapproving glare of Zebedee, who felt only the greatest contempt for the Master.

But John did not look back. Jesus alone filled his eyes, his mind, and his heart.

So this was what it was like to be reborn! This was what it meant to find life!

Only a stretch of sand lay between him and the Lord. This he crossed breathlessly, coming at last within reach of the Nazarene.

"Master!" he cried, throwing himself into the waiting arms.

The warmth of the reunion was all encompassing, and happiness flooded John's heart such as he had never known possible. "It is a joy to find life . . ." echoed the Baptist's words.

Jesus raised his disciple's tear-stained face to his, holding him tenderly before him. The Master's eyes were also wet with joy, and John read in them a volume of love unspeakable.

"Lord . . ." he whispered.

"John . . . welcome home."

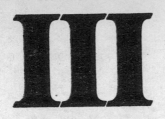

III

THE TRUTH

*Abide in me, and I in you. As the
branch cannot bear fruit of itself,
except it abide in the vine; no more
can ye, except ye abide in me . . .
for without me ye can do nothing.*
JOHN 15:4, 5

Chapter 1

John had made his decision, but the remolding of his character had only just begun. While it was indeed a joy to find life, the process of living out that life would demand transformation.

What was to happen immediately after his conversion, therefore, served as a seal of assurance that Jesus was indeed the Messiah. John had seen the Lord perform miracles before, both at Cana and at the feast in Jerusalem. But now they came in such dazzling and rapid frequency that he could barely take them in.

The first, and one of the most spectacular, involved the releasing of a man from the chains of demonic possession. That had happened on a Sabbath day, in the middle of a synagogue meeting, when Jesus had been invited to speak to the people. In a voice like that from the underworld, a strange, wild-eyed, and disheveled man had interrupted him, crying out, "Let us alone, Jesus of Nazareth! Are you come to destroy us? I know who you are . . . you Holy One of God!"

The congregation stared in horror at the spectacle, and John was filled with fear. Though the poor unfortunate was a local citizen, known to all, he hardly seemed recognizable in this condition. But the Master had calmly and with sure authority looked at the man, and had then spoken as if to another being, "Hold your peace! And come out of him!"

The crowd had watched, mute with wonder when, at that instant, the demoniac had been thrown, as if by a power beyond himself, into the midst of the gathering, and onto the floor. He had lain thus for some time, writhing and clutching at himself, leaving great gashes where his nails scraped across his chest. Then, after

one unearthly shriek, which had made John's hair stand on end,
the fellow had suddenly become limp and quiet, lying as one dead
before them all.

John remembered looking at Peter, whose face was white, and
after some time had passed the two disciples approached the man,
and lifted him to his feet.

He had stood shaking, but he was a whole man, and the crowd
was astonished.

"What is this?" they had murmured. "What kind of thing have
we seen? Even unclean spirits obey this Jesus of Nazareth!" And
from that moment, the fame of the Master had begun to spread
with even more energy than before, up and down Galilee.

That same afternoon, in a very real way, he confirmed himself to
John's friend, Peter, and his wife. The disciples had retired to the
big fisherman's house in Bethsaida. When they arrived they were
greeted at the door by an anxious Deborah and the household
servants. It seemed Peter's mother-in-law, who lived with them,
had come down with a terrible fever. The Master wasted no time
going to her bedside.

There the old woman lay, unconscious. John had watched as
Jesus stood over her, looking tenderly at her flushed, hot face.
Then, with the same voice of authority he had used in the
synagogue, the Master said, "Fever and sickness, depart!" And
reaching his cool hand toward her, he touched her forehead,
taking hold of her, and raising her up. Instantly, before the eyes of
all present, her face lost its fevered appearance. Her breathing
became calm, and strength flooded back to her. The fever had
gone! And she rose, astounded, rejoicing, and busied herself with
the entertaining of her guests.

It seemed Jesus even knew how to mend a strife-filled home, for
if Deborah had had misgivings concerning her husband's itinerant
wanderings with the Nazarene, they vanished with her mother's
healing. Peter, who until that moment had struggled with the
problem of leaving his new bride, now found that she was urging
him to do whatever the Master might ask.

Indeed, it seemed the whole world was bowing to Jesus' power.
That night the street in front of Peter's home was so jammed with
people seeking the Nazarene and his miracles that John wondered
how the Master could face so many needs.

But it was only beginning. From that day, individuals from all
over Palestine and nearby lands would search the Lord out. It
would become virtually impossible for him to find solitude. They

would swarm over him, they would hound him like a hunter's dogs, bringing the sick, the deranged, the maimed, the helpless of every kind to be touched by the Master's hand. But he would not cease to heal them, and always, when they came to him, his face would bear a depth of compassion which the disciple had not begun to fathom.

Chapter 2

John was bone weary. Not since the night he had crawled up on Jordan's bank in search of the Baptist, had he been so utterly spent of his strength.

For weeks Jesus and his disciples had been trekking around Galilee, going from town to town as the Master preached and taught the people who massed about him. For more days than John cared to count, they had lived off the generosity of those who would give them food to eat and a place to lay their heads. And, though it was always energizing and exciting to observe the Lord's miracles, to listen to his powerful words, the schedule the disciples kept was enough to weary even the most spiritual of men.

"And I am not the most spiritual of men," John thought to himself, laughing. "At least not yet!" In his present condition, he was feeling, indeed, very fleshly. All he could think of was a soft bed and a good night's sleep. He would have chastised himself, but he lacked even the energy to do that.

They were nearing Capernaum again. His great weariness was made worse by the realization that he and his fellow fishermen would put in long hours on the sea when they reached home. It was necessary for them to maintain their trade whenever they were in the home port. The crews needed their supervision, and it was best not to leave them unattended any more than necessary.

It was a relief that James had decided to join partnership with Peter and Andrew, rather than return to Zebedee. In the wisdom which came with his few years, the first born of the Pharisee knew his father would not welcome John and himself as long as they remained disciples of the Nazarene.

Still, the thought of those long, dark hours ahead weighed John down like an anchor. He leaned back against the trunk of a great palm which shaded the oasis along the shore road, where they had come to rest. The other disciples dozed contentedly, and Peter's uninhibited snoring kept an even rhythm with the swaying sea breeze. It was the perfect temperature and atmosphere for a nap, but John was so tired that sleep eluded him. The more he tried to attain it, the further it slipped from his grasp. At last, with a disgusted sigh, he sat up and decided to wait out the time.

The disciple tilted his head back and gazed into the vivid blue sky. A small cluster of clouds passed lazily overhead, and watching them he grew drowsy, but a rustling at his side brought him back to consciousness.

"Did I waken you?" the Master whispered.

"Not really, sir," John said, sitting up alertly. "Sleep seems beyond me today."

"There are times when it flees me, too." Jesus nodded.

"You, sir?"

The Master laughed softly and picked up his tone. "Why are you surprised? Do you think I cannot sympathize with such things?"

John looked away, somewhat ashamed.

But the Master smiled kindly and said, "Friend, how can I sleep when there are so many faces constantly before my eyes?" His voice was full of a strange note, and John found himself listening with a heavy heart as Jesus explained something of what it was to be in his position. "Even in my dreams they come to me, John. The crowds, the thousands who mill about me as I walk. I cannot seem to escape them, even in rare moments of quiet." He then looked at his young follower questioningly. "Is it a wonder I do not sleep?"

John shook his head. He had never given much thought to the burden of being sought after. "But, sir," he answered, "you do not seem the anxious sort."

Jesus gave his laughing smile again, and John found himself reevaluating the last statement. "Friend," the Master replied, "one does not have to be anxious or full of worry to be restless." But then he sobered and looked out across the road and down to the shore. "Even now I can see them," he sighed, "the lonely, empty faces, and pleading hands . . . grasping at me from all sides." Then he turned silently to his disciple. "Don't you see? There is much work to do."

"But you do not seem to slow," John insisted. "I am much younger, and yet *I* lag behind *you*. Where do you get your strength? How do you go on, day after day, without rest, without proper food?"

"It is a hard life you have chosen, John—to follow me," the Master answered. "I understand your weariness, how it seems you cannot put one foot in front of the other. As for myself, of course, I know what it is to feel such things." Jesus' eyes took on a far-away look. "Do you remember how you wondered where I spent my time after my baptism at the Jordan—how you questioned the reason for my strange, haggard appearance?"

John nodded in reflection.

"I said we would one day speak of it," he went on, "that it would have seemed too incredible to you then." Jesus studied him carefully. "Perhaps you should hear of it now . . ." he suggested.

John stirred eagerly. "Yes, Lord. I am ready!"

The pain of those days was apparent as the Master spoke: "I wandered in the wilderness without food for forty days," he said.

The disciple shuddered. He had heard of fasts of extended length. But forty days—and under such conditions? He listened breathlessly, envisioning the Lord's ordeal, and the climb through terrain which had torn his hands and tested his body. But as the Master continued it became clear that hunger and pain had been the least of his temptations.

"Satan tormented me in that time," Jesus went on.

The Lord's voice was heavy as he described the agony of those hours. And John, who had often doubted the very existence of a personal devil, found himself not only believing every word, but scarcely able to bear it.

When, at last, however, Jesus stopped, and his eyes closed in relief, John sat silent with the awe of the revelation. Then the Nazarene turned to him again. "Yes, John, I grow weary, just as you. But I must not slow. I cannot stop when there is so much to do."

The Master's words called up Peter's account of Jesus' teaching at the well in Samaria. When the crowds had come rushing out to meet the Nazarene, the Lord had compared them to a great field of wheat, ready to be harvested. Undoubtedly, this was the urgency in his gait, the awesome responsibility which occupied his every waking moment.

Such a duty, John thought. Such a burden of labor. Even Zebedee does not work so hard for his religion.

At the thought of Zebedee, however, John shuddered afresh. And though it shamed him to question again, he wondered, "Could it be that Jesus' way of life is no more than another form of Pharisaism? Full of works and good deeds which can make a man old before his time?" But then, as if in answer to his unvoiced thoughts, the Master was speaking again.

"John, I can do nothing of my own self. Do you see? My power is from above, from my Father, who is in heaven. In my own energy, I am nothing. It is his strength which I call upon. If I do not slow, if I do not show weariness, it is because my Father's strength is my power."

John was stunned by this response, and he looked at the Nazarene incredulously. Never had he heard such words. "Jehovah helps you not to grow weary?"

The Master laughed compassionately. "Are you a child of Israel, and you do not know of such things?"

John shook his head. "I cannot recall that I have ever learned such a concept."

Jesus gazed down the road with a broad smile, and then, as if chanting to himself, he began to quote words which should have been very familiar to the young Jew. "The Lord is the strength of my life . . . Blessed be the Lord my strength . . . He gives power to the faint and to them that have no might he increases strength. . ."

At this, the others of the company took up the chant and joined the Master in his song, one by one, until the chorus was loud and jubilant.

"Even the youths shall faint and be weary," they sang, "and the young men shall utterly fall! But they that wait upon the Lord shall renew their strength; they shall mount up with wings as eagles. They shall run, and not be weary! And they shall walk, and not faint!"

The tempo had climbed until, at the end, James and Peter were full of ecstatic laughter, and John's eyes were wide with delight.

"Master!" John smiled. "I guess I *have* learned such things. At least, I have *heard* such things. Why did I never think of them before?"

Jesus' eyes were full of loving patience as he studied his young follower. "Why had Nicodemus never learned the things I taught him? He had read the Scriptures all his life, and yet had failed to see what they were saying."

They stood to go, and John looked at the road which passed now beneath his feet. Clasping his hands behind him, he meditated on these concepts, his brow furrowed with intensity. "Lord," he said finally, "could it be that masters of Israel have missed something all along? And if they have missed this, perhaps they have missed many things. But, Lord . . . my father and his kind are the righteous of Israel," he insisted. "They do all the right things. They are the backbone of Judaism! Why, everyone looks to their ways as *the* ways! And yet . . . they do not teach what you teach. They hate you, Master. They say you have come to destroy the Law!"

"Do you believe that, John?"

The disciple turned to him confusedly. "Master, no! I cannot believe that!"

"And why not?"

"Why . . . " John stammered, "because . . . because your words are truth! They are from the Scriptures! No Jew can refute them."

"But," the Master asked, "does not a Pharisee quote the Scriptures?"

"Oh yes, sir! As often as he breathes!" John responded. And then he gave a perplexed shrug. "But he finds a laborious, burdensome teaching in them, Master. How can that be?"

Jesus suggested, smiling, "Perhaps the Scriptures contradict one another?"

The young disciple was horrified. "Surely you do not believe that?"

"What other answer can there be?"

John detected from the Master's secretive look that indeed he did *not* believe the Scriptures contradicted one another, but that he was tickling his student's mind. "Well, sir, I do not know. The Pharisees follow the Scriptures, and you follow the Scriptures. Who is right and who is wrong? And how *can* one be right and the other wrong?"

Jesus gave no answer but only waited. Then, slowly light began to dawn in John's mind. "Could it be that the men of the Law have seen only a part of the truth?" he asked.

Jesus' eyes brightened. "Well said, John! You are an apt pupil!" John was elated. How he reveled in such praise! But then the Master sobered. "Tell me, then, John, what part have they not seen?"

The disciple studied the sky thoughtfully. "They follow the Law, my Lord . . . "

"They try," Jesus corrected him.

"Yes . . . " John was confused, but then remembering the Baptist's words, he said, "You are right. They try, but they fail in peace and mercy. And their way is burdensome, unlike yours, my Lord. What have they missed? How does a man attain God's help, God's righteousness?"

At this, Jesus spoke the strangest words his followers had heard since the night with Nicodemus. Looking at them intently, he proclaimed, "I am the way to the Father, for the Father and I are one. Come to me, if you labor and are burdened, and I will give you rest. Apart from me you can do nothing."

Chapter 3

The silver light of the moon painted bright specks on the ripples of the sea. John worked beside James silently, hauling in the net and tossing it out again. His mind was deep in thought, going over and over the Master's teachings.

Such concepts were extremely difficult for a Jew of orthodox background to readily grasp. He could assent mentally to such truths, but to actually live in such a way went against his nature.

All his life John had been taught, along with every other Jewish schoolboy, that a righteous man is a man who *does,* who *works,* who *strives,* and who *performs.* But here was Jesus saying that a truly righteous man is one who does *not* do, who does *not* work, who does *not* strive or perform, but who trusts in him.

John looked at his brother and the others as they labored at the nets and oars. Their faces shone with glistening sweat in the moonlight. All of them were strangely silent, apparently, like himself, deep in thought. Jesus had stayed in Capernaum this evening, where he had been invited to dine with a prominent citizen. John wished he were here. He had so many questions.

When the small vessels pulled onto the shore in the gray light of dawn, the hulls were resoundingly hollow. Hours of backbreaking labor had yielded only trash fish, and these had been thrown back before the men entered port.

As John hung the nets out to dry, anger grew in him. "Spiritual platitudes are one thing, but if the Master truly wants to free us from our burdens, he should help us with our fishing! That would be proof to me!"

The sun worked its way up slowly to morning, and the sea birds scanned the water in the gradual light, spying for fish which might come too close to the surface. John watched them and muttered, "Good luck!"

But with the brightening of day, the sound of many voices could be heard from the direction of town. The fishermen looked up from their nets to see a great crowd swarming out from the city gates.

On inspection, it became clear just what was causing the excitement. They were following after Jesus, who, for some reason, seemed to be leading them down the beach. It appeared all Capernaum was at his heels, and the fishermen looked at one another curiously. "Why would he bring them out here?" they questioned.

Apprehension filled the disciples as they watched the oncoming throng. With growing clarity, they could see that the Master was not at all "leading" the crowd down the beach. He was in fact being jostled and pressed by the great, swelling numbers who had come to hear him preach this morning. Apparently the congregation, including many from outlying towns and villages, had been too great for the synagogue, or for even the city square. Jesus had been forced to go beyond the city gates to speak to the people, and now they sought him with such energy, the sick, the infirm and their families begging his touch so voraciously that he was being forced further and further down the sandy coast.

"Make room! Make room!" Peter cried to his friends. "See how they are coming on!"

John's heart beat fearfully. "They will trample him if they are not careful!" he shouted above the growing din.

Jesus had given up speaking. The congregation was so loud that he was not being heard any longer. Pleading hands reached to him from all sides; his cloak was tugged and pulled by the clutching mob and it seemed, from his expression, that though he could have driven them back with a word of divine power, he was bent on some other method of handling the matter.

He had nearly reached his disciples, when he turned his attention to the boats moored beside the lake. The disciples could not imagine what he had in mind. Tearing himself from the reach of the crowd and beckoning for Peter, he went quickly toward the vessels.

"This is yours?" he called to the big sailor.

"Yes, sir!" Peter replied, running to him.

The Master wasted no time getting into the ship. "Thrust out a little from the land!" he commanded. Peter hastily complied, his burly arms shoving the vessel down the sloping sand and into the slapping shallows. Wading a way into the water and still pushing the boat, the fisherman jumped in and began rowing.

"Enough," Jesus said. "Thank you, Peter."

John looked on in amazement. He never would have thought of such a thing. The Master was going to preach to the crowds from across the barrier of a few feet of water. The hindrance would be just enough to hold the people in restraint while he caught his breath and rested a moment. "Very good!" the disciple thought.

Jesus, seated in the bow of the boat, glanced at his devoted friend with a smile. Wiping the sweat from his own brow, he then turned to Peter with a sigh. "Good work," he commended. "This will do fine."

It was late afternoon when Jesus finished speaking to the crowd. The fishermen were exhausted, for they had worked all night and had then stayed with the Master all day. Sometime during the morning as the congregation had continued to grow, John and the others had gotten into the second boat and pushed out onto the water to be near the Lord. After the crowds finally departed, Jesus spoke to his men. Observing the empty hulls, he said, "It appears you had a poor night on the sea."

John smiled wearily. "Yes, sir. The poorest we have ever had."

Jesus turned toward the bow of the ship and looked for a long time across the water. John could not guess what was going through his mind, though he tried very hard to interpret the Lord's expression. Finally Jesus spoke to Peter, who was the master of the fleet. "Launch out into the deep," he pointed, "and let down your nets for a draught."

Peter stared at him in white amazement, as did John. What could the Lord be thinking? Didn't he understand their trade? They did not fish at midday! Besides, there was no harvest to be had. Peter spoke John's thoughts when he said exhaustedly, "But Master, we have toiled all the night, and have taken nothing!"

Jesus did not reply, but looked from face to face, deep into the eyes of his men. When he came to John, the young follower's cheeks burned with the penetrating gaze. And as the Lord again turned to Simon Peter, the big fisherman cleared his throat and looked at the boat's floor, stammering, "All right, Master, at your command, I will let down the net."

Feeling very foolish as they rowed onto the lake in the middle of the day, the hardy sailors said nothing. Fellow tradesmen undoubtedly watched from the shore, if there were any who were not home in bed. The jokes would surely fly thick and fast in the streets tonight, and the brothers Bar Jona and Bar Zebedee would be the brunt of them. Nevertheless, they found it difficult to say "no" to Jesus.

"Let it down!" Peter called when they had reached the deepest section of the sea. At this, Andrew and the other men of the crew let fly a great round throwing net. It was unheard of to lower such an instrument unless a school of fish had already been spotted, but today they would obey a different rule.

The sinkers had barely begun to plummet into the depths, taking the lighter skein down with them, when the men of the ship began to feel a great tugging on the loops. Suddenly, out of nowhere, hundreds of fish were swarming the net, sleek, glistening, silver-bright. So many, in fact, had mysteriously found their way into the hemp that some of the thick twine began to break.

Peter, Andrew, and their helpers found themselves straining to keep hold of the unmanageable haul. Their arms shone with sweat and their backs bowed painfully as they attempted to drag the catch into the boat before the net gave way completely.

"James! John!" they called. "Come and help us!"

The younger son of Zebedee was dumbfounded; he and his brother were so awed by what they witnessed that their reaction was slow. "Yes!" James called at last, and the second boat was brought alongside. The four fishermen and their crews were barely able to raise the splitting throw net, and when this was accomplished, another net, and another, were flung into the sea, resulting in the same phenomenon.

Jesus lent his strength to the task, working right alongside the disciples to bring the sparkling trophies into the hull. When several more nets brought in still other fish, the second boat was needed as an additional carrier. But even it was not enough. So numerous were the fish that the slats which girded the undercarriage of the vessels were straining, the rivets beginning to protrude from the ribs.

"Lord Jehovah!" Peter was shouting. "How can this be?"

John's breath was labored and heavy. A sense of exhilaration mixed with the expenditure of his energy, and tears coursed down his cheeks. "Jesus! How can this be?" he echoed.

Still the fish came, and still the boards of the boats creaked, until the men feared the ships would sink.

"It is enough!" Peter shouted. "Take no more!"

Within the holds lay flopping, glittering mountains of the most gorgeous fish the men had ever seen. Their trained eyes, quickly scanning the miraculous haul, told them that every edible variety available from the sea was represented in their ships. Broad comb fish, with their high fins; long, sleek barbels; gray mullet; and carp—all were here. And to their further amazement, not a single catfish, which were forbidden by Jewish kosher laws, and which would have been sorted from the rest when they reached shore—not a single one was to be seen in the catch!

It was a perfect haul. Never had they seen the like! Indeed, Jesus had proven himself as John had desired, in the mundane realm of the fisher's world.

Staring up at the Master from the rocking vessel, the young disciple cried again, "My Lord! How can these things be?"

Peter stood shakily in the bow of his ship and stared with growing awe at the glistening hoard. In the wake of the thrill he had just experienced was coming another, more profound emotion. John communicated with the feeling etched upon his friend's face, for he too felt an overwhelming fear, a tremor of speechless wonder at what had transpired.

It was Peter who spoke for all of them. Looking tremblingly at the Master he found himself struggling for speech, and he fell to his knees on the mound of sea-silver. "Depart from me!" he cried, tears flowing down his face. "Depart from me, for I am a sinful man, O Lord!"

But Jesus' face was full of compassion as he gazed down on the rugged fisherman and said to all of them, gently, reassuringly, "Fear not. From now on you shall catch men."

And when they had brought their ships to land, they forsook all, and followed him.

Chapter 4

Stars hung like tiny, vivid lanterns in the blackness above the lonely Galilean terrain. Behind him, John could hear the laughing voices of the other disciples as they stayed close to the night fire of the campsite. The young son of Zebedee waited silently alone for the sound of the returning Master.

Since leaving the sea the day of the miraculous draft of fish, Jesus had ministered for a few days in coastal towns and villages, but recently he and his men had been forced to find seclusion from the hounding masses who everywhere sought his touch. The necessity of withdrawing into the wilderness of the province, however, had come only as a last resort after a most frustrating incident.

One recent afternoon, in a small seacoast town, Jesus had been approached by a beseeching leper. This had occurred during a very rare moment when the Master had been free of a crowd. Had it been otherwise, the poor man would not have been able to come anywhere near, as lepers were outcast from any congregation. The man had crept through the city's alleyways unheeded, and had caught the Master as he passed a secluded corner. The disciples had stood well out of the way, looking on bewilderedly when the Lord did not retreat.

The pitiful leper had come in his stinking rags, bowing and scraping before Jesus, his filthy bandaged hands full of festering wounds, outstretched beggar-like. "Jesus of Nazareth," he had called hoarsely, "if you will, you can make me clean! Lord, I know you can make me clean!"

The man had drawn within only a few feet of Jesus, still crying out his misery. But the Master had not stepped away. John had looked on in horror, recalling the day at Jerusalem when he had seen Jesus gazing upon the lepers clustered outside the gate. He had thought then that Jesus looked as if he wished to reach out to them, and he had been relieved when he did not.

But what would he do this day? the young disciple had wondered. Such a look of compassion had etched itself upon the Master's face. Surely he did not mean to converse so closely with this man! Surely he would not . . . touch him!

John cringed even now as he relived the moment Jesus' hand went out in love to that poor, helpless man. Yes—the Master's touch had been granted even a crippled and deformed leper, and what had followed was not, to John, a greater miracle than the incredible love he had seen in that one gesture. The fact that before his eyes John had watched the scars and stinking disease of leprosy fade into nonexistence—the fact that ravaged flesh had given way to skin as fresh as a baby's—none of these realities moved the disciple more than Jesus' unthinkable compassion.

It had seemed strange, when, following this great healing, Jesus had said to the fellow, "See that you say nothing to any man, but go your way, show yourself to the priest, and offer for your cleansing those things which Moses commanded, for a testimony to them." John and the other disciples had looked incredulously at one another. Surely this curing of leprosy had been one of the Master's greatest works. If he were the Messiah, would he not want the news of the event to be heralded far and wide? It would certainly convince even the most ardent skeptics that his claims were true.

But the Lord had been wiser than they. He had foreseen what would happen if such word should get to the masses. The jubilant recipient of the healing had given his promise on the matter, but apparently unable to contain the secret of his marvelous cure, and the joy of the event, he had publicized the story the instant he got the chance. The tale had spread so quickly that all of Galilee fairly buzzed with the affair, and the Lord became so sought after that he could not even enter the city openly again, for his own safety.

Instead he had been forced to remove himself and his disciples into the wilderness of Galilee, where he would spend much time in prayer and meditation. But even now they continued to hound him, and he found himself moving from place to place in the outlands to find peace and quiet.

Thus it was that John sat in the wilderness tonight, awaiting the Master's return. The silence was interrupted only by a chirping cricket somewhere in the distant brush, and the disciple remembered the hours he had spent in a similar posture listening for the footsteps of the Baptist returning from his solitude to the Bethabara cave. So much had happened since the last day John had been with that mighty man. Though he was ever-present in John's heart, the disciple had had little time recently to dwell on what might have become of the great preacher.

He ached now with the thought. Was his old companion quartered in some dank prison under Herod's cruel hand? Surely he must still be alive, for had it been otherwise, the news would have traveled rapidly. John rested somewhat in that assurance. Nevertheless, the realization of what might await a man taken captive by Antipas chilled his soul, and he wrapped his robes close about him.

The Baptist, however, was not his only concern. He was beginning once more to have deep questions about Jesus' teachings. He had learned from the miraculous haul of fish that Jesus could truly lift a man's physical burdens. But the Master had implied, in his roadside lesson the day before, that more than physical help came from God, that through himself a man could stand spiritually righteous in the Father's eyes. Even the

Pharisees, he had indicated, for all their striving, failed the Law. "I am the way to the Father. Come to me and I will give you rest," he had said. But how could a sinful man be accepted by God? How could Jesus accomplish such a thing for any man? John's mind boggled at the thought.

The sight of Jesus coming at last over the ridge above camp relieved John's spirits.

"It is a warm night," the Master called.

"Yes," John nodded.

Jesus took a place next to him, and the two sat in silence until the Lord said, "It seems your custom always to be waiting for me, apart from the others."

"I guess I like to think alone sometimes."

"And what are your thoughts tonight?"

John straightened his back and reflected. "They concern many things. Just now I was wondering about the Baptist . . . Sir, what do you think has become of him? Did you send me to be with him in Samaria because you knew it would be . . . because there would be no more opportunity after that?"

Jesus knew the heart of John's question: would the Baptist survive Herod's intentions?

"You love him greatly, don't you?"

"Yes."

"He is in my Father's hands," Jesus replied. "He is sheltered with God's protection. Do you believe this?"

"Sir, I believe God protects his servants."

"There is hesitation in your voice."

John could not disguise his fears. "You know the reputation of the Herods."

Jesus looked across the desert horizon, and the disciple thought he could make out the glimmer of tears in the Master's eyes. Was it sorrow for the Baptist that provoked them?

"Master, how well did you know the preacher?" he inquired.

Jesus continued to gaze far into the distance. "We met for the first time at my baptism," came the answer. "But, he is my cousin."

"Your cousin?" John stammered.

Jesus turned slowly to him. "He is the son of Elisabeth, my mother's relative."

John had no words for his surprise. "Why, sir! He never said a word about this."

"If he had, would you have accepted his testimony of me so easily?"

John thought. "Perhaps not, sir."

"There is probably much he did not tell you about himself. There are many strange things concerning his birth and mine—things which my mother has told me. Perhaps one day you will learn of them."

John's ears burned to hear these things, but he sensed it was not the time to question. Instead he only shook his head in amazed contemplation. "Then, sir, your love for the Baptist must be as great as mine."

Jesus smiled compassionately. Drawing near to his disciple, he placed an arm around his shoulders, and held him close. John felt himself enveloped in the warmth of the Master's love, full of security and contentment. It seemed more true all the time that Jesus had singled him out for a special kind of friendship, for a closeness none of the others had been afforded. He had once denied such an idea, thinking it too unlikely, even impossible. But with the growing evidence had come a tremendous sense of his own unworthiness.

"My Lord," he confessed, calluses of pride falling away from his heart, "I have so many questions. I have hidden them for days, trying in myself to find the answers!"

"I know," Jesus said gently.

John felt relief in the confession. "You *know*, Master?"

Jesus nodded.

The disciple sighed, and rested his head upon his knees. "For days Peter's words to you have pounded in my ears. 'Depart from me, for I am a sinful man.' "

The Nazarene waited quietly for John to explain.

"He spoke for me, as well as for himself, Master. I have never felt more unworthy of anyone's love than I feel of yours. Oh, Lord . . . I am a sinful man—full of so many wrong ways." This was hard for John to admit, almost as hard as turning to Jesus in the first place. But his heart swelled with the acknowledgment, for he had never put in words the extent of his own shortcomings. "Master," he went on, "you know my nature. I feel that somehow you know me better than anyone ever has, that you have read my soul more deeply than it has ever been read."

Jesus was only silent in affirmation.

"And," John continued, gaining courage with each syllable, "you know my bigotry, my tendency to rebellion and anger, my stubborn pride. I believe that somehow when I trusted you, you made me right with the Father. You told Nicodemus that belief in you gives eternal life. But how can such things be? How is it that I am right with God? How can he say I am righteous when I am not, when he knows I am full of evil and wrong ways? What has he done with my sins? Has he swept them under a rug? Has he winked at them? Does he say arbitrarily, 'This fellow is now clean'? Why, even Jehovah would be unjust to do that!" He sighed wearily. "Oh, I don't know! Perhaps these are stupid questions. Perhaps they make no difference."

But they did make a difference. They were the questions which kept human beings awake at night, questions concerning man's purpose, his destiny, his relationship with the universe. Perhaps they were worded differently in every man's mind, but, ultimately, they were the same. "Why am I here? How can I be all I want to be? What do I do with my failures?"

Jesus stood to his feet and paced the brow of the ridge. "John, do you remember the leper who came to be healed the other day?" he asked.

"Yes, Master . . . "

The Lord studied his friend's face for a long time. "Do you remember what he called out as he approached?"

John reflected. "I believe he said, 'Lord, I know you can make me clean.' "

Jesus waited for the truth to dawn upon his disciple. "All men are leprous, John. Full of the disease of sin. If a righteous God can touch and cleanse the stench of leprosy, can he not cleanse the filth of the soul as well?"

John felt a surge of joy and hope well within him, but just as quickly, intellectual doubts rose to suppress it. "But how, Master?"

"With him all things are possible, John. Believe, and you shall see the salvation of God."

Chapter 5

For an autumn day it was very warm outside, and on this crowded gallery it was suffocatingly hot. Jesus had only a few hours ago returned to the port city of Capernaum, and was lodged once again at Peter's home. Within moments of his arrival, the news that he was in the house had been heralded throughout the town, and virtually everyone in the city had come to seek him out.

John stood beside the Master with the other disciples, attempting to keep some order to the gathering, so that the Lord might be heard. Pushed and shoved from all sides by sticky, perspiring bodies, John found himself wishing for just one breath of fresh air, but he had to keep his mind to the task at hand. Latecomers were still vying for a passage into the already over-packed courtyard and entryway below and a great crowd stood in the streets outside the house, straining to catch the words of the Master.

When he was done speaking, as always, the masses began bringing their sick and infirm to him for the miracle of his touch. To this point there had been nothing unusual about the afternoon, except that numerous Pharisees and doctors of the law had come from every town in Galilee and Judea, even from Jerusalem, to witness what might transpire. John and the others had been most wary of this upon first seeing their arrival, and all the Lord's followers kept a careful watch on them, knowing they could mean no good for the Master.

Perhaps because he was the owner of the house, Peter was the first to notice something strange occurring in the ceiling above the gallery where the Lord stood addressing the people. Surely no one else would have been concerned with a few flakes of plaster and dust; Palestinian roofs needed repair from time to time. But Peter sensed there was more to this. He nudged John, but the young Jew only shook his head quizzically, seeing no reason for great concern.

When the flaw in the ceiling began to widen, however, John's eyes grew large and round, and Peter fidgeted uneasily. Now those gathered under the aperture joined in his apprehension. When they found that there were more than a few flakes of loose plaster floating down from above, that they were in fact brushing large chips from their heads and shoulders, a noisy shuffle of feet and voices ensued. Above the preaching of the Master and the murmur of bystanders could now be discerned a scraping and clawing sound overhead. Meanwhile, a wide aisle was being formed on the gallery as those beneath the descending debris pushed their way back, and the attention of the house was drawn to the curious hole.

Peter forced his way through the crowd to get a better look at his ceiling. Though it was obviously not the roof which was at fault, but some intruders, he was nonetheless embarrassed that such a thing should be happening at such a time, and on his premises. Angrily he glared at the opening, feeling helpless to do anything, and frustrated that he did not understand what he witnessed. Yes—someone, or something, was breaking through, removing the heavy, resonant tiles and chipping away at the rolled earth, gravel, and mortar.

Eventually sunlight pierced the opening, filtering through the dust and blinding Peter's vision. By now the crowd was laughing. "Who goes there?" the big fisherman bellowed, lifting an ominous fist to the hole.

The Master stepped up to him and persuaded him to stand aside. "It is all right, Peter," he whispered.

John had made his way to his friend's side, and had caught the Lord's words, but was just as baffled as Simon. Incredibly, the hole continued to grow. Several pairs of masculine hands were working from above, ripping and tearing at the rim of the aperture.

And now, to the amazement of all, something was being lowered through that hole. It was a cot, a stretcher, suspended by ropes, and upon it lay a sick man!

The bed was lowered all the way to the floor of the gallery, right in front of the Master, and the invalid looked up at him with wide eyes. The crowd murmured, fascinated. John studied the feeble man on the stretcher, and determined that he must be stricken with the palsy. He appeared to be paralyzed in several parts of his body so that he was full of uncontrolled tremors and unable to sit, stand, or walk. There he lay, helpless, spastic, without speech. John's heart ached for him.

Above, there now appeared four faces, those of the friends who had brought the poor man to the Lord. Peter stared up at them silently, his anger quelled by sympathetic insight. What other access had been open to them in this crowd, but the rooftop?

Jesus gazed compassionately on the man before him, then, turned to those men who peered down from the roof, and for a long moment studied their expressions. Apparently their devotion to their friend, and their obvious faith that the Master could heal him, impressed the Lord greatly. For, it was only after considering their faces that he returned to the palsied fellow.

The paralytic was young, and his contorted features betrayed fear of the circumstances in which he found himself. Perhaps it had been against his will that he had been brought here. Perhaps he had had no will at all in the matter. But Jesus seemed to sympathize with his feelings, for he reached out to him and said in his gentle way, "Son, be of good cheer. Your sins be forgiven you."

The Master's words caused a great stir throughout the crowd. Even John and Peter were bewildered. What could Jesus mean, "Your sins be forgiven you"? No one had power to forgive sins but God himself! And why did he even broach such a subject, when the man had been brought for a healing?

The most violent reaction to the Lord's statement, however, came from the scribes and Pharisees in the courtyard below. John cast a wary glance their way and found them staring wildly up at Jesus, whispering among themselves in bitter tones. Hadn't the Master realized they were here? the disciple wondered. Why wasn't he more careful of himself?

Jesus turned from the sick man and looked at the accusers. Seeming to read their very thoughts, that they were calling him a blasphemer, he answered from the gallery, "Why are you thinking such things in your hearts? Is it easier to say, 'Your sins be forgiven you,' or to say, 'Arise and take up your bed, and walk' ? "

He had now approached the railing and confronted the scribes and Pharisees in direct challenge, his countenance stormy with indignation, as on the day he had driven the moneychangers from the Temple. His voice, low but ominous, allowed them no time for rebuttal. "But that you may know that the Son of Man has power on earth to forgive sins . . . " he said, and then gestured to the palsied man. "I say unto you, arise! And take up your bed, and go your way into your house!"

And immediately he arose, took up the bed, and went forth before them all. And they were all amazed, and glorified God, saying, "We never saw it on this fashion!"

Chapter 6

Jesus' commentary on the disease of sin had been dramatically reinforced the day he had healed the paralytic. He had taken the opportunity of that incident to illustrate the point he had made when speaking to John in the desert only a few evenings before. Yes—man was sick, if not physically, always spiritually. And who was to say God could not cleanse the soul as well as the body?

Indeed, the concept was not foreign to Jewish doctrine. The Scriptures, especially the songs of King David, were heavy with references to divine mercy and forgiveness. And if Jesus claimed to be the Son of God, it naturally followed he would claim for himself the same powers that the Almighty held. If Jehovah could forgive sin, so could the Master. The "hows" of the issue still eluded John. For a mere mortal to pass over another's transgression was understandable, for he would recognize his own imperfections. But for a perfect God to dismiss sin—it seemed somehow unjust. Should not a righteous Deity punish evil—not simply disregard it?

It was the construction of John's soul to investigate, to never rest until he had found the solution to a mystery. For the present, however, he would find no clear-cut answers. He would have to take on faith something very elusive, just as the men of Scripture had done since the days of the patriarchs.

Jesus would not be free of a crowd the rest of that afternoon. Leaving Peter's house, he and his disciples directed their steps to the city gates. There would be more room and a cooler environment at the sea.

To pass this way necessitated that they go by the custom seat, where the tax collectors scrutinized all traffic. And today, Matthew Bar Alpheus was again in charge, the despised young Jew who had done so well for himself as a publican deputy.

The very sight of him repulsed John. He represented the acid hand of Caesar more profoundly than could any native Roman, for he was a traitor to his own kinsmen. The disciple's hate for Matthew and his kind was unbounded, and he felt no remorse for it. It was an acceptable hatred, he thought, a righteous hatred.

The Master was not able to move quickly past this station, for the crowd which surrounded him was immense. At first John had only to bear with a glimpse of the haughty revenuer, but when movement through the gates was delayed, he found himself detained just short of the receipt bench.

He could sense Matthew's penetrating and prideful gaze. Glancing as casually as possible in his direction, John determined that the publican's distaste for him was just as great as that which he himself harbored. "Well," John thought, "he can go his way and I shall go mine."

But it seemed the crowd was ridiculously sluggish. "Why aren't we moving faster?" he asked James.

"It appears the Master has stopped."

"Stopped? But why? Why here of all places?" John's hands fidgeted nervously with his robe.

"See for yourself," was James' only answer. Indeed, Jesus was not proceeding. He was, in fact, directly in front of the tax seat, where he stood looking up at the young publican.

Revulsion shot through John. But before he could react, Matthew had been caught by the Master's loving gaze.

No! John rebelled internally. Not a traitor like Matthew! Lord, I have learned to bear with your acceptance of the Samaritans—even of a Samaritan whore. I have stood by silently while you touched a leper! But Master, not a publican! I can never accept a publican!

Still, it was happening. Jesus' countenance reflected the same compassion at which John had marveled again and again, and this time for such scum as Matthew!

Undoubtedly the publican knew who the Rabbi was, and he eyed him with disdain. But his cold, stony facade seemed to weaken as he studied the face of Jesus. John never would have believed what was transpiring had he not witnessed it firsthand. The hard exterior of the hated Bar Alpheus was cracking under the Master's look of love, and his expression was growing soft, almost warm.

John shrank from the reality. Was there no one Jesus could not love?

"I cannot tolerate this!" he told himself, the venom of loathing flooding him.

But he had no hand in the matter. The Lord was calling out to Matthew the same words with which he had enlisted John, James, Peter, and Andrew.

"Follow me," came the gentle, compelling command.

John watched breathlessly as the publican in his fine red robes turned from the money table, stepped down from the customs house, and followed after Jesus.

Chapter 7

The mountain above the little town of Tabigha was gently swept by fingers of wind descending to the sea. Though it was midnight, the waters below could be seen clearly, rippling under the moonlit sky, and Capernaum's lights could be distinguished, though they were a mile up the shore.

John had been asleep a good while, but stirred now restlessly, wondering how much longer the Master would be away. Jesus had asked to be alone so he might pray, and had retreated some distance up the hillside, seeking a measure of seclusion.

The disciples had been asked to keep guard over his privacy. They were positioned at intervals along the hill's flank, alternating the watch against the intruding masses who now followed Jesus days at a time, even camping overnight wherever he might rest.

Sounds of the day still rang in John's ears, and dreams of recent events had wakened him before his turn as sentinel. Below on the hill sat Matthew, keeping the guard. The disciple was convinced he would never grow used to the idea of a publican following his Lord. John had avoided the revenuer ever since he had joined the group, and he turned his eyes from him now, trying to put him from his mind.

Of late, the throngs had become so immense that they nearly drove the disciple to distraction. Multitudes came from all parts of Galilee, from Decapolis, Jerusalem, Judea, Syria, Idumea, and notorious cities of the Mediterranean, like Tyre and Sidon.

Their tramping, their pleas, cries of misery from the sick, and elation from the suddenly healed—all this John could yet hear. Even the shrieks of demons haunted him, spirit beings within the possessed, screaming, "Jesus—you are the Son of God!"

A great part of the disciples' daily concern now lay with the

Master's well-being. When Jesus was near the sea, they kept a boat ready at his request, lest the crowds press in on him too closely.

And even the Lord himself took precautions, repeatedly admonishing those who had been healed, especially those who had been delivered of demons, to keep silent about it.

Still the multitudes grew, and he had collected quite a sizable following of men, and even of women, who had left homes and occupations to devote themselves to him, though he had not singled them out.

The clamor of each day badgered John. There were times when he felt lost in the shuffle. But, in a way, he was grateful for his recent anonymity, grateful that the Lord had less time for him. For his inner peace was disturbed by more than the noisy throngs. Awareness of his own shortcomings and unworthiness had escalated since the calling of Matthew. At that moment, more pointedly than ever, the gulf of difference between himself and Jesus had been illustrated.

He had tried in vain to feel as the Master felt. Still, he loathed Matthew, he hated Rome, he despised the Samaritans. Though, in his youthful rebellions, he had read and admired the Greek philosophers, he had done so, many times, merely to spite Zebedee. In truth, he had no great love for the Gentiles, and retained a hot Jewish pride.

But even certain Jews were anathema to him. Having eliminated the poor, the greatly diseased, the very wealthy, the uneducated, the Pharisees, the Sadducees, the Herodians—any who did not suit him—John had defined his world, he suddenly realized, very narrowly.

He sneered at the irony of it all. Indeed he was no better off than the Pharisees with their stringent code. In his own way he had been just as self-righteous, just as insufferable as they. He could almost understand why they reacted so bitterly against the Master. Though it was not his purpose to do so, Jesus shamed them. He shamed them with his very way of life, for he was so good, so unquestionably right.

But while the Pharisees turned their shame into hatred for the Nazarene, John turned his inward. And he found himself shrinking further each day from the exposing power of the Master's love.

John laughed miserably, closed his eyes, and rested his head on his updrawn knees. "Yes, I hate even myself," he whispered. "Myself—most of all . . ."

John's self-recriminations were temporarily interrupted by a tap on the shoulder. Looking up he found Matthew. The publican had no more use for John, than John for him, and his voice betrayed as much. "Your turn," he said sharply.

The disciple glared coldly at the hand which had dared to touch him, and drew his shoulder back with disgust. Saying not a word, he rose to his feet and took the guard position down the hill.

As soon as he was seated, the realization of what he had just done, the realization of yet another failure set in upon him. John Bar Zebedee—destined to follow the Messiah? What use could he possibly be to a good and gentle man like Jesus?

A strong wind swept suddenly toward the sea and down the brow of the hill on which he rested. With it returned the words of the Baptist echoing his own thoughts: "You respond with the fire of lightning, John. Your soul roars with thunder at the least provocation."

Chapter 8

It was still John's watch when the sun arose and dawn stretched across the lazy sea. A soft footfall startled him and he turned to find the Master heading his way.

The other disciples were asleep, and Jesus did not waken them, but came directly to John. The young disciple attempted a smile, and tried to put from him the disconsolate thoughts which had hounded him through the night. "Good morning, Master," he called.

"Good morning, John. I have a favor to ask of you." The Lord's voice was decisive, as that of a man who had spent many hours in the formulation of some great plan, and who was eager to see it carried out.

"Yes, sir," John answered, jumping to his feet.

The Master wasted no time in explaining, and said simply, "I want you to gather up all the men who have been following me steadfastly the past few weeks."

John knew he referred to those who had joined Jesus, apparently determined to make him their Teacher. "I will, sir," he replied.

"Bring them, along with Peter and the others, to the top of the mountain."

John was indeed curious as to the Master's reason for this, but he asked no questions. It took the better part of an hour for him to locate and call all of those the Lord wanted. Word was passed from mouth to mouth, and finally a large gathering was assembled on the ridge of the hill, including men from every district and background in the region of Israel and beyond.

John joined the other disciples near the head of the throng, and waited with James to hear whatever the Master might present. At last Jesus stepped before the select crowd, and they fell silent, a tremor of excitement evident in their breathlessness.

"My friends," Jesus began, "I have been in prayer all night for my work. The ministry has become a great one, and its burden is also great."

Men here and there nodded appreciatively, realizing that the pressures had been tremendous for the Rabbi. "I have decided to portion out the task at hand, as the Lord instructed Moses when the burden of leading this nation became so great. I will choose from among you twelve men to be closest to me, and I will ordain them to preach the gospel of the kingdom, to heal the sick and cast out devils." His eyes now scanned the congregation, and he said, "These shall be my apostles."

The crowd marveled. Heal the sick? Cast out demons? Could anyone but Jesus have such power? When they saw that the Master was sincere, many wondered if they might be among the ones to be chosen. They wondered what credentials the Lord might consider important. Certainly any who had the background of a rabbi would be among them, they reasoned. And the well educated, the well known. True, he had called fishermen, even a small-town schoolmaster and a tax collector, as disciples; but surely, for these special positions, he would be more selective.

As for John's thoughts, he held little hope of the Master's consideration. He knew that he was not worthy. He had been privileged with the Nazarene's confidences on occasion, but he had not even merited that much.

Jesus was now surveying the multitude. In his introspection, John barely heard the names he called. He did recognize, to his delight, that his friend Simon Peter had been chosen. And to the surprise of the skeptics in the gathering, Jesus did single out other close followers, despite their dubious credentials. "Andrew," he called gently, "Philip, Nathanael, Matthew . . ."

The last name burned in John's ears. One by one the loyal followers stepped to his side, each greatly humbled by the awesome responsibility he had been given.

There were others less familiar to John, though he had been aware of their presence in the masses the past few weeks: Thomas called Didymus; James, Matthew's brother; Lebbeus called Thaddeus; Simon, a Canaanite Zealot; and a very handsome young man by the name of Judas Iscariot.

John stood silently in the midst of the great crowd, staring at the ground, and wishing that all of this might be over soon. He did not know how many the Lord had called. He had not kept count. His body and mind seemed detached from one another, and emptiness filled him such as he had never known.

He wished to turn and run, to be gone from the Nazarene entirely. He, who had been closest to the Master, could not bear the thought that others would share a keener communion with Jesus than he would be afforded. Though in his self-hatred he had been grateful for recent separation from the Lord, permanent loss of direct access pained him to the quick.

Only the day he had been forced to leave the Baptist at Bethabara had he felt such loneliness, and even that did not compare to this.

Still, the assurance that he was not worthy seared him like a refiner's fire. Scenes from his childhood, the explosive confrontations with Zebedee, leaped before his eyes. "Curse you, John . . ." he maligned himself. "When were you *ever* worthy?"

Without being fully aware of it, he was turning to leave, his head down, his shoulders stooped. But then, he heard the voice of the Nazarene. "James . . ." he was saying.

John wheeled about quickly. Had Jesus singled out his brother?

James was incredulous, and John, in a momentary flash of selflessness, wondered if he might also feel unworthy. But his brother had nothing of which to be ashamed, John reasoned.

As the red-haired fisherman stepped up to join the other apostles, the younger son of Zebedee watched longingly, but was determined not to linger.

Just as he began to depart, however, one last name was voiced. "John!" it rang like a bell. The disciple stopped dead in his tracks. "Do you mean to leave me?" Jesus was calling.

John slowly turned to face him, loneliness and sadness in his eyes. The Lord drew near through the crowd, and beheld him tenderly. "My impetuous, stormy young friend," Jesus whispered. "Did you think I could not use you?"

John looked away silently.

"Truly, you are a son of thunder," the Master said. "But let me harness that energy, John. Let me make you an Apostle of Peace."

Chapter 9

John stayed very close to his Master for several days, fearful that any distance between them might wake him from the dream of the Lord's promise. If John's fiery spirit were to change, let no time be wasted. If John were to be a new creature, let it happen now!

The eagerness with which he clung to Jesus was a sight to behold. More than a year he had been with the Master, yet he had not taken in so much teaching as in the days immediately following his call of apostleship.

That very afternoon the Master had spent several hours intensively training his chosen followers. John had drunk in his mountain sermon in great gulps, hungry for all the instruction he could receive. The soft sky of Galilee was a calm field of sea-blue as Jesus had spoken, and the breeze had carried his words, messages from God himself, directly into John's heart.

"You have heard it said, 'You shall love your neighbor and hate your enemy,' " he called. "But I say to you, love your enemies, bless those that curse you, do good to those that hate you, and pray for those who despitefully use you, and persecute you. For if you love those who love you, what is your reward? Do not even the publicans do this? And if you salute your brothers only, what more are you doing than others? Do not even the publicans do this? Be, therefore, perfect, just as your Father, who is in heaven, is perfect."

As the words had continued, John had thirsted for such inward qualities. Later that afternoon when the sun had begun to set in a purple haze, Jesus had insisted ". . . if you forgive men their trespasses, your heavenly Father will also forgive you. But if you do not forgive, neither will your Father forgive your trespasses.

Judge not," he had said, "so that you will not be judged. For with
the judgment that you judge, you will be judged. Why do you
consider the sliver which is in your brother's eye, but not the beam
which is in your own eye? And how can you correct your brother
when you are more at fault? Hypocrite! First cast out the beam
from your own eye, and then you will see clearly to cast the sliver
out of your brother's eye. Therefore, all things that you would
have men do to you, do the same to them. For this is the law and
the prophets."

Never had such words been spoken, or with such authority.
John had felt that the Master spoke to him alone, so intensely did
the message burn his soul.

But he would not wallow again in his own mire of failures. When
the sermon was ended, John resolved that he would be all the
Master wanted.

"I *will* be your servant," he told himself. "I *will* change. You
will see. I will be a *different* man!"

At first, the Master's words on the mount had charged John with
zeal and determination. But as the days passed, and as Jesus'
ministry brought yet other questionable characters across his path,
John found himself just as incapable of keeping the Lord's ways as
ever he had been.

When Jesus had finished teaching the multitudes for the day, he
retired to Peter's house and his apostles sat with him discussing the
meanings of the parables he had spoken. John drew especially
close to him, and waited for the others to complete their
discussion. Despite the fact that Peter and James would overhear,
he could no longer refrain from asking his questions.

"Master," he began, "I have fears."

Jesus looked at him quietly. "And what are your fears, John?"

"You remember the parable of the soils, which you spoke by the
sea? How the farmer scattered his seed, but some fell on the
wayside and was eaten by birds, and some fell on shallow ground
and sprung up quickly, but withered without root?"

"Yes, John. And some was choked by weeds, and some fell on
good ground and was fruitful,'" Jesus answered patiently.

"Well, sir, I have fears that . . ." John paused and looked
hesitantly at Peter and James, who were leaning forward in
curiosity.

"That what, John?" Jesus encouraged him.

". . . that I am like the shallow ground or that I am full of weeds." His voice cracked. "Master, I love your words, but they seem not to grow in me. I must be bad soil, for I do not bring forth the fruit of peace which you said I should."

Jesus smiled with understanding. "Son, have you, in all this time, failed to see what I have been trying to teach you? Did I not tell you to but ask, and it would be given you? To knock and the door would be opened to you? If no man can keep the Law of Moses, how shall he keep the law of the Spirit in his own strength? It is not the seed alone, nor the soil alone which is of consequence. It is the Master who must bring them together and tend to their husbandry. The part of the soil is to yield to the Master's plow."

Chapter 10

It was evening once again on the Sea of Galilee. Jesus had asked the disciples to take him to the far side of the lake and was now asleep in the stern of the ship. The steady slap, slap, slap of Peter's oars and the night breeze which ruffled the canvas sails should have had John asleep as well. But a storm was raging in the young disciple's heart.

Had he understood correctly? Did he simply have to yield? He looked across the waters to the distant fields toward which they journeyed, and thought of the many times he had seen native farmers work their soil. The shallow layers had to be built up, given more depth, the soil full of weeds and tares cleaned of impediments, and even the best of earth filled with nutrients to make it richer.

The lesson was becoming clear, but was still hard to accept. Jesus, who could heal diseases, and who claimed the power to forgive sins, was now also claiming the most impossible of all things, John reasoned: mastery over the design and character of the human heart. Only one condition was required of the man wanting to change:

"The part of the soil is to yield . . . to yield . . . to yield," the words returned.

"If only I could believe," John whispered, looking at the door to the hold where Jesus lay. "Such power seems impossible . . . even for you, my Lord."

But now something drew his attention to the horizon. The twilight could deceive even experienced eyes like his, but he was certain he saw thunderclouds gathering behind their backs.

Turning to Peter he found that he, too, had noted them and the great fisherman's brow was knit with concern.

"It doesn't look good, John," he said.

Theirs was not the only boat nearby. Many of Jesus' followers and all his apostles were divided among a fleet of vessels. What would happen if a storm were to come up when so many of the men were totally inexperienced in the ways of the sea?

As the clouds grew in density and moved in their direction, so did anxiety grow in the hearts of the fishermen. Quickly they began the task of lowering the riggings and rolling down the swollen sheets of their little schooner, and the rest of the fleet followed suit.

James and Andrew crept forward. "We're in for a bad one," James said in low tones, not wanting to frighten the passengers, Philip and Nathanael.

"I fear so," added Andrew.

Peter's dark eyes betrayed mounting apprehension. "Is the Master still asleep?"

"Yes," said John.

"He won't be for long. There's a real squall brewing."

Peter's rugged arms had at last grown tired, and John took control at the oars.

The wind was becoming colder and more forceful. Whitecaps could be seen forming on the water miles away, and as they spread, the sea heaved in humps of gray and green.

John rowed with all his might and called for help. Each disciple in the ship took up oars, even the two who had never before manned a boat.

"Ho!" James called in a rhythmic chant. "Ho! Ho!" and the tempo of rowing increased with his commanding cadence.

They must go faster, faster. The storm approached with uncanny speed. Could it be that the Master remained asleep? Was he so weary that even a Galilean gale could not waken him?

Suddenly great swells of dark water surrounded the boat, lifting it and casting menacing fingers toward the sides. Any moment the waves would enter the ship itself.

The boat's bow was rocketed upward, and John was thrown back, the oars ripped ruthlessly from his sturdy grip. As the ship plummeted down again, the waves came, frigid, bone-chilling, swirling and cascading over the bow. And Peter cried aloud with the wrenching of the helpless vessel.

The little ship was now thrust like a cork from wave to wave, coming very close to striking broadside against another boat. John looked above fearfully. The sky loomed copper and gray, gigantic thunderclouds mixing with the moody shades of sunset.

"God, help us!" bellowed Peter. Splintering lightning had struck a nearby vessel, the one carrying Matthew and Thomas. Cries of calamity filled the howling air as the men of that crew fell back from their fire-struck mast. Rain left only a small cloud of steam at the target, but the men's fear would not evaporate so easily.

"Lord!" cried John. "Can he still be asleep, Peter? Waken him!"

It seemed impossible. No man could sleep through such a storm, tossed about in the hold as surely he must be.

John had long ago given up seeking the oars. There was nothing to do but hold onto the ship's sides for dear life. He was cast to the floor again, his neck aching from the perpetual up and down movement of the galloping sea. If the storm did not abate they would all be lost!

Peter had apparently not heard John's plea that he waken the Nazarene, John thought. Still, as yet other icy waves deluged them, covering the ship, and as the boat filled with the overwhelming sea, the young apostle could think of nothing but his Master's name. "Jesus!" he cried. The sound was a comfort. "Jesus!" And now he found himself faltering his way to the Master's side.

The door to the compartment in which the Lord tarried had come unbolted, and slammed back and forth with the ruthless wind. The disciple inched his way toward it, more than once being thrust backward just as he came to the entry.

When he did finally attain it he peered helplessly inside, restraining the flashing door. Incredible as it seemed, the dim light of the hold revealed a sleeping man, seemingly immune to the ravages above.

"Lord!" John cried. "Save us, or we die!"

By now, Peter had also crept to the hold, along with the others. "Master," he shouted into the doorway, "do you not care that we perish?" And cries of "Lord, save us! We perish!" "Master, Master, we perish!" challenged the howling wind.

Strangely, though he had slept through ear-shattering storm and drumming waves, the Master woke to the voices of his men. Stirring from the pillows which lined the compartment, he looked through the opening, peering out at the sky, and quickly assayed the situation.

Then his compassionate eyes surveyed the helpless cargo before him, six terrified Galileans, at the mercy of a relentless sea. But his countenance bore a mark of disappointment, a cast which John had no strength to analyze.

"Master, Master!" James called, gripping the bowing sides, "save us!"

What they expected him to do, they did not know. Still John felt, as did the rest, that if there were any hope, it lay with Jesus, or nowhere at all.

But there was little nobility in this. Theirs were cries of desperation, more than of belief. And strangely, this, and not the storm, must have been Jesus' concern. For in his gentle but penetrating way he said just loudly enough to be heard above the wind, "Why are you fearful, oh you of little faith?"

The rebuke stung the young apostle, and tremblingly he watched the Lord as he arose and stepped from the hold onto the deck with them. John could not take his eyes from him, though it required all his stamina to manage one position, and though his hands were ripped repeatedly from their hold.

For a brief moment the Master looked above, the sea-spray lashing at his hair and robes, and then he shut his eyes, as if in meditation.

Once again, he opened his eyes and gazed at the sea. Taking one hand away from the door and stretching it over the waters and into the wind, he inhaled deeply. Three short words followed, the most beautiful John had ever heard, as Jesus directly, personally rebuked the howling gale and blustering waves.

"Peace, be still."

Suddenly there was nothing—nothing but the most tangible of stillnesses. There was not even a gradual departing of the wind. It simply ceased, as if it had never existed. And the sea was as flat as a newly minted coin.

Clouds still hung above, but they appeared suspended by invisible strings, like gray cotton, and just as harmless. Had John not had the voiceless but awestruck witness of a hundred friends and onlookers in the ships nearby, he would have questioned his own ears and eyes.

But more incredible yet was the quality of the silence. It was unnatural, a peace beyond description. More than soundlessness: it was calm.

John gazed at the Master and found him studying his men once more. Sorrow still marked his face, as when he had responded to their voices. Though moments intervened before that look again found audible expression, John felt the source of his Lord's disappointment keenly. Yes—his men had called to him in their time of need, but their cries had been virtually vacant and faithless.

The lesson must be driven home *now*, at this moment of soul-searching quiet. Again came the words, not fully grasped when spoken in the howl of the storm:

"Why are you so fearful? How is it that you have no faith? Where is your faith?"

John looked away, overwhelmed by awe and unable to face the Nazarene. "How indeed?" he trembled, surveying the water and sky. "What manner of man is this, that even the winds and sea obey him?"

Chapter 11

The banquet hall of Matthew Bar Alpheus' house was a riot of lights and finery. As John stood on the threshold, somewhat hidden behind the Master, he shuffled awkwardly, attempting to disguise his uneasiness.

He had dreaded this evening ever since a week before when the ex-publican had invited the twelve to dine. "A reception in your honor," he had told Jesus. But who besides the Lord's disciples would join Matthew's feast? The only other friends he could claim were of his old profession.

"A houseful of the heathen!" John muttered, as he glimpsed the roomful of guests. But as soon as the thought voiced itself it was followed by a dagger of guilt, and then by fresh affirmation. He would not fail again! He was determined to let his weaknesses rest in Jesus' hands. He had not discussed this with the Master. He had felt no need to. If Jesus were indeed the Son of God, he need not be told verbally of John's needs.

Still, the disciple was new enough to the idea of full surrender to take great security in the Lord's bodily presence.

"Master . . ." he whispered.

"I am here," Jesus returned.

In that instant the apostle knew the Teacher understood. He knew the Lord had control.

The next hour unfolded events John never could have imagined experiencing. He found himself, the son of an orthodox purist, being led into a hall teeming with sinners. He felt himself sitting in the midst of Roman dogs. He heard their voices, was jostled and surrounded by them. He found himself conversing with them. And ultimately, as the food was set before him, he found himself participating in a hitherto anathema activity—he was eating with publicans!

The hours passed almost without his realizing it, and he nearly forgot the stigma of his surroundings.

Only one incident made itself of special note. And it served to drive home the privilege he had in being here. A group of Pharisees had dared to enter the hall, to spy on the Master's activities. "How can he eat with such as these?" they questioned. The Lord was not ruffled by their criticism, but answered with uncanny wisdom, "They that are well do not need a physician, but they that are sick. For I am not come to call the righteous, but sinners to repentance." With that, the stamp of God's purpose was on the evening.

But it was not until night verged on morning that the apostle realized God's purpose in his own life. This had been an enjoyable feast. No bolt from the sky had struck him for consorting with outcasts. His tongue had not grown leprous for speaking with sinners. He had in fact found them to be quite like him-self—human, and full of great, great needs.

As he once more evaluated the scene before him, a hand reached over his shoulder, bearing a plate of wine and fruit. Taking from it graciously, he turned with a smile to thank the gift-bearer. What met his eyes at first unsettled him and then filled him with wonder. It was Matthew.

The two apostles studied one another hesitantly. Apparently the same Spirit had been at work in them both, for, softened, mellowed with the refining fire of God's love, the two men found tears difficult to suppress.

"Thank you . . . friend," John managed.

And now, spontaneously, they reached for one another, embracing with the love of brothers.

As they did so, John caught a glimpse of the Master, and his heart rejoiced at the memory of Jesus' reassuring words. "Yes, my Lord, you *are* here."

Chapter 12

John the Baptist, the mighty prophet of Israel, strained his vision toward the last rays of sunset which leaked through the solitary aperture in his dungeon wall. He then turned with a dark, furrowed brow to the stone slab upon which he would sit out the night.

This marking of the day's end had become a ritual with him, one of only three contacts he had been afforded with the outside world. The other two—a daily bowl of gruel thrust between his bars, and a weekly message to and from his disciples, were the only human contacts.

He drew his knees up and stared into the twilight darkness. As it did so often, his mind wandered back to the months at the Jordan when young John had been with him. The happiest time of his life, that had been. Now here he sat, a shadow of his former self.

A whistle of hot desert wind shot through the dungeon's high slit of a window. Only with great difficulty had the Baptist ever been able to inch his way up the precarious juttings of the wall to gain a glimpse of the world outside. The few times he had done this had tired him of the view quickly.

Machaerus, the mighty castle-fortress in which he was imprisoned, was located within a deep rift east of the Salt Sea. Access to the remote Perean station, provided by a narrow, guarded roadway, cut through terrain as desolate and geography as forbidding as any in Palestine.

The Baptist need not look outside his fortress to imagine the sea as it changed from coral red with sunset, to black and silver beneath the rising moon. Under other circumstances such a scene might have been considered beautiful. But the desert canyon, though brilliantly colored by day, became shadowed at night, and at all times was vacant of life, as though God had forgotten it.

"Fitting," the Baptist often thought, "for I, too, am forgotten."

Only one memory ever relieved his distress: the thought of John the disciple. But even it pained him at times. Did the son of Zebedee remember his old master? In his new life with Jesus of Nazareth, was he ever inclined to think on the Baptist? To the mighty prophet, confined these long months without solace within walls of stone, it seemed the world had written him off—the world which had once sought him out, often trekking through barren reaches to hear his voice.

Now he was alone—more alone than he ever had been during fifteen years' solitude. Now his voice was silent, useless and unnecessary. Then he had had a purpose, a goal, a future toward which to work. Now it seemed, as he sat at the mercy of his own mind, that all those years had been a cruel joke—all his great expectations a hollow dream.

That a once-great herald of truth could have fallen into such a pit of hopelessness would have been a tragic sight to behold. But none beheld it. No one knew his torment, for it was endured behind impenetrable walls, within a cold fort, beyond reach of loving hands.

Even God was distant. If there was a God.

The prophet leaned his head against his rocky pillow and closed his eyes. The miracles of Bethabara were very far away now—from another lifetime, and so intangible, he often doubted their reality.

"Are you the one?" he asked the cold blackness. "Jesus of Nazareth, are you the one I said you were? Why do you not act? Why do you not establish yourself and justice?" His throat was tight with longing. "Is there a Jehovah—is there a Messiah?" he cried. And peering up at the narrow window, he felt like the last man on earth. "Is there even an Israel?" he pleaded.

Night settled in, and he paced the cell, glimpsing now and then toward the blue shaft of moonlight which filtered across the ceiling. "Out there! Is there an Israel? Or is the entire world this single dungeon—and God the hand I see between the bars one time a day?" His mighty voice shook the walls, but no one answered. He walked toward the grid of the door and held the iron rods in a stranglehold, but no comfort could be wrung from them.

Madness tempted him. It would have been a relief to give in to it, to let his mind escape reality. But the shuffle of guards' feet within the corridor beyond jolted him into the misery of the present. He knew it must be midnight, for the jailers changed shifts at that hour.

He lay down again upon his bed and savored the sound of their footsteps. There was some comfort to be had in the assurance of other human existence, even if it was alien to him. "You prepare a table before me . . . in the presence of my enemies . . . " he whispered, and a vague, ironic smile crossed his face.

"Tomorrow . . . " he thought, "tomorrow . . . I must think about tomorrow . . . "

His mind's eye concentrated on what he knew would take place near the gates of the prison the next day. His disciples would be descending the narrow road of the steep hillside which led to the castle. They would be approaching the walls of the fort and seeking any message the Baptist might have for them this week. He envisioned the scenario of their arrival, and wondered what word he would give.

His first weeks here, his men had come eagerly to receive his communications. His spirit had been strong, his words full of hope. "Tell them I am well; Jehovah triumphs. Tell them to make straight his paths, for he has come to this land!"

But with the passing days, the words had grown less confident, the spirit of the man less assuring.

"Nothing . . . " he thought now. "I have nothing to say. I am a man no longer of truths, but of questions . . . "

And then it came to him. A single, daring ray of light afforded in this dark time. "Questions? But questions *are* something! How can we find truth unless we first ask questions? Did I not tell young John he must not fear questions?"

His heart sped and he rose to pace the room once more, his chain clattering behind him as he moved. Pounding his fists against his thighs, he walked back and forth across the floor with determined strides. "Yes . . . I will make demands with my questions! I will send my men away with questions! And perhaps, O God," he looked toward the window, "perhaps there will be answers!"

Quickly, now, he set to work. What did he most want to know? What answer would bring him the most comfort? Should he ask about the state of the nation? Should he ask about Herod's plans for him? It was not far from possible that whatever answers he received would be the last words he would ever hear.

Suddenly, he knew what they must be his. He knew what truth must be his if he were never to hear afterward.

"Jesus . . . " he whispered, stopping and gazing out at the sky. Tears came to his eyes, and he trembled. "I must know. Are you the one? The one I said you were? Or do we look for another?"

Chapter 13

It should have been the happiest day of the disciple's life. He and the other apostles had just returned to Capernaum from an extended tour of Palestine. The Lord had commissioned them to go out two by two into all the region preaching the gospel of the kingdom, and he had promised them powers unimaginable. Eagerly they had sought Jesus to tell him of their experiences: healing all manner of disease, casting out demon powers, even raising the dead!

But John sensed, as he and the Master's followers sat in Peter's house, enthusiastically expounding upon their adventures, that Jesus was strangely silent and greatly burdened. And it seemed, though John could not discern the cause, that the Master's sorrowing eyes fell frequently on him.

What the reason might be for the Lord's depressed spirits eluded John. He wondered if the others noted the Teacher's heaviness, but observation told him they did not. They were so elated over recent marvels, they appeared oblivious to such nuances of feeling.

Perhaps John, too, would have missed the Nazarene's mood had Jesus not looked so often in his direction. But, under this sad scrutiny, John lost his enthusiasm and grew apprehensive, afraid to know what the Master had for him.

At last, after a long session with his apostles, the Lord commended their faithfulness, and assured them of the joy he felt upon this occasion. Then, giving his apologies, he rose and excused himself from their presence. Though they grew silent a moment, wondering at his strange behavior, excitement for their testimonies overcame the stillness and within seconds the room was abuzz with conversation once again.

Apparently Jesus knew John would be following him into the courtyard, for he stood waiting beside the well as the disciple approached.

No words were spoken for some moments. John was torn between the desire to know and the fear of hearing what was to come. He shuffled uneasily as all manner of thoughts posed themselves. Was the Master angry with him for some reason? No—it did not seem likely. Did he have news from the house of Zebedee which would greatly sadden him? He envisioned some family member ill, or—dead . . . But no, would not James have been summoned as well?

What might concern John more than the other apostles? Suddenly an iron weight descended with crushing heaviness upon his heart. The Baptist! Had something happened to the Baptist?

Fearful to even look toward the Master, John swallowed with difficulty, and at last broke the silence. "Lord, what is it?"

The Nazarene drew close and gazed compassionately into his eyes. "You have sensed it, John."

"The Baptist?" he asked shakily.

"The greatest of the prophets . . . " Jesus' voice was soft and low.

"Lord?" John waited breathlessly.

"He is dead . . . at the hands of Herod."

Suddenly, the world was gray. All color had vanished, and the taste of life was sand. John could not move, speak, or feel. Rigid and white, he scarcely perceived the Master's embrace, only superficially realized that Jesus pressed his head to his bosom. And it was with leaden ears that he heard the Lord's words:

"You loved him greatly, John. For he was more than a prophet. Among all those born of women there has never been a greater prophet than John the Baptist. But the kingdom of heaven suffers violence, and the violent seek to take it by force."

Chapter 14

It was little consolation for John to know that the Baptist had died in the knowledge of the truth. The mighty preacher's desire for assurance had been granted when his disciples had returned with Jesus' answer to his question. After working many miracles in their presence, the Lord had sent them back saying, "Go your way, and tell John again what things you have seen and heard—how the blind see, and the lame walk, the lepers are cleansed, and the deaf hear, the dead are raised up, and how to the poor the gospel is preached. And blessed is the man who will not be offended by me."

But after days of crushing sorrow, it was a mercy that tonight John was being forced to physically exert himself. Without his realizing it, rowing the boat against a contrary sea, working against boisterous winds, and convulsing billows, was helping to draw out the cry of his soul.

"Row!" he bellowed. "Pull, pull!" His unfettered voice mixed with the elements and with the chants of his fellow oarsmen. There was relief in this expression, however much it camouflaged despair.

He was fully aware of the Baptist's death. He was fully in tune with grief. But he had progressed from stony silence in the arms of the Lord, to the release of outrage.

"Row!" his voice cried. "Unjust!" was his soul's intention. "Pull!" was his audible word. "There is no justice!" his heart's translation.

Blasphemous though it may have seemed, there was healing in such honesty. Tears came freely, and he found relief in their flow. He was grateful for the darkness which hid him from the scrutiny of his friends. But it was a blessing to cry. Though his indignation was directed heavenward, it at least expressed the essence of faith that Someone might hear, that Someone might be listening.

He had been spared the details of the Baptist's execution until the Lord knew he could receive them. He had not immediately been told that the method had been beheading, or that Herod's decision to commission the deed had followed the request of his wife and her daughter. Herodias, Herod's unlawful spouse, had desired the end of the Baptist for months. She had so despised his condemnation of her illegitimate marriage to her own brother-in-law that she had demanded his death.

John could almost see the events which had transpired at Machaerus. Salome, the sensual daughter of Herodias, had been summoned to dance before Herod and his cohorts at a feast. When the tetrarch had been intoxicated with incestuous delight in her display, he had offered her anything she might ask, up to half his kingdom. "Give me here John the Baptist's head in a bowl," she had returned, following the advice of her mother.

And so it had been done. It had actually been a sorrow to Herod, it was reported, for he had come to fear and respect the man of God. But it had been done, nonetheless.

And so, "Row!" John cried. Could there be a loving God?

What he had witnessed today on the eastern shore of the sea was no consolation. The Master had miraculously turned five small barley loaves and two fishes into more than enough food to feed the hungry multitude which had followed him, five thousand men and their families. After seeing this, the crowds had been eager then and there to crown him as their king, but such a miracle had not fed John's bereaved spirit.

Knowing the intent of the multitude, the Master had bid his men return to Capernaum without him, and, sending the people away, he had departed alone into the mountain. He would come to his apostles shortly, so he had said. John had not questioned him. He had not really cared.

But now he wished the Master were here. "O Lord," he whispered into the wind, "is there justice? Is there a God who cares?"

The sea was riotous. Great sheets of slate-gray water flooded the vessel, and the men found their work increasingly frustrating. They had rowed almost four miles, but it seemed they fought an invisible hand. The waters and the night wind mocked their every effort, and they made no progress.

It was in the fourth watch of the night, when John noticed that, despite the urgency of the moment, Peter had ceased to row. Incredibly, he sat without lifting a hand, staring wide-eyed across the sea. "Row, you fool!" John cried, as he himself tugged viciously at the oars. But still Peter stared blankly across the waters.

John followed his gaze, and what met his eyes left him numb. Something, some form or figure was advancing toward them actually walking upon the water!

A chill of dread swept through John, causing the very hairs of his head to bristle. "It is a spirit!" Peter cried. And shouts of fear came spontaneously from the crew as they gazed at the phantom figure.

For a stunned moment no one thought to row. The vessel was left to flounder like driftwood on the swollen sea. Then, with the full impact of terror, all hands took madly to the oars.

"Go!" John shouted. "Row this boat!"

Frantically the iron-muscled sailors sought to flee whatever it

was that approached them. There was no time for disputing as to
the nature of the phenomenon. They all saw it, and that was
enough.

But their efforts were still frustrated. The winds were too much
against them and they could make no headway. Without a pause
the figure drew closer and closer, and its shape became more
distinct. It was plain to see now that it had the form of a man, his
cloak and robes slapping about him with the gale. And his feet
were actually treading the face of the waves, as though they were
just so many stepping stones.

It was useless to fight the resistant seaway. The boat simply
would not go forward. Any distance gained was quickly lost as the
vessel was tossed to and fro.

John's heart nearly gave way for fear. Never before had he seen
a ghost. He had not even believed in their existence—until now.

As fear became panic, it was John who first heard a strange
sound mixing with the howl of the storm. It seemed to be a
voice—and he stared wide-eyed at the oncoming figure.

"Peter—do you hear that?" he called.

The bulky fisherman looked at him curiously and then hesitated
in his mad rowing long enough to listen.

There it came again—a man's voice—from the direction of the
strange form.

"Be of good cheer," it was calling, "it is I—be not afraid . . ."

John's heart sped. "My Lord . . . can it be?" he whispered.

Indeed, as the figure drew within close range of the vessel they
could see that it was Jesus. Awe and wonder overtook the crew,
and John found the horror which had gripped him suddenly
banished.

As it so often happened, it was Peter who spoke first. His dark,
excited eyes bore only a trace of doubt. "Lord, if it is you, bid me
come to you on the water!"

"Come," was the simple reply.

John looked on incredulously as Peter made up his mind to do
just that. "What faith!" he thought to himself. "If only I had such
faith!"

And then he watched in amazement as Peter in fact stepped
onto the face of the heaving sea as onto solid ground, and began to
walk, boldly, confidently toward the Lord, not once taking his
eyes off him.

One step—two, three. John's mouth fell open. Could this really
be happening? Should he, too, attempt such a thing?

But suddenly, it seemed Peter's confidence teetered. John

noted his apprehension as wave after wave slammed against him, and as he began to study the wind and water.

The big fisherman appealed to his comrades for help, his eyes wide with fear. And John cried out desperately, "Peter! Peter!"

"Lord, save me!" came the helpless plea of the burly Galilean as he looked desperately to the Master. For now he was beginning to sink.

Immediately Jesus stretched forth his hand and caught him, raising him up again and embracing him upon the wild sea. "O you of little faith," he said gently, "why did you doubt?"

Then bringing Peter to the ship, Jesus helped him aboard, and suddenly the wind ceased.

John clung in speechless amazement to the side of the now gently rocking vessel, surveying the sea and sky, and then stared in wonder at his Lord. Trembling with awe, he came forward and knelt before the Master, grasping him about the knees. Tears of joy coursed down his young face. "Truly," he cried in broken tones, "you are the Son of God!"

Chapter 15

It was with a joyous heart that John walked close to Jesus the day following. The cool spring breeze which blew up the shore near Capernaum swept the Master's hair away from his face, and the disciple studied the beloved countenance silently.

The assurance he had gained through the witness of Peter's rescue from the sea would remain indelibly with him. Indeed, there was a "saving hand," and that knowledge had drawn him from his own waters of despair.

How the apostle ached to embrace the Lord, to say just how much the Master meant to him.

It was at times like this that a strange notion came to John. It seemed that none of the other eleven followers related to Jesus in quite the same way he did. Though the very idea smacked of conceit, John felt the reason for their special relationship was no flattery to himself. If he were truly to know him "as no one else would ever know him," he believed it would only be due to his more critical need for reformation.

As the nature of John's inner man had been revealed over the long months of discipleship to the Baptist and to the Master, it had not been a pretty sight. True, the other apostles had their failings. Peter was flamboyant, unthinking at times, full of faith and then full of doubt. James was prone to intellectual practicality. Andrew was perhaps too quick to accept what he was told. Matthew had to fight the call of worldly comforts and Thomas was a hard-nosed realist.

But John's shortcomings were, it seemed, more subtle, more elusive and harbored in the dark chambers of his heart. As the bigotry and self-righteousness of his nature had come to light, he had been thrust into despairing dependence upon the Master.

How well he had begun to learn what the Lord would seek to teach the multitudes today!

It was Sabbath morning, and not long after they had entered the synagogue crowds from the eastern shore began to collect about Jesus. "Rabbi!" they called to him, "when did you come to this side of the sea?"

But Jesus read the true concern of their hearts, and rebuked them. "You do not seek me because of the miracles I do, but because of the bread I gave you to eat. Do not work for food which does not last, but for food which lasts forever. I alone can give that to you, for the Father has given me the power."

The multitudes were confused. "But Master, what shall we do, that we might work the works of God?"

Jesus said to them, "This is the work of God, that you believe on him whom he has sent. I am the bread of life. He that comes to me shall never hunger, and he that believes on me shall never thirst."

The fire burning in the hearth at Peter's house was a comfort after a day on the windy beach. But John, along with the other apostles, stared into it silently. Though the Master was with them, there had been little conversation all evening. Deborah and her mother did their best to cheer the men, but as the night wore on, they retired to their womanly duties behind the scenes, frustrated in their cause.

That anyone could reject the Lord and his teachings, after having followed him so long, seemed incomprehensible to John. Yet this was exactly what he and the others had witnessed. By the dozens, men who had waited on Jesus' words, men who had trekked the face of Palestine with him for months, had today, in a moment, decided to leave him.

The young disciple retraced the events of past hours, trying to understand what had happened. Had the Lord gone too far in his parable of the bread? Could he have used a more palatable illustration to drive home his point? Why had he chosen such an offensive way of expressing the truth?

"I am the bread of life . . ." To John those had been beautiful words. Why had the Lord felt it necessary to take the analogy to the extreme: "The bread that I will give is my flesh, which I will give for the life of the world."

The striving of the crowd over such a statement had troubled John. But as if that had not been enough, Jesus had gone even further. "Verily, verily," he had exclaimed, "except you eat the flesh of the Son of Man, and drink his blood, you have no life in you. Whosoever eats my flesh, and drinks my blood, has eternal life . . . and I will raise him up at the last day!"

John shuddered. Of course that had driven them away. He, himself, might have been driven away by such words had he not already, in some measure, learned to trust the Lord's wisdom.

Still, the concepts haunted him. The Master had gone on to explain, "It is the spirit that gives life. The flesh is worthless. The words that I speak unto you are spirit, and life." But what had he meant by "giving his flesh for the life of the world"?

John wished to question Jesus, but was not sure he wanted to hear the answer. As he studied the pensive face of the Nazarene, it occurred to him how much it must have hurt the Lord to see so many turn away. Reaching out, John placed a hand on the Master's shoulder, and Jesus looked up from the fire.

For a long moment the Lord's attention was on John, and then his gaze traveled about the room from disciple to disciple. At last the crackling of the fire, the only sound for most of the evening, was joined by his voice, heavy and low, addressing the twelve. "Will you also go away?"

John's heart raced, and Peter was quick to exclaim, "O Lord, to whom shall we go? You have the words of eternal life. And we believe and are sure that you are the Christ, the Son of the living God!"

All the men appeared to be in unanimous agreement, and murmured approval for Peter's words. It came as a mighty blow then, when Jesus gave his response.

Looking deep into the fire so as not to identify the culprit, he said, "Have I not chosen you twelve, and one of you is a devil?"

Chapter 16

It suddenly seemed everything was happening too fast. Only days after Jesus' baffling pronouncement at Peter's hearth, rumors were spreading concerning a plot to kill the Master.

It had been known for months that the Pharisees were bitter against the Nazarene for his overt rejection of their ways and teachings.

When Jesus repeatedly demonstrated his ability to heal, it was difficult to deny the truth of anything he might say. But despite ever-growing popularity among the common people, he was increasingly unpopular with religious leaders.

Since the healing of the paralytic, when he had challenged them openly, the Pharisees had lain in wait, determined to trap him in his own doctrine. Once victorious, they planned to silence him, as they had the Baptist.

Their reasoning was the same as it had been at Bethabara: this man was dangerous, not only because his teachings contradicted theirs, but because he questioned their righteousness.

Two incidents in particular disturbed them. They had caught the Master in the fields one Sabbath, and had rebuked him for allowing his followers to pluck the grain. "The Law says we are not to work on the Sabbath!" they insisted. After pointing out scriptural evidence to the contrary, Jesus had said, "The Sabbath was made for man, and not man for the Sabbath. Therefore, the Son of Man is Lord also of the Sabbath!"

If this enraged them, however, even more did an incident of healing. A man with a withered hand was present in the synagogue where Jesus had entered. Hoping to catch the Master in a web of inquisition, the Pharisees asked, "Is it lawful to heal on the Sabbath day?"

"I will ask you one thing," Jesus responded. "Is it lawful on the Sabbath day to do good, or to do evil? to save life or to destroy it?" Then he told the man, "Stretch forth your hand." And when he obeyed, it was made completely whole.

Seeing this, the Pharisees had been filled with madness. And, as they had done when frustrated by the Baptist, they went out and immediately took counsel with one another, then with the Herodians, as to how they might destroy the Nazarene.

Even more flagrantly, Jesus continued to denounce them. "Hypocrites!" he would cry. "Blind leaders of the blind!" It seemed he sought occasions to transgress their laws and to expose them, but it was also apparent that they watched him like wily foxes. Only the outraged citizenry would delay attempts to take him.

For this reason Jesus temporarily confined his ministry to Galilee. It was safer here than in Judea where the capital harbored his staunchest opponents.

Now that so many followers had turned from him, however, it was little comfort even to be in his native province. The discourse on the "bread of life" had added fuel to the fires of his enemies at home as well as away.

John was alone this morning. He had left the group where they lodged at Peter's house, and had sought the sanctuary of the shore, where he could think in private. He remembered having sat on this beach, after returning from his first trek to Bethabara. His spellbound heart had been so captivated by thoughts of the Baptist, he had not even heard Peter call out to him.

In contrast to that distant morning, his mind today was full of unpleasant things. For the Master's closest apostle, these were especially trying times. Recently he had faced the fact of the Baptist's death. Rumors of plans against Jesus chilled him to the bone.

And crowning all of this were the Lord's words: "One of you is a devil . . . "

Dark feelings enveloped John as he stared out at the blustery sea. One by one the apostles' faces came to mind as they had been frozen in his memory that day beside the hearth. Peter, James, Andrew, Matthew . . . he went around the room. "Who, my Lord? Who is the devil?" he whispered. Philip, Nathanael, Judas, Thomas . . . from face to face he called up the images. But no answer came. And then he remembered Jesus' sad eyes as they had fallen on each one . . . and on him.

A jolt of breath was taken. "No!" he cried. "Master—can it be me?"

The past week's miseries overswept him. None of the apostles had been exempted. He least of all. Life itself was death, betrayal, and deviltry.

"My Lord," he whispered, trying to shake his ugly imaginings, "I only know I love you . . . "

Chapter 17

Not until the Feast of Tabernacles did Jesus leave Galilee and appear once again in Jerusalem. John and the others had been full of apprehension when he announced he would attend the late autumn festival. And it seemed their fears were well founded, for during the holidays such commotion had fomented about him that his life had been in jeopardy.

As he had done in Galilee, Jesus spoke too boldly for the likes of the Judean hierarchy. John had watched helplessly when the Pharisees and chief priests sent officers to take the Master.

Incredibly, Jesus had, with a few short words, sent them away empty-handed. But tonight John stood at the window of the upper room in which the Rabbi and the apostles lodged, staring across the rooftops to the Temple cloisters of the Sanhedrin. He knew that his father was in the distant marble hallway, conspiring with the other predators against the Nazarene.

It seemed a lifetime since the portentous night when he had paced the Temple court awaiting some word of the council's plans for the Baptist. So much had transpired since then, yet it returned to him vividly.

Turning downcast from the window, John's eyes fell upon the Master. Jesus drew near. "What is it, John? You are troubled."

The young disciple could not withhold his opinion, and in a burst of passion directed his anger toward the very one for whom he sorrowed. "You have leveled stormy seas! You have routed disease and hunger with a mere motion of your will!" he cried. "Why do you not destroy those who take counsel against you?"

The scene in the Sanhedrin chambers was a virtual reenactment of the struggle which had taken place over the Baptist long before. The forces were divided along basically the same lines. The majority was bold and ready for blood. But a scattered few, like Nicodemus, would defend the rights of the subject. To this small group had been added of late a rabbi named Gamaliel, and a wealthy lawyer called Joseph of Arimathea. And then there were those who, for private reasons, did not care to offer an opinion.

One character in the drama, however, had changed roles. Zebedee of Capernaum would not shrink from the spotlight as he had done before. He had now lost two sons to renegade rabbis, and this time he would fight.

James' decision to follow the Carpenter had tempted the old man to withdraw even further into bitter loneliness. But at some uncertain point, his attitude had changed. Angry, with seemingly nothing more to lose, he would use his influence and position to crush the enemy, Jesus of Nazareth.

Tonight he was alert to all that went on. He stood at the head of the crowd, seeking the opportune moment to make a statement.

The floor was open. Annas and Caiaphas waited for anyone who wished to speak. But confusion reigned, many desiring to lead out.

At last it was Nicodemus who gained the platform. "Your honors," he addressed the high priests, "it should be recognized at the outset that many people of Israel are saying this Jesus is a prophet. There are even those who are saying he is the Christ . . . the Messiah."

Nicodemus had known his statement would be applauded by only his little band of comrades, but he had never imagined it would be Zebedee who would rise against the challenge. "Ha!" the old fisherman snarled. "Shall the Christ come out of Galilee?"

The source of opposition stunned Nicodemus, but his reply was well calculated. "Why, Zebedee, you are a Galilean. Do you besmirch your own countryman?"

"Well said, I am a Galilean," Zebedee answered, "but I am one Galilean who knows the Scriptures! And do not the Scriptures say the Messiah will be a descendant of David, and that he will come from the town of Bethlehem where David was? This Jesus is of Nazareth!" The last word hung rancidly in the air. The very suggestion that anyone of import might come from such a slum elicited laughter throughout the chamber.

Nicodemus looked disconcertedly at the floor. He had never told anyone of his night visit with the Nazarene. He knew many

present suspected his growing allegiance to the man. But it was not
fear of censure which pained him, nor the sorrow that Zebedee,
his old friend, should turn so violently against him. What brought
a tremor to his old heart was the likelihood that support for Jesus
would be overrun, just as defense of the Baptist had been.

Even now, in the midst of the noisy throng, he could visualize
the quiet scene in the upper room. He would never forget the
peace that encounter had brought. Desperately he longed to shift
the tide of opinion in this hall, but he knew it was beyond himself
to do so.

"Sirs," Caiaphas' voice commanded attention, bringing instant
silence. "It shall not be long before we hear from the Nazarene
himself on these points."

The council listened expectantly. "You all know," he continued, "that certain of your spokesmen, and we ourselves, recently
commissioned officers to find the Nazarene and bring him before
us. This is the night they are to appear."

The majority received the news eagerly, but Nicodemus
cringed. That a good man like Jesus should be subjected to
harassment was, to his mind, a travesty.

At that moment, however, his attention was drawn to the rear of
the room, where a new cast of characters was entering. A hush fell
over the crowd as half a dozen court officers worked their way
toward the high priests.

Though they made a sterling spectacle in their armor and gear,
hesitancy marked their bearing, and soon it became apparent why
this should be. They had no prisoner, no Nazarene.

Annas and Caiaphas were wide-eyed. But quickly, incredulity
turned to angry humiliation. The elder, who normally remained
aloof from direct involvement with chamber proceedings, lurched
forward in his chair. Slamming his fist upon the platform rail, he
demanded, "The Nazarene! Where is he? Why have you not
brought him?"

Every councilman was asking the same question, and Nicodemus' heart sped. The officers shuffled uneasily, and one of them
answered, barely audibly, "We went to take him, sir, but . . . no
man ever spoke as he does."

The crowd murmured disgust, and Zebedee confronted the
guards wildly. "Are you also deceived? Have any of the rulers or
the Pharisees believed on him?" Then turning in rage to the high
priests, he threw his arms into the air. "We had expected court
officers to have better sense. But the old saying is true, 'people
who know not the Law are cursed' !"

Nicodemus had heard enough. "Gentlemen," he addressed the boisterous throng, "I see that we are conducting ourselves with the same consideration to propriety we brought to our sessions on the Baptist. We have tried, judged, and condemned the Nazarene without giving him an audience." Then, facing the bench rigidly, he expounded, "Does our Law judge any man before it hears him, and knows what he is doing?"

It was Master Jacob Bar Harsha who picked up Zebedee's tune. "Are you also of Galilee?" he sneered at Nicodemus. "Search . . . and look! For out of Galilee arises no prophet!"

This seemed to be the last word. Without ceremony, the high priests rose to dismiss the session, and disappeared into their quarters.

The leaders of Israel dispersed in baffled contemplation, each going to his own house.

When even his few comrades had departed, Nicodemus stood alone at the platform rail. Zebedee lingered nearby, but only long enough to flash a triumphant smile at his opponent. His point had been won without a contest.

Chapter 18

Had anyone told John he would one day dwell again at Bethabara, he would never have believed it. Yet this was where winter found him. It was, in fact, once again Hanukkah. As he looked back to the first such season he had spent here, it seemed life was repeating itself.

This time, however, he had not come by choice. Though the Sanhedrin had allowed Jesus to dwell two more months in Jerusalem, they had made their intentions obvious, repeatedly attempting to trap the Master in his own teaching.

John would always remember the day a cluster of scribes and lawyers had brought to the Lord a fear-wracked woman they had found in the act of adultery. "Moses in the Law commanded us that such should be stoned," they had insisted. "But what do you say?"

Jesus had replied, "He that is without sin among you, let him first cast a stone at her."

One by one, beginning with the eldest, all the commissioners had turned to leave in shame. The woman, who had lain shaken and tearful upon the road, had raised herself, looking incredulously about her.

Lifting her up, the Lord had sent her on her way. "Neither do I condemn you," he had said. "Go, and sin no more."

John stood with his back against the cold night wind of the gorge. A vicious irony, he told himself, that shortly thereafter the same men had sought to stone the Master himself, in the Temple. That time Jesus had escaped, but at the Feast of the Dedication they had tried once more to take him, so he and his men had sought sanctuary in the wilderness hills.

All of this had been much for John to bear. But what disturbed him most was the Master's resigned acceptance of such things. Even Jesus' words made it seem he was bent on his own destruction. "I am the living bread," he had proclaimed. "The bread that I will give is my flesh, which I will give for the life of the world. I am the good shepherd," he had declared. "The good shepherd gives his life for the sheep. I lay down my life for the sheep."

There had been other statements, too, which unsettled John. Jesus had spoken of laying down his life, "that he might take it up again." "No man takes it from me," he had asserted, "but I lay it down of myself. I have power to lay it down, and I have power to take it again. This commandment have I received of my Father."

John did not know what this could mean. It dogged his thinking, it pestered at the back door of his mind, like a scratching cat. Still, worrisome enough were repeated references to the Master's demise.

The apostle tried to refute the possibility, but the words returned persistently, and he glimpsed a fragmented picture of himself one day without his Lord. "No!" came the spontaneous response. "It shall never be! I, myself, shall die before I will allow it to be!"

Looking once more at the turbulent water swarming past his feet, he turned angrily toward the path leading back to camp. Near the fire he saw the Master watching for him.

The apostle's heart burned at the sight. He could not take another step, but stooped to the ground in a huddle of despair. He would plead with anything—the earth, the rocks, the sky. Only, let not his Lord be taken from him!

John's storehouse of unvoiced fears at last found expression. Staring wildly about him, his eyes wide with madness, he found a gnarled, weathered root, torn from its rightful place. Reaching forward, he raised it in shaky, spasmed fingers, lifting it above his head like a pathetic banner, and calling hoarsely toward the Nazarene. "It cannot and it shall not be! I will see to that!"

At the sight of his love-torn apostle, tears brimmed in the Master's eyes. Quickly he left camp, descending the path toward him. Without a word, he reached for the son of Zebedee and held him close.

There was bittersweet assurance in Jesus' love.

John sat beside the highway, cold and weary in spirit. When the time had been right they had left Bethabara and had been on the road since, trekking long distances despite the winter winds, as far as Mount Hermon in the land of Herod Philip II.

The campfire light accentuated lines of heaviness in his young face. As they traveled, the Master had spoken to them of the "kingdom," as he called it, and of the "Son of Man coming in his kingdom." Whatever he meant, glorious references to some obscure future did not appease the agony of John's heart.

"The Son of Man must go to Jerusalem, where he will suffer many things," Jesus told them now clearly, "and be rejected of the elders, and of the chief priests and scribes, and be killed." To this he added a most peculiar proclamation: "The Son of Man shall then rise the third day." Again, John was at a loss to decipher the meaning. But, as always, he reacted violently against the notion of Jesus' death. And he was not the only one to do so.

A few days before, when they had been camped near Caesarea Philippi, Peter had rebuked the Master for such talk. He had echoed John's words at Bethabara when he had said, "Be it far from you, Lord! This shall not happen to you!"

How unlike Jesus it had seemed, when, forcefully, he had turned to Peter, declaring, "Get behind me, Satan! You are an offense to me, for you do not savor the things that are of God, but those that are of men!"

John shook his head. How that must have pained his friend, Peter. The big fisherman had not been the same since. He, who usually walked confidently at the head of the group, seemed to have lost his vitality. Even tonight, as John studied him, he was stooped beside the fire, staring into it blankly.

At last Peter stood and walked away from the company heading for the solitude of a nearby grove. John's heart went out to him, but he waited a while before following.

Simon was hunched against the trunk of a great cedar when the disciple found him, and John could easily detect tears on his face. Never, even as children, had he seen the burly fellow cry, and he pretended not to notice.

"Friend . . . " John whispered.

Peter lurched at the sound and quickly wiped his eyes with the sleeve of his robe. "John." He attempted a smile. And then nervously, "The fire was a bit warm, don't you think? I thought I'd cool off . . . "

But the sham was useless. He knew John read through it. "You have been thinking of what happened the other evening, haven't you?" The disciple sought to console him.

The big man looked shamefaced at his companion. "Yes . . . I have been . . . a great deal."

John was torn between love for Jesus and loyalty to Peter. "I just don't understand," he said at last, taking Simon's part. "I said the same things to the Master at Bethabara, and he did not react to me as he did to you. You were only expressing concern for him, and he turned on you!"

There was relief in stating what John had held back for a week. He was sure Peter would rally at his defense, but he was in for a surprise.

"No," his friend corrected. "It is not the same at all."

John was bewildered.

"Oh, I would like to think the Master was unjust in his rebuke," Simon continued. "But I realize now that my words were not prompted by love, but by pride."

Still John did not understand.

Peter sighed and looked high into the starlit sky. "It is possible to say the same words with different intentions. The night you cried out at Bethabara, all of us knew it was despair which drove you to it, and the Master reacted accordingly."

"But you, Peter . . . what motivated you?"

Simon's voice was full of feeling. "John, he claims to be the Messiah. Only days before rebuking me, he praised me for calling him the Christ, the Son of God. He often speaks of a kingdom, and of his glorious reign." Here he hesitated, caught up by his own zeal. "Friend, don't you see . . . if he is to be king, as he claims, and as so many hope he will be, how can he destroy Rome and take the throne if he is . . . "

"Dead!" John finished, suddenly comprehending.

Silence gripped them both. John had sometimes thought of the

Master's "kingdom" in this way, but it had not been of major interest to him, as perhaps it had been to Peter. During his months with Jesus, John had been so embroiled in spiritual lessons that his contemplation had not often been politically oriented.

"Of course . . ." he whispered. "So that is what he has meant by his 'kingdom.' " And now he began to pick up Peter's spirit. "Why, then, he cannot die! We cannot allow it!"

His heart beat excitedly. But to his great confusion, Peter suddenly quelled it. "No, John! Don't you see? It was for just such a statement that he corrected me."

John bristled. What did Peter want? First he had thrust politics at him and now he was rebuking his enthusiasm.

Perhaps one thing had become clear. A man could, indeed, say the same words twice with different motivation. Pride, the desire to see Jesus ruler of his enemies, had prompted John's last words. They contained none of the love which had sparked his cries at Bethabara.

But, in a quandary, John rebelled at his dilemma. "Motivation be hanged!" he spat. "One thing alone is important to me!" Looking back at the campfire, he singled out his Lord. "Peter," he said, trembling, "what are we to do?"

The burly fisherman sighed again, obviously as frightened as John. "Though we don't understand, we must let the Master have his way . . . whatever the cost."

Chapter 19

Had it not been for a strange incident the morning after Peter's confession to John, the big fisherman might have felt forever rejected by the Lord.

It was not yet dawn when the Master woke John, James, and Simon and called them aside. Jesus asked his three most intimate companions to accompany him, despite a winter gale, on a journey up Mount Hermon.

Dubiously, the fishermen looked at one another, and then shruggingly accepted.

The way up the mountain was steep and precarious. The mammoth landmark, nearly ten thousand feet high, and the

greatest in the region, established the upper limit of eastern
Palestine. Forty miles northeast of Gennesaret, Hermon's
perennially snowy heights were visible as far south as the Salt Sea,
which marked the end of Jordan's one hundred twenty miles.
From its triple-peaked summit, glacial waters descended, merging
into the river's primary source.

Frigid blasts of cold forced the disciples to bury their faces in
their mantles. John looked over his shoulder once or twice as they
ascended, bracing himself against the dizzying view. Still he kept
close to his Lord, and at last they reached an open place.

Remnants of ancient Baal-worship littered the site, this
mountain having been the sanctuary of that cult. Eros pillars and
broken altars stared grimly at the four Galileans. John felt alien
and uneasy.

Jesus had given no explanation concerning this venture, and he
remained silent now, kneeling in the unsheltered space. The men
had been with the Master before, when he had gone apart to pray.
But why he had chosen such a day and such a location baffled
them. And the sight of their Lord meditating in this ancient house
of Baal set badly with them. They knew this was not the time to be
questioning, however, so they stepped a few feet away, huddling
beneath a nearby ledge.

Since they had been awakened out of sound sleep at camp, it was
difficult for them to stay alert. John may have dozed an hour
before strange voices jolted him to consciousness once more.

The sound was coming from the open space where Jesus had
been praying. Supposing that some of the other apostles had come
in search of the Master, John stirred himself and left the overhang.
What met his eyes upon emerging, dazed and dumbfounded him.

The spot where Jesus stood was flooded with radiant light. The
Master's clothes appeared white and glistening, like new fallen
snow, and his face shone as the sun. Two men stood with him,
whom John had never before encountered. They, too, were
arrayed gloriously, and John shielded his eyes from the brilliance
of the scene.

The voices which had wakened him were those of the two
strangers speaking with the Lord. John could not make out their
words, for they talked in low tones, but they seemed to be giving a
message of encouragement to one who badly needed it.

Trembling, John stumbled back into the cave and roused his
companions. Something in his face must have persuaded them to
follow quickly, for he could not describe what he had just
observed.

Coming upon the scene, Peter stammered, "What is this?"

James, wide-eyed, nudged the big man. "Listen! Perhaps we can make out what they are saying."

Only a few words could be determined, but they were sufficient to raise John's skin in gooseflesh. "Jerusalem . . . Pharisees . . . Herod . . . death . . . . "

They spoke of the Master's death!

The apostles looked on in horror. Who were these men? they wondered.

Momentarily that mystery would be solved, for the listeners would hear Jesus address the two strangers as "Moses" and "Elijah."

At this pronouncement John grew taut with fear.

But now the Lord caught a glimpse of the apostles, and the two figures with him vanished before their eyes.

Though awestruck, Peter was the first to find words. As if not knowing what else to say, he looked at the repugnant Baal sanctuaries and offered, "Master, it is good for us to be here. Let us make three tabernacles . . . one for you, and one for Moses, and one for Elijah."

But before the statement was completed, a new phenomenon was taking place. A cloud of indescribable brightness descended, settling around them, and the same voice John had witnessed the day of Jesus' baptism at Bethabara now issued from the vapor. "This is my beloved Son, in whom I am well pleased," it said. "Hear him."

Terrified, the three apostles fell to the ground, burying their faces in the dirt.

"Rise up. Do not be afraid," Jesus spoke softly, drawing near and touching them.

John could barely bring himself to move. But as he and the others did so, they found the Master standing alone beside them, and the scene had returned to normal.

As they came down from the mountain, shaken and numb with wonder, Jesus charged them, saying, "Tell the vision to no man, until the Son of Man be risen again from the dead."

Chapter 20

If the witness of the Transfiguration was meant to cheer Peter, it had certainly had its effect. As he and James walked together today they were full of talk, questioning between themselves what Jesus' reference to "rising from the dead" could mean.

The Lord had gone ahead of the group a way, and John was left to listen in on the conversation. James and Peter assumed he was part of their discussion and attempted to include him, but the young son of Zebedee had his own thoughts and only occasionally offered a word.

What the Master could possibly mean by "rising the third day" completely eluded him, as it did the others. He saw no purpose in deep examination of the statement, for it was nothing but alien to him. He did not like the sound of it, and so had shuffled it into the back drawers of his mind.

The vision on Mount Hermon had not had the elating effect on John that it had had on Peter and James. But this was not why he walked, lonely and full of dark brooding, apart from his friends.

Jesus had made it clear once again, in discussion with his men, that someone was going to betray him into the hands of his enemies for the accomplishment of his demise, and the words he had spoken at Peter's house continued to haunt John: "One of you is a devil."

Still, bits of his companions' conversation did occasionally slip into the disciple's thinking. Could it be that he actually heard Peter speak of the "kingdom" once again? What did it matter which of the twelve would be greatest in that vague future of which the Master so often spoke? Yet this was what they disputed, Peter and

238

James. And now the others who followed behind were picking up the issue, grappling with it like greedy children.

John turned on them all angrily. "Here you are wasting your time with such stupidity!" he confronted them. Unprepared for this attack, the eleven looked at him in silent surprise. " 'Which of us will be the greatest?' " he mimicked. "You can speak of such things seriously? What you should be asking is 'Which of us is the betrayer?' "

Peter did not hold his tongue for long. "Who do you think you are? Why, all these months you have set yourself apart from us. Going off for long hours to sulk—so concerned with your own problems, you have not even been involved in promoting the Master's kingdom!"

Any onlooker would have thought the two apostles had reverted to adolescence. As adults in the fishing trade, Peter and John had often engaged in verbal warfare, but it had been years since they had sunk to physical confrontation. John's old nature had reared itself, however, and his fists were clenched and ready for action. With quickness of tongue uniquely his own, he retorted, "At least my head is not in the clouds. It appears I alone am left to protect the Master here and now!"

"Protect him from whom?" the big fisherman roared. "Are there Pharisees behind each bush?"

John would not tolerate mockery. Lunging at Peter with the advantage of surprise, he knocked the giant of a man sprawling to the ground. The wind taken from him, Peter lifted himself, shaken, angry and humiliated. "You little flea!" he bellowed, raising a fist. "Come closer and I will crush you with my thumb!"

John stepped back, surprised at his own action. But he bared his arms for defense. "Indeed there are Pharisees behind the bushes!" he cried. "And enemies to the Lord of all sorts! Can you say there are not?"

Peter did not pursue the challenge, but watched in amazement as John looked wildly about him.

Always there were those who trailed along behind the apostles wherever Jesus went. There were the curious, the scoffers, the would-be disciples, those who were loyal to the Master, but whom he had never called to be his special students.

John had come to suspect anyone not familiar to him. In his desperate desire to save Jesus from the fate he seemed so bent upon, he had often had to restrain the urge to drive them all away.

One in particular troubled him: a certain Joshua, of Arbela, a small town west of the sea. This character was frequently seen pacing behind the Lord's company, and it was rumored that he could work miracles in the name of Jesus.

Today John sought this figure among the scattered faces along the road. He would show Peter he meant business. He would make an example of Joshua and roust an undesirable element at the same time.

At last he saw him, and his muscles tensed. Joshua, small of stature, inconsequential in appearance, was coming around a bend in the road behind. No one but John had ever considered him a threat.

With the little man was a flock of miracle-seekers from nearby towns. Not realizing he had a hostile observer, Joshua began to cast out devils in the name of the Master.

Instantly, John was after him, running headlong down the highway, as the eleven and a stunned audience looked on. "Who are you?" John demanded as he drew near. "You are not one of us!"

Joshua of Arbela glanced up in bewilderment. "What?" he stammered.

"Who are you?" John cried again. "How are we to know you are not one of Jesus' enemies? You are not one of us!"

The baffled miracle-worker had no reply, so unexpected was the challenge. "Why, I am no enemy!" he asserted.

"You are alien, wandering about like a shadow, using our Master's name! I forbid you to do these things any longer!"

Joshua recognized his accuser. Though he was innocent, he dared not resist the command of John, the son of Zebedee, the closest of Jesus' companions. Crestfallen, he took the order as directly from the Rabbi, and, sorrowfully, he replied, "I was never chosen as you were, but I have meant no harm. I only wanted to be of use to the Nazarene . . . " Then, looking sadly at the ground, he said, "Tell the Master I am sorry he feels as he does, and beg his pardon for me."

Then, turning about, his slight frame bent with heaviness, he made a quiet retreat and disappeared down the road.

John stood silent a moment, somewhat shamed by his own actions. But as he sensed the crowd watching for his next move, he straightened his shoulders and started back to the company.

Surely, he pondered, he had done the right thing.

Chapter 21

It was not until they had risen from dinner in Peter's house later that day that Jesus questioned them concerning the incident along the road to Capernaum. Calling them into the parlor, he asked, "What was it you disputed among yourselves as we traveled?"

For a long moment, no one spoke. Shame silenced them. But it was James who at last answered. "We were wondering, Lord, which of us will be the greatest in your kingdom when you establish it. Who is the greatest in the kingdom of heaven?"

Jesus sat down and looked steadfastly at his men, perceiving the thought of their hearts, that each, even John, hoped it would be himself. Then he called them to him, saying, "If any man desires to be first, he shall be last of all, and servant of all."

Peter fidgeted uneasily and John leaned against the wall, feeling now very justified in his criticism of his friend's ambition. But the Master went from face to face silently, knowing the pride each heart harbored, and then motioned a little servant boy to come close. Innocent of the role he would play in the Lord's teaching, he nevertheless came eagerly and Jesus drew him up, held him close, and motioned the men to be seated.

"Truly I tell you," he began, "unless you be converted, and become as little children, you shall not enter into the kingdom of heaven. Whoever, therefore, shall humble himself as this little child, the same is greatest in the kingdom of heaven."

The message was pointed. Even John was shamed. Everyone looked at the floor, each aware of his own guilt in the matter. The Lord continued to speak, but John did not really hear his words.

He was deep in recollection of the event which had followed the disciples' roadside dispute.

Had he been wrong to assault Joshua of Arbela? His conscience troubled him. But suddenly his chin assumed a stony angle, and he rationalized his behavior. Of course, he had not been wrong. The Lord's safety was his motive. Someone must look out for him!

But Jesus' words filtered through to his conscious mind, exposing the self-exaltation which lay behind his actions. "Whoever receives this child in my name receives me, and whoever receives me receives the one who sent me . . . for he who is least among you all is the one who shall be great."

Joshua of Arbela had received Jesus. Would the Lord feel John had been wrong to reject him? A lump formed in the apostle's throat, but at last he found courage to speak. "Master," he said, "we saw one casting out devils in your name, and he does not follow us . . . and we forbade him . . . because he does not follow us."

John's confession was not strictly honest. He alone had reprimanded the miracle-worker. Nevertheless, no one challenged him. They had been sufficiently silenced by the Lord's message.

Jesus perceived the facts, however. Looking patiently at the apostle, he answered, "I know you were only trying to protect me, John, but do not forbid him, for no man who does a miracle in my name can lightly speak evil of me. He who is not against us is for us."

The Master's compassion was evident, and John warmed to it. However, coupled with it came a warning against the kind of pride which had crept into the love he felt for Christ. "And whoever shall offend one of these little ones that believe in me, it is better for him to have a millstone hanged about his neck, and be cast into the sea . . . .

"Salt is good," he added, "but if the salt has lost its saltiness, with what will you season it? Have salt in yourselves, and have peace with each other."

The words might have seemed harsh except that Jesus' eyes were full of love for the disciple he corrected. John was silent with thought.

And now the Lord turned his attention to another matter, addressing the twelve. "Moreover," he was saying, "if your brother sins against you, go and tell him his fault between you and him alone. If he hears you, you have gained your brother."

Peter looked uneasy. Glancing awkwardly at John, he drew near the Master, not wishing the others to hear. "Lord," he said, "how often can my brother sin against me, that I must forgive him? Seven times?"

Jesus knew the contents of his heart. "I tell you, not 'Seven times,' but, 'Seventy times seven!' "

Chapter 22

For the stranger to Palestine, Samaria would have seemed a beautiful place in many respects. Hills ribboned with terraces, vineyards and groves of olives, valleys with antique highways, and delicately clouded slopes—surely Jehovah had meant this to be a pleasant province.

But no Jew could see it this way. It was enemy territory. John's eyes did not dwell on the riots of red flowers bunched beside its stone fences, or on the beauty of its olive-skinned women. And if he viewed the villages at all it was only with disdain for their terrible poverty.

Why Jesus had once again chosen this route between Galilee and Judea, rather than the more popular one through the Jordan valley, John could not imagine. Either was about seventy miles long, and took four to five days to travel.

Being in this province recalled for John the incident at Jacob's Well. He never had come to grips with his attitude toward Samaritans. Perhaps he had hoped he might never be faced with them, that he might not have to deal with his prejudice. But now, here he was again in their very homeland.

Jesus had been determined to head for Jerusalem. Ever since the encounter with Moses and Elijah on the mount, when they had spoken of the accomplishment of his death in that holy city, he had intended to leave Galilee for Judea. He had even sent messengers before him, bearing news of his coming to all villages marking the way he would travel.

Through the towns of Galilee great throngs had gathered, everyone hoping to catch a glimpse of the most newsworthy man of the day. Hundreds vied for his touch of healing, or to be in earshot of his teachings. Generally the people's mood was one of applause, of desire to show honor for the famous Nazarene. True, there were the Lord's enemies, for whom John watched. But the common folk stood in awe of the Teacher who could work miracles and who claimed to be more than a man.

By the time Jesus and his disciples had reached the southern borders of Galilee, John was not a little proud of the reception his Master had experienced. It served somewhat to soothe the ache of fears embedded in his heart—fears for what lay ahead in Jerusalem.

When, therefore, they came to the village of Ginaea, in Samaria, John was not prepared for the reaction of the citizens. For some reason this population had never come to share the enthusiasm for Jesus which had characterized the folk near Jacob's Well. Most of the province, like Galilee, had accepted the Nazarene since he had been so gracious to them at the beginning of his ministry. This town, however, retained antipathy for the Master. He was a Jew, and whatever his reputation, they wanted nothing to do with him.

As Jesus and his men approached the hamlet, the messengers he had sent ahead met him on the road. "Master," they called, "perhaps you will want to skirt this town. The people are not friendly toward you. They will not receive you here."

John's eyes flashed and he confronted the two heralds as though they were to blame for this insult. "What do you mean they will not receive him!" he challenged, stepping in front of the Lord. "Everywhere we go he is received!"

Jesus pulled him back and silenced him with a look. "We will enter," he asserted.

The messengers stood by, shaken and apprehensive, but did not question. It was obvious the Master would not be deterred.

The village gate was little more than a door. The walls, composed of broken stone and rubble, could not have kept a child out, let alone the Son of God. If he was determined to enter, let it be in style, John thought, and he raised his head austerely as he followed the Nazarene.

A crowd was gathering, but from their expressions, they held no reverence for Jesus. When they saw that his face was set for Jerusalem, they began to hiss and boo. Here and there spittle struck the ground before him, and he hesitated, but then walked across it as if he had not seen.

John's heart burned white-hot with hatred. His eyes cast spears at the spectators. Surely the Lord's murderers lay in this very crowd. And even if they did not, who did the rabble think they were, to treat the Messiah this way?

John stayed close beside the Master, certain to defend against any who would come too near. There was no question in his mind that his attitude was right. This was not a matter of any Joshua of Arbela. These were Samaritans—the scum of the earth! Christ had tolerated them once; he had even kept company with some of their people—but that day was not this day, and those folks were not these folks. Perhaps one could endure even a Samaritan, if he had accepted Jesus. But—not these!

The crowd was becoming more boisterous. Small pebbles were flung at the Master, and John looked behind him fearfully. The other disciples were just as concerned. James' fists were clenched in readiness, and Peter walked with heavy strides, his eyes cloudy with warning.

"Dogs!" John snarled.

And James picked up his note. "Watch them! Keep them at arm's length."

Such a stench they brought to John's nostrils. "They must bathe in their own sewers!" he jeered, and James laughed derisively.

Suddenly, from deep in the crowd, someone was taking up that challenge. A meat merchant, massive in size, bearded and wearing a blood-stained leather apron, made his way toward John and the Nazarene.

"He has a cleaver in his hand!" Peter shouted, and the crowd went wild. It all happened too quickly for John to register it mentally, but the flash of steel and the grappling speed of the big fisherman against the attacker told him he and his Master had just been spared an awful fate.

Peter had the Samaritan on the ground, and James ripped the brutal instrument from his knobby hand. Then the elder son of Zebedee turned to John. "Is the Lord safe?"

John's dry mouth could find no words, but he nodded silently. James shook the dust from his robes, as Peter flung the merchant aside like a net of rejected fish.

When John regained himself, he throbbed with anger. James drew near, supporting him with his own hot zeal. "Scabs!" the elder whispered. "They are pestilence on the Lord and on us!"

"Why did we come this way?" John demanded, his teeth clamped in disgust. James could only shake his head.

Throughout the incident the Master had said nothing. But now he approached, and the two brothers, breathing heavily, looked to him for praise on their valiance. After all, any educated Jew knew that centuries before, at the word of Elijah the prophet, God had twice sent fire from heaven to consume Samaritan troops.

John, his chin lifted and his arms flexed, stood ready for just that. "Lord," he said, "do you want us to command fire to come down from heaven, and consume them, even as Elijah did?"

But there was to be no commendation from Jesus on this count, and no encouragement of any kind. His eyes were full of rebuke, and before their very enemies he spoke with anger and sorrow. "John, I have rightly called you a Son of Thunder," he said, "and I see that James is one as well!" Then directing his gaze at each, he asserted, "You do not know what spirit you are of. For the Son of Man has not come to destroy men's lives, but to save them!"

Chapter 23

The small town of Bethany, about two miles from Jerusalem via the Mount of Olives, held in store a refreshing interlude for John. Though weary from travel and unending crowds, and though still fearful of nearing the Holy City, he was encouraged by Bethany's warm spirit.

As often happened when Jesus traveled, there were those eager to have him visit their homes. Today the Master accepted the invitation of a certain Lazarus, a man about James' age, tall and very thin, with a pointed wisp of a beard.

A clothmaker, Lazarus was well known in the community, being one of its most industrious citizens. Pilgrims going to and from Jerusalem gave him a good business, as his wares were famous for their quality, appreciated by Jew and Gentile alike.

His home, which sat like the other buildings of Bethany, in a cluster along the hill, was one of the most well appointed in town. Though it was modest in proportion to Zebedee's Capernaum residence, John found it immediately to his liking. Beyond the gate, a small courtyard was filled with the music of a bubbling fountain, surrounding which were small stone boxes of well tended flowers. A table, already prepared beneath the gallery, was arrayed with tempting food. John saw only two servants, and having heard that Lazarus was a bachelor, he wondered how he managed so fine a home without more assistance.

Soon he received his answer. At the gallery rail there appeared a woman not much younger than Lazarus, shaking out a rug. Not having expected the Master just yet, she looked greatly embarrassed and quickly ducked inside the house, brushing the dust from her skirts.

"Martha, it is all right," Lazarus called. "Come, meet our company."

Flustered and crimson-cheeked, she descended the courtyard stairs. Though not striking in beauty, she was a well-groomed woman, probably in her early thirties. But most noticeable was the mood of anxiety which seemed to permeate her. While being introduced, she perpetually smoothed her hair and straightened her garments, as though they were in disarray.

"Master," Lazarus said good-naturedly, "this is my sister, Martha. She is such a good hostess, she threatens to wear herself to the bone."

Jesus smiled kindly, and attempted to put her at ease. "Your home is beautiful, Martha. We are happy to be here."

With this she sighed heavily, as if greatly relieved, but then left to "see to the servants," as though they had not done their work.

At her departure, the original calm returned to the court, and John found the tension easing from the back of his neck.

How did Lazarus live with such a woman? he wondered. Strange couple, he thought. Bachelor brother and spinster sister living under the same roof. But soon his thoughts were distracted.

"Mary?" Lazarus was saying.

John looked up to see whom he addressed this time, and his heart stood still. In a doorway off the courtyard a young woman peered quietly out at the men. Standing in shadow, she had probably assumed she was hidden from view, but what John could make of her was very pleasing to the eye.

She appeared to be even younger than the apostle, and was small and delicate of stature, perhaps a bit too slender, but beautiful nonetheless. Simply attired, the girl wore just one ornament, a tasteful jeweled pendant strung about her forehead. Her features were fragile and fine, but her eyes, by contrast, were large and dark, emphasized by the slightest touch of eye paint.

The fine white linen tunic which hung to her feet was drawn in to her tiny waist by a blue sash, and her graceful cloak was wine in color. This she drew up as a hood when Lazarus beckoned her to approach the men. But dark locks of lustrous hair could still be seen where they fell about her shoulders, and to her hips, completing the most beautiful picture John had ever seen.

"My younger sister," Lazarus introduced her.

Amenities were passed between Jesus and Mary, but John did not really hear what was said. How clearly he admired the girl must have been obvious, for when he at last tore his eyes from her, he found Peter giving him a cat-like grin, as though to say, "Sworn bachelors should not look at women in such a way!"

Red-faced, he stared at the ground, but as long as the girl was present, he could not resist frequent glances in her direction.

All Mary's attention, however, was on the Master. Wouldn't she just once look John's way? But what would he do if she should?

Mary did not stay long. It was not the place of women to remain at men's gatherings. Bowing her head, she backed away after the Master had finished speaking, and slowly she left the courtyard. John watched her departure sadly, his breath coming heavily.

But again he caught a glimpse of Peter's mocking face, and a scowl crossed his brow.

For the first time in his long discipleship, he would sit in the presence of the Nazarene without registering a word of his teachings. Though he chastised himself for the way his eyes roamed toward the door of Mary's exit, it did no good. "This is not right," he considered. "She is undoubtedly like other women I have known—lightheaded, silly-minded. I must concentrate on what is really important."

With much effort, he was able to subjugate his "lower instincts," as he thought them to be. There was no place for women in the life of an apostle—at least not in *his* life. Let Peter have his Deborah, and the others their wives and family ties. He was determined to remain free of such involvement for the sake of "greater things."

But though John's conscious mind was on the Master's discussion with Lazarus and the men, the doorway was kept in view. And suddenly he thought he saw her.

Yes—Mary had returned and stood where she again felt no one would notice, apparently trying to catch what she could of Jesus' words.

She remained thus for some moments, and then, to John's surprise, she began inching her way into the courtyard, keeping well against the wall. She adored the Master, it was apparent. She clung to every syllable he pronounced. Like a powerful magnet, his presence drew her to come slowly, ever so cautiously, near the group.

Perhaps no one beside John had observed. But he was keenly

aware of her approach, though he tried not to let on. He knew it must be difficult for women to stay always behind the scenes, especially when such a great Visitor as Jesus graced their homes. Occasionally Mary darted glances toward the house, as though feeling guilty for not staying where custom dictated. Still she continued to draw close. Due to her humble attitude, she did not attract the attention of the men who sat listening to Jesus, even when she seated herself on the courtyard floor, just outside the gathering.

John lifted his hand to straighten his sun-bleached hair, in case she might notice him. But then he caught himself. "Fool . . ." he muttered, "what does she matter?"

Besides, it appeared there was no chance of such a thing. Without even attempting to do so, Jesus had captivated her. John felt a stab of jealousy.

For nearly half an hour Mary remained motionless, studying the Master, drinking in his lessons like a thirsty child. If nothing else, John found in this an opportunity to satisfy the craving to look on her. His eyes went down her form slowly, and his masculine heart skipped erratically. As she had entered, her mantle, unbeknown to Mary, had fallen back, and she sat now draped gloriously in rich dark hair, so long it nearly touched the pavement. Greatly moved, he thought, "She is beautiful!"

John could have watched her indefinitely, but Martha had entered the courtyard with the servants, bustling nervously and distracting the guests with her intense "hospitality."

Mary seemed to jump as Martha came in and sat rigidly, torn between the desire to stay with Jesus, and the knowledge that she would be in trouble if she did not rise to help her sister.

Presently Martha's eyes were on her, hot and glaring. Displaying audacity John could scarcely believe, the older woman approached the Master, interrupting him in midsentence with a didactic tone. "Lord," she addressed him curtly, "do you not care that my sister has left me to serve alone? Tell her to help me!"

Mary was crestfallen, and John's hackles rose. Fortunately, the Master interceded. While other men would have put Martha firmly in her place, Jesus looked first at Mary, assaying her pure motive for being seated at his feet: the desire to learn of him. Then he addressed the elder sister with amazing tenderness. Shaking his head, he sighed. "Martha, Martha, you are anxious and troubled about many things. But only one thing is really needful, and Mary has chosen that good thing, which shall not be taken from her."

Chapter 24

The Judean night was cold, but lit beautifully by the harvest moon. Jesus and his apostles were in the countryside beyond Bethany.

Tonight as they rested, John was full of thought. Jesus' words to Martha had shamed him, though the Master had not intended them to. "Only one thing is needful, and Mary has chosen that good thing," he had said. Only Jesus and his teachings were really important. John had rebuked himself soundly for his distraction at Lazarus' house, and was determined not to let it happen again.

Looking out toward the hills of Jerusalem, he was filled with fresh dread of the future. It seemed the awful prophecies of the Lord's death approached fulfillment with the marching feet of a relentless army. Would nothing dissuade the Master from venturing into the realm of his enemies?

And what of John? At Ginaea, once again, his nature had revealed itself. What had all the teaching been for, the weary months of discipleship, if the Lord were to leave him while he still had no strength?

He thought back to a few days before, when, on the road through Judea, a scribe had challenged the Master. "What shall I do to inherit eternal life?" he had asked, testing him.

"What is written in the Law?" Jesus had countered.

"You shall love the Lord your God with all your heart, and with all your soul, and with all your strength, and with all your mind . . . and your neighbor as yourself," had been his quick reply.

"You have answered correctly," Jesus had said. "This do, and you shall live."

The lawyer had been silenced for the moment, knowing he had

not been able to do this. But, wishing to justify himself, he had asked flippantly, "And who is my neighbor?"

At this the Master had taken a seat along the road, and had proceeded to tell a parable about a certain man who had been robbed, beaten, and left for dead beside a highway. By chance a priest and then a Levite had passed that way, but seeing him lying there, had not deigned to help the man. Only a Samaritan had stopped and taken compassion on him. Binding his wounds and carrying the fellow upon his own donkey, he had brought him to an inn to care for him.

"Which, now, of these three do you think was neighbor to him that fell among thieves?" Jesus had questioned the scribe.

"He that showed mercy."

"Then," said Jesus, "go, and you do the same."

John drew his knees up and stared into the night sky. The Lord's choice of a Samaritan for his example of love had driven the lesson home.

Suddenly he wished to be with the Master, to spend any time he could at his side. Standing, John walked down the slope to where Jesus was meditating.

The Lord sat at the edge of a grove. His white robe had caught the moonlight, and his uplifted face, marked so often with heaviness, of late, seemed serene and peaceful.

Across the meadow at the foot of the hill, fields heavy with grain promised bounty for winter, and scattered flocks of sheep rested complacently. Jesus could have been the shepherd of the scene.

"I am the good shepherd, and I give my life for the sheep . . ." John sensed there was no turning from the reality of that statement. The Master would not be with him always.

He stood back, waiting for the Lord to complete his prayers, but he was glad for the chance to mark this image of the Nazarene on his table of remembrance. As if Jesus' form and features were not already an inextricable part of his memory, he drank in every detail of the picture.

At last the Master stood and turned toward camp. But John stepped out from the shadows and called to him.

When Jesus caught a glimpse of his disciple, he smiled warmly. "John, shouldn't you be asleep by now?"

"I cannot, my Lord."

The young son of Zebedee drew near, and the two sat together beside the grove. There was much John wanted to say, but fearing he might sound overly sentimental, he retained manly restraint.

"You pray often, Master," he said. "The Baptist tried to teach me how to pray, but I was always very awkward at it." The Lord said nothing, but let John go on. "I guess I am awkward at many things . . . Perhaps I am a slow learner when it comes to things spiritual."

Here his voice trailed off and he wondered how to continue. "You see, Master . . . I want to be like you. And yet I have no power. Once you told me I could do nothing of myself, that I must lie like a field beneath God's plow and let him turn me over. But still I seem to lack so much of what you have. And how can I do better if you . . . "

"If I go away?"

John nodded silently.

"If I go away, John, the Father will not leave you comfortless. He will give you the Holy Spirit and his power if you but ask."

"But how am I to ask? I cannot pray as I should, for I have never learned the way."

They were interrupted by footsteps behind them, the other disciples having come out from camp.

"Lord, teach us to pray, as the Baptist taught his disciples," John said when the others were seated.

Jesus looked at them all compassionately and then complied. "When you pray, say, 'Our Father who is in heaven, hallowed be your name. Your kingdom come.' " His voice was reverent and full of feeling. " 'Your will be done, as in heaven, so in earth. Give us day by day our bread. And forgive us our sins, for we also forgive every one that is indebted to us.' " Here he paused, allowing the thought to sink into their ears. " 'And lead us not into temptation, but deliver us from evil. For yours is the kingdom, and the power, and the glory forever. Amen.' "

They had heard these words once before, when, at the beginning of his ministry, Jesus had given his sermon on the mount. As John dwelt silently upon them, the profound implications which lay beneath their simplicity began to strike him. God had all power. His will in heaven and earth, and in the life of the disciple was all that was necessary.

"Is it truly his will to grant me his Spirit?" John wondered. "Must I only ask?"

But Jesus was speaking again. "And I say to you: Ask, and it shall be given you. Seek, and you shall find. Knock, and it shall be opened to you. For everyone that asks receives. And he that seeks finds, and to him that knocks it shall be opened. . . .

"If you then, being evil, know how to give good gifts to your children, how much more shall your heavenly Father give the Holy Spirit to those who ask him?"

Chapter 25

It was of some relief to John that Jesus decided to retreat into the wilderness before finally going into Jerusalem. But his reason for doing so would be clear only in retrospect.

The second morning of this voluntary seclusion, as the men finished their dawn meal, a stranger raced breathlessly over the hill toward them. Prepared at all times for the approach of Jesus' enemies, the apostles started anxiously. "Stay where you are!" Simon shouted.

"It is all right, Peter," the Master assured him, motioning the frightened newcomer forward.

In the gray light the big fisherman had not seen that the supposed foe was but a boy, and upon evaluating his stature, Peter looked quietly at the ground.

The young fellow walked toward them, sweat glistening on his face from a long run through difficult terrain. "Jesus of Nazareth?" he asked.

"I am."

The boy, obviously awed by the renowned Rabbi, tried to be as businesslike as possible. "I have a message for you from the house of Lazarus in Bethany."

Rarely did hired messengers bring good news, and John fought the fear that something might have happened to Mary.

"Speak, son," the Master said.

The lad was apparently close to the family who had sent him, for the pain of the message showed in his face. "I have been asked to tell you, sir," his voice quavered, "Behold, he whom you love is sick.' "

The announcement concerned Lazarus, and not his young sister. John felt a sort of guilty relief at this, but noting Jesus' sorrow, he shared some of his sentiment. If the sickness had been anything but urgent, no runner would have been commissioned.

Walking up to the Lord, the apostle wished to comfort him, but could find nothing to say. Instead, it was the Master who spoke, and such strange words they were.

"This sickness is not unto death," he said, "but for the glory of God, that the Son of God might be glorified thereby."

At this, he motioned the lad to leave, thanking him for the message. The boy hesitated, expecting some answer to the pronouncement. Wouldn't the Master be coming to Bethany?

But Jesus only turned to go, wandering silently away from his men and deep into the hills.

It was not until another two days that the Lord returned to camp. Meanwhile, the disciples waited in confusion and questioning. They were glad he did not go to Bethany. It was dangerous for him in the province of the capital. But did he not love Lazarus? How could he be so callous?

John was especially torn. Scenes of Mary in her anguish came frequently to mind. For him there were mixed feelings when the Lord returned to his men, having fasted the two days, and said, "Let us go into Judea again."

The apostles murmured loudly. "Master," Peter objected, "the Jews recently sought to stone you. And you go there again?"

"Are there not twelve hours in the day?" was Jesus' strange reply. "If any man walks in the day, he does not stumble, because he sees the light of this world. But if a man walks in the night, he stumbles, because there is no light in him. Our friend Lazarus sleeps, but I go, that I may awake him out of sleep."

No one had understood his first statement, but the latter part they thought they comprehended, and James responded, "But, Lord, if he sleeps, he will get better."

Then Jesus said to them plainly, "Lazarus is dead."

John's heart sank, and the apostles turned to one another. Of course, the Master had power to know such a thing, and they were pained by the news. But why would Jesus feel it necessary, now, to go to Bethany? All he might do is mourn with the family. And if he was determined to go, why had he not gone earlier than this? He might have healed Lazarus!

Sorrow, bewilderment, anger—all these were evidenced as the disciples whispered among themselves and shook their heads.

But the Lord spoke again, and his voice was heavy with rebuke. "I am glad for your sakes that I was not there, as now you will have reason to believe in me."

Seeing their further confusion and doubt, the Lord sighed and gathered his robes about him, making ready to depart. "Let us go to him," he said.

Realizing that he would venture ahead without them, the apostles were shaken with fear, and Thomas said, somewhat sarcastically, "Yes—let us also go . . . that we may die with the Master."

Chapter 26

It took four days to travel back to Bethany, but well before Jesus had come to the town, news of his approach got out, and crowds began to collect about him while he was yet some distance from the place.

The reaction of the people was mixed. They had undoubtedly expected him much sooner. Some mocked him for his tardiness, jeering and calling him a false prophet for his "callous neglect" of Lazarus. Others were very quiet, not wishing to pass judgment on the great Teacher too quickly.

As John absorbed this, he noted that the Master was greatly troubled, heavy-hearted in a way new to the disciple. His sorrow seemed to relate directly to the attitude of the crowd, for the more they taunted him, the more depressed he became. Could it be that he was ashamed he had not arrived earlier—that he was having second thoughts about his decision to remain those two days in the wilderness?

"Four days Lazarus has lain in the grave!" a nasty voice pierced the crowd. "Jesus of Nazareth, do you lack power to heal those who love you? Perhaps it is dangerous to love you too much!"

Four days? John thought. Lazarus had passed on the exact date Jesus had said he was dead!

Suddenly the Master wheeled about, leveling stormy eyes at his assailant. John could clearly see it was the accusation itself and not the reference to Lazarus which so troubled him. Indeed, it appeared that none of Jesus' sorrow related to the death of his friend. And now the apostle found even himself questioning the Lord's concern in this whole affair, for Jesus seemed to value his reputation more than the deceased.

Many people of the capital had come out to mourn with Mary

and Martha, for Lazarus was well-known in all these parts. And so, the crowd was full of the Master's enemies. While John questioned the Lord's motives, he was also on guard for his safety. It startled him, therefore, when, as they neared Bethany, a sudden jostling in the throng indicated someone was trying to push through to Jesus.

John was relieved to find that it was Martha, nervous and distraught as ever. Mary, who mourned in isolation, had not heard of the Rabbi's coming, but Martha had run out from the town the moment she received word of his approach.

"Lord!" she cried as she made her way to him.

Appearing ten years older than John remembered her, the woman stumbled forward, brokenness and despair in her haggard features. The Nazarene embraced her, and she cried again, "Lord . . . if you had been here, my brother would not have died!"

Though she was, in typical manner, presuming to correct Jesus, it was apparent that grief had softened her nature, and John could feel only sympathy for the mourner. Silently the Lord lifted her face, and looked upon her with an intensity of compassion shown but few times in his ministry.

Martha grew quiet, and as the Lord's love enveloped her she spoke words of faith unlike herself. In a voice full of assurance, she said, "But I know that even now, whatever you ask of God, God will give it to you."

John was amazed. Could it be that she expected the Master to . . . No—it could not happen! But with Jesus' reply, the apostle was filled with wonder.

Calmly, definitely, the Lord answered, "Your brother shall rise again."

John's skin stood in gooseflesh, but Martha's face was radiant. Almost as quickly as her joy had come, however, it began to fade, for her mind refused to accept what she wanted so to believe. "I know," her voice faltered, "that he shall rise again . . . in the resurrection at the last day . . ."

The Master studied her solemnly, and John detected the glint of tears at the corners of his eyes.

"I am the resurrection, and the life . . ." the Lord responded in measured, heart-heavy tones. "He that believes in me, though he were dead, yet shall he live . . . and whoever lives and believes in me shall never die."

Martha, wide-eyed, trembled at his words.

Sighing deeply, the Master demanded, "Do you believe this?"

"Yes, Lord," she stammered, "I believe that you are the Christ, the Son of God, who was to come into the world."

She had made no commitment. Jesus shook his head and Martha turned away, going back toward home.

But as she departed, the Lord called out, "Tell your sister I want to see her."

The house was full of mourners from throughout the region —friends, acquaintances, and business associates of the late departed. Mary sat in a private room, her face hidden in shadow as she dwelt apart from these who had come to comfort her. Lazarus had been the dearest and best friend she had ever had. No man, save perhaps Jesus of Nazareth, had ever held her adoration as had her brother, and even the Master had not seen fit to come when she and Martha had so badly needed his touch.

Though smothered in despair, she sometimes recalled how her heart had thrilled to Jesus' teachings the day he had graced their home. Could she have been so mistaken about him? Even now, it was hard to believe the Master could have anything but the truest love for them all. Yet . . . he was not here.

Curtains shrouded the window of the dark room where she sat. Morbid thoughts haunted her. She could still see the dead form of Lazarus as he had lain on the cot the last time she beheld him.

Suddenly a sound at the door brought back the present, and she lurched in her chair. "Mary . . ." her sister's voice was calling.

The young girl turned about and found her only remaining relative straining to see through the shadows. "Yes . . . Martha . . ."

The elder's voice bore a strange mixture of excitement and shame. "I have good news for you," she said.

"Yes, sister. What is it?"

"The Master has come . . . and he has asked for you."

Mary's heart jumped. He had come! He had not failed her! Moving more rapidly than she had in days, she walked hastily to the door. "Where, Martha? Where may I find him?"

The elder sister told her the way, and followed after. The others in the house, likewise, when they saw that she rose up hastily and went out, followed her, thinking she was going to the tomb to weep.

As she went, her body pulsed with excitement, but after she had traveled down the road a distance, she was overcome by confusion, and then by something akin to anger and resentment. Why had Jesus waited until now? Hadn't he known how much they needed him? She loved the Master, yet had he not been intolerably delinquent, inexcusably cruel to his friends?

Jesus had not left the site where he had called for Mary. Something in the realization of this began to melt the icy thoughts which had been crystallizing in her young mind. She was broken with the sight of him, and fell at his feet, weeping, "Lord, if you had been here, my brother would not have died."

Though Mary's words to the Master were the same as her sister's, John knew there was no rebuke in them—only genuine sorrow. Jesus reached down to embrace her, and she clung to him limply.

How the disciple wished to comfort her.

For a moment Jesus was silent, looking at the weeping form he held so close, but as his eyes traveled from face to face in the sobbing, heartbroken crowd, he could no longer contain his own agony. Only later would John realize what the Master must have gone through, but the apostle quaked when he heard his Lord groan audibly.

Then, gazing once again upon the throng, Jesus said, "Where have you laid him?"

Some answered, "Lord, come and see."

The Master followed them up a nearby hillside, Mary and Martha close at hand, and John endeavoring to walk beside him. As the disciple drew near, he trembled to see that Jesus wept.

"Behold how he loved him!" said some who followed after.

And others, "Could not this man, who opened the eyes of the blind, have prevented his friend from dying?"

When Jesus heard this he again groaned deeply, and John placed his arm about him.

Lazarus' grave was a cave set in the hillside. A stone covered the entrance. The Master stood for some moments staring at the tomb, tears coursing down his face and into his beard. John stood by in agonized helplessness, wishing for all the world that there were something he might do to comfort his Lord. But suddenly Jesus spoke the strangest words John had ever yet heard.

Turning to the men who had led the way, he said deliberately, so as not to be misunderstood, "Take away the stone."

As they might look on a madman, the strangers stared

incredulously at him, and Martha was quickly upon him with her old manner. "Lord," she was saying, "by this time the odor will be great, for he has been dead four days!"

Jesus eyed her stormily, refusing this time to tolerate her attitude. "Did I not say to you that if you would believe, you would see the glory of God?" he demanded.

Martha fell back, stunned at his response, and Jesus turned again to the strangers. The glint in his eyes warned them, and without a further word, they pressed themselves to the task of rolling the stone from the cave's mouth.

John could scarcely believe what was happening. It took them some minutes to move the stone from the trench in which it rested. It ground against the earth stubbornly as the men rocked it back and forth, gaining momentum for a final shove. One, two, three—it bashed against the side of the tomb, and the strangers had to begin again. Heave, push, push—at last it rocked with a jolt, nearly crushing one fellow's foot, and came to a thudding halt beyond the ditch.

Instinctively, Mary, Martha, and John lifted their sleeves to cover their faces, certain that the stench of death would come spilling forth from the cave's dank dingy recesses.

The Master stood silently again some moments, and then gazed above to the heavens, saying, "Father, I thank you that you have heard me. And I know that you hear me always, but because of the people which stand by I say this . . . that they may believe that you have sent me."

The apostle was speechless as the Lord stepped up to the tomb and rested his hand against its opening. As if gathering strength for some great task, Jesus stared into the dark cavern and John shivered with anticipation.

At last, the Master cried aloud into the cave, his voice moving the mountain, "Lazarus! Come forth!"

John, Mary, Martha, the strangers, and all the company of Jerusalem and Bethany gathered on the hill and in the streets below, were captives of the unthinkable, not one of them taking his eyes from the black mouth of the tomb.

Could it actually happen? Could Jesus perform such a miracle?

No one spoke, no one breathed. Seconds passed, but they seemed an eternity . . .

And suddenly . . .

From the depths of the house of death a hint of moving white was seen, and as all looked on it became clear just what it was. . . .

Lord, Jehovah!—John shook violently—it cannot be!

As if from a single body a gasp of astonishment rose from the crowd below.

And he that had been dead came forth, bound hand and foot with graveclothes, but with no stench of any kind . . . his face wrapped about with a napkin. . . .

And Jesus said to them, "Loose him, and let him go."

Chapter 27

Though many believed on Jesus after having seen this most miraculous of all his works, some witnesses took the news immediately to the Pharisees in Jerusalem. Within hours of Jesus' great display of power, a council was called by the chief priests, and the men who had sealed the death of the Baptist once again discussed how they should handle the Nazarene.

"This man is doing many miracles! If we leave him alone," they concluded, "all men will believe on him, and the Romans will come and take away both our place and nation."

And Caiaphas added, " . . . it is expedient for us that one man should die for the people, that the whole nation would not perish!"

From that day on they took counsel together to plan the death of the Master. For a while, therefore, Jesus was forced to avoid the Holy City, but he would not put off his destiny indefinitely.

Today, John and James walked together behind the others. They were silent, as were all the Lord's men, and deep in contemplation of what they had witnessed at Bethany. They sensed the inevitable push toward Jerusalem, and they knew the plot for Jesus' life.

Why must this be? John thought to himself. If only he might stay with us always! Why must he die—now of all times, when he has just proven himself to the world!

He recalled the times Jesus had spoken of his kingdom. Whatever it meant, John knew it was to be a reality. He could no longer doubt the Master on anything. But, if the Lord were to die, how could he reign as he said he would?

Still, all power clearly rested in the Master's hands. The miracle at Bethany had confirmed that.

Suddenly, pieces of the puzzle came together, and John's heart thrilled within him. "Lord," he spoke silently, "can it be that you will rise again? Like Lazarus?"

All at once, nothing seemed impossible. The sight of Lazarus walking forth from that grave could leave no room for doubt. Had Jesus not spoken of the Son of Man "rising from the dead"? If he were to die, was it necessary that the grave must keep him?

Of course not!

The thought must have struck James at the same instant, for as though he were in tune with John's very mind, he was suddenly speaking. "Of course not! Why, brother, how stupid of us! How could we have failed to see it?"

John looked curiously at the elder, but when he caught the gleam in James' eyes he knew that he had received the same burst of insight. Laughing uproariously, they embraced and shouted for joy. "Praised be Jehovah!" they cried, and the others turned to see what possessed them.

"They would think us insane!" John grinned.

"Yes—wouldn't they!"

But before they could share the vision, a voice called their names. Scarcely believing their ears, they stopped short. "James, John!" it came again. Yes—it was their mother!

Wheeling about quickly, they found her pursuing them down the road, followed by a handful of servants from the home in Capernaum. Though baffled at her sudden appearance, the two sons received her with open arms. "Mother!" John cried, enfolding her. "What are you doing here?"

Women had followed Jesus during his ministry, but it had been months since the brothers had seen Salome. And they could not recollect her ever leaving Capernaum except to accompany Zebedee to feasts in Jerusalem.

Wiping tears of happiness from her eyes, she explained her presence, and the strange breaking of the tradition which had always bound her to her home. "Sons," she breathed heavily, "your father left for Jerusalem some days ago, to go meet with the council."

John's heart grew cold at the thought of Zebedee's treachery, and Salome read the disdain in his eyes. "Try to understand," she pleaded. "Your father is not the man he once was. He cannot find it in his heart to forgive the loss of you and James."

The disciple wished to ask what great change that was for Zebedee, for his father had never been a forgiving man. But he curbed his tongue this time.

"Mother, that does not explain your presence here," James

floundered. It was highly unorthodox for a woman to leave home apart from her husband, and his eyes were wide with bewilderment.

Salome looked at the ground. "I have heard how the Master raised a man who had been dead four days . . . " She hesitated, finding it difficult to go on. "I can no longer doubt that this Teacher of yours is who he claims to be," she faltered.

James took her in his arms, and John was radiant.

"I could not stay behind in that lonely house another day . . . " Salome whispered. "I felt I had to come to you! Zebedee no longer cares what I do. He has made it clear he has no need of me. He only stews in bitter memories, or thinks on how he may destroy the Nazarene. I know I have gone against custom, against the traditions of Israel. But I could not live as I was living!"

At this the servants nodded in affirmation of their mistress' suffering, and James consoled her. "We will care for you, mother," he said. "I am sure our Lord will not send you away."

Salome lifted her head, grateful for this assurance. But urgency marked her features. "Please, James! We cannot let them kill the Master!"

The brothers looked secretively at one another, the elder indicating that it was time to share their recent thoughts. "Mother," John began, "the Lord has often told us he must die."

Salome shook her head angrily, but he went on. "That does not have to be the end, though, don't you see? If he raised Lazarus . . ."

The meaning of John's words did not dawn quickly, but when they did, Salome's eyes brightened, and though her mind balked at the thought, her soul was filled with excitement. "John! Are you saying . . . ?"

"Yes, mother!" The disciple smiled. "Why not?"

Salome's imagination reeled. "Can he actually come back from the dead?"

"Surely you have heard of the Master's kingdom," James asserted. "He has spoken of it often, and of his ultimate reign over it."

Salome nodded enthusiastically. "Then . . . death cannot keep him!" she exclaimed.

The three stood silent as the revelation infused them. But Salome's interest took a curious twist, and she studied her sons with womanish intrigue. "I have heard it said that the two of you are the closest to the Lord of all his disciples. Is that true?"

John and James did not know how to answer. But remembering the Transfiguration and the times the Lord had shared his friendship with them privately, the elder gave a straightforward response. "Perhaps so, mother, if you include Peter in our number; for Jesus has taken the three of us into his confidence more than the others."

Salome tingled with motherly pride. "Well, then!" she insisted, taking them both by the arms. "If he is to have a kingdom, who should reign beside him but my two boys!"

The brothers were perplexed and a little embarrassed, wondering what she had in mind. "I want you to ask Jesus for this," she prodded. "Who deserves it more than you?"

Her face shone as she took them in hand and began leading them down the road toward the Master. It all happened so quickly, neither one of them could account for the next few moments, but somehow, by the time they had nearly reached the Nazarene, she had them committed to complying with her request. Could they deny her anything, on this reunion day? They were to ask the Master for seats beside his throne!

Anyway, they reasoned, was it such a bad idea? Why should they not desire such a thing? Someone would surely occupy those choice positions. Why not the sons of Zebedee?

Coming upon the Master, mother and sons alike made obeisance, and Salome, who had remained a few steps behind, now nudged James and John.

Face to face with Jesus it was suddenly difficult for them to voice their request. They looked at their mother and then at the Lord, saying only, "Master, we want you to do for us whatever we shall desire."

Jesus studied them thoughtfully, and then replied, "What do you want me to do for you?"

The words came out very slowly. "Grant us that we may sit, one on your right and the other on your left, in your glory," they faltered.

An answer did not come immediately. Instead, Jesus turned to the mother. As if asking her mind on the matter, he put the same question to her. "What do *you* wish?"

The two sons had never seen such boldness in Salome. She had always been the one to stay behind the scene when they were at home. She had never spoken up for the things she wanted, no matter how Zebedee had gone against her. Amazed, the two men watched as she came humbly but straightforwardly to the point.

Bowing before Jesus, she confirmed their request. "Sir, grant that these, my two sons, may sit, the one on your right and the other on your left, in your kingdom."

Jesus looked at his two apostles curiously. "You do not know what you ask," he said. "Are you able to drink of the cup that I shall drink, and to be baptized in the same way I shall be?"

John turned red-faced to his elder brother. They did not know what to say, but as Salome eyed them, they replied, "Lord, we are able."

Sighing deeply, Jesus gazed compassionately at them and shook his head. "You shall drink indeed of my cup," he answered, "and be baptized with my baptism. But to sit on my right hand and on my left is not mine to give, but it shall be given to those for whom it is prepared by my Father."

The two apostles were numb with shame, and Salome pondered the ground at her feet.

Of course the others had overheard, and a rumble of indignation against James and John rose from among them. Peter especially was put out with them for what he considered great gall on their parts.

But Jesus called them all unto him and said, "You know that the princes of the Gentiles exercise dominion over them, and those that are great exercise authority upon *them*. But it shall not be so among you. But, whoever will be great among you, let him be your minister, and whoever will be chief among you, let him be your servant."

At this the group fell silent, each one weighing his own soul. And then Jesus spoke with great heaviness, "Even as the Son of Man came not to be ministered unto, but to minister . . . and to give his life a ransom for many."

THE LIFE

"In him was life; and the life was the light of men. And the light shineth in darkness; and the darkness comprehended it not."
JOHN 1:4, 5

Chapter 1

The Passover feast once again drew close, and people of Palestine were converging on the Holy City from all directions. Much excitement centered on conversations concerning the Nazarene and whether or not he would attend the festivities. Jews from all over the Roman world hoped to lay eyes on the man who raised the dead.

The chief priests and Pharisees, however, had issued a commandment that if anyone knew where Jesus was, he must make it known.

Six days before the feast the Master was on the last leg of the journey toward Jerusalem and his destiny. He made only one final stop along the way, to dine with his friends in Bethany.

At supper that night, in the house of a man named Simon, Jesus and one other were the guests of honor. That other man was Lazarus, alive and well, and celebrated for the great miracle which had restored him. As usual, Martha served, but Lazarus sat at the head table with his Lord.

Despite the warm surroundings and the fine array of food, John could not bring himself to eat. He could think only of the days ahead, and wonder how much longer he would behold the face of his beloved Master. Lazarus' beautiful sister, Mary, did not capture his thoughts, nor did Jesus' possible resurrection cheer him tonight. Only fear for the dearest and best man in the world consumed him.

It was not until an unusual occurrence that John took in the activities. The meal was nearly completed, and the Lord and his disciples reclined at ease around the table, when Mary entered once more, uninvited, into the midst of the generally male gathering. At first, this disturbed some of them, especially Simon, the host. But when it became apparent that the Lord was pleased to see her, no one challenged her presence, and John was struck afresh by her unique character and beauty.

Mary said nothing, but her face revealed a heart full of love for the Master, and she set about silently to show just how much he meant to her.

From under her cloak she drew a gem-studded box of carved alabaster, opening it so that the pungent odor of costly spikenard ointment filled the house. She began to anoint the Lord's head with the fragrant balm, and then knelt at his feet and soothed them in the same manner, going so far as to wipe them with her rich, dark hair.

Now such commodities as this ointment did not come inexpensively, and one of the disciples became indignant at what he considered a "waste" of the spikenard.

John had never paid much attention to Judas Iscariot. A quiet man, he had never stood out among the Lord's followers. No one thought ill of him. He was a handsome fellow, seemingly trustworthy. The Lord had, in fact, appointed him group treasurer. There had been little reason to doubt his integrity, though John did recall a time or two when the till seemed lower than it should have been. Still, all in all, he appeared to be a good manager, as far as the others could tell, with their limited interest in such things.

But today he called unusual attention to himself by his strange response to Mary's actions. "To what purpose is this waste?" he asked suddenly, his eyes full of anger. "This ointment might have been sold for three-hundred pence and given to the poor!"

John was taken aback by his challenge, and even more so when some of the other disciples began to agree with the words. As the murmuring rose, Mary looked, shamefaced, at the floor, and tears spilled from her eyes. John glared bitterly at Judas, finding it incomprehensible that he could be concerned with such a thing at this time.

But then the Master called for silence and turned to Mary, taking her hand in his. "Leave her alone," he answered. "Why do you trouble this woman? She has done a good thing for me. For the poor are always with you, but me you will not always have."

The reality of the Teacher's coming death hit them once again, and they were silent with shame and sorrow—all but Judas, whose feelings John could not ascertain from his stony face.

Again Jesus spoke, looking tenderly at the lovely girl before___ him. "For in anointing me, she has prepared me for my burial," he said. At this Mary studied him in horror. But then he blessed her with assurance, saying, "Truly I tell you, wherever this gospel shall be preached in the whole world, the story of what she has done will also be told for a memorial of her."

Chapter 2

Excitement in Jerusalem had reached fever pitch. News was out that Jesus was on his way to attend the Passover. Since the raising of Lazarus, so many had come to believe in him as the expected Messiah, that a virtual mania to make him king had taken hold.

John had no idea what to expect as they approached the Holy City. He knew only that great crowds would be awaiting the Master.

As they drew nigh to Jerusalem and to Bethphage, to the Mount of Olives, Jesus called for Peter and John. "Go into the village over there," he said, pointing to a small hamlet which bordered the mountain, "and you will find a donkey tied, with a colt beside her. Loose them, and bring them to me."

John looked quizzically at Peter, but realizing that there had to be a good reason for this request, they hastened to obey the Lord. As the apostles raced away, the Master called, "If anyone questions you, say, 'The Lord has need of them,' and he will send them."

Upon entering the village, they found the animals tied outside a doorway, and as they began to loose the colt, the owners, standing by, watched them incredulously, wondering at their nerve. "What are you doing?" they demanded.

John gulped, but then remembered what Jesus had said, and answered, "The Lord has need of them." The strangers were obviously taken aback, but did not question them further, and Peter and John went free with the creatures.

Still not knowing what use the Master had for the animals, they were surprised when, upon returning with the beasts of burden, they found that the Lord was going to enter Jerusalem by this means. The two apostles removed their cloaks and threw them across the donkey and her colt. Did Jesus actually mean to come before the worshiping masses, riding on something so lowly as a donkey?

The gates of the Holy City were not yet in sight. The Lord and his men had not even reached the crest of Mount Olivet, before the thundering crowd was upon him. At first hint of his approach they had swarmed out from the villages and the capital like bees from a hive. In all the Lord's ministry John had never experienced such a pressing, ear-shattering mass of humanity.

Not only were their numbers more magnificent, but their mood seemed to be one of pure adoration, pure worship of the Messiah. There were no cries for healing—no pleas for his miraculous touch. The people were, instead, full of nothing but unquestioning praise and loud acclaim for the man of Nazareth. As he came, they spread their clothes in the way; they cut down branches from palm trees and used the fan-like foliage to pave the highway before him and his lowly steeds.

"Hosanna! Hosanna!" they sang. "Blessed is the King of Israel that comes in the name of the Lord! Blessed be the kingdom of our father David, that comes in the name of the Lord! Hosanna in the highest!"

As John took all this in, he could not be an impartial observer. The dynamics of mass worship swept him up in their path as easily as an irresistible wind sweeps up a leaf.

It frightened him to be so helpless—

But why not praise the Lord? he thought. Truly he was the Messiah! Truly he would triumph! For the first time in these months of journey toward the Lord's terrible destiny, John felt exultant, ecstatic! As they began the descent from the mount, he found himself removing his own cloak, throwing it before the Master, and shouting with the crushing throng, "Blessed be the King that comes in the name of the Lord! Peace in heaven, and glory in the highest!"

Like John, all the apostles had been caught up in the spirit of the moment. But the Master sat upon his beast silently, his eyes unswervingly directed toward the city, as though contemplating his purpose there. Noting this, John quickly put it from his mind. This was not the time to think of such things, he persuaded himself. So he danced and sang along with the multitude, exuberant and free.

But somewhere along the way, Pharisees came out from the

crowd, hot with anger and disapproval. "Master, rebuke your disciples!" they ordered him.

Suddenly a pall fell over the throng within range of these words. They feared the Lord's enemies. And John especially felt a twinge at this sudden interjection of what he wished so to forget.

But the Master did not cease his journey. Steadfastly, he kept his eyes toward the city, letting his gaze fall only briefly upon the adoring crowd. At that instant, the compassion which was so typical of him filled the masses with renewed joy. And directing his accusers to look at his followers, he said, "I tell you, that if these were to hold their peace, the stones would immediately cry out."

Chapter 3

John and all the Lord's men were lodged at Bethany tonight, as they had been each night since the Master's glorious entry into the Holy City. Despite the pleasant surroundings, however, the apostle found it impossible to sleep. For two or three hours, he had been pacing the roof and galleries of Lazarus' home, hoping not to waken anyone, but so restless he could not stay in bed.

Much had happened since Jesus' triumphal entrance into Jerusalem. The next day, the Master had reenacted the scene with which he had started his ministry. He had gone to the Temple and proceeded once again to drive out the moneychangers. The overturning of tables, the freeing of sacrifices . . . line by line, the drama had been the same. Had John not known better, he would have thought history was repeating itself. In a sense the Master had been trying to show just that. Despite his teachings throughout Palestine, nothing had really changed in the hearts of its people, at least not in the hearts of its leaders. In his eyes, their righteousness was still filthy rags.

And then, once again, the healings had commenced—the blind, the lame made whole by the touch of his hand. When the children had praised him in song that day, the chief priests and scribes had tried to squelch them, but to no avail.

The Master had begun to teach daily in the Temple, meeting with droves of people early in the morning. He spoke by parables, and in allegory, stories which showed up the hypocrisy of his enemies. The Pharisees were not slow to realize the intent of the Lord's words, but when they sought an opportunity to destroy him, they could not, because of his adoring masses. They tried repeatedly to entangle him in his own talk, but to no avail. When they found over and over that his answers were too wise, or that he was able to turn their questions against themselves they at last gave up that strategy and retreated from the battle for a while.

The Master, however, did not retreat. His attacks on the opposition grew more pointed, more scathing. It was a wonder that he survived them. Just today he had flung incredible disparagements their way. "Woe unto you, scribes and Pharisees, hypocrites!" his voice had carried thunderlike through the Temple courts. "You blind guides! You fools! You are like whited sepulchers, full of dead men's bones! You serpents! You generation of vipers! How can you escape the damnation of hell?"

John's hair stood on end at the memory of that voice and those words. Truly, the Lord was making his own deathbed!

The apostle was on the roof, and he cast his eyes toward the Mount of Olives which separated Bethany from the capital. The sky westward was illuminated by the lights of the great city, and as more of the Master's words were recalled, tears came to John's eyes.

When Jesus had finished his rebuke of the Pharisees in the audience of the people, he had gone to the edge of the court and looked over the city at his feet. His voice suddenly broken, and as though his strength were spent, he had cried heavily, "O Jerusalem, Jerusalem, you that kill the prophets, and stone those who are sent to you . . . how often would I have gathered your children together, even as a hen gathers her chickens under her wings . . . and you would not!"

John finally fell asleep near a corner of the roof, only to be awakened by Peter. It was still dark when the big fisherman shook him.

"What do you want?" John snapped.

"Why should you sleep when I cannot?" Peter retorted.

John sat up and stretched his cold, cramped legs. "So what's troubling you?"

Simon was incredulous. "You can ask such a question?"

John stared across the roof. "Of course, I know," he sighed. "We all fear for the Master."

Peter looked at him blankly, and then a blush of shame, hidden by the dark, rose to his rugged face. "Of course," he muttered. His tone of voice, and the silence which followed, indicated that such things had not been the source of Simon's unrest. That anything else could, at this time, dominate a disciple's thinking was unbelievable to John, who could barely bring himself to pursue another topic.

"There is more on your mind than this?" he asked.

Peter stirred uneasily. "Have you forgotten Jesus' words to us yesterday afternoon?" he queried. "Do they not trouble you at all?"

John quickly sifted through the impressions which had bombarded him of late, and he lit upon the conversation to which Peter apparently alluded.

As Jesus had left the Temple, following his rebuke of the Pharisees, some of the disciples had been marveling at the beauty of the sacred edifices. The Lord had taken opportunity from the moment, and turning to look at the courts and marble pillars, had spoken a mystery. "See all of these great buildings?" he had begun. "Truly, I say unto you, there shall not be left here one stone upon another, that shall not be thrown down!"

So astonished had the disciples been at this statement that they had not questioned him regarding it. But Peter, James, John, and Andrew had gone to him privately later that day as he rested on the Mount of Olives. "Tell us," Peter had asked, "when shall these things be? And what will be the sign of your coming, and of the end of the world?"

That the strange discourse which followed had not taken preeminence in John's mind showed only that his concern did not presently lie with such things. Now, however, as he contemplated it afresh, an eerie sensation overcame him. It seemed the Master's words had pointed to the future—whether near or distant, John could not be sure. But the portent had been full of disasters—wars, famines, earthquakes. Jesus had warned his four listeners of impending doom, saying that some of his disciples would be delivered up to councils, and that some would even be killed for his sake. He had talked of the sun being darkened, and of Jerusalem being surrounded by armies, and trodden down. He had related that he would return in glory, triumphant . . .

Truly, the Lord's message must have been important, or he would not have shared it at such a time as this. "Like the words of a dying friend . . ." John whispered.

"What?" Peter asked.

"Nothing . . ."

"Well, John, what do you think the Master was talking about?" Evidently Peter was eager to discuss the topic in detail. Still, though John could relate in part to his fascination with the subject, other things seemed much more urgent.

Knowing no other way to rid himself of the intruder, he feigned a look of terrible sleepiness and settled into his corner with closed eyes. "We will speak of it in the morning!" he grumbled.

Peter stood disgruntledly and spat upon the rooftop. Peering through a slit of his eye, John watched as the burly fisherman trudged away angrily. Then he leaned his head back, staring into the black, diamond-studded sky.

Too-familiar tears came once again to cloud his vision. "Should all the stars fall and the moon turn to blood . . ." he whispered, "what would it matter, my Lord, once you are gone from me?"

Chapter 4

It seemed that only a few minutes passed before John was once more wakened against his will. Opening his eyes in anger, he was surprised to find dawn's gray light above, and the Master bending over him.

"John . . . " came the familiar call.

Scrambling instantly to his feet, the disciple returned the greeting. "Sir, I was only now thinking of you."

Jesus walked to the edge of the roof and leaned against the balustrade, heaviness in his bearing. "But you were sleeping, John."

"It does not seem to me I slept at all," he insisted. "But even so, you filled my thoughts."

The Rabbi turned to his beloved follower. "And what were your thoughts?" he asked.

The apostle scanned the horizon toward the Holy City. "Surely nothing is hidden from you, Lord . . . You know my concerns."

Jesus studied him compassionately. "It would be good for you to speak of them, my friend."

John was confounded. "You can be mindful of my well-being even at such a time as this?"

Jesus understood. "Don't you see, John. It was for just such a time that I came into the world. I have been preparing for it all my life. You do not know what lies ahead, and so only fear has been your companion."

Once again the Master had plunged to the core of John's soul. How better to describe the haunting horrors of his days and nights since he had first begun to realize that Jesus was going to die? Fear had been his bedfellow, hanging like a loathsome parasite upon his spirit.

Unspeakable was his love for the Nazarene. Looking at him, he trembled. "Do you not fear, my Lord? You endure all of this with such resignation! Has fate dictated the ledger so that it cannot be challenged?"

Divine though Jesus was, he was also human. Turning away, he surveyed the hills over against Jerusalem, and his face twitched.

Suddenly John realized his Lord had not come up on this roof only to comfort him. The Master himself sought consolation.

John stepped closer to Jesus and put an arm about his shoulders. He felt totally inadequate to ease the pain, but the fact that his mind had been turned, however fleetingly, from his own misery to that of the Nazarene seemed to comfort the Son of God.

"You know that after two days is the feast of the Passover . . ." Jesus replied, "and the Son of Man is betrayed to be crucified."

John jolted involuntarily, staring wildly at the Nazarene. Crucified! No, Lord! Was this to be the way? "Master . . ." his throat was dry as the desert, "how . . . when . . ."

John, the "comforter," was failing miserably. Black fear enveloped him, and he could not look at his Lord. Somehow he restrained his emotions, but Jesus knew the storm of his soul.

As always, the Master had to bear the burdens. Reaching for his beloved companion, the Lord spoke tenderly. "You fear, my friend, because you do not believe. You fear because you do not know with certainty that you will see me again."

John had, indeed, recently lost hope for such a thing. Though he and James had temporarily reveled in the possibility of the Lord's resurrection, the imminence of lonely terror had overwhelmed such expectancy, and present anxiety had overshadowed thoughts of the "kingdom."

Looking anxiously at the one he loved more than life, John desired and feared to hear more.

"All things are in my Father's hands," Jesus was saying. "In a little while the world will not see me, but you will see me. Because I live, you will live also. I will not leave you comfortless. I will come to you."

John turned to the railing and a large tear splashed down upon his hand. "Truly, Master? Will you come again? Will I see you for myself?"

Jesus embraced him warmly. "Do you remember what I said to you long ago, that afternoon in the upper room?"

Could John ever forget? Falteringly he spoke the promise. "Yes, my Lord. You said that I would come to know you . . . as no one else would ever know you."

Suddenly the sky awoke with the coral glow of sunrise. Somewhere in a distant tree, morning birds began their songs, and a thrill of new life surged through John's being. He did not know what those words had meant. It would be years before he would fully understand them. But they would be his strength and his hope.

Jesus lifted the disciple's face in his hands. "Do you believe this, John?" he asked.

With fervent devotion, the apostle looked up into his Lord's eyes and smiled. "Master, I do believe."

Chapter 5

This was the first day of the feast of unleavened bread, the Passover. Millions of men, women, and children, descendants of the patriarchs and their proselytes, crowded the streets of Jerusalem. They were dressed strangely, as though for a journey, like their ancestors had been that night long before. There was no great exodus to be made, as after the first Passover. Nonetheless, the Jews remembered the event by dressing the part.

John followed Peter's lead through the noisy masses. The two apostles had been given the mission of locating a place to eat the feast, and of preparing the Passover. This was no light responsibility. It was true that Jerusalem opened its homes hospitably to travelers during the holiday. But the huge throngs could have made it extremely difficult to find lodging for a Rabbi and twelve disciples. Had it not been for Jesus' special insights, Peter and John might have found the task impossible.

The Lord had been very specific. "Go into the city, and there shall meet you a man bearing a pitcher of water. Follow him. And wherever he shall go in, say to the goodman of the house, 'The Master says, Where is the guest chamber, where I shall eat the Passover with my disciples?' And he will show you a large upper room furnished and prepared. There make ready for us."

It would be unusual to see a man performing the womanly task of bearing water; but the room had been found. Now the second phase of the mission was being carried out.

Thousands upon thousands were making their way to the Temple at this time. Confusion was compounded by the bleating of uncountable sheep housed in innumerable pens lining market-places, leading all the way up to the sacred mount.

As Peter neared the ascent to the Temple, he began to study the animals offered for sale. "This one," he directed a keeper, and pointed to a beautiful he-lamb about a year old.

John had followed Zebedee through this process of selection every Passover when he had lived at home. Somehow, except when he was very small, it had never affected him as it did now. Perhaps due to his recent preoccupation with death . . . perhaps due to the Master's talk of crucifixion . . . John felt a chill of helpless pity. He found himself looking sympathetically into the round, black eyes of the lamb, which stood confused, fearful, full of a sense of danger, yet helpless.

A she-lamb would have been just as frightened at the strange, noisy surroundings, just as apprehensive as she was passed to a stranger for some unknown and dread purpose. But she would have been paralyzed, and would have made no sound. The young ram, however, began to kick and bleat vainly as Peter grasped him in his rugged arms. "There, little fellow . . . " the big fisherman tried to soothe him, "it will all be over very soon."

John was nauseated at the sound of those words. All too true they were, and not only for this small creature.

The spring sun filtered through the columns of the Temple courts and onto the pavement where its rays could find room between the thousands who congregated there. No one noticed. All was abustle with the errand of the moment, the slaying and offering of the paschal lambs. Since Peter was the eldest of the two disciples, it fell to him not only to select the sacrifice, but to offer it up. John was glad for this. He had never had to do this thing, and knew that today, especially, he would not have had the stomach for it.

They waited in one of the dozens of long lines, as the hundreds quickly dispensed with the gory duty, and went to make their burnt offerings. Only one reared in the tradition could endure it without utter revulsion. Fresh warm blood spilled from the carcasses of the he-lambs who were slain in rapid succession. The smell of this, mingled with the sickeningly sweet odors of incense and burning flesh, would remain in a dark, smoky haze blanketing the city for days to come.

The ear-splitting cries of the animals, the pressing of the throngs . . . the heat of the sun . . . on this particular Passover John came close to leaving the Temple.

But now, Peter's turn came. He had reached the head of the line. A priest stood before him, his sleeves rolled up, his arms covered with layers of dried blood. He held a great golden bowl under the creature as Peter drew near. Lowering the frantic animal down to the pavement and straddling it with his mighty legs, the big fisherman grasped its muzzle and pulled its head back tight against his own body. John did not want to look, but somehow he could not ignore the lamb's horrified countenance. Its eyes were wild as Peter took from his belt the gleaming knife with which he had always cleaned his catches. And then . . .

It was over quickly. The little fleece-covered body was quiet now, its eyes glazed and lifeless. Only the gaping slash at its throat told the ordeal it had gone through. The priest caught its life-source in the great basin as it spilled forth, and passed the bowl down a line of attendants toward the altar, while Peter took the lamb to be sacrificed.

It was midafternoon when the two apostles finally gave up their offering. The priest in charge of the altar dipped his hand into the golden bowl, sprinkled the blood toward the base of the altar, removed the entrails from the carcass and flayed the sacrificial form.

As the fire licked at the entrails of the paschal lamb, the sparks ascending heavenward carried John's mind beyond the present.

"So quickly it has happened . . . " he thought. " . . . life has given way to death."

And then he recalled the words of the Master which would

sustain him throughout the coming days: "In a little while the world will not see me, but you will see me. I will not leave you comfortless. I will come to you."

Chapter 6

The sun had fully set and dark had descended. John and Peter were in the banquet room taking care of the final preparations for the feast. The court was filled with the odor of lamb roasting on a spit. Servants, graciously provided by the goodman of the house, bustled about making ready the rest of the traditional fare.

The upper room in which the meal would be served was a beautifully decked apartment elevated above the floor of the court. The first sight to greet the visitor, this room had furnishings of the finest carved woods and pillowed upholstery. In this month of Nisan, it was cooled by the breezes which swept gently past the patio fountain.

In the center of the room three tables were arranged in a "U," and on the outer edges were three cushioned couches. Peter and John had decided that the twelve would be divided equally upon these, with the Master reclining at the head table, where they had also positioned themselves.

It was the custom to meditate before the feast, and so the apostles began to filter into the dining room in random succession. It came as a surprise, however, that Judas seated himself only two down from the Master's station. John and Peter had expected that Andrew and James would occupy the remaining two places with them. Now only one vacancy was left, and Andrew, being the younger, would probably sit elsewhere.

As the men arrived they stretched out upon the beds, their heads elevated toward the table. In this manner they would converse and eat, resting upon their elbows.

Traditionally, the governor of a feast arrived last, but it seemed some time before Jesus finally appeared in the court. John knew the reason for the look he bore, as did they all. Just yesterday he had shared with the rest what he had told John on the roof in Bethany. They knew his time was at hand, and the mode of death which would be his. Exactly when and how all of this would come about, they had not ascertained, and they feared to speculate. It seemed it must be very soon, though most of them hoped even yet that something might alter the terrible destiny.

John did not have that hope. He had resigned himself to the inevitable, and he felt detached, emotionless, as he had upon hearing of the Baptist's demise. But his unmoved exterior served to cover a heart which lay only momentarily still. Like the clapper of an immense bell, with the right touch it would be set to thunderous drummings within his breast.

Jesus took his seat, as John had planned, next to the beloved disciple. Peter reclined beside John, and James sat on the other side of the Master, with Judas, who had never been one of the inner circle, occupying the far seat next to him.

"With great longing I have desired to eat this Passover with you before I suffer," were Jesus' opening words, "for I say to you, I will not eat of it again, until it is fulfilled in the kingdom of God."

Following the ritual of Passover, he filled his cup with wine, blessed it and passed it to his disciples. But his words were not traditional. "Take this, and divide it among yourselves, for I say to you, I will not drink of the fruit of the vine, until the kingdom of God comes."

Sorrow pierced the protective shell John had built around his heart. But he must not give in to his pain—not here, not now.

Bitter herb salad, unleavened bread, charoseth sauce, and the meat of a special peace offering were brought in. Jesus took a small dish of the sauce, commemorative of the mortar made by the Jews during their Egyptian bondage as brickmakers. In this substance he dipped a swatch of herbs and said thanks to God for the fruits of the earth. After tasting it, he passed small bits to the four at his table, and so all likewise partook.

John remembered having asked his mother, when he was but a child, "Why do we rest upon couches when we eat?"

Her answer had been simple, yet profound. "It is to show that we are free men and no longer slaves."

Finally, the unleavened bread was to be passed, the lamb placed before the host, a second cup of wine drunk, and the explanation of the feast given. However, the Master again departed from custom. Instead of distributing the bread immediately, he hesitated and studied the faces around him. He then took the loaf, gave thanks, and broke it. The yeastless dough was tough but pliable, and John watched the crumbs fall to the table.

"Take, eat. This is my body which is given for you," Jesus said. "Do this in remembrance of me."

The thought was powerful and difficult to absorb. "I am the bread of life," the Lord had once said. "Unless you eat my flesh and drink my blood you have no life in you." Many disciples had left him on that day, but to those who stayed he had explained, "It is the spirit that gives life. The flesh profits nothing. The words that I speak to you are spirit, and life." Therefore, though John did not now fully comprehend the significance of the bread, he ate willingly, hoping one day he would understand the meaning.

Steam from the roast lamb rose up to the Master's face. As he lifted the second cup of wine, he quoted Moses: "And it shall come to pass, when your children shall say unto you, 'What does this service mean?' that you will say, 'It is the sacrifice of the Lord's passover, who passed over the houses of the children of Israel in Egypt, when he smote the Egyptians and delivered our houses.' "

The wine warming them, the apostles sang the first part of the *Hallel*, as Jews had done at this point for generations.

Always, in the past, John's heart had thrilled to this song. Now it sat still like a stone.

The rest of the ceremony would consist mainly of eating the food set before them. John did not have much stomach for it, but ate as best he could. Due to the crowded arrangement of the dinner bed, his head, as he rested on his elbow, often came in contact with the Master's chest. It was a comfort to be so near the one he loved more than life. But it was torture, as well, for all too soon that physical closeness would be inaccessible. John held his food numbly. Sorrow overcame him and he blinked back his tears.

Apparently the Master sensed his distress, for he whispered, "Do you fear again, John?"

With a heavy sigh, the apostle looked up into his face. "I love you, Master."

Jesus smiled at him sadly. "I know you do, John.

"I speak not of you all," the Master addressed the twelve. "I know whom I have chosen. But so that the Scripture may be fulfilled, 'He who eats bread with me has lifted up his heel against me.' Truly, truly, I say to you, that one of you who eats with me shall betray me."

The disciples looked on one another, wondering who the culprit might be, and there arose a clamor among the men, as they questioned who would do this thing. As Jesus peered into their faces, however, each seemed to sense his own capacity for evil, and with great sorrow they began to ask him, "Lord, is it I?" Even John found himself choking out the words.

The Master would not expose the traitor openly. He answered only, "It is one of the twelve. He that dips his hand with me in the dish, the same shall betray me." That could have been any apostle sitting at the head table, for they shared a common bowl! But, were not Peter, James, and John the Lord's most intimate friends? Surely he was not accusing one of them! And who else was left, besides Judas? Surely the Lord could not mean him. Why, Jesus had entrusted him with the treasury all these months!

John's mouth was dry. And then Jesus was speaking again, as if his first words had not been enough. "But behold, the hand of him that betrays me is with me on the table. And truly the Son of Man goes, as it was determined and as it is written of him. But woe to that man by whom he is betrayed! It would have been good for that man if he had never been born."

John and the others jerked their hands away instantly. But it was too late. Jesus clearly meant any one of them. They dared not look up. Each too much feared he might find the Master's eyes upon him. But the Lord left the description as it stood. And now all the apostles began to murmur among themselves.

As Jesus left off speaking, John's heaviness grew intolerable. Not knowing what the response would be, he nonetheless once again leaned his head on the Master's bosom. Jesus did not shrink from him, and so the apostle found courage in this.

Apparently Peter noted the Rabbi's acceptance of the young disciple, and so beckoned to John. "You are close to the Lord's heart," he seemed to be saying. "Perhaps he will tell you who the traitor is. Ask him."

Sighing deeply, John looked at the Master and whispered low, "Lord, who is it?"

At that moment, John caught a glimpse of the confidence Jesus placed in him, for he answered him privately, "It is the one to whom I shall give a sop, when I have dipped it."

Then, taking a piece of unleavened bread, the Master dipped it into the sauce and handed it to Judas. John could scarcely believe his eyes, yet at the same time, he was filled with relief.

It was an honor to be given a sop by the host of a banquet. Judas reached for it hesitantly, however, sensing the intent of the gesture. Looking sadly at Jesus, he whispered, "Master, is it I?" Jesus answered quickly, "You have said."

Judas held the sop to his mouth as though it were poison, but after he ate it, a strange expression came over his countenance, a look of evil, as though some alien being had entered into him. And he stood up rigidly. A chill went through John as he contemplated the destiny which had driven Judas to sit where he had.

And now Jesus spoke to the betrayer, words which no one but Judas understood: "That which you are doing, do quickly."

Peter and John were the only others who had an inkling what Jesus' direction concerned, and even they could not know the full intent. The rest of the men assumed the statement related to an innocent business errand, as Judas had the treasury bag in hand.

Quickly he departed for the exit and disappeared into the night.

As John watched the door close, he had a great compulsion to leap from the couch and run after Judas. Visions of dragging him into a dark alley and beating the life from him darted through his mind. His muscles tensed with the thought.

But now a hand was on his shoulder. "There is yet much I have to say to you, John. Stay with me," came the Master's voice.

John looked at the remainder of the meal before him. As the other apostles finished the bread and herbs, the peace offering and the lamb, he sat stonily, staring into space. It would not be long until midnight, and finally the third and fourth cups of wine were to be drunk. He managed the third, but with the last, the Lord once again spoke words untraditional and frightening.

Raising the chalice, he gave thanks, and passed it to the men, saying, "Drink all of it. For this cup is the new testament in my blood, which is shed for you and for many for the remission of sins. But truly I say to you, I will not drink again of this fruit of the vine, until that day when I drink it new with you in my Father's kingdom."

John let the wine slide quickly down his throat and passed the cup to Peter.

The big fisherman's mind was definitely on the Master's instruction, but it seemed to strike a different chord within him. There was a trace of sorrow in his eyes, as was only fitting, but John was sure he read the same ambition there which had always colored Peter's countenance at mention of the kingdom. Could it be, John wondered incredulously, that even now his old friend contemplated who should be greatest in that nebulous future?

As the big sailor drank the cup, and as it went around the table, the Master studied the son of Jona intently. Peter did not sense the Lord's insight into his thoughts, nor the concern they brought to Jesus' heart. By the time all had partaken of the wine, he was in a discussion with the other apostles, debating and defending his qualifications to be the Rabbi's right-hand man.

But Jesus would no longer tolerate such squabbles. Speaking sternly, he confronted them. "Haven't I told you before that he who would be greatest among you must be your servant? The kings of the Gentiles exercise lordship over them and . . . are called benefactors. But you shall not be so, but he who is greatest among you, let him be as the younger, and he who is chief, as the one that serves. For who is greater, he who sits to eat or he who serves? Is not he greater who sits to eat? But I am among you as one who serves."

The Lord was angry, full of contempt for their hardhearted pettiness. Shamefaced, they looked away from him, struck with their folly. Seeing this, the Master now spoke more softly, assuring them, "I know that you are my friends. You are the ones who have continued with me in my temptations. And I appoint unto you a kingdom, as my Father has appointed unto me, that you may eat and drink at my table in my kingdom, and sit on thrones judging the twelve tribes of Israel."

Peter knew that the reprimand had been directed primarily at him, for he had been the instigator of the debate. Therefore, it was only with the Lord's next words that he found courage to speak aloud. Jesus was looking sadly toward the door of Judas' exit, and with a sigh, he said, "Now the Son of Man is glorified, and God is glorified in him. . . . Little children, I am with you just a little while. You shall seek me, and as I said to the Jews, 'Where I go you cannot come,' so now I say to you." Then, gazing on them all, he continued, "A new commandment I give to you: love one another. By this all men will know that you are my disciples. . . . "

Simon Peter was deeply troubled. "Lord, where are you going?" he asked.

Jesus looked again with concern on him. "Where I go you cannot follow me now, but you shall follow me afterwards."

Peter, greatly saddened, protested strongly. "Lord, why can't I follow you now? I will lay down my life for your sake!"

Tears came to Jesus' eyes. "Will you lay down your life for my sake?" he asked. And then with a groan of sorrow, he asserted, "Simon, Simon, behold, Satan has desired to have you, that he may sift you like wheat. But I have prayed for you, that your faith does not fail. And when you are converted, strengthen your brothers."

The mighty Galilean stared at the Master in shock. "Lord," he objected, "I am ready to go with you, both into prison, and to death!"

Jesus shook his head despondently, and met his rebuttal. "Truly, truly, I say to you, a cock shall not crow until you deny me three times."

John's heart ached for his crestfallen friend. It was unbelievable that Peter would do such a thing. Yet, this night it had been impressed upon the son of Zebedee that any one of them was capable of any manner of treachery, that not one of them merited the Lord's love.

The disciple sensed that it would not be long now until Jesus' hour would be upon them. The Master's next statements were clearly his last instructions. John's broken heart could take in only so much of what he was delivering. The rest would come back to him over the hard days ahead.

"Do not let your heart be troubled," the Lord was saying. "You believe in God; also believe in me. In my Father's house are many mansions. . . . I go to prepare a place for you. And if I go and prepare a place for you, I will come again, and receive you unto myself, that where I am, there you may be also. . . .

"I am the way, the truth, and the life. No man comes to the Father, but by me. . . . He who has seen me has seen the Father. . . . Believe me that I am in the Father and the Father in me. . . .

"And I will pray to the Father, and he shall give you another Comforter, that he may abide with you forever, even the Spirit of truth. . . . I will not leave you comfortless. I will come to you. . . . At that day you shall know that I am in my Father, and you in me, and I in you. . . . These things I have spoken unto you, being still present with you. But the Comforter, who is the Holy Ghost, whom the Father will send in my name, he shall teach you all things, and remind you of all the things I have said unto you."

Then his voice plumbed the very depths of John's soul. "Peace I leave with you, my peace I give to you. Not as the world gives, do I give to you. Do not let your heart be troubled or afraid."

The Lord rose from the table. John sensed that they would be leaving, probably to go into the Garden of Gethsemane, where the Master loved to pray.

Before they departed, however, Jesus led them in the closing hymn of Passover. Tonight, as John sang the words, he realized their true meaning for the first time, though he had repeated them year after year all his life. The phrases were terrible yet beautiful, painting a clear picture of God's purpose with the Nazarene. And as they were harmonized, they surrounded John's heart with peace, fear—a kaleidoscope of impressions—but most of all with understanding.

The Master's mellow baritone enhanced the minor notes of the Jewish music, and his eyes were closed as he led the song:

"I love the Lord, because he has heard my voice and my supplications. . . .

"The sorrows of death compassed me, and the pains of hell got hold upon me: I found trouble and sorrow.

"Then I called upon the name of the Lord; O Lord, I beseech you, deliver my soul. . . .

"God is the Lord, who has shown us light: bind the sacrifice with cords, even unto the horns of the altar. . . . "

It was difficult for John to go on. Flashes of the struggling he-lamb at today's altar came vividly to mind, and he could barely sing as Jesus finished:

"O give thanks unto the Lord, for he is good: for his mercy endures forever."

Chapter 7

The old gnarled olive trees of the Garden of Gethsemane cast odd shadows in the moonlight which managed to filter through foreboding clouds overhead. On this damp, tepid night, a breeze spasmodically wrestled with the treetops. Occasional flashes of lightning far to the west were followed by low rumbles of ominous thunder. Save for the fickle moon and the rare light of the storm, it seemed to John an exceptionally dark evening.

The disciple walked with the Master to the center of the garden. Peter and James were nearby. When Jesus and his men had arrived at the wooded area, the Lord had asked that only these three accompany him into the interior. The others had been told to stay near the edge of the grove while he went to pray.

The three apostles were very silent. As they sensed growing heaviness and sorrow in their beloved Master, they knew it was not the time to be speaking—that nothing they could offer would ease such pain as he was evidently feeling. For a long time Jesus stood without moving, looking up into the foliage, perhaps listening to the rustling of the branches. John pulled his robe about him and tried to adjust his vision to the blackness. The only sounds were the wind and the rushing of the brook Kidron which flowed nearby. But fearful thoughts drummed inside his head like a marching army.

The Lord's face was etched with agony, terrible to behold. John longed to embrace him, but felt too helpless.

At last, Jesus, having studied the heavens, dropped his head forward, a groan of torment escaping his lips. John shuddered and reached for him. "My soul is exceeding sorrowful," the Lord said brokenly, "even unto death!"

John held him close, but after a moment the Master pulled away and looked at the three men.

"Wait here and watch with me," he managed in a constricted voice. Then, falteringly, he walked away, evidently wishing to spare them further misery.

Jesus was gone for what seemed a very long time. John sat in the shelter of a great boulder, resting his head upon it. His ears strained for any sound the Master might make. The air was very silent, but occasionally it seemed he caught the faint sounds of weeping. He listened closely. Yes, there it came again. "My Lord!" he trembled. "He cannot go through this alone!"

Peter and James rested nearby. Perhaps they had fallen asleep. Neither questioned him, so John slipped away quietly and fumbled in the darkness toward the Master's agony. As he came to a clearing not far from the boulder, the moon shown momentarily through the clouds, revealing a sight he would never forget. Prone upon the ground with his face to the dirt and praying in unspeakable torment, lay the Master.

John's immediate impulse was to go to him, to lift him and take him from this place. But he dared not. Somehow he knew all this must be, that he would be wrong to interfere. The apostle stood for some time watching his Lord. But it was torture to witness such a thing, and so at last he turned to rejoin the others, stooped with a greater feeling of inadequacy than he had ever known.

When he had gone a few feet, however, he stopped. The Master was speaking, and he could not help but listen. The words carried a chill to his heart. "O my Father," the Lord wept, "if you are willing . . . if it be possible, let this cup pass from me! Abba, Father, all things are possible with you! Take away this cup from me!" John shuddered, and scenes from that evening came to mind, of the Lord raising the Passover cup and saying , "This is my blood which is shed for you . . . "

John stood still and waited for more. The darkness enveloped him like a grave. He wanted to run, but as in a nightmare, his feet would not move. A long interval of silence transpired. At last the Master spoke again, and the apostle's heart sunk. "Nevertheless," the Lord submitted, "not as I will, but as you will."

Suddenly, John was going, tearing through the darkness. He managed to find the boulder, and sunk to the ground beside it. Burying his head in the folds of his cloak, he too wept bitterly. He did not care if Peter and James heard.

What seemed hours passed, and the Lord was still away. The apostle grew weak with weariness and despair. His vigil apparently useless, he at last leaned his head against the rock and looked up at the black vault of heaven. How empty it appeared!

As his salty tears began to dry in the night breeze, his eyes grew heavy with sorrow. Stuporous sleep overcame him, and he could not keep watch another moment.

He did not know how long it was before a voice pierced through to his consciousness again. The Master had returned and was speaking to Peter. Looking down upon the sleeping form sadly, Jesus was saying, "What, could you not watch with me one hour?"

One hour? Was that how long the Nazarene had been praying? Why, it had seemed an eternity even before John had returned and fallen asleep! Peter jolted awake and rubbed his eyes. "Lord . . ." the big fisherman stammered, "forgive me!"

Jesus studied him knowingly. "Were you not the one who would die for me, Peter?" came the gentle rebuke. "Why do you sleep? Now rise, watch and pray, that you do not enter into temptation. The spirit indeed is willing, but the flesh is weak."

John and James knew he spoke to them as well, but they had no answer. When the Lord turned again to the place of his prayers, John tried desperately to stay awake. But he could not find the strength for more than a few moments. His eyelids weighed heavily from his crying. Try as he might, he could not keep them open. Perhaps if he allowed them to close, but kept his mind active . . .

He would not realize the error of that way until later. Almost instantly, sleep again drugged him.

The evening was a blur of tormenting dreams and fitfulness. One nightmare in particular terrified him, but he could not rouse himself from it. He saw the Master in a most horrible agony, so dreadful that the sweat of his brow was like great drops of blood falling to the ground.

At last, when dawn was still a good way off, the men stirred from their lethargy. A note of resignation colored the Master's voice as he woke them. "Sleep on now, and take your rest," was his ironic rebuke. And then, shaking them with a gentle hand, he pointed the way toward the edge of the garden. "It is enough. Behold, the hour is at hand," he said, "and the Son of Man is betrayed into the hands of sinners. Rise up, let us be going. Behold, the betrayer is here."

Chapter 8

John emerged from his hazy stupor quickly as he followed the Lord to the edge of the grove. Assembled there already was a great band of soldiers and officers carrying all manner of weapons, lanterns, and flaming torches.

The apostle thought he recognized some of the troops. It was evident they had been sent by the chief priests and the Pharisees, for he had seen them in times past on duty in the Temple courts. And with them were chief priests themselves, captains of the Temple, and elders.

Then John's eyes fell upon the one who had led them to this place—Judas Iscariot!

"Scum!" Peter snarled bitterly, his fists clenched and eager. Had the big fisherman made a move, however, the horde of soldiers would have squelched it easily. John shook with anger and looked at his elder brother. James' eyes flashed ominously, but there was nothing to be done against so many, and so the apostles held themselves in check.

As though his treachery had not been enough, Judas stepped forward quickly and greeted the Lord. "Hail, Master," he said, his voice a mixture of deceit and shame. He drew close and, as Jesus studied him, Judas trembled saying, "Master, Master . . . " But then, as if bound by some unbreakable resolve which even he did not seem to understand, he embraced the Lord and kissed him upon the cheek.

John could scarcely believe the Master's response. Obviously the gesture had been planned as a sign to identify Jesus to the soldiers. But, with incredible gentleness, Jesus looked at his betrayer knowingly and asked, "Friend, why have you come?" Judas shrunk from his gaze, and the Master shook his head. "Judas," he whispered, "do you betray the Son of Man with a kiss?"

John wished to clutch the traitorous dog about the neck—to strangle the life from him.

Peter lurched forward, drew his weapon from its sheath, and cried, "Lord, shall we kill him with the sword?" But Jesus turned to the impetuous sailor, and, without a word, told him such behavior was not his will. Angrily, the big fisherman obeyed and let the weapon hang idly from his hand.

Just how far from his mind it was to resist his enemies, Jesus showed them by stepping forward. "Who is it that you seek?" he questioned the officers.

Startled, and realizing the Rabbi must know it was himself they sought, they nonetheless answered, "Jesus of Nazareth."

"I am he," was the Master's unflinching reply.

But then a strange thing happened, and one which clearly displayed the Lord's control of the situation. As soon as he had spoken the words, Judas and his other enemies were suddenly pushed backward by an unseen force, and they fell to the ground like a toppling row of harvest sheaves, one against another.

The apostles looked on, stunned. The entire retinue of soldiers, some fifty in number, the officers, the priests, the elders—all lay in a confused mass upon the ground. Swords, spears, and shields were in disarray, and as the leveled horde came to their senses, they were jolted quickly to their feet by flames of the torches which, having fallen with them, now licked at their clothes.

John blinked his eyes, but the Master stood gazing at the scrambling pile coolly. When they had regained some dignity, they studied the Nazarene fearfully, apprehensive of making any move to take him. They would have left quiescently had it not been for the Lord's next words.

"Whom do you seek?" he repeated the question.

One of the priests stirred uneasily and looked for support from his followers, but finding none, responded shakily, "Jesus of Nazareth."

The Lord did not take his eyes from him for an instant. "I have told you that I am he."

The priest and the troops braced themselves at these words, fearing the same force might display itself again. But when a few seconds had passed without any ill signs, their relief was evident.

Then to the amazement of all, Jesus said, "If I am the one you seek, let my followers go their way."

He could have destroyed his opponents with a syllable. They knew it. But he was, of his own accord, giving himself up. As if taking pen in hand to sign his own death warrant, he was laying down his own life, and he was turning what was intended to be a shame to him, into an embarrassment for his enemies.

The remainder of their role in the drama was merely mechanical. As though it would be a sin to depart from convention, the priest motioned two men to step forward and bind the Master's hands with rope. Making a mockery of themselves, they laid hold on him and began to do as they were told, taking him into their doubtful custody.

Perhaps, despite the display of power, Peter did not really believe the Lord was in control. Perhaps his love for the Nazarene overcame his reason, for he could not stand idly by any longer. At the sight of Jesus being handled by aliens, he leaped to his defense. Pushing the Master aside, he drew his sword and, with a whistling blow, brought his weapon crashing down upon the high priest's attendant.

With terror and agony the servant slumped to the ground, grasping the side of his head. A torrent of blood rushed through his fingers, and on the path next to him lay his right ear, severed from his body.

Jesus looked stormily at his well-meaning apostle, and commanded, "Put your sword again in its place! For all those who take the sword will perish with the sword! The cup which my Father has given me, shall I not drink it? Do you think that I cannot now pray to my Father, and he will give me more than twelve legions of angels? But how then can the Scriptures be fulfilled?"

Peter shook shamefully. John stepped up beside him, but he knew the Master had said rightly.

Jesus' attention now, however, was on the wounded man who lay weeping in torment at his feet. Leaning over, he took into his hand the lifeless ear. Looking again at Peter, he said somewhat angrily, "Allow this to be." He then touched the ear to the servant's head, and instantly the man was restored, the pain gone, and the severed flesh whole again.

In all his months of discipleship, John had not witnessed so much of the Lord's mercy and power. He listened awestruck as Jesus brought the matter to its conclusion.

Speaking again to his enemies, he said, "Are you come out as against a thief with swords and staves to take me? I sat daily with you teaching in the Temple, and you laid no hold on me. But the Scriptures must be fulfilled. This is your hour, and the power of darkness."

Then, stretching forth his hands, he allowed officers to bind them.

Despite the Master's evident control, John and the others were overcome with fear. And all the apostles forsook Jesus and fled.

Chapter 9

John stood shakily in a patch of brambles somewhere in the darkness beyond Gethsemane. He did not know what to do, or where to go. He cursed his cowardice in having left the Master when he needed him most. But what must he do now?

Wind from a brewing storm whistled about his ears. He was helpless and alone. "I will go to him," he told himself. At the thought, however, trepidation filled him. He knew what might become of any disciple of the Nazarene who dared show his face in the city. "The servant is not greater than his lord. If they have persecuted me, they will also persecute you . . ." So had the Lord spoken at the Passover. And as the words returned to John, he stood staring into the black night, mute as a roadside stone.

But scenes of the Master haunted him. What were they doing to him—Judas and the others? What torment did they have in store for the Son of God?

At the memory of Judas, John was suddenly spurred into action. "I will be no better than he if I do not go to Jesus!" Without further hesitation he scrambled out of the undergrowth and onto the highway. Pushing personal safety out of mind, he ran madly toward the Holy City.

He was grateful for the darkness which camouflaged him, but as he drew close to Gethsemane, the moon broke periodically through storm clouds overhead, and once he thought he caught the form of a man coming down onto the road. The cold hand of terror then spurred him on even more quickly.

But almost as soon as he passed the questionable figure, a voice hailed him. John was paralyzed in his tracks. "Lord Jehovah . . ." he trembled, "if this is the end, let it happen quickly." Fully expecting the hand of a Temple soldier to grasp him, he stood rigid. What a relief when the voice came again. "John!" It was Peter. Wheeling about joyously, John met the embrace of his friend. Something in the fisherman's eyes indicated that he too had resolved to enter Jerusalem. "You know what may become of us," John tested him.

Peter looked determinedly toward the walled city. "I know," he answered.

Day was still hours away, yet the courts of the Temple were dotted with servants scurrying to and fro about their errands. Much work had been necessary to put the buildings in order after Passover the evening before. Altars and steps had to be cleaned of blood spattered from the myriad sacrifices. Debris left by swarming crowds had to be cleared before winds drove it all about the city.

Peter and John were grateful for the bustle of the courts. They would be less conspicuous on their way toward the High Priest's palace, where, due to the unusual nature of the matter at hand, the Sanhedrin would be meeting.

John might have little difficulty gaining access to the palace. Being the son of a Sanhedrin member was all the credentials he normally needed. Peter, on the other hand, would have to wait outside. When they reached the gate, John showed his seal to the young woman who kept the door, and he was allowed to enter. "Wait here," he whispered to Peter. "I will see if I can get you into the courtyard."

As the door shut behind John, Peter suddenly felt very much alone, and fear filled him afresh. He slumped against the wall and waited in the cold night air.

John did not mean to forget Peter. He had fully intended to speak with the doorkeeper the minute he was inside. But the moment the gate was shut a commotion at the far end of the court caught his attention. It appeared that a band of soldiers was ushering a man from the house of Annas to the house of Caiaphas. Upon inspection, John recognized their captive. Jesus was being pushed and shoved through the breezeway like an ox under correction.

The young apostle no longer cared what might happen to himself. He raced through the court toward the group of soldiers. Cursing bitterly, John tried to push his way through to the Master's side, but was flung rudely to the floor by the armed men. As he lay sprawled on the pavement, he looked up into the face of his Lord. Jesus' eyes were full of love for his faithful friend, but he did not encourage his attempts.

"Let me go into the hall with him!" John begged the commanding officer. For his trouble he received a vicious kick to the stomach, and he doubled over in agony. Tears of torment filled his eyes, but he strained once more to see the Master. Violently, the soldiers grasped the Nazarene and led him away, but as Jesus was turned from him, John saw that his face had been bruised.

"Animals!" the apostle shrieked. "What are you doing with him?" he cried after them. But it was no use. Coldly they marched to the gate of the High Priest's quarters and a great carved door shut behind them.

John sat helplessly on the pavement for several moments. Back at the door where he had entered, a group of servants and guards was starting a fire. Suddenly he remembered. "Peter!" Staggering to his feet, he slowly made his way to the courtyard gate.

"Miss!" he called to the doorkeeper, attempting to stand with dignity. "I have a friend waiting outside. It is a bitter night. May he warm himself by your fire?"

The maid looked at John skeptically. "You are the son of an elder?"

"Yes, I told you I was."

"Very well," she said hesitantly. "But he may not come beyond the court."

She opened the gate for John, and he summoned Simon. "Peter," he called, "you may come in."

The burly fisherman was obviously relieved at the opportunity to escape from the chill night air. As he looked on the men huddled around the flames, however, a certain uneasiness overcame him. John began to explain his delay, but Peter hushed him and peered carefully about. "Not so loudly," he cautioned. "Do you want them to know we are his disciples?"

John stared disbelievingly at his friend. "I want the world to know!" he asserted.

"*Shhhhh!*" Peter motioned to him. "Fool—do you not know what they will do to us?"

"Fool?" John returned venomously. "You are the fool!"

Peter looked anxiously at the officers. "You go your way,

then," he said under his breath. His resolve to die with the Master had quickly waned in the face of so many onlookers. John turned angrily and walked alone toward the gate where Jesus had been taken from him.

The strangers about the fire studied the big fisherman curiously, and Peter gave them a nervous smile.

Chapter 10

It was unheard of to hold a trial in the middle of the night. Yet this was Jesus' lot at the hands of his enemies.

It was only the grace of Jehovah which allowed John to witness the proceedings. When he left Peter he found his way to the gate of Caiaphas once more, where he had seen the soldiers disappear with his Lord. By a strange oversight the guards had failed to lock the door behind the prisoner, and John found himself able to walk into the empty hall which led through a maze of vaulted corridors to the meeting place of the Sanhedrin. He remembered, as a small lad, having come with Zebedee through these hallways, when the proud Pharisee had shown his two sons the buildings in which his duties as a councilman were carried out. John had not forgotten a turn in these cold passageways. He wondered if James would remember them as clearly.

The thought of James struck him sadly. What was he doing at this moment? Had he, too, repented of deserting the Lord? John wished he were here.

Sound carried easily through these echoing stone walls. John was careful to muffle his footsteps. Bending over, he removed his sandals and bundled them under his arm. So far no one had seen him. No one had been anywhere near. When he at last glimpsed the heavy wooden door of the council chamber, his heart leaped. It was ajar.

Inching his way up to the opening, he peered carefully through the crack. There must be well over a hundred men assembled inside, he considered, including the elders, the scribes, and the chief priests, to say nothing of the false witnesses against Jesus who had undoubtedly been enticed from the streets for a fee.

There was very little discernible at first in the rumbling confusion which met John's ears as he listened in by the door. At last the voice of Caiaphas brought a degree of order to bear.

"I am made to understand," he addressed the defendant, "that you dishonored the High Priest Annas with your disrespectful answers when he questioned you. And that for this reason you were smitten on the face. Is this correct?"

John could not see Jesus, but his reply told the disciple he was not intimidated by the accusation. "When your father-in-law asked me of my doctrine and of my disciples, I answered him truthfully," he said. "I told him the same things I would tell you: that I have always spoken openly to the world, that I have always taught in the synagogue, and in the Temple, wherever the Jews congregate. And in secret have I said nothing. If you have a question concerning these things, you need not ask me. Ask those who listened to me. They know what I said."

John could imagine the rage in Caiaphas' face. "You are fortunate I do not have you scourged for such insolence!" he shouted.

"If I have spoken evil, bear witness of the evil. But if I speak the truth, why would you have me scourged?" Jesus challenged them.

"Indeed! You have spoken well, Carpenter. You have called for witnesses, and so you shall have them!" Caiaphas leered triumphantly.

What followed did not surprise John. The mockery of a trial turned into a virtual Roman circus of misunderstanding, misquotes, and outright lies concerning the Nazarene.

One witness claimed to have overheard a plot to stage the death and raising of Lazarus. According to his report, Mary, Martha, and their brother had been in league with the Lord and his disciples to pull off the hoax.

Another claimed to have inside information proving that the Master's rise to national attention had been carried out through a detailed scheme laid by the families of John the Baptist and the Nazarene himself.

Witness after witness bringing other false tales came forward, but none seemed to have evidence or testimony conclusive enough for the council's purposes, or witnesses' testimonies did not agree, and so were invalid. After the outrage of the people over the mishandling of the Baptist's trial, the Sanhedrin knew it must be more careful to have adequate reason for destruction of the Nazarene. And indeed, this was their intention—to put him to death.

There were not many charges warranting the death sentence

which could be brought against a man. The only one which could reasonably be brought to bear against Jesus would be to prove he had claimed himself equal with God. So far, the testimonies had not shown this, though every man present knew the Nazarene had come close to claiming such things repeatedly.

At last another witness, who had perhaps at one time been a follower of the great Teacher and had then turned from him, brought charges that Jesus had claimed magical powers for his physical body and blood. "I heard him tell the multitudes that if they would eat his body and drink his blood they would have eternal life!" he declared.

This was very close to blasphemy. Only the Lord God had the power of life and death. To claim such was to make oneself equal with God. But, unfortunately for the sake of the council, two witnesses were needed before such testimony could be accepted.

Until now, Caiaphas had held back his two best witnesses. He had known the preceding testimonies would not be enough to bring the intended sentence, but he had wanted the crowd to hear them nonetheless. At last, however, he called on a member of the council to produce the desired spokesmen.

"Yes, your honor," a councilman answered. "I have brought with me from Galilee two honest and respectable men who claim to have heard blasphemy from the lips of the Nazarene."

John's skin crawled. He knew that voice. It was Zebedee's. His own father was bringing the witnesses who would attempt to seal the fate of his beloved Master. He had not recognized the voice at first. It was unusually rough and coarse, like that of a very old man, much older than John's father. In fact, it sounded as if it issued from the throat of a dying man—a man who, even in his last moments, was bound by some fury of hatred and revenge.

The disciple crept close to the door and tried to single out the form of his father. But it was no use. He had to listen blindly to the hideous statements of the lying accusers.

Directing Caiaphas' attention to Jesus, they swore, "Your honor, we are witnesses that this fellow said, 'I am able to destroy the Temple of God, and to build it in three days!' " And, "We heard him say, 'I will destroy this temple that is made with hands, and within three days I will build another made without hands.' "

John shook angrily. Jesus had never indicated he might destroy the Temple. His words to his enemies on that occasion had been, "Destroy this temple, and in three days I will raise it up." But, be that as it may, it only served to enhance a very damaging testimony. Jesus *had* claimed power over the Temple of God. John had never understood the Lord's words. But he had feared, when Jesus had first spoken them, that they would one day bring grave trouble.

The disciple sensed the victory of the Sanhedrin. Two men had given their word on this statement. Nothing else would be necessary, he reasoned.

As the witnesses were questioned, however, it became clear that even their testimonies did not agree. Caiaphas, angry and frustrated, called a halt to the proceedings.

Looking for a long moment at Jesus, he seemed to be calculating a way to rescue victory from defeat. Perhaps, he seemed to be thinking, if he could catch the Nazarene in a verbal trap, he could yet use the false statements against him.

At last Caiaphas addressed the Master once again. Rising, he said, "Do you answer nothing? What is it which these witnesses have against you?"

The crowd fell silent, waiting for the Nazarene's response. But he gave none. Stormily the High Priest demanded an answer, coming quickly to the central issue. "I adjure you by the living God," he commanded, "that you tell us whether you be the Christ, the Son of God! Are you the Christ, the Son of the Blessed?"

For another moment Jesus held his peace, but at last he answered plainly, "You have said. I am. Nevertheless, I say to you, in the future you shall see the Son of Man sitting on the right hand of power, and coming in the clouds of heaven."

Feigning righteous horror and indignation, Caiaphas lifted his voice in lament toward heaven, and tore the silken robes which covered his body. The rending of the glorious fabric, the drama of his priestly mourning, would have filled an innocent onlooker with sympathetic dread.

"He has spoken blasphemy!" Caiaphas cried. "What further need have we of witnesses?" Then, calling for an immediate verdict, he addressed the throng, "Behold, now you have heard his blasphemy! What do you think?"

"He is guilty of death!" was the answer of the hundred voices.

With this, John heard a loud scuffle in the middle of the crowd. The men who held Jesus were mocking and striking him, spitting in his face and beating him with their fists. He was blindfolded and struck upon the cheek. "Prophesy to us, you Christ!" he was taunted. "Who is the one that struck you?"

As the blasphemies continued, John held his rage in check. How he wanted vengeance! But now the doors flew open, flinging him out of the way. None of the men saw him, as, in their blood-fury, they dragged the Master from the hall. When the disciple saw Jesus he longed to cry out to him, but he passed too quickly, and John stood shakily leaning in lonely despair against the marble wall.

He had seen these men before, all of them. They were the elite of his father's profession. As a child, he had revered them. Tonight, he could scarcely recognize them. They were like mad beasts, with no dignity of any kind.

Interestingly, those who might have been sympathetic to the Nazarene were not found among them. Apparently uninformed of the trial, moderate men like Nicodemus, Gamaliel, and Joseph of Arimathea were not present tonight.

At last the remaining members exited the room on the tail of the angry crowd. One, being carried on a stretcher, smiled despicably at those who bore him out. Zebedee—old, sick, hate-filled—John would not have known him on casual observance.

As the bitter old Pharisee disappeared down the hall, his son looked after him miserably. "This *is* your hour," John cursed, "and the power of darkness:"

Chapter 11

It was early Friday, the morning after Passover. An unseasonably hot sun beat fiercely upon a crowded Jerusalem street, and a violent, enraged mob lining the way added to the unbearable heat. The throng which had only days before lavished praise and honor upon the Nazarene at his entrance into the Holy City, now teemed with hatred and the desire to see him destroyed. Only an observer who could recount all that had transpired in the interval would be able to explain the ironic shift in mood. Perhaps, though he did not think on it now, John was the only one, besides the Master, who could claim such a full witness.

But no one sought explanations now. John was alone in a crowd of thousands, pushing his way madly through the multitude, desperately determined not to let the Lord pass out of sight. Often Jesus fell beneath the weight of a heavy, wooden cross which his enemies had given him to bear. Repeatedly, John had forced through the masses to offer his assistance. But his appeals had been in vain. The guards had thrust him back, and so he had been swallowed by the throng.

Trial after mocking trial had brought the Nazarene to this moment. The scenes before Annas and Caiaphas had been only the beginning. Following that the Master had been taken before an official gathering of the Sanhedrin, where the verdict of death had been ratified. Since, however, the Jews had no legal method of performing an execution, Jesus had been taken next, like so much chattel, to the palace of Pilate, the Roman governor. The confused Gentile had not known what to do with a case so religious in nature. Upon learning, therefore, that the accused was a Galilean, he had sent him to Herod Antipas, at that time also in Jerusalem, in hopes he would handle a problem which was clearly under his jurisdiction.

Though John had not been able to witness this inquisition, it was not difficult to imagine the ridicule and shame heaped upon Jesus at the hands of "that fox." Quickly, Herod had returned him again to Pilate, having had nothing more than merriment at the procurator's expense.

A weak-willed and frustrated Pilate had debated to no avail with the multitudes who had come to the final trial in his palace yard. A mob whose spirit had been turned against the Master by the elders and their paid rabble rousers demanded the death of Jesus. Pilate had not wished to give in. But when the throng, at the instigation of the Lord's enemies, had warned him that Caesar would not take kindly to one of his governors protecting the so-called "King of the Jews," he had backed down. Ordering a pitcher of water, he had washed his hands in sight of all. "His blood be on us and on our children!" had been the cry of the people. "Crucify him! Crucify him!"

And so it was about to happen. Jesus was being led to Golgotha, the ignominious Mountain of the Skull, also named Calvary, outside Jerusalem. The events which had transpired since the betrayal in the garden had come and gone so quickly that only a matter of hours had passed between the Lord's Passover and the event of this, his destiny. Even now, John wished to deny the reality of what he witnessed, to waken from this terrible dream. Yet he knew it was not a dream, for the Master had spoken of this very hour, time and again during his ministry.

Two other men were to be executed on this day. John did not

know them. The inscriptions on their crosses signified that they were charged with thievery. It was Roman custom to clear the death house on a regular basis, and it was not unusual, in many parts of Caesar's crime-ridden empire, to see numerous crosses erected on any given afternoon.

The Roman soldiers in charge of today's executions treated Jesus as brutally as they would any common criminal. In fact, it seemed they drove him more fiercely toward the gates than they did the other two men. Perhaps their anger was whetted against him by the roar of the blood-crazed crowd; perhaps it was the inscription Pilate had lettered for his cross which enraged them so. "This is Jesus of Nazareth: King of the Jews," it read.

When the priests had questioned Pilate's choice of titles, asking that he put rather, "This man *calls* himself 'King of the Jews,' " Pilate had answered only, "What I have written, I have written."

And so the Master had been forced into the midst of the howling mob, to bear his cross to Calvary, scourged, smitten, spat upon, with a crown of thorns adorning his head.

There were friends of the Nazarene scattered in the multitude. Oddly, it was mainly the women of his following who had mustered courage to show loyalty on this day. John did not see a single apostle, though perhaps, somewhere, they trailed behind. If so, they were keeping well out of the way.

By the time Jesus and the throng had come to the Jerusalem gates, the Master's strength had almost been spent. The great wooden cross was too much for him to bear any longer upon his bruised and beaten back. More and more often, he fell beneath its weight. It was not for mercy, however, that the soldiers relieved him of his burden. It would be a poor example to let a man die on the way to his own execution, and so they grabbed hold of a stranger whose ill fate led him to cross their path at that instant. He was a black man, perhaps a proselyte from Ethiopia, here only to celebrate the Passover. He was exiting the city as the soldiers and their charge approached the gate. Laying hands on the unsuspecting Cyrenian, they forced him to carry the cross of the Nazarene all the way up Golgotha's slope.

John cursed them vociferously, pushing his way up to the Lord's keepers. "You know I would have carried it!" he cried. But the troops pretended not to hear, and thrust him once more ruthlessly back into the throng. How John loathed them! "Swine!" he shouted.

His voice was lost in the din of the crowd, but he did manage one quick glimpse of the Master's face. Jesus had known he was there. The Lord had heard his desperate pleas to be allowed to aid him. Jesus' eyes, searching out his disciple, at last met John's gaze.

Instantly, the apostle reached out toward him, straining, stretching his arms over the head of the intruding masses. Pushing and forcing his way to the front once more, he came within but a few feet of his beloved Master, and the Lord, too, reached forth his hand. For the fraction of an instant their fingertips met, and then Jesus was torn violently from his grasp.

John moved like an automaton with the surge of the crowd the rest of the way up Calvary's mountain. Securely he held to his breast the hand which had touched his Lord, not allowing it to be tainted by any other contact. The disciple who had cradled his head on the Master's chest only the night before knew he might never again touch the Lord of Life.

Chapter 12

The torture of crucifixion lay not so much in the piercing of the hands, nor in the ripping of the flesh as the body's weight pulled on the pegs. Indescribably painful as that was, the crucified must fight against the despair of ultimate suffocation, raising himself upon the spikes repeatedly to exhale. Here the greatest torment found its source. Through this continual action, the horror of the spikes was amplified, and the body utterly exhausted. Only when no longer able to lift itself, and only by sinking into breathless oblivion, would it at last be freed from its ordeal.

John did not want to look, and yet he could not take his eyes from the one he loved more than life, from his Master who hung now, pinned to the hideous Roman tree. It seemed that nothing had ever happened before, that no history had led to this moment, or would ever lead from it. Time had begun here, and ended here, so it seemed to John.

Transfixed with horror and awe, he had stood motionless since the resounding thud of wood against hollow earth had told him the Master's cross had found its foothold, and since the instrument of torture had reared its ugly head toward heaven.

There was no telling how long a man might endure such torment as Jesus was going through. And the Nazarene, who had spent his ministry homeless and itinerate, his body hardened by daily travel and exposure, might last a good deal longer than the average man.

"King of the Jews . . ." the name was etched, as though by the hand of God himself, on the placard above Jesus' head. Hebrew, Latin, Greek—all the common languages shouted the words from the top of the cross, for so Pilate had seen fit to tell the whole world.

But other words haunted the son of Zebedee, burning into his heart like brands. "Father, forgive them, for they do not know what they do!" Such had been Jesus' sentiments as his cross had been lowered into its standard. That incredible statement tormented John's coal-hot heart.

Occasionally the events transpiring near the cross dawned upon the apostle. In sight of the cross, the careless Roman guards divided the Master's clothing, gambling for the only item of value, a seamless tunic. The crowd continually taunted and ridiculed the Master. Passersby reviled Jesus, shaking their heads, and hooting, "You who destroy the Temple, and build it in three days, save yourself! If you are the Son of God, come down from the cross!" Even the chief priests, scribes, and elders were lowered to such devices. "He saved others. Himself he cannot save!" they spurred the onlookers. "If he is the King of Israel, let him now come down from the cross, and we will believe him! He trusted in God. Let him deliver him now, if he will. Isn't this man the Son of God?" The soldiers, even the thieves crucified on either side of the Master, derided and railed at him.

Forgive? The very thought was repugnant. John gritted his teeth as he surveyed the Lord's assassins. "Never," he swore.

Some of the women who had followed Jesus today, and who had been loyal to him these many months, managed to make their way to the cross. Among them was John's mother, Salome. They had been watching from afar since the beginning, but now felt it imperative to draw near. As John observed his Lord, he found him looking on the grief-stricken women. He seemed to study one in particular, and John, turning to see who she might be, recognized her as Mary, the mother of Jesus, the lovely lady he had met at the wedding in Cana.

What torment it must have been for her, John considered, to be here on this day. Instantly, his heart went out to her, as through tearful eyes she beheld her beloved son.

That the sight of her agony deeply distressed Jesus, it was evident, and that he found the strength to speak, a miracle. It was only fitting he should address his mother when he did. "Woman, behold your son!" he cried, his voice dry and rasping.

John wondered how she could endure what she saw. But at this command, instead of continuing to watch Jesus, Mary directed her eyes to the disciple himself. John turned in confusion to the Master, and found his Lord gazing on him lovingly. "Behold your mother!" Jesus called.

Bewildered, the apostle looked to Salome. No jealousy marked her countenance—only sympathetic concern for the poor woman who had given birth to the Nazarene, who had reared and cared for him throughout his first young years. John's mother drew near to Mary, her sister Galilean, and held her close, answering her son's doubts. Jesus was not stripping Salome of her rightful station, but was directing Mary to let John fill the place he would vacate. He was giving Mary into John's charge. The apostle had been like a kinsman to the Nazarene, so well had they loved one another. For Mary, then, whose other male children, James, Jude, Joseph, and Simon, still held her firstborn in contempt, John could be a truer son. As the apostle, therefore, considered his Lord's dying request, the honor of it struck him profoundly.

Humbled beyond measure, John turned again to Jesus, nodding his assurance that he would fulfill the Lord's desire, and stepping up to the lonely woman of Nazareth, he enfolded her in his arms.

Mercifully, after three hours the apostle was shaken from his stuporous vigil. As if nature itself could no longer bear the horror of this day, the ground began to quake with warning tremors. It was about noon, yet suddenly the sun was black. Darkness spread eerily over the land of Palestine. An unnatural wind blew up from the four corners of the sky, howling and whistling a dry, unearthly wail.

John looked skyward and his heart froze. The heavens were an ebony shroud, admitting only enough light to distinguish the three crosses on the horizon and the people fallen back in terror. Women sobbed and strong men cried out. John slumped to his knees and buried his head in his hands.

Gradually the earth tremors died away, only occasionally succeeded by the distant rumble of thunder and the rocking of the ground in spasms. The crowd became quiet, the mockers speechless. John at last found courage again to look on his Master's disfigured countenance. Tears fell from the apostle's eyes as he grasped the base of the rough-hewn cross and wept bitterly. He had no words. The full weight of soul-rending sorrows crushed in upon him, and only wracking convulsions escaped his lips.

For three hours the sky was black, and around three o'clock the quaking of the earth, which had died out for a time, resumed in fuller force than before.

The mountain heaved, white lightning blistered the heavens, and from the height of the cross came the most unearthly words John would ever hear. "My God! My God!" the Master was shrieking. "Why have you forsaken me?"

For an interval the world was silent. Nature and the universe waited. Not a breath was taken, not a muscle moved, not a breeze bent the head of a reed.

Then, with a cry of relinquishment, the man of Nazareth looked toward the black vault of space. "Father!" he cried. "Into your hands I commend my spirit! It is finished!"

With a sigh, the Master's life left his body, his head falling forward, his eyes glazed and lifeless.

Tearing toward the foot of the cross again, John clung to it madly, his soul afire with indignation. Grief-bedeviled, he groveled and pleaded that the inanimate structure return his beloved to him. But his voice was lost in the elements, as the momentary silence in earth and space was ripped by a gale-force.

The mountain rocked, the city below was split asunder by a quake. Monstrous boulders were cleft in two, and cobbled streets shattered as though struck by a colossal blade.

"Lord! Master! Jesus!" John wailed. "My God! My Lord!"

Splinters of the despised cross embedded themselves beneath his nails and in his hands as he beat out his agony upon the unfeeling pillar of death.

But no one heard him. No one cared for him. Each man on earth had his own life to keep, and God in heaven was deaf to him

Leaning his head back, he studied the lifeless form of his dear Teacher, and wished that he might have died with him.

Chapter 13

The house where the Master and his apostles had eaten the Passover was as welcome a retreat as any could be at such a time. But John would not have found rest in a palace.

Having seen to it that the Lord's mother was made as comfortable as possible in the crowded rooftop hideout, he had crept shadowlike into his own corner.

By the second night after the Master's death he had still barely moved from that place. It was like John to react so to grief. The same one whose soul responded with fire and vengeance when aroused by anger, withdrew into shock and behind a flinty facade when his heart was broken. This had been his condition since the last hour on Golgotha's slope. Leaving the cross, the young rebel, the young seeker, had stumbled down the icy skids of disillusionment, and his spirit, once so confident, had become the prisoner of labyrinthine caverns, captive behind rocky bars of gall and gloom.

Sitting immobile for long hours at a stretch, he did little but stare blankly into sequestered space, cradling his soul in hopelessness, and nursing black despair. Only rarely did he allow a question to pose itself within him. And always, when he did, it was the same: "Why? Why did you have to die, my Lord? What purpose was served by your death?" Bewildered, empty, he found himself sometimes chiding the very one he had lost. "You could have stopped them, Master! You had the power! How could you leave us? How could you leave *me?*" But no answers came. No gentle voice reached through his shroud of bitterness to relieve the agony of his heart.

It was not for fear that he kept close in the obscure room. Unlike some of the others, he did not concern himself with the dangers lying in wait for Jesus' disciples in the streets below. To him nothing was very important now—not even his own life. All he wished was solitude, though he did seek it in the proximity of his acquaintances.

The thought of most of his comrades, however, struck him ironically. How could they be considered allies when they had not seen fit to minister to the Lord in his last hours, when they had left that task to John and the women, and had slithered into anonymity when needed most? Many of them seemed alien to John now.

James and Peter, he had learned, had watched the Lord's death, though from a distance. He was glad for their token remembrance.

Peter, however, still left the disciple with mixed feelings. As John looked on his oldest ally, who sat beside him deep in sonorous and rumbling sleep, his heart went out to him. Earlier the big sailor had admitted that during the Master's trial some had recognized him as a follower of Jesus, and he had vehemently denied it several times. It was clear that the Lord's prophecy had come true. The apostle who had vowed he would die for the Master had insisted he did not even know him.

In his sleep, Peter occasionally jerked and murmured as if plagued with the memory, his face contorted in harrowed and weary lines. John had to credit Peter's willingness to admit his wrongdoing frankly, and he had to forgive his shortcoming as Peter had forgiven him for questioning the scene at the Samaritan well.

One candle burned low at the far end of the room, the only light the fugitives allowed themselves. In the dim glow, John continued to study the faces of his companions.

He wondered what thoughts had been the apostles' since the night they had fled the garden. One was not here to give his story. It had already been told when his lifeless form had been found at the foot of a cliff, in an open field. Judas Iscariot, unable to live with his treachery, had hanged himself in lonely dejection only hours after the betrayal. His sash serving as a noose tied to a protruding root, the traitor had plunged headlong into the black of night. But even in death, he was to find no dignity. His sash had broken, sending him careening onto the pointed granite below, where his body was found burst asunder and disemboweled.

Not far from John were the women who had followed the Lord. Occasionally low weeping could be discerned as they mourned the Master's death and attempted to comfort his mother. Salome was among them, and the beautiful Mary of Bethany.

Another Mary, of Magdala, out of whom the Lord had cast

seven demons, and whose previous reputation had been anything but spotless, was sitting somewhat apart from the group. Her grief seemed especially profound, though it did not manifest itself in tears and audible mourning. How dear the Master must have been to her, John considered, as Jesus had done so much for her.

She and the other women had gone out earlier that evening to purchase spices for the burial preparation of the body. One of the few Pharisees who had sided with the Master in his trials, the wealthy Joseph of Arimathea, had gone boldly to Pilate the evening of the Lord's death, asking permission to have the corpse for interment. He and Nicodemus, also by now a secret disciple, removed the body from the cross and placed it in a new tomb near Mount Calvary, closing the doorway with a great stone. The women had been obliged to postpone the final preparation until after the Sabbath. They had spent the better part of the late evening, since having purchased the spices, mixing and making them ready for use as ointment compounds. They would go at dawn to anoint the body.

But John noted Magdala's anxious glances toward the window. She seemed restless, as though she hoped to see the first rays of the sun now, hours before they were due. Her obvious desire to go to the Lord's side, even though he lay cold and still, touched John deeply.

At the thought of Jesus' lifeless form, however, the agony of John's own grief closed in upon him once again. Suddenly he was chuckling madly, hysterically, rocking back and forth, his head weaving from side to side.

Peter stirred and looked his way. One by one the others turned their attention toward him, studying him with fear and apprehension.

"Fools!" he called, raising his fists to the ceiling and laughing maniacally. "We are all fools!"

Thomas rushed to the window to be sure no one heard his raving. "Hush!" warned Andrew.

"Why are we here?" John continued desperately. "What are we thinking to achieve by this hopeless seclusion? You men wait in fear for your lives!" he faced them wildly. "Do you not know that your lives are worthless now? You women wait to put the final stamp upon a death already accomplished!" he cried. Then, his eyes wide, he groaned, "And some of us seem to wait for something more—as though there is a hope to be realized! We are insane!"

A cursory slap from the hand of Peter set John back in stunned silence.

James crossed the room and blew out the flickering candle flame. As blackness overtook the room, a pall of uneasy rest would intervene before the haze of morning.

Chapter 14

Sometime during the long hours before dawn, John at last found a measure of troubled rest. But in his dreams he was haunted by the memory of the Lord's marred visage as he had hung upon the cross. John saw himself, in his restless sleep, running madly through mazelike corridors, crying out for his Master, but at every dead end, finding nothing save the horrid Roman tree erected before him, and bearing upon it the dead form of his dearest friend.

It seemed to his unconscious mind that he would stumble through those black and terrifying hallways for the rest of eternity. He saw the phantom of himself at last slumped hopelessly against one of the imaginary walls, peering bleakly into the infernal blackness ahead. At that moment the weak cry, "Master," escaped his lips for what he supposed would be the last time, and he turned his face downward in lonely resignation.

But just as he did so, his dreaming eyes were caught by the beam of a tiny light barely discernible somewhere in the tunnel ahead. As it grew, apparently coming his way, he thought he heard a voice. Shuddering with great fear, he kept his eyes riveted to the light, which he had determined to be the flame of a candle. Now and again it seemed he heard the shuffle of soft footfalls, and he knew that somebody was carrying the taper, as one who would light his way through the passages of a deep dungeon. "John," the voice came clearly, though from a long distance.

There could be no doubt. John knew the source. He sat absolutely motionless. "Master . . . " he whispered, fearing too-loud speaking would make the moment vanish.

"Do you not remember what I said to you?" the gentle voice called. "All things are in my Father's hands. The world will not see me, but you will see me . . . . "

John found himself reciting, along with the Lord, the words he had clung to in times past: "Because I live, you will live also. I will not leave you comfortless. I will come to you."

John was weeping as he echoed that promise. He could not see the form of his dear Teacher, but the light confirmed his presence. In his sleep, John remembered others of the Lord's words. "I am the light of the world. I am the resurrection and the life. He who believes in me, though he were dead, yet shall he live."

When John could no longer speak for the joy he felt, Jesus waited. The apostle could sense his warmth almost tangibly.

"Did I not tell you that you would come to know me as no one else would ever know me?" the Master inquired gently.

"Yes, Lord . . . " John cried. And at that encouragement he thrust his hands into the blackness, fully trusting that the touch of human flesh would greet him.

And so it did. John opened his eyes instantly. The contact had jolted him from the vision and into the world about him. Still, for a moment he did not know whether he was asleep or awake. Someone was bending over him, holding his hands, as in the dream. "Master . . . " he again cried. He could see the robed form of the one who touched him. Yet strangely it did not seem to be Jesus. What hideous cruelty was this?

"Sir," the figure spoke softly. "I am sorry to waken you, but I must speak with you and with Peter!"

The voice was that of a woman! John was fully conscious now. He drew back his hand from her grasp and brushed away the tears which remained from the all-too-real encounter in his sleep. Gaining his composure and covering his disappointment that the vision had not carried over into this world, he strained his eyes in the darkness to determine who she might be. "What is it?" he muttered angrily.

"It is I, Mary Magdala." By now Peter was stirring also, for she had shaken him from his repose as well.

"Speak, woman," the big fisherman growled.

"Sirs, I have been to the tomb. I could not wait until dawn. I had to go." Her story came breathlessly, urgently.

"When I arrived I found the stone rolled away from the mouth of the cave! Entering, I found that the body of our Lord was missing!"

"Missing?" John blurted, shaking her violently. "What do you mean, missing?"

"Someone has stolen the Lord out of the sepulcher! We do not know where they have laid him!"

Peter and John, their eyes having adjusted to the dark, looked at one another incredulously. Without further hesitation, they were up and running madly from the room, down the outside stairs of the house, and into the street. Not caring what dangers might lie in wait for them should they be discovered in Jerusalem, they fled through the main roads, to the wall of the city, and through the gate.

The tomb was even yet a good way off, but they did not slow their pace. As they neared Mount Calvary, white-hot anger spurred John onward. "Pharisee dogs!" His heart pounded erratically. "Was it not enough for you to take his life! Could you not rest until his body was taken, too!"

Anxiously, he passed Peter, and flew down the last remaining slope before the destination. Without a pause he headed straight into the garden graveyard of Joseph of Arimathea. An eerie moon sent just enough light filtering through the trees to reveal the sepulcher at the far end of the grove. John's heart stopped at the sight of it, but he kept running, and at last he stood directly before it.

Just as Mary Magdala had said, the great stone had been rolled away. The yawning maw of the tomb gaped at him like an aperture of hell. Gripping himself, he went forward and stooped his head into the doorway. In the dim light of the moon, he saw just enough to make his stomach turn. He had glimpsed the empty linen graveclothes which had once swaddled the body of his dear Lord, and he could not look further. Falling back against the side of the hill which cradled the cavelike hold, he stood mute and white.

Peter raced breathlessly to the site. He could see that John was badly shaken, but displaying the boldness which so often characterized him, he went directly into the house of death. A long moment passed, and John began to wonder how Peter could endure such a place. "John, come here," Peter called at last.

Something in his voice sent a chill down the apostle's spine. "Why?" he asked hesitantly.

"Come here! This is very strange!"

Doubtfully, John collected his courage and looked inside again. "Come in, fool!" Peter bellowed once more. "Look at this!"

"It is only as the Magdalene said. The body is not here," John snarled.

"But why would robbers take the time to remove the clothes, and leave such fine material as this?"

Curious now, John did as Peter had bid and entered the dark cave. Fearing to look, he studied the clothing carefully. "And see," Peter continued, awestruck, "the graveclothes and the napkin for his face lie separately, and the napkin is folded quite deliberately! What robber would take the time for such a thing?"

The sight of the arrangement did indeed strike John as peculiar, but this evidence suggested to John an even more startling thought. It appeared to him, by the way the clothes lay, that the body had actually passed through and out of them.

"My Lord!" the apostle sighed. Suddenly the image of Lazarus coming forth from his tomb leaped before him. And then he noted that this sepulcher, like that at Bethany, had none of the stench of death.

Words from the Master's teachings flooded him afresh. On the Mount of Transfiguration had he not commanded them, "Tell the vision to no man until the Son of Man be risen from the dead . . ."? One by one, impressions, before so vague, became suddenly interpretable: this was the third day . . . hadn't the Lord alluded to it on many occasions? "Destroy this temple," he had said, "and in three days I will raise it up . . ." Why, the temple he referred to was his body!

How could they have been so blind?

Trembling, John slumped to his knees. Peter stared at him inquisitively. How John yet feared to believe what his heart told him. It was too awful . . . too wonderful!

Vividly his dream returned to him. "I will not leave you comfortless . . . I will come to you." He had always felt that could be true in the spiritual sense. But could it be that Jesus had meant he would see him again in the flesh?

"Lord, was it a dream? Or were you preparing me?"

Looking once again upon the vacant slab which had so recently held the Master's body, John saw, as if for the first time in his life.

And he believed.

Chapter 15

John, James, Peter, and Andrew, the fishermen of Galilee who had forsaken all to follow the Nazarene, had now returned home. Today they and three others of the Lord's disciples walked quietly down the beach from Capernaum. Their voices, when they did speak, came in whispers. Often they stopped and gazed wistfully across the waters in the direction of Judea and the Holy City, now so far away.

They spoke carefully yet excitedly on the only subject which had filled their minds and hearts for nearly two weeks. They had seen Jesus! Yes—he was risen from the dead! And they had seen him with their very eyes!

At first it had been hard to accept, even for John, who had believed in the resurrection. When Mary Magdalene had claimed to be an eyewitness of the Master's bodily presence in the garden that first Sunday morning, no one had received her testimony. But later that day, Jesus had appeared to Peter, and then to two travelers heading for the small village of Emmaus, not far from Jerusalem. The attestations of the two had been scorned. Then at last, that evening, and eight days following, the Lord had appeared in the closed room which housed his men.

Adding to the drama were eyewitness reports of encounters with saints long dead. Their graves had been opened during the earthquake which had occurred the day of the crucifixion, and they had been seen by many since the Lord's resurrection, appearing in the Holy City and speaking the things of God.

Dared anyone disbelieve now? Only a fool would do so!

Still, the stunning reality of it all had not fully hit them. They were in a state of suspended shock, and had been so for days. Their nerves had been so jarred, their perception of life and of the natural world so turned about, that everything and nothing seemed real. All was joy and glory, yet the impact of it was nearly too much to bear, too overwhelming for the human heart.

Yes—they did believe, but they felt so strange. They found it somehow comforting to be back in touch with the sea and the air. There was something very reassuring in seeking out the common and the ordinary after having been exposed to so much of the supernatural.

Should not the appearance of the Lord have been enough? He had eaten before them on one occasion, had even allowed Thomas, the doubter, to feel his hands and side as a token of proof concerning his identity. Should not this have been enough?

Yet—John found himself craving more. He longed to embrace his Lord, to hold him tangibly before him once again. He longed that he might appear and never go away. But this did not seem to be the way destiny had planned things.

The sea, therefore, and the old familiar things, were a solace to him. And they seemed to be so for Peter, as well. Suddenly the big fisherman was running down the beach. "I am going fishing!" he shouted back at them, his feet kicking up sand as he went.

John's heart thrilled. It felt good to think of such a thing. "We will come with you!" he called, the others joining him eagerly.

Immediately, they were in one of Peter's ships, taking up oars, even the least experienced of them, and rowing like excited schoolboys toward the center of the sea.

The rocking of the vessel upon the night waters had at first warmed John's Galilean heart, returning to him his days of youthful seamanship. But all night they had caught nothing. The voyage which had begun as a liberating escape had turned into tedium and futility. How he longed, just now, for the Lord to appear, so that he might ask him to his face: "Why, Master? Why did you have to die? You live! It is true! But it seems you only come to leave again. Your death has changed everything for us all . . ."

When the first rays of morning crept over the horizon, the boat full of hungry sailors was very near the shore. John could think of nothing but going home, eating, and crawling into bed.

In the distance a stranger could be seen warming himself beside a small coal fire on the beach. Had he been more alert, John might have wondered who he was and why he sat solitary on the sand at the crack of dawn with no net or ship nearby. As it was, all the apostle could question was whether the small gray curl of smoke ascending from the flame might bear the scent of some morning meal. How hungry he was!

The stranger poked at the coals with a stick, and then stood up, looking out across the waters toward them. "Children, have you caught any fish?" he called.

The disciples were puzzled. Why should a stranger address them so familiarly? "No," they responded.

"Cast the net on the right side of the ship," the stranger called again, "and you will find fish."

How ludicrous that anyone would know such a thing! The fishermen laughed aloud, but something in the directness of the instruction whetted their curiosity. "Why not?" Peter shrugged. "What have we got to lose?" And so the net was sent flying in its wide, spectacular arc, over the orange dawn sea. No sooner had it descended into the liquid depths, however, than the laughter ceased. Suddenly the hemp became heavy as an iron anchor. It was flooded with the most enormous school of Galilean silver the crew had ever seen. Their arms strained, but to no avail. Nothing would budge the heavy load.

Wide-eyed, John looked at the stranger on the shore, and his mind registered his identity. "Peter!" his lips trembled. "It is the Lord!"

Simon halted incredulously, but then a spark of fresh belief filled his eyes. Without hesitation he wrapped his cloak about him and flung himself into the sea, swimming as fast as he could until he reached the shore, where he threw himself prostrate at the Master's feet.

How John longed to do likewise, but if they were all to drop the net they would lose the catch which the Master had so graciously provided. Instead, he was left to row and drag the heavy trap toward the beach. His breath came laboriously, anxiously. Memories returned of the first time he had hurried from the sea, when Jesus had called him to be his follower upon this very shore.

"I will make you fishers of men," had been the Master's words that day long ago. And that very hour John had been born again, in the Lord's loving arms.

At last the bow of the boat scraped against the waiting sand, and the men leaped overboard. Upon the shore the Master's fire burned low with the tantalizing aroma of frying fish which he himself had caught, and with the fragrance of toasting bread.

Tenderly Jesus raised Peter to his feet and sent him back to help with the haul. "Bring some of the fish you have just caught," he instructed them. Then, the net having been brought to shore, Jesus said, "Come and dine!"

John did not run. He was too overwhelmed by awe and joy. With Peter and James he walked up to the Master and seated himself silently beside the fire.

When all the men had settled themselves, Jesus stirred the coals and smiled at them, knowing their minds and hearts. "Surely you are hungry," he said warmly.

That somewhat broke the tension of the moment, and eased their awestruck countenances. This was their Master, their beloved friend, just as he had always been—gentle and companionable. They laughed freely in response, and the Lord set out to meet their need. Breaking the bread, he passed it to them, along with mouth-watering hunks of the broiled fish.

John watched those beloved hands as they went about their work, and his heart ached with passion and sorrow. The nail prints were very evident, and he could not restrain his swelling emotions.

Questions again flooded his mind. "Why, my Lord?" But as the Master came around to John, serving him his portion of the meal, the questions were pushed momentarily aside, and the apostle looked up at Jesus with love unspeakable. The dream of the dark tunnel returned vividly, and like the helpless one who had sat there, John thrust out his hands toward his Lord.

This time the dream would be realized. The apostle's plea would be greeted by the touch of God's own Son. Jesus laid the fish and bread upon the sand and embraced his beloved disciple.

V

THE ACTS

*Then said Jesus to them again,
Peace be unto you: as my Father
hath sent me, even so send I you
. . . . And ye also shall bear witness,
because ye have been with me from
the beginning. . . . Love not the
world, neither the things that are in
the world. If any man love the
world, the love of the Father is not
in him. . . . If ye were of the world,
the world would love his own: but
because ye are not of the world, but
I have chosen you out of the world,
therefore the world hateth you. . . .
These things I have spoken unto you
that in me ye might have peace. In
the world ye shall have tribulation:
but be of good cheer; I have
overcome the world.*
JOHN 20:21; 15:27;
1 JOHN 2:15; JOHN 15:19; 16:33

Chapter 1

The steps of the Jerusalem Temple swarmed with excited and enthusiastic men and women. As John and Peter made their way through the crowds they were cheered and grasped at from all sides. The city which had only weeks before killed their leader seemed turned inside out with approval and acceptance of these, his two chief apostles.

But much had led up to this moment.

John's heart thrilled as he relived, even now, the incidents which had given him the courage and confidence of recent days. After the morning on the shore of the Galilee Sea, when Jesus had enfolded him in his arms, the apostles had returned to Jerusalem. One evening, as they had sat at dinner, the Master had appeared again, and had answered the questions which had tormented John's heart and mind since the crucifixion.

What had impressed John most was the gradual realization that he should have seen, he should have understood the Lord's purpose in the world from the outset. Had not his first teacher, the Baptist, tried to tell him? Hadn't he said, "Behold, the Lamb of God, who takes away the sin of the world"? Had not the Judaic traditions tried to tell him? Must he, like so many of his countrymen have been blind to their meaning?

Born to die! John shuddered at the thought that Jesus had walked steadily toward the cross from the first day of his ministry. He had had the power to avoid death, but he had taken up his cross from the beginning. Men had killed him with their sin, but not with their own hands. He had died for their iniquities of his own volition.

As Jesus had unveiled all of this for his apostles, still other previously undeciphered clues jumped into John's mind. He remembered how his stomach had revolted when, at the Lord's last Passover feast, the closing hymn had been sung. "Bind the sacrifice with cords, even unto the horns of the altar. . . ."

John had choked on those words that Passover night. Now they comforted his soul. They had enraged him once. Now they filled him with wonder.

As Jesus had continued to expound the reasons for his suffering, he had recounted his own words to Nicodemus. "For God so loved the world, that he *gave* his only begotten son, that whoever believes in him will not perish, but have everlasting life." "You must be born again," he had told the Pharisee.

John had been born again when he had first flung himself into the Master's arms that long-ago day at the Galilee Sea. He had been born again, but he had not understood it. Now it was clear how such a thing could be. If Jesus truly were his Lord, his death was his and his resurrection was his. New life, rebirth, was truly his! "Because I live," Jesus had told John repeatedly, "you will live also! I am the resurrection and the life! Whoever believes in me, though he were dead, yet shall he live!"

Jesus at the last had charged the disciples, saying, "And you are witnesses of these things. Go into all the world, and preach the gospel to every creature. He who believes and is baptized shall be saved. But he that does not believe shall be damned. And these signs shall follow those that believe: in my name they shall cast out devils, they shall speak with new tongues, they shall take up serpents, and if they drink any deadly thing, it shall not hurt them, they shall lay hands on the sick, and they shall recover."

Jesus paused at that moment, as if his next words were of special import. And then he said, "And, behold, I send the promise of my Father upon you, which you have heard of me. But wait in the city of Jerusalem, until you be endued with power from on high. For John the Baptist truly baptized with water, but you shall be baptized with the Holy Ghost not many days from now."

"Master," Peter had spoken for them all, "you talk of power . . . Lord, will you at this time restore again the kingdom to Israel? Will you now, at last, crush Rome?"

How they had longed to hear his answer! Surely now was the time for that glorious reign of which he had so often spoken during his years with them.

But Jesus' response had been somewhat disappointing. "It is not for you to know the times or the seasons, which the Father has put in his own power," had been his gentle but firm reply. And then, returning them to the subject at hand, he had continued, "But you shall receive power, after the Holy Ghost has come upon you. And you shall be witnesses unto me both in Jerusalem, and in all Judea, and," he said, to John's surprise, "in Samaria, and unto the farthest region of the earth."

Then, leading them out from the evening meal, Jesus had taken them to the Mount of Olives overlooking Bethany, where he had raised his hands in blessing over them. "All power is given unto me in heaven and in earth," he had said. "Lo, I am with you always, even unto the end of the world." And before their very eyes, as he gave his benediction, he was parted from them, and carried up into heaven, and a cloud received him out of their sight.

"You men of Galilee," two mysterious, white-clad strangers had stood speaking to them, "why do you stand gazing up into heaven? This same Jesus, who is taken up from you into heaven, shall come in the same manner as you have seen him go into heaven."

There had been, then, no room for sorrow at his leaving. Awe, wonder, worship, joy had filled the onlookers—but not sorrow. Jesus *would* come again. And, surely, very soon! His kingdom would be established, and they would reign with him, as he had promised!

But Jesus had told them to wait. And so they had returned to Jerusalem, as he had instructed.

The same upper room in which the Master had eaten his last Passover, and the same house where they had hidden after the crucifixion, was their station. In all, there had been about one hundred and twenty waiting.

Evidence for the resurrection had convinced even Jesus' brothers, James and Jude, to believe on him, and they were with the church in those hours. Although, for their earlier unbelief, they had forfeited the care of their mother to John Bar Zebedee, the love of Christ had now restored that family's unity. James, especially, would become a pillar of the Jerusalem church, and John rejoiced with Mary of Nazareth for all these things.

They had not known in what way the Holy Ghost would "come upon" them, as Jesus had said. As they had sat together on the day of the Jewish Feast of Pentecost, fifty days after the Passover, praying in one accord, suddenly there had come a sound from heaven as of a rushing mighty wind, and it had filled all the house. Then there appeared unto them cloven tongues like fire, which sat upon each of them. And they were all filled with the Holy Ghost, and began to speak with other tongues, as the Spirit gave them the words.

Of course, since it had been a feast time, devout Jews from every nation were staying in Jerusalem. When the news got out that this strange event was taking place, multitudes came together to witness it, standing in droves in the courtyard and out in the streets beyond the great house. Oddly, every man claimed he heard the disciples speak in his own language. Amazed and marveling, the crowd questioned the phenomenon. "Behold, aren't all these which speak Galileans?" they had said. "And now we hear every man speak in our own native tongue."

Taking a census among themselves, they had found that Parthians, Medes, Elamites, men from Mesopotamia, Judea, Cappadocia, Pontus, Asia, Phrygia, Pamphylia, Egypt, Libya, Cyrene, Rome, Crete, and Arabia—both Jews and proselytes, were represented. Yet each heard the disciples speak in his own tongue of the wonderful works of God. "What does this mean?" they had asked. "They are full of new wine!" others had mocked.

Hearing the commotion in the streets, Peter and the other apostles had gone forward to explain. "You men of Judea," Peter had called out boldly, "and all of you that dwell at Jerusalem, know this, and pay attention to my words, for these men are not drunk, as you suppose, since it is only the third hour of the day. But this is what was spoken of by the prophet Joel . . ."

Continuing with Scripture, he had preached the first sermon in the history of the infant church.

And thus Jerusalem had been taken by storm. The supernatural might which had filled that first bold message had ushered three thousand into the Lord's fold that day. Indeed, the Master had made his apostles "fishers of men."

And the Lord confirmed his word with signs following. Many wonders and miracles were done by the apostles in the name of Jesus. Believers began to share their possessions, and held all things in common. Continuing steadfastly in the apostles' teachings and fellowship, in the breaking of bread and in prayers, they sold their belongings and goods, and distributed them to all that had needs. In joy and unity they praised God daily in the Temple and from house to house. And the entire city received them with favor, the Lord adding daily to the church those who would be saved.

So it was that Peter and John met with such enthusiasm today as they passed up the Temple steps to enter just at the hour of prayer. John's pulse quickened at the reception. So much had happened so quickly in the past few days, he could scarcely comprehend it. He had been swept up, like all the Lord's followers, on a tidal wave of joy and elation, and he hoped it might be this way always, until the Master's return.

The Master's return . . . that thought alone would have filled him with rapture. But he had not had much time of late to contemplate it.

As the two apostles reached the Gate Beautiful where they would enter the Temple, an old man was being carried upon a stretcher and placed on the steps near the great doorway. He was a lame man, a beggar, and he had found that this was a choice spot at which to gain a lucrative income, as those going to and fro were in a religious and therefore, perhaps, a more giving mood. Neither apostle had ever taken much note of him.

The old fellow had probably seen John, and also Peter, pass through these gates many times over the years. John could recall him begging here when, as mere children, he and James had come with Zebedee on feast days.

Something today, however, brought him to the special attention of the two Galileans. Perhaps it was the way he addressed them as they were about to pass by. "Men of Jesus," he called, "will you give alms to the poor?"

The fact that he referred to the Nazarene caught their ears. Peter turned to John and whispered, "Do you think he is a believer?"

"I don't know," John returned, "but I wish we could do something for him . . ."

"We have no money . . ." Peter shrugged.

But then a gleam came to their eyes, as a marvelous thought struck them. Stepping up to the withered man, they looked at him carefully, compassionately. He stretched out his hand expectantly. Surely such notable men would give generously, especially with so many observing.

But Peter, seeing the old man's mind was set on what he might draw from his purse, directed him differently. "Look on us," the apostle said.

The man raised his eyes in bewilderment.

"I have neither silver nor gold," Peter said soberly, "but what I have, I give you. In the name of Jesus Christ of Nazareth, rise up and walk!"

A hush came over the crowd as the poor man studied him dubiously. Lame from his mother's womb, the cripple had never taken a step in his life, but had been carried everywhere. Nevertheless, as he looked on Peter and John and considered their matter-of-fact command, the light of trust and faith illumined his pale, old eyes.

Instantly, reading that ray of hope, Peter reached out and grasped him by the hand, lifting him up. Immediately, his feet and ankle bones received strength, and the man literally leaped to a standing position.

Stunned, but still believing, the old man looked down at his previously weak and withered limbs. He had never been able to stand, had never felt the full weight of his own body. For a moment he trembled, overcome with joy and unspeakable elation. Then he was walking, like a small child, somewhat shakily, but excitedly.

Tears coursed down his cheeks, as he leaned in Peter's direction, nearly falling as he stepped quickly toward him. Peter and John caught him, laughing with the crowd in celebration.

Entering with the apostles into the Temple, he was eager to step out on his own, and after a number of successful steps, he began walking, running, and at last leaping through the courts. "Praise God!" he cried, his legs now straight and strong as a young man's. "Praise the Lord!" he laughed joyfully, cavorting and jumping like a child, weaving his way through the multitudes and between the massive pillars.

Strangers who had not seen the healing looked on in amazement, recognizing the old beggar. And as he returned to Peter and John, embracing them and kissing them ecstatically, throngs came running to find the source of the excitement.

When Peter saw the stir all this had created, he took the old man up on the steps where he might be seen of all. "You men of Israel," the apostle cried, "why are you amazed at this? And why do you look at us, as though by our own power or holiness we have made this man walk? The God of our fathers has glorified his Son Jesus! And through faith in his name this man has been made strong. Yes—faith in him has given him this perfect soundness in the presence of you all! Repent therefore and be converted that your sins may be blotted out! God, having raised up his Son Jesus, sent him to bless you, in turning away every one of you from your iniquities!"

Chapter 2

John had heard that beneath the splendid Temple courts of Jerusalem's Holy Mountain were dungeons for prisoners suspected of gross religious heresy and attempted anarchy. Jesus himself would have been confined in one of these places, had his trials not been held in such rapid succession.

The son of Zebedee was being allowed firsthand experience with the cavernous hold. In the middle of Peter's speech in Solomon's Porch, the priests, the captain of the Temple, and other leaders had come upon the two apostles and had ruthlessly taken them off to prison in sight of the congregation.

Brutally thrust, without benefit of rights, into a dark, barred cell, they sat now, bound and cold, awaiting the dawn. It would have been untrue to say they felt no fear. But the exhilaration of the day's events in the courts above had given them spirit to endure the hours with a measure of hope and peace.

Excitedly they spoke of the miracle and its reception. Even the reaction of their enemies, hostile as it was, confirmed the certainty they felt of God's hand in the matter.

"Jerusalem is being rocked to its foundations!" Peter asserted.

John smiled broadly in the darkness. "And *you* are the one who is shaking it, Peter."

The big fisherman was silent a moment. "John, it is *not* me . . ."

The disciple knew what he meant. "Yes—of course. The *Lord* has used you, it is true. It is not you, but his Spirit in you who speaks. But, Peter . . ." John reflected, "never have you stood so firmly for so long!"

At this, he caught himself, fearing he had offended his friend. But Peter reassured him. "You speak the truth, John. I have always vacillated. Time and again I have failed the Master . . . I, who so often boasted of my loyalty to him."

John regretted the turn the conversation had taken, but he sensed Peter found some relief in such admission. "We all have times of weakness . . ." he attempted to clear the air.

"But, John, weakness is most glaring in a cocky fool!" Peter declared.

An interval of silence passed. John had known Peter too long to deny his self-effacement persuasively. Peter *had* bragged too often in days gone by, but John wished to turn his thoughts to better things. Choosing his words carefully he said, "What then has changed you?"

The burly fisherman sat huddled in a dark corner of the cell for a quiet moment. The faint glow of moonlight from a very small barred window high above their heads illumined his face. "The knowledge that the Master accepts me," he asserted. "When he appeared to me after his resurrection, apart from all the others, he did not speak. But I knew he had chosen to show himself to me, alone, to reassure me of his love, despite my cowardly denials of him." The mighty man's eyes showed tears at the corners, but he did not brush them away. "And then the words he spoke to me beside the sea when he called us that last morning . . . they have changed me."

John's curiosity was whetted. "Peter, what did he say to you?" he urged. "I followed behind as the two of you walked down the beach after breakfast. But I could not catch a syllable."

Peter's voice came low and trembling. "Three times the Lord asked me if I loved him. Three times I told him I did so. I was grieved that he asked again and again. He knew all things. He knew I loved him. I suppose he wanted me to resolve my loyalties once and for all. He knows how weak I am. And each time he heard my answer, he said, 'Feed my lambs . . . feed my sheep . . .' " Here Peter paused, as if fearing to go on. "I did not know what he meant by that," he continued. "I think I am beginning to know."

John could not help but interject his own thoughts at this point. "Peter," he exclaimed, "do you remember when, long ago, he said 'on this rock I will build my church'? Was this what he meant? It is happening now!"

Peter did not comment, his mind already on another matter. "But John, this is not all he said that morning. He told me something very strange, which I do not understand . . . nor do I think I want to understand . . ."

John listened respectfully.

"He said to me, 'Truly, truly, I tell you, when you were young, you girded yourself, and walked wherever you wished. But when you shall be old, you will stretch forth your hands, and another shall gird you, and carry you where you would not go.' " Peter shook as he repeated the words. They obviously troubled him greatly. "And then the Master insisted, 'Follow me.' I cannot deny him again, John. I must not—and I cannot. I love him—and I need him, too greatly."

John contemplated his confession carefully. This had been the difference between them from the beginning. John had *always* felt his need of Jesus, even before he had met him or known of his existence. Peter had only recently recognized such need. *This* is what had changed him.

John's heart reached out to his friend. After all their years of camaraderie, they were at last truly one in the Spirit, brothers in Christ. The voice of Jesus at the Last Supper came to mind. "But I have prayed for you," he had said to Peter, "that your faith does not fail. And when you are converted, strengthen your brethren." At last, the big fisherman had experienced the true commitment which John had found so long before. And he was, indeed, strengthening his brethren.

But what had the Lord meant by his fearsome reference on the shore? "Peter," John whispered, "I am amazed that you have tolerated this imprisonment so easily. Do you not fear this may be the fulfillment of the Master's words?"

Peter smiled. "I am certain it is not," he asserted. "The Lord's church is only beginning. There is much yet to come!"

John breathed a sigh of relief. "I suppose you are right," he said. But then as he reflected on that morning at the sea, he falteringly reached out a hand to his fellow-prisoner. "Peter, that dawn, as you walked with the Master, you turned about once or twice to look at me, and your face bore a very singular expression. What did it concern?" he asked hesitantly. "Did the Lord speak of me?"

Simon looked at John uncomfortably. "I had hoped you would not ask. Not because the Lord spoke terrifying things for you," he added quickly, "but because I have analyzed his words again and again, and cannot imagine what they mean."

John's eyes were wide. "You cannot think to keep such a thing from me!"

After much consideration, the Son of Jona at last explained, "I was very fearful when the Lord told me of my strange future. It filled me with apprehension. I did not know if I wished to follow such a course. Hoping to justify my own weakness, and wanting to turn his mind away from me and my needs, I saw you walking behind us. 'But Lord,' I offered, 'what shall this man do?' Of course, I was really saying, 'Can't you use him, instead of me?' "

John appreciated Peter's candor, and laughed sympathetically. "And how did Jesus respond?" he asked.

Peter looked at the cell floor blankly. "The most peculiar words, John . . . he said, 'If I choose that he tarry until I come, what is that to you? You follow me!' "

The young apostle took a sharp breath. What could be the meaning of such a statement?

"Do you see?" Simon continued. "Does it not sound as if the Lord intends that you will never die?"

John shook his head vigorously. "Of course not, Peter! It cannot mean such a thing!"

But the Son of Zebedee wondered at the saying and would not shake it easily.

Chapter 3

John and Peter stood alone in the center of the great Sanhedrin courtroom, their hands bound with rough cords behind their backs. Annas, Caiaphas, and their kindred accusers sat at the head of the room. More rulers, elders, and scribes were gathered here today, to try the two apostles, than had ever attended the sessions on John the Baptist or Jesus. As Peter had said, Jerusalem had been rocked to its very foundations.

John wondered where Zebedee might be in the crowd. Was he still borne about upon a stretcher, sick and hate-filled? His son's heart ached at the thought of him, but standing tied and guarded he could not look about to locate him.

When the throng had assembled, the man who had been healed the day before was brought in to be seen of all. No one could deny the miracle. Everyone here had seen the helpless beggar many times over the years. No testimony was necessary to support what had taken place. Instead, the defendants were to be questioned directly.

"By what power, or by what name, have you done this?" Annas commanded, pointing a long finger in Peter's face.

The great fisher of men looked at him squarely and answered, "You rulers of the people, and elders of Israel, if we this day are examined concerning the good deed done to this man, let it be known unto you all, and to all the people of Israel, that by the name of Jesus Christ of Nazareth, whom you crucified, whom God raised from the dead . . . by him this man stands here before you—healed! Jesus is the stone which you builders rejected, and he has become the chief cornerstone! Nor is there salvation in any other, for there is no other name under heaven given among men, by which we must be saved!"

The mighty words echoed through the silent hall. For a long time no one spoke, but at last the high priests and their cohorts on the platform began conferring together. The angle of their heads, and the way they spoke with one another showed they marveled that such profound words could have been heralded by a Galilean fisherman. Compared with such doctors of the Law as lined the walls, Peter and John were indeed "unlearned and ignorant men."

After due consultation, Annas again questioned them. "You were disciples of the Nazarene, were you not?"

"Yes, we were," Peter declared, "and we *are!*"

Again, the magistrates conferred, this time their attention being directed at the beggar. Shaking their heads incredulously, and unable to deny or refute what had happened to him, they sent the apostles from the room until a decision might be reached.

Peter and John stood between two armed guards outside the courtroom. Nearly half an hour passed, as the Sanhedrin debated the best solution to the "problem." How John wished he might catch a word or two of the proceedings.

At last they were summoned again before the council, and Annas glared down upon them threateningly. "That a marvelous and unexplainable thing has happened to this man is undeniable," he granted, knowing he would be a fool not to do so, "but there is no cause to thank anyone save Jehovah for that." Then, straightening himself, he declared, "We have determined to release you. However," he paused for effect, "it is from here on our ordinance and command that you will not speak at all or teach in the name of this Jesus of Nazareth!"

Thus far Peter had done all the talking. Now John took the initiative. "Is it right in the sight of God to listen to you more than to God? You are the judges! For we cannot speak anything but the things which we have seen and heard!" he cried.

Annas was shaken by the retort, but rebounded quickly. Piercing John with his flashing eyes, he warned, "We are the instruments of Almighty God! Challenge us and you will pay dearly for your treachery!"

Chapter 4

The joy John experienced as he walked free from the courtroom that morning was immeasurable. As he and Peter passed through the streets of Jerusalem they were applauded and cheered by throngs of onlookers who had heard the news of their trial. Never in the memory of Israel had two commoners so easily shut the mouths of the ruling hierarchy.

But, more thrilling even than that victory, was the story which reached the apostles' ears along the way. Other disciples had been eagerly awaiting their release, and as soon as they saw them, they told them excitedly, "Because of the lame man's healing, over five thousand men have joined the faith!"

John's heart sped. By custom, the males of a household were the key figures in any census. "Five thousand men" might actually mean ten thousand or more living souls, for their wives and children were undoubtedly swayed by their beliefs. This number, plus the three thousand who had trusted Christ on Pentecost, and all those who had joined the church in the interval, might well total twenty thousand people! Jerusalem was indeed being split asunder!

Peter threw an arm around John's shoulders as they strode boldly and excitedly for the house of the upper room. "Can anything stop us now?" he declared.

John smiled in response. "It would seem not!" he answered.

But already, something had dampened his spirits. He had expected to see James, and all along the way he had searched for his brother's face. However, the elder son of Zebedee was not to be found among those who had come out to celebrate their release. Sensing that something was wrong, John tried to convince himself of better things.

The great house of the upper room was filled with fellow believers, waiting breathlessly for a detailed account of all that had transpired. To John's relief James met him at the door.

"How I have needed you, brother!" the red-haired rabbi asserted.

But there was no time now for explanations. Though John wished he might be alone with his elder brother, he must wait on the demands of the people.

John glanced about. Where were Salome and Mary of Nazareth?

When Peter had at length reported all that the chief priests and elders had said to them, James stepped between the two celebrities and placed his arms about them, praying aloud as the congregation lifted hands in worship and voices in praise and joy to heaven.

"Lord, you are God, who made heaven, and earth, and the sea, and all that is in them!" James began. "Grant unto your servants, that with all boldness they may speak your word, by stretching forth your hand to heal, and that signs and wonders may be done by the name of your holy child Jesus!"

Upon the completion of that prayer, the people were so moved with praise, John had not heard the like since the day of Pentecost.

So fulfilling was the moment, John nearly forgot his previous anxieties. But once again he studied his brother. Only rarely had James ever been so bold, and those times had usually been in relation to some entanglement with his father.

Urgency compelled John to know the source of his brother's heaviness, and to find Salome. Quietly, as those about him centered their interests on prayer, he slipped out of the room and headed for the quarters which had housed his own family and the mother of Jesus.

When John pushed open the door it led to a darkened, quiet room. There was something very ominous in the mood which filled the scene as he entered. As his eyes adjusted to the darkness, he saw that Mary, the mother of Jesus, sat beside Salome, who lay weeping upon her bed. The woman of Nazareth spoke to her softly, words which John could not discern.

But as he was about to approach, a voice behind him halted his progress. "John. . . " it whispered brokenly.

"James!" he responded, turning to face his elder brother. "What is it? What has happened?" He wanted to go immediately to Salome, supposing she was sick or injured, but James restrained him.

"Brother, we have bad news," he explained. "Our father is dead."

John grew cold. As the story unfolded it brought terrible

pictures to his mind. Zebedee, the hate-ridden, bitter old Pharisee, had died in seclusion, cut off, of his own volition, from all friends and family. One by one, since driving Salome away from home in Capernaum, he had dismissed his household servants, discouraged visitors, and rejected acquaintances. For weeks he had dwelt as a recluse at the family's private home here in Jerusalem. Coming out only for meetings of the Sanhedrin, he had had dealings with those who carried his stretcher, and none else. He had apparently died alone, in the bedroom of his empty house, being discovered days afterward, a horror of bloated and blackened flesh.

John shuddered. "Then," he whispered, "he was not even present at today's trial."

"No—he was not," James answered.

The young apostle looked up at his elder brother with aching eyes, knowing, now, the source of his heaviness. Though the two sons of Zebedee had always been distinctly independent personalities, though their years together had been checkered with contention, they loved one another greatly. At this moment John felt as he had when traumas of childhood had sent him running to James. How he longed for the strong hands of his big brother to set everything right.

Looking in need to one another, the two embraced and went to Salome's side. "John!" she whispered. "You are with us?"

"Yes, mother. Rest now."

The sight of her younger son, safe and free beside her, seemed to calm Salome greatly, and John bent over her with a kiss. Leaving her to Mary's charge, he rose and looked out the chamber window, voicing the question which had weighed on them all. "James, what of father's soul? Where do you think he is now?"

The elder son of Zebedee answered not a word.

Chapter 5

It had been years since John had been inside the family home at Jerusalem. Indeed, he had not even seen the house since he had gone to follow the Baptist. Standing before it today brought back many happy memories, for this had always been one of his favorite places.

The family had used the home mainly during feasts and holidays, leaving Capernaum to celebrate in the Holy City. Here John had partaken of his first Passover; here he had celebrated his first Hanukkah; nearby he had received his Bar Mitzvah, at which time he had been formally ushered into manhood.

The apostle stood in the street for some time before entering. He wanted to remember the house as it had been before seeing it in its present state. Doubtless, in his last days, Zebedee had neglected it. John did not want to witness it that way, and did not want to think on those terrible hours.

But, summoning his courage, he stepped through the portal, removed his mantle, and kissed the mazuzah on the doorpost.

Several of the church women had come today with Salome and Mary of Nazareth to clean the house. Life in the commune of the great hall, where the apostles and unattached converts had been staying, had become virtually unbearable for Zebedee's widow and the Lord's mother.

Mary in particular had found it difficult. Because of her relationship to the Master, she had come to be a sounding board for all matters of debate or question in the young church. Repeatedly she had attempted to avoid such issues, explaining that being the mother of Jesus did not necessarily qualify or prepare her for such things.

And then, the zealous converts and the apostles themselves had found it all too tempting to constantly examine her regarding their Lord's history. What had he been like as a child? they wondered. How had it been to raise him? Had he been unusually bright, terribly mystical? What of his relationship to the Baptist? Was it true they were cousins? On and on the questions went.

At first, perhaps, such discussion had been a blessing to her, filling her lonely hours and somewhat alleviating her grief at the loss of her son. But over the weeks she had come to long for peace and privacy, commodities impossible to attain with such a living arrangement.

And so, the death of Zebedee had proved beneficial in one respect. John and James, inheriting his estate, were able to provide good lodging now for Salome and Mary. And the church rejoiced in the fact.

The young apostle had dreaded setting foot in the old family home, for fear of what he would find. But the busy chorus of women's laughter flooding the gallery and rooms around the court, the flurry of activity which filled the house, caught him so unexpectedly he soon forgot his apprehensions. Life and sound abounded. He had come to oversee matters, and found himself only in the way.

Even Salome's voice, amid the chatter, sounded happy for the first time since Zebedee's death, and John smiled broadly.

Wandering almost unnoticed throughout the grand old house, he stopped from room to room reminiscing over his childhood. It seemed so long since those days. So much had intervened of good and ill. Memories like specters and poltergeists peeked at him from the corners of each hallway, sad and happy recollections at each turn.

As he came to the last room in the gallery corridor, however, his attention was captured by yet another train of thought. Two young women stood precariously upon a broad stool attempting to take down the tattered curtain from a high window. At first he thought no more of them than he had of the others in the house. But as they busied themselves, the light mantle fell back from the head of one, and he recognized her as the fair sister of Lazarus—Mary of Bethany.

Unprepared for this, his heart was caught in mid-beat. Standing in the doorway, he watched her silently, taking in her beauty like a balm. As the two girls, the other a servant of her household, giggled and struggled vainly with the rag-like drapery, he crossed his arms and leaned against the doorpost with a private chuckle of satisfaction.

At last the ugly fabric came loose, sending dust and debris through the air. "There," Mary sighed, holding the offensive scrap far away from her, "take this thing and dispose of it!" The servant-girl left the room quickly to do just that, looking rather surprised at the sight of John in the doorway. Mary still had not seen him, but he had not taken his eyes from her. She stepped down from the stool, brushing the dust from her hair and shaking her skirt gingerly.

"You look just fine to me," John interrupted.

Mary glanced up in astonishment. "Good day, sir," she said softly, color rushing to her face. Quickly she raised her mantle, as it was improper for a woman's head to be uncovered before any man save her husband or close kin.

But John looked on with delight. "Leave your mantle down, Mary," he said, smiling. "I like it better that way."

Chapter 6

Miracles at the hands of the apostles were coming in ever-increasing numbers. Daily since their trial, Peter and John had been going into Solomon's Porch to preach the good news, and no one had laid hold on them. In fact, so powerful had been their ministry that the sick and the deranged were brought from nearby cities, lining the streets up to the Temple each morning in hopes that the mere shadow of an apostle might fall upon them. For it had been reported that healings had come even in such a way.

The hierarchy would not tolerate this revolution much longer. Today, in the Porch, countless miracles had taken place since the arrival of John and Peter before dawn. By noon, however, the Sanhedrin had met once again, and officers had been commissioned to seek and take the Lord's men, by force if necessary.

Soldier feet could be heard in the distant corridors. A great band of troops suddenly appeared between the columns, pushing the crowds aside as they came. They must have numbered in the hundreds, and were of the Temple guard and Roman contingent. Doubtless the rulers had sent so many fearing an uprising when the apostles were taken.

It all happened very quickly, forcefully, and without explanation. Once again, John and Peter found themselves incarcerated, this time in a common prison, large enough to hold all the apostles and a number of church leaders.

John sat as before, bound beside Simon, but this time his brother James sat with them. It was cold inside these walls, despite the noonday heat outside. The only view to the external world was through the grates on the double door of the prison, and then only the hallway and the station guards could be seen.

Despite the circumstances, however, spirits were high. Someone in the group began singing, and soon the dungeon rang with choruses of praise and exultation.

But just as the worship had started, without prelude or introduction, it was brought to an abrupt halt, as from the hallway, one of the guards stood peering in at them and shouting: "You'll not be so glad when they come to take you away!" His tone was ominous, and it brought a chill to the hearts of the prisoners.

"Explain yourself," Peter demanded.

"What need is there for explanation? The word is, the magistrates mean to have you all disposed of!"

Disposed of? John looked fearfully at his big friend, and a pall fell over the gathering. But James, the elder Son of Thunder, faced the guard squarely and spoke words which overwhelmed John's heart. "If this is true," he called, "we could not be more greatly honored, for we shall join the ranks of the Baptist and the Nazarene!"

Hearing this, the apostles were stunned. But as the concept bore into their hearts, it infected them with martyrs' zeal. "Praise the Lord!" Stephen, a deacon, cried out. And the rest responded in kind, with new songs and praises to God.

John's countenance was radiant. Might he be destined to die for his Lord? Could it be that James and Peter and all the rest would die for Christ? The thought was fearsome but somehow full of attraction.

Suddenly, however, the Master's words concerning the apostle returned in haunting cadences to his mind: "If I will that John tarry until I come, what is that to you?"

During the night the guards were to be changed. The apostles had been inside the hold for over fifteen hours. Most of that time had been devoted to loud and celebrative worship. Now, however, many of them slept. James' head lay on John's shoulder, where it had come to rest during the long dark evening. His heavy breathing was a comforting sound. John was glad his elder brother was so near.

But as black night had crept through the dungeon, leaving only dim torchlight in the hall, terrible thoughts had plagued John. He wondered how much longer he might be with his friends. If they were all to die together, they would be present with the Lord at once, and no sorrow would be felt. But what if he were to lose James, Peter, and the others, yet be left to grieve behind them? He could conceive of nothing more lonely.

"Jesus," he whispered, "spare me that! Whatever your words meant, spare me that!"

His prayer was suddenly interrupted. Hearing the guards leave the hallway, he waited for the replacement shift to arrive. But before the sound of any new sentinels was discerned, there came a peculiar rattling at the iron doors.

John lurched forward, waking Peter and James. "Listen!" he answered their confusion, "the doors are being opened!"

"This is it," James said soberly. "They are coming to take us."

Fear gripped the gathering, but John hushed them. "This is very strange, brothers," he whispered, as the doors continued to be worked by unseen hands. "There is no one in the hall; at least no one I heard. The guards left, but no shift has yet come to replace them! And see the eerie torchlight at the bars. It is not of fire, unless fire is now blue-white!"

There was no time to contemplate this. Instantly the doors were flung open, and a brilliant creature, unearthly in its beauty, greeted them.

They needed no introduction. They knew it was an angel. Its presence seemed to fill the entire prison, flooding it with irridescent light. "Go," the figure commanded, "stand and speak in the Temple, to the people, all the words of this life!"

As the apostles exited, quietly looking back in awe and wonder, the prison doors shut resoundingly behind them, and the angel disappeared from sight.

The next morning the high priest and his men summoned the council. When they had assembled, Caiaphas sent officers to the prison to have the apostles brought forward.

Minutes later, the emissaries, white-faced and shaking, returned, empty-handed, bringing only the two morning prison guards. The keepers, who had arrived at their post just moments after the night's strange event, stood mute before the high priest.

"Where are your prisoners?" Caiaphas demanded.

The poor guards shook their heads bewilderedly. At last one of the officers answered for them, "The prison we found safely shut, and the keepers standing outside, in front of the doors. But when we opened the hold, we saw no men!"

Consternation and fear overcame the council, and as the high priest consulted with his baffled cabinet, another officer entered the courtroom.

"Your honors," he addressed the platform, "behold, the men whom you put in prison are standing in the Temple and teaching the people!"

Chapter 7

Despite the miracles of recent days, these were fearsome times for the church.

"We ought to obey God rather than men!" had become the byword of Christ's followers. For this had been the sentiment of Peter, James, and John, when once again, the morning after the angel's intervention, all the apostles had been taken before the Sanhedrin.

Enraged by such a statement, Caiaphas had had Jesus' loyalists beaten with flesh-ripping whips. Then, due to the wisdom of one Pharisee, the learned Gamaliel, the apostles had at last been set free. "Refrain from touching these men," he had counseled, "and let them alone. For if their work is of men it will die away. But if it is of God, you cannot overthrow it, for then you would be fighting against God!"

Gamaliel's insight had been providential. The council had accepted his advice, and had sent the apostles away with a warning not to speak in the name of Jesus again. Upon departing the chambers, however, the men of Christ had only rejoiced in their suffering. And they continued daily in the Temple, and in every house, to teach and preach the gospel. Many were added to the Jerusalem church as a result, and even a great company of the priests themselves were obedient to the faith.

But, ironically, the same man who had rescued the apostles from death at the hands of the council had also recently introduced into leadership another Pharisee who, unknown to the good rabbi, would prove to be the greatest persecutor the church had yet known. Saul of Tarsus, one of Gamaliel's pupils, had, on his teacher's recommendation, been given membership in the Sanhedrin. And he now filled the very post left vacant by the death of Zebedee.

Having come from a distant northern port city in the province of

Cilicia, Saul had not been well known in Jerusalem. But within months of his initiation into the council, his fame and influence were spreading furiously. Short, stocky, fearsome in appearance, with eyes full of zeal for Judaism and hatred for the followers of Jesus, he set about to make havoc of the church. One of his first deeds was to encourage the killing of the deacon, Stephen, one of the mightiest leaders, orators, and miracle-workers of the infant congregation.

The day of his martyrdom had been one of the most horrifying in John's life. The Sanhedrin had now gone beyond threatenings and scourgings. They had forgotten Gamaliel's advice, and at the instigation of Saul had cast Stephen out of the city, where they had stoned him to death.

John had been spared the witness of that most hideous torment, but the description, brought by those who had been present, had both terrified and awed him. It was reported that as the stones had been thrust upon Stephen, the godly man, bloody and broken, had looked heavenward, and as if seeing the face of God, had cried out in relinquishment, "Lord Jesus, receive my spirit!" Then, as he had been battered to the ground, he had pleaded, "Lord, lay not this sin to their charge!" and had died instantly.

Tonight John stood in the gallery of the great house of the upper room, looking down on the fountain and taking in its music. His thoughts, however, ranged beyond the walls of the building, seemingly the only sanctuary for the apostles in Jerusalem. Every other house containing followers of Christ had, upon the authority of the chief priests, been ransacked by Saul and his men, and wherever believers were found, whether male or female, they had all been committed to prison. Saul was known for forcing blasphemies from the weak, tormenting the strong, and ultimately seeing that many were put to death.

For some reason, the Lord had seen to it that no apostle was taken, and this house had become an island of refuge for any who were inside during Saul's raids.

Thousands of believers had fled Jerusalem, and more were leaving every day. They were scattered as far away as Samaria, deeming even that despised province more desirable than the Holy City.

John and James had seen to it that Salome and Jesus' mother were secretly ushered to Capernaum, where they would stay in the family house until it was safe to return—if ever that day should come. Mary of Bethany, Martha, and Lazarus had gone with them to care for their needs.

Now, it seemed, only the apostles remained. Actually there were hundreds of believers in the city, but communications were kept to a minimum. Compared to the joy and excitement of the church's first months, this underground experience was lonely and fearful for John.

He did take comfort in the presence of James and Peter. He had never appreciated his two companions more.

Footsteps on the gallery behind brought his mind to the moment. James had joined him and stood silently watching the cascading fountain below.

"You are full of thoughts," John perceived.

"I suppose . . . " James offered.

"They concern the church?" John urged.

"They concern its persecutor."

John's face clouded at the mention of Saul. "I despise him!" he snarled. "To think that he has taken father's station in the Sanhedrin!"

James was silent, but finally said, "My thoughts exactly." Then came words not typical of the elder brother. "Wouldn't father be pleased? Saul is achieving what he himself would have attempted with half the youth and strength!"

Chapter 8

It had been years since John had first been in Samaria, and he had passed through the province then only to see the Baptist at Aenon. He remembered vividly his revulsion when he had found Jesus with the harlot at the well. His second journey had been with the Master during the final stages of his ministry, and at that time a native with a meat cleaver had threatened his life. Had anybody told John then that he would one day serve the Samaritan people, he would have called him insane.

But such was the case. He and Peter were traveling to the district to minister to converts within its alien borders. Many Samaritans had come to believe on Jesus, due to the witness of Christian refugees who had sought sanctuary from Saul by fleeing there—the one place they knew he would not set foot. In fact, like seeds blown on a fearsome wind and taking root in fertile soil, the church had grown wherever its witness had been scattered. Saul's determination to destroy the cause of Christ had only driven it to greater success, forcing it into regions as yet unresponsive to the gospel.

It had been very hard for John to digest the thought that Samaritans were now his brothers. When the deacon, Philip, had evangelistic success in the region, and when the cry for further teaching came from the converts, John had been rankled. It seemed the Lord had not finished developing tolerance in him upon his acceptance of Nicodemus the Pharisee, Matthew the tax collector, and Joshua of Arbela.

Peter and John traveled by night through Judea. The darkness would provide some degree of camouflage, should Saul's men be in wait along the way. His spies seemed to know each move of the infant church, and word would surely have reached them concerning this missionary journey. Though the Lord had protected his leaders until now, they were ever mindful that they were key targets for the persecutor.

Each unexpected sound along the road sent chills down John's back. Scenes of torture and bloodshed filled his mind as he walked close to his friend. The big fisherman's great strides were rapid and determined. John wondered if he, too, was anxious for the Samaritan borders.

"How ironic," he thought, "that we should long for the stench of that province!"

No word had been spoken between the two apostles since sunset. Only the rhythmic slapping of Peter's cloak against his staff filled the night air, sometimes lulling John into lethargy. But always he was on guard. And, as much as he dreaded the land to which they traveled, he found himself fearing Judea more.

Chapter 9

John did not know what to think of his Samaritan brothers and sisters, even after a week's ministering in their towns and villages. He and Peter, themselves outcasts of Palestine, had been warmly received by many of the converts. And the presence in the province of Judean refugee believers took some of the edge off John's uneasiness at being here.

Still, it was not to be expected that all would go smoothly.

John was apprehensive, today, as they approached the great fort city of Sebaste. Philip had cautioned them concerning a certain Simon, a famed sorcerer, who resided here. Curiously, the wizard had claimed belief in Christ under Philip's ministry. But the deacon had never been sure of the man's true allegiance, wondering if miracles had attracted him, rather than the gospel.

Upon entering the gates of Sebaste, the first sight to fill the apostles' eyes was the magician's black tent, decorated with colorful symbols of the occult.

By now a crowd had gathered to greet the Lord's men, having heard in advance of their coming. The reception was cordial and eager, but as the noisy welcome filled the streets, John glanced toward the tent. A head appeared between the door flaps, and a spangled turban caught the sunlight. Black eyes beneath it sent a chill to John's heart.

"Men and brothers," the sorcerer's voice cleared the crowd, and he stepped forward forcefully. The natives obviously respected this man greatly. Before their conversion, he had been their foremost leader, and many still esteemed him highly. "How pleased we are that you have come," he smiled with gleaming teeth. "Our brother Philip has told us much about you," he flattered, bowing low before them.

Peter looked nervously at John. The wizard knew he need not introduce himself, and so came directly to the subject which most interested him.

"Philip has wrought many signs among us. I am certain you will verify your credentials in the same manner."

"We need not prove ourselves," John asserted. "Our Lord will do that for us. We will but pray for his power in the lives of our brothers and sisters. If signs follow—they will follow. If they do not come—we will praise him anyway."

The sorcerer had no reply, but followed silently behind as the throng led Peter and John into the local synagogue. Only the strength of Christ carried the young apostle through those portals. Never in his wildest dreams would he have considered entering a Samaritan house of worship.

But as the Lord's men began to lay hands on the people, praying aloud for them, here and there in the crowd the same phenomenon which had occurred on Pentecost manifested itself again. Men and women were speaking in new and strange tongues, until all those assembled were filled with the Spirit. John had not expected such a thing. That God should anoint Samaritans as he had anointed Jews shocked his sensibilities, and shook him to the core.

But he was not the only one overwhelmed by the witness. The sorcerer stood at the back of the synagogue looking on and listening, fascinated by the strange dialects. Philip had wrought many miracles, but nothing like this!

His defenses down, the magician now showed his true colors. Working his way up the aisle of the building, he approached the apostles, crying above the glorious din, "I will give you money, sirs, more money than you can imagine! Only give me also this power, that whoever I lay my hands on may receive the Holy Ghost!"

At this the rejoicing died away, and the congregation waited in amazement, wondering what the apostles would say. But Peter scrutinized the sorcerer confidently. "Your money perish with you!" he rebuked him. "Because you have thought that the gift of God may be purchased with money! You have neither part or lot in this matter, for your heart is not right in the sight of God!"

The wizard gazed at him red-faced, not knowing what to say, and was shamed to the depths of his soul. "Repent, then, of your wickedness, and pray to God, that the thought of your heart may be forgiven!" Peter demanded. "You are in the gall of bitterness and bound by your iniquity!"

John watched as the sorcerer seemed to become visibly smaller. Shrinking back, the hypocrite who had posed as a believer could no longer look Peter in the eye. He had nearly persuaded Philip of his sincerity, and until now he had been given the benefit of the apostles' doubt. But he had not fooled the Holy Spirit.

"Sirs," he said, barely above a whisper, "pray to the Lord for me, that none of these things which you have said will fall upon me." Then, hunched down like a mongrel dog, he slunk out of the synagogue and away from public view.

Chapter 10

By now, John and Peter had been in so many Samaritan villages that they had all begun to look alike—dirty and impoverished. The young apostle did not note the name of the town they were approaching this evening. He had lost track of their specific whereabouts.

Until now, they had been afforded the hospitality of small communes of Jewish refugees, eating and sleeping in hostels where they had, by the grace of God, found lodging. Reportedly, however, no Jewish converts resided in this little city. John wondered where he would stay tonight. He did not relish the idea of sleeping out, for storm clouds were gathering in the sunset sky. But less did he savor the thought of dwelling in a Samaritan house.

"Peter," he whispered as they entered the city's low gate, "do you find it difficult to accept these people?"

The big fisherman smiled. "You know me, John! Of course I do!"

"That comes as a relief!" the young Galilean sighed. "Still, I suppose it is not a good way to feel. I know the Master would not approve . . . "

Peter thought a minute, caught by John's concern. Then, forthrightly, he walked ahead, striking his staff against the earth. "Well," he asserted, "we shall pray about it!"

They did not pray together, but individually, for no sooner had they entered the town, than they were swept apart by its enthusiastic greeting.

As local deacons introduced themselves, as the women of the town brought gifts and the children sang and danced, John remembered the Lord's words at his Last Supper. "A new commandment I give unto you, that you love one another . . . "

"Lord, help me to love these people," he whispered. "Love them through me!"

Darkness descended, and they were informed that lodging had been offered by a deaconess, Sister Rebekah. Dubiously they assented, and when the evening's festivities began to taper, they were escorted to her home.

The building was modest, but well lit and warm. The woman and several servants met them at the door, the pleasure they took in this honor evident at every gesture. When John entered, he found himself almost instantly at ease. The inhabitants were true believers, he could feel, for the spirit of Jesus permeated them.

The house was very clean, unlike most Samaritan hovels. Sister Rebekah bade the apostles sit, and brought in platters heaped with simple but delicious fare.

John watched as the woman served. She had struck him as

strangely familiar from the outset, and even now it seemed he had seen her before. "Impossible," he reasoned. "She has probably never set foot outside this town."

Her face, now so peaceful, betrayed lines of a hard life, and he wondered how she had lived before her conversion. What impressed him most pointedly, however, was her maturity. Rarely had he seen a new convert with such spiritual grace.

"I am beginning to have second thoughts," he whispered to Peter when she had stepped from the room.

"Concerning?"

"The Samaritans . . . "

"Oh." Peter's voice was secretive, a gleam of sly humor in his eye.

Not knowing how to account for it, John went on, "This Sister Rebekah is a remarkable woman. Not at all like a Samaritan!"

Peter chuckled.

"I mean, I would have guessed her to be Jewish . . . " he stammered. But this was no better.

Peter roared with delight. "John—you are the bigot, aren't you?"

At this John warned, "Shhh! She will hear us!"

The gracious woman entered once more, this time with a pitcher of wine. "I must apologize for the quality of the beverage," she said humbly. "I am not a wealthy woman, and I find I must often dilute what I have with water. But," her eyes sparkled, "our little town has a good well."

She grew very quiet for a time, and Peter smiled as though he knew her thoughts. Gradually the story unfolded. "You will remember that your Master spoke with me once in private," she reminisced. "He called himself the 'living water' and said that if I should ask of him, I should never thirst again." Tears rose to her eyes as she related line by line the story of that long-ago day beside the Sychar well.

John was caught in mid-breath. Was this *that* city? Was this the Samaritan harlot he had once run from the very sight of?

Peter had known all along. John grimaced. But he could not hold the jest against him. It had worked to John's good, for only shock could have fazed his petty provincialism.

When they had gone to their quarters for the night, the young apostle lay awake for hours. The hard-core Jew who had prayed for tolerance had received more than he had bargained for. Not only did Samaritans merit love, but he would do well to emulate some of them.

"Lord," John prayed silently, "if I become half of what this woman has become, I shall be grateful."

Chapter 11

The church was about two years old, and had grown so rapidly in that time that the entire Roman world was feeling its impact. It had spread far beyond the boundaries of Palestine, into Syria, Ethiopia, and, indeed, to all parts of the empire, wherever Jewish Christians had carried it.

But as it had spread, Saul's terrible persecution had followed. No one knew how many believers had been put to the sword in his name. Day after day news was brought to the apostles in Jerusalem concerning his latest conquests.

That Peter and John had returned safely from Samaria was nothing short of miraculous. Saul's men had doubtless watched for them along the way.

"Why are we spared?" John found himself questioning. "Why are others taken and not we ourselves?"

He feared for the women in Capernaum. When the persecutor's activities had centered in Jerusalem, it had seemed the safest thing to send them there. But with the dispersion of believers from the Holy City, Saul had carried his vengeance into Galilee.

News of hostile action in that province always spelled agony for John. Daily, during such times, he would wait anxiously at the gate for word from home. "Messenger—how is Capernaum?" he would ask. Thus far the answer had been, "Saul has not gone there as yet," or "Saul has spared it thus far."

Still, thoughts of Salome and Jesus' mother—alone, frightened, defenseless—haunted him. And naturally with them came visions of Mary of Bethany. Time and again he had determined to go to them, but the other apostles had convinced him it would be a foolish venture. His chances of making it that far, barring God's intervention, were nearly nonexistent. And even if he were to arrive, would he attempt to escort the household back to Jerusalem with Saul's men on the roads?

His hands had been tied. Helplessly he passed the days, relieved only when he heard the persecutor's efforts had been turned some other direction. Though it grieved him when any city was struck, at least the ones he loved most were temporarily safe.

Recent word was that Saul had asked the high priest to send letters to the synagogues of Damascus, in Syria, warning them that the marauder was on his way. "If any be found in your congregations who hold to the heresy of Jesus of Nazareth," the notices stated, "whether they be men or women, Saul has authority to bring them bound to Jerusalem. The resultant punishment is death for those who will not recant."

The letters had gone out nearly two weeks before, stamped with the seals of Annas and Caiaphas. Saul was doubtless in Damascus now, ravaging and devouring the church. In fact, John and the others had fully expected to hear word from that distant city several days ago. But so far no messenger had arrived.

John sat tonight with Peter and James in the courtyard of the great house. Their thoughts were identical, though not one voiced them. "When will we hear? What will the news be? Do we really want to hear?"

Presently a knock at the gate brought the long-awaited herald. Fully expecting the sorrowful countenance of one who bore bad tidings, the three apostles were not a little surprised when the man entered. His expression was strange—not sad, not joyful, but rather perplexed, as though he did not really believe the news he had been commissioned to bring.

"Speak," Peter addressed him. "What is the word from Damascus?"

The messenger shuffled nervously. "Sir, the word is that Saul has been converted!"

Peter, James, and John looked at one another bewilderedly.

"Again, fool! What is the news?" Peter demanded.

"Sir," the herald repeated, "they say Saul has become a believer and abides with the disciples of Damascus!"

Chapter 12

Had the messenger not been one of their own people, the apostles would have thrust him from the house bodily. As it was, they certainly gave his story no credence. Either the poor fellow had been deceived or was sadly confused. In either case, they would not be taken in by such nonsense.

Still, as days passed, more and more rumors concerning the "conversion" of Saul were coming to their ears. These they passed off as part of some great scheme to delude the church. If Saul were to be accepted as a believer, if he were to be admitted into the underground of their society, he could spy on it very conveniently, learning much about its activities and the whereabouts of the various dispersed congregations.

The most elaborate part of the "charade," as they judged it, began with rumors that the Sanhedrin was now determined to destroy Saul.

"How far will they go in this hoax?" Peter snarled one evening at supper. "They must think us the greatest of fools!"

John laughed with him, but their mood was interrupted by a voice from the courtyard. "Not fools! Just stiff-necked!" it called. Approaching the upper room was a fellow believer whom they had not seen in some weeks, Barnabas, a Levite of Cyprus, who had joined the church at its inception. Having had much land, he had sold it upon his conversion, giving the proceeds to the brethren. Under Saul's persecution he and his family had taken leave of Jerusalem, and the apostles had not since known their whereabouts.

"Barnabas!" John called. "We had almost given you up!"

"Praise the Lord!" James greeted him. "How good to see you!"

Only Peter did not rise to greet him. Glad to know that Barnabas was alive and well, he nonetheless sat stunned at the man's introductory remark. "Stiff-necked!" It rang in his ears, and he wondered at the accusation.

Barnabas embraced the sons of Zebedee. "Grace and peace to you! How I have longed for this day!"

"Where have you been?" they queried, leading him to the table. "Damascus."

The apostles were awestruck at first. Then their questions came tumbling forth.

"Brothers," Barnabas quieted them, "I have the most wonderful story to share. I know you have heard of Saul's conversion." His brilliant eyes were joyful, but the apostles were silent. "I also know you have not believed what you have heard." He smiled.

John turned to James dubiously. What was Barnabas up to?

"I have come to give you a firsthand report, brothers, to assure your hearts that Saul is indeed one of us!"

Peter stirred angrily, and Barnabas read his posture. "Brother, you are offended that I called you 'stiff-necked.' I apologize. But have we not all prayed for rest from our persecution? Have not all the saints prayed for this?"

The apostles were pricked by his questions. "And has there not been just the reprieve we longed for? When did word last reach you of a single believer imprisoned or put to death?"

They could not recall any such incident since before Saul had gone to Syria.

"I have been with the man for several weeks, brothers," Barnabas continued. "Let me tell you what transpired as he came to Damascus."

The strangest tale John would ever hear was recounted: how supposedly Saul had seen a vision of Christ, as he had been on the road to Damascus; how a brilliant light had thrust him to the earth, blinding him, and how a voice had cried from heaven, saying, "Saul, Saul, why do you persecute me?" Barnabas told how that voice, being the Lord's, had then directed Saul to go into Damascus, where he would receive his orders; how a disciple, Ananias of that city, had also seen a vision, in which Jesus had informed him of Saul's conversion, and had told him to locate and pray for the persecutor; how Ananias, at first very skeptical, had nonetheless obeyed, and how Saul's blinded eyes had been healed when prayed for; how Saul had spent several days with the church at Damascus, and had then begun to preach boldly in the synagogues.

When the story was finished the apostles were at a loss for words. They neither believed nor disbelieved.

It was Peter who retained the strongest skepticism. "Brother. Barnabas, how are we to know for ourselves?" he responded. "Possibly, by a miracle of God; what you say is true. But without confirmation in our own hearts, we cannot trust it to be. For all we know, to accept Saul would be to take a viper to our bosoms."

Barnabas laughed, but his laughter carried a trace of anger. "Do you really *want* to know for yourselves?"

For a long moment no one answered, but John was constrained to say something.

"We do . . . " he replied hesitantly.

The Levite studied him carefully. "Then let the Spirit of *Christ* bear witness in your hearts that what I say is true!" he declared. At this, he turned from them and headed for the courtyard door.

The apostles stirred uneasily. No one made a move to call him back, and Peter spat noisily upon the floor.

John's conscience was troubled, however, by Barnabas' injunction. Certainly, the Spirit knew the truth of the matter, and as John allowed it, his soul was flooded with compassion. Scenes of the Samaritan harlot flashed to mind. Had he learned nothing from her conversion? Could Christ not receive and change anyone? Yes—even Saul?

"Brother Barnabas!" he called. "Wait!"

The other apostles watched in astonishment as John went forward.

At first Barnabas eyed him warily. Carefully, John chose his words. "Brother," he said, "do you return to Damascus?"

"Yes," was the cautious reply.

John resolutely thrust out a hand of acceptance. "Then, greet Saul in the name of Jesus!"

A smile slowly came to Barnabas' incredulous face. And, by proxy, Saul's hand, which had sent saints to their deaths, met John's in believer's fellowship.

Chapter 13

These were good and pleasant days for John. There had been rest for the people of Christ for about nine years now. Since Saul's conversion the church had seen prosperity and growth, greater even than that of its first months. Of course, the Jews were still antagonistic, but Gamaliel's advice to leave the apostles and their followers alone had taken on new importance since the strange reversal of Saul's attitude. And no new persecutor had arisen to equal him.

The man currently occupying the Judean throne was Herod Agrippa, grandson of Herod the Great, and nephew of Herod Antipas who had slain the Baptist and mocked the Nazarene. But thus far he had been surprisingly kind toward the Jews and tolerant even to the Christians of his realm.

After several months of doubt, even Peter had come to believe in Barnabas' testimony of Saul's regeneration. Saul, the great persecutor, who now called himself "Paul," meaning "little," had at last come in person to Jerusalem to meet the big fisherman. As expected, his visit had been met by fear in the church. But Barnabas had managed to gain him an interview with Peter, and after another accounting of the man's strange conversion, the apostle at last had accepted him.

At first opportunity John had gone to Capernaum to fetch the women of his house and all the family servants. Salome and the Lord's mother had so praised the service rendered by Mary of Bethany during their confinement in Galilee, that John had asked her to stay with the two elder women as long as she wished, to be a companion to them in their advancing age. Devotedly, the girl, now a woman herself, had complied, and had been in the family's Jerusalem home ever since, as had been Lazarus and Martha.

The great house of the upper room had been willed to the apostles by the wealthy owner, and he had passed on shortly after Saul's conversion. A believer himself, the hospitable man had done a fine service to the church, providing its headquarters for years to come.

And these were busy times for John. The days, though peaceful, were filled with activity. Because Peter often left Jerusalem to see to the well-being of disciples elsewhere throughout Palestine, John and James had become pillars of the Jerusalem believers' community. It was their lot, and a comparatively pleasant one, to care for the ministry in the Holy City, while Peter, Saul, and Barnabas took on missions further afield.

There had been, to be sure, difficulties with the church at Jerusalem. From time to time internal squabbles had arisen between brethren which required the attention of the apostles. But generally, it was a peaceful society, held together by common belief, unity of spirit, and, sadly, a common fear: the ever-possible emergence of fresh persecution from their enemies.

The Lord had taught them one vital lesson during these years, the subject of which had brought about a crisis of controversy before it was accepted. In one of Peter's stints outside of Jerusalem he had preached the way of Christ Jesus to Cornelius, a Gentile of Caesarea, and a Roman Centurion, at that.

This had been a major about-face for Peter, who had always avoided association with Gentiles, especially Romans. He, like John, was being taught tolerance by unmistakable persistency on the part of the Holy Spirit. To his amazement, Cornelius and his house believed one and all, their conversion being confirmed immediately by the same sign which had fallen on Jews and Samaritans, as well: they spoke in new and unknown tongues.

While all of this should have been cause for celebration in the Jerusalem church, it had met, instead, with bigotry and rejection. Upon his return, Peter had been severely challenged for having had such intimate dealings with uncircumcized Gentiles. Only after detailed rehearsal of all that had transpired was the apostle able to persuade them of the truth, "that God is no respecter of persons." At last they had acknowledged, "Then God has, also, to the Gentiles, granted repentance unto life."

So the church had grown out of its strictly Jewish background, and had become the faith of Jews, Samaritans, and Gentiles alike.

So great, in fact, was its influence, that the world gave believers a title: "Christians," the Christ-ones, for they were proclaiming his power everywhere.

A note of fear had been introduced when a church leader had prophesied a famine which would affect the entire Roman Empire. But active faith replaced fear, and the prophecy fell to the good of the church, bringing Christians from across many miles into contact through mutual aid and assistance. John and the elders in Judea had been encouraged when food and provision had been sent from Antioch, in Syria, by the hands of Paul and Barnabas, who ministered there.

John had been on a rare mission outside Judea when Paul had met with Peter for the first time. But this second visit of the renowned convert and his partner allowed John the long-wished-for introduction. The son of Zebedee would never forget that day, for the proof of God's transforming power had been seen clearly in the now-softened eyes and peaceful demeanor of the ex-persecutor.

There had been times when John had envied the lot of the more-traveled apostles. Sometimes he found himself yearning for their adventuresome style of life. But he knew it was his mission to care for the Lord's mother, and he did not resent that obligation.

Today he entered the courtyard of the family home in a preoccupied mood. His duties with the church had kept him busy and away from the women of his charge for several days. He sat down beside the fountain between Mary of Nazareth and Salome.

"You are working too many hours, John," Salome insisted, studying his tired and somber expression. "Why do you push yourself so?"

"Because I want the church to be ready when the Master returns."

"Perhaps your work would be easier if you had someone to help you," Salome teased.

John looked at her with a sigh. "You aren't going to start that again, are you?" He rested his chin on his hands and stared angrily at the courtyard floor.

"Now, John," the Lord's mother joined in, "we are only thinking of your happiness!"

"And hers," Salome added, sending the two women into peals of laughter.

Time and again, since the day John had brought Mary of

Bethany into the house to care for the aging matrons, they had found opportunity for attempted matchmaking. It had nearly become their chief joy in life. They were determined the bachelor would not remain so forever, and they were persuaded that Mary, Lazarus' sister, was his match.

"Don't be angry," Salome soothed him. "I must admit I have something at stake in all this. James is beyond hope. First it was his rabbinical studies; then it was the Master; and he was in his late twenties then. But," she drew close to him, "you are not so old, John. Of course, most men are married at eighteen . . . but thirty-five is not so old. You are not beyond hope at least! And Mary—she is yet a young thing . . . "

John stood to his feet. "That will do! You have seen the kind of life Peter has given his poor wife. Left alone most of the time—childless. Would you have me curse any woman with such an existence?" He threw his hands up in disgust. "What's the use? We've been through it all before! Look at the two of you—mature widows—one of you the mother of our Lord! I should think you would be above this!"

With these words he saw instantly that he had wounded them deeply, and caught himself short, but it was too late. Mary of Nazareth could not look him in the eye, and his mother's face bore a pained expression.

John groaned in frustration, "Forgive me. I didn't know what I was saying!"

Salome gazed at him tenderly, her eyes full of mother-love. "Son, we truly think of your happiness. Don't you realize we have seen the way you look at that girl? Don't you suppose we know how lonely you must be?"

At that moment, light footsteps were heard on the gallery. John turned to see none other than the very subject of their conversation. Mary of Bethany, older now, was nonetheless even more beautiful in her maturity. Her form, once very slender, was more womanly; her face, if possible, more perfectly defined. Excitement filled him, as it always did on his viewing her.

Mary looked down into the courtyard, not expecting John to be there. It was obvious, by her undefended expression, that the sight of him touched her heart as well. She paused a moment, gazing at him, as their eyes met across the way. But then, catching herself, she withdrew into a gallery room.

John had forgotten, temporarily, the presence of the two elder women. When, upon descending into reality, he found them peering at him with knowing smiles, he stood instantly. Shaking his head as if to say "you are mistaken," he turned hastily and left the house.

Chapter 14

Freedom from persecution was not to last forever. The conversion of Saul had squelched it for much longer than the church had dreamed possible. But just when they were beginning to accept peace and rest, and the Christian community was starting to forget the pains of its birth, the hand of the enemy came upon it again.

This time the persecutor was not an unknown in the world.

Though his reign had, until now, been peaceable, Herod Agrippa, who loved the praise of his subjects, and who realized that their leaders despised the Christians, began an assault on the church.

What more appealing targets for his evil gluttony than the apostles themselves? They had been spared the terror of Saul. To Herod this was delightful. Their fate was reserved for him, he reasoned. And he would not set his nets for the smaller fish, but would go directly for the leaders, the Lord's inner circle—Peter, James, and John.

On this particular day, only a handful of the apostles and their servants were in the great house of the upper room. The majority were about the business which had occupied their days during these years of peace: visiting from house to house, praying for the sick, rejoicing with those who had some recent blessing, counseling the needy, sorrowing with the grief-stricken, bringing strength of spirit to the downcast, preaching the good news of Christ's salvation to all who would listen.

John himself sat today at the bedside of a young mother whose first child had been stillborn. Somehow he found himself speaking words which quieted her weeping. Many times he had been called upon to bring a healing message when he felt helpless to do so. At such moments Jesus spoke through him. He knew it, and he took no credit.

After nearly an hour at her side, John stood and spoke softly to the watching family. "She will do well. She is sleeping." The woman's husband thanked him with a broken voice, and her mother embraced him tearfully. Situations like this were very fulfilling for the young minister, and had taken him from day to day these several years, with little sleep and little time to himself. When he left this house, he would be going to yet another needy residence, one of many thousands served by the apostles and elders.

As he entered the street, the sun was beginning to set. The strength which had sustained him through the ordeal with the childless woman began to subside. He had experienced this on innumerable occasions, an effective reminder that nothing in his own ability or wisdom could see him through such a crisis.

It was nearing Passover again. This was always a difficult season for the apostle, recalling too clearly the Master's trials and death. A cool spring breeze whistled down the narrow viaduct, and as John passed the vicinity of the Holy Mount, he remembered that on a similar night eleven years previous, he had made a fearful trek through these passages in quest of Jesus at Caiaphas' court. He shivered at the memory.

Street torches accentuated the lines time had brought to his face. He was no longer the nineteen-year-old boy who had left the fishing nets in search of the Baptist. Often he longed for those more carefree days. "One more visit," he pushed himself. "Only one more and I can go to bed."

Frequently James accompanied him on his rounds, or when Peter was in Jerusalem, they ministered together. But James had business at the great house, and Peter was not in the city this month.

John wished for a partner in these lonely hours. It was on nights like this that Mary of Bethany came most painfully to mind. It would be a comfort to know a beautiful woman waited for him at home, a balm for his weary spirit. Still, he reacted defensively to Salome's entreaties that he marry. Though other apostles had their wives and families, he could not consider his way of life anything fit for a woman to endure.

And then, the next needy parishioner would come to mind, supplanting such pleasant thoughts, just as happened now. Down the street he saw the house of the intended visit, this one containing a family in desperate want of food and clothing. As he approached the low door and was about to knock, the sound of rushing footsteps greeted his ears from the shadowed street. Not knowing the source, he ducked into the doorway and waited. Expecting the trampling feet to bring nothing more than a gang of rowdies speeding past, he, nonetheless, could not be too careful.

To his fear and surprise, the noisy group stopped short in front of the very house he was about to enter. "There he is!" one shouted.

John's heart leaped to his throat. He braced himself for a confrontation with some dread enemy. It was dark here, and he could not make out the faces of those who hailed him, but suddenly the voices took on a familiar sound. "Brother John, we hoped we would find you!" It was a young convert who greeted him, and gradually John could make out that all the men before him, some ten or twelve, were of the Jerusalem church.

"What is it?" the apostle asked, hoping in his misery that they did not bring news of some other need to be attended this night. Had he known the report they bore, however, he would gladly have taken a thousand errands instead.

"Sir, it seems Herod has stretched out his hands to vex the church," the young disciple said breathlessly. "Tonight soldiers from his palace broke into the great house, and have taken James captive!"

John looked at them blankly, as if not hearing. The messenger reached for him, but he drew back angrily. "No," his soul raged, "tell me it is not so . . . "

The family he had come to visit, upon noting the stir outside, had ventured to the door, and had caught the news. They beckoned to him silently, but he turned from them uncomforted.

Somehow the apostle found stamina to push past the little crowd, and began making his way down the narrow street. "Where are you going?" they called anxiously. "Don't you know Herod will want you, too?"

But John did not answer. To his conscious mind, he wandered into the darkness aimlessly. But his heart took him toward the palace of the enemy.

Chapter 15

By the time John reached the palace of Herod, throngs of Christians had already congregated at the gates. Rarely had all the Jerusalem church gathered in one place. Their numbers had grown so that when joined together they made a formidable force. The hierarchy of Judaism would think long and hard before sending armed men against such a host, for though most Christians were unarmed, they were too numerous, and had too many sympathizers.

It had been years since they had been challenged to lock hands against an enemy. As the multitudes grew at the spreading news of James' capture, the air was charged. The smoke of a thousand torches ascended into the night sky outside Herod's house, while the people of Jesus shouted and chanted in unison:

"The Lord is my rock, and my fortress, and my deliverer; my God, my strength, in whom I will trust; my buckler, and the horn of my salvation, and my high tower.

"I will call upon the Lord, who is worthy to be praised: so shall I be saved from my enemies.

"For he has girded me with strength for the battle: he has subdued under me those that rose up against me.

"He delivers me from my enemies: he lifts me up above those that rise up against me: he has delivered me from the violent man!"

Over and over the words rang through the outer courts of Herod's palace, tens of thousands of voices protesting his tyranny.

Long before John was within view of the place, he heard the chorus, and his previously terror-numbed gait took on more confidence. As he came upon the scene his heart swelled with pride and hope. Surely Caesar himself could not go contrary to this ominous throng.

John stood on the edge of the gathering, fully expecting at any moment to be granted the sight of his brother James, brought forth free and unharmed. The crowd was continuing to expand, and the singing was becoming louder, more insistent: " . . . so shall I be saved from my enemies! . . . He has delivered me from the violent man!" On and on went the rhythmic chant.

When more than an hour had passed and the blackness of night had fully descended, John was growing anxious again. Thus far he had been unnoticed, standing in the background, but now he began making his way forward, pushing through the multitudes like a persistent wedge. When those nearby recognized him, they greeted him with reverence and compassion. "Brother John! Praise the Lord! James will be protected! You will see!"

John smiled at the sea of faces which parted as he went, but his heart was a heavy weight. How he wished to believe the words of encouragement they spoke!

Perhaps he would have been more convinced if he had not lost, already, two masters at the hands of Agrippa's uncle, Antipas. From time to time, as he listened to the chants, he found himself full of faith, but then would come the memory of the Baptist's tormentor and Jesus' mocker, or then he would glimpse afresh the stony walls which loomed so unfeelingly between himself and James. Were these people not fools to think any Herod capable of mercy?

All about him were his brethren, those who supported him. But John felt very much alone. As he approached the front of the crowd, however, a familiar voice rang out. "John! Over here!"

"Peter! Thank God!" he cried. For some reason which John would not question, the great fisherman had returned to Jerusalem this night, ahead of schedule. The son of Zebedee found tremendous comfort in his presence. The mighty man embraced him, saying, "Friend, you must believe that everything will be all right!"

John nodded, desiring more than anything to know such confidence, and picking up some of Peter's enthusiasm.

But another hour passed, and still no sign of response came from the palace. Armed guards looked down upon them from the porch outside the gate and from the mighty turrets overhead, yet even they were silent.

At last, John's patience being stretched to the breaking point, he pulled away from Peter, asserting, "I can endure it no longer! I am going in!" Peter reached for him, but already John was on the steps leading to the gate. The guards lowered their spears, barring his entrance, and Peter ran after him, shouting, "Fool! They will kill you!"

The gleam of brandished steel stopped John in his tracks, but then, disregarding his life, he made a dive for the doorway. One quick flash of the cold metal would have settled his misery. Perhaps that was the hidden desire of John's heart. But it was not to be fulfilled. The doors were flung open before him, just as he made his move.

A hush came over the crowd in that instant. Though John stood closer to the scene than any onlooker, he was the last to fully comprehend its meaning. The hands which had opened the gates were those of the assassins which had, only moments before, wielded the sword of James' death.

The eldest son of Zebedee, the mighty apostle, and the beloved brother of John, lay in grisly display upon a bloody bier, his head borne alongside on a platter.

John sunk into mindless oblivion. No man could follow him there. No enemy could touch him. Yet in that void of darkness, even in the retreat of that sad, black haven, sounds of a distant refrain, soft, but persistent, reached him:

"The Lord is my rock, my fortress, my deliverer, my God, my strength, in whom I will trust . . . "

Chapter 16

Faith alone took John through the days which followed. Nothing else could have given him the strength to uphold his mother through this time, to go about the ministry when believers were held in the grip of new terror, or to fulfill his role as one of only two remaining chief apostles of the church.

John had not thus far had time to lick the wounds of grief suffered at the loss of his brother. For days he had been forced to apply the energy which would have been expended in mourning toward greater labors than he had ever known.

Unity was the byword now. Because James' murder had greatly

pleased the Judaic hierarchy, Herod might instigate fresh persecution at any moment. Peter, John, and all the apostles had devoted many days to the task of preserving the church, gathering supplies and establishing hideaways throughout the city. In other towns and villages of Palestine, and indeed, throughout the Roman Empire, Christians had undertaken preparations. The object was not to make war with the enemy. All measures were of a defensive nature.

There were those who fled Jerusalem, but this time the Christians were determined, for the most part, to hold their own. John gave his household members the option of going back to Capernaum, but unanimously they decided to stay put.

Since even the great house of the upper room was no longer a sanctuary, James having been captured there, the apostles were lodged in various quarters about town. Peter and his wife were in the house of a prominent young convert, John Mark, who had accompanied Paul back to Antioch. John Bar Zebedee stayed with his people in the family home.

Most of the preparations were now made for the safekeeping of the church. John had worked long and hard hours, seemingly endless days. Tonight, for the first time since James' death, he had a moment to be alone, to reflect upon what had happened.

He sat in the porch of the court beneath the gallery. The servants, under the direction of Lazarus' sister, Martha, kept busily out of sight, knowing the master needed time to himself.

John sensed the presence of his Lord very keenly this evening, as he had ever since the realization of James' death. That presence had thus far shielded him from the blow. But the Lord knew John needed more than shielding. He had to be free to release his sorrow. It could not be suppressed indefinitely without ugly consequences.

Quietly the tears began to flow. Tears of loneliness and grief. Though the church would miss the elder apostle terribly for a while, the years would gradually take him from their memories, and his role would be a minor one in recorded history. But John would not forget him.

The stabilizing influence of James' calm and deliberate personality had complemented John's more fiery, impulsive spirit. The quieter son of Zebedee was, as Jesus had called him, just as much a "Son of Thunder" in his own right as John. James had exemplified the thunder of strength and determination; the thunder of capability and stamina. John had come to a greater appreciation of these qualities now that his brother was gone.

He harbored no bitterness at this loss, as he had with the deaths of Jesus and the Baptist. He did not wallow in selfish despair. Perhaps he had grown beyond that. But as he sat in the empty court, the Lord his only audience, he simply whispered brokenly, "Why, Jesus? Why was he taken, and not I?"

Chapter 17

It was Passover, about one month following the death of James. John was rudely shaken from sleep by a loud knocking at his chamber door. "Sir!" a female voice roused him, "please wake up!"

It was highly unorthodox for a woman to go near the sleeping quarters of any man, save that of her husband. John sat up groggily, pulled on his outer tunic, and stumbled to the door.

"Sir!" the cry came again.

Now fully alert, he recognized the voice. It came as a pleasant but rather unnerving surprise to think that Mary of Bethany greeted him from the hallway. Opening the door, he cleared his throat and tried to attain a measure of poise. "Mary?" he said bewilderedly. "What is it?"

"Sir, forgive my coming here . . ." she answered, making it certain she would never have broken the taboo, had it not been for unusual circumstances. "I had just risen to tend the parlor fire, when a messenger arrived from John Mark's house. They have taken Peter!"

John eyed her wildly. "They! What do you mean—they? Who has taken Peter?"

Shaken by his tone, Mary nonetheless explained. "Herod's men! Not half an hour ago!"

John's head reeled. But trying to think clearly, he considered the young woman who waited in awkward silence at his rebuff. "You have done well, Mary," he assured her. "Wake the others and come quickly."

Upon John's orders, the church did not come together en masse, as it had at the capture of James. The hour had come for full use of planned defenses. Believers were charged to keep close to their homes and hiding places, and to pray unceasingly for Peter.

James, the brother of Jesus, led a prayer meeting on one side of town, and a large gathering, which included apostles, key elders, leaders of the church, and their families, met secretly under John's instruction, at the home of John Mark and his mother, from whence Peter had been taken.

The burden of leadership was heavy on the apostle's shoulders. Herod did not move quickly this time. For three days and nights believers prayed for Peter's protection and release. While Judaism observed the Passover festival, Christians were on their knees in fasting and arduous petition. It was part of Herod's plan to thus demoralize the church, making it chafe in torment while the world outside celebrated a holiday.

John had no power to transmit hope to the people of Christ. The Holy Spirit alone upheld them in those hours. It would have pleased the apostle greatly had he been able to take a census at this season, for the church, rather than diminishing under persecution, was multiplying. Hardly a man or woman who had claimed allegiance to Jesus had turned away, and even now, the ranks were swelling.

But Peter's capture had been a great blow to John. When Mary had brought word of Herod's move, the apostle's immediate thought had been of Jesus' words to the big fisherman that last day on the beach: "When you were young you girded yourself, and walked wherever you wished. But when you shall be old, you will stretch forth your hands, and another shall gird you, and carry you where you would not go."

Though Peter could not be considered "old," the death of James made it difficult for John to pray with confidence that he would be spared.

The apostle surveyed the faces in the gathering. Hope and sorrow were mingled in their expressions. He dared not tell them of the Master's words.

Lost in lonely and dejected thoughts, John was stirred by movement near the central fire. Mary of Bethany had risen to tend it. It was like her to think of such a thing. All about, men and women prayed earnestly, while some slept for weariness, their energy depleted from the three-day vigil. Soon they would rise and take over the intercession, relieving those now on duty, and the room had to be kept warm for the next shift.

John observed the beautiful woman silently. These days spent in her presence had caused his admiration to grow. Even now, he wished he might take her in his arms, and speak his feelings forthrightly. Such thoughts did not seem out of keeping with the moment. He truly cared for Mary, yearned for the comfort of her society, and desired to share his lonely fears with such a woman.

How long he sat watching her he did not know. But when she rose from the fire, she glanced his way. Always before, these many years, when caught by one another's eyes, they had turned as if in shame from further communion. But this time John gazed upon her steadfastly, and though color rose to her warm cheeks, he smiled at her tenderly.

Her face spoke volumes, but John could not ascertain the interpretation. Did she care for him, too? How he wished he might touch her, but this was not the hour, or the place.

Peter must be the central concern. They must turn their minds to him.

Chapter 18

The days of Passover had come and gone. Word now had it that Herod intended to bring Peter out for public execution the next morning. Filled with fresh motivation, the church prayed even more earnestly.

John paced the room continually, pleading with God for the release of his friend. He could not bear the thought of life, if Peter, too, were taken from him.

With sunset, time seemed to double its pace. Hours passed too quickly. Dawn would arrive too soon.

Exhausted, John ceased his vigil and walked to a parlor window. The night streets were silent, but the apostle's fears crowded his mind with sound.

As he peered outside, bloodstains upon the doorposts of a nearby house affirmed that this had been the Passover season, and the anniversary of the Lord's resurrection. Always before the most celebrated of Christian events, it had passed nearly unnoticed by the Jerusalem church this year, as they had awaited news of Herod's actions.

It came to John that Jesus, too, had once prayed in agony. In the Garden of Gethsemane he had pleaded with God to spare him Calvary's torment. It comforted the apostle to know his Master could sympathize with his pain. But then came the memory of Jesus' ultimate cry of relinquishment, "Nevertheless, not as I will, but as you will . . ."

John trembled. Must he relinquish his fear for Peter, and give his desires over to the will of God—whatever the consequences?

He stared, motionless, at the dark street, struggling with his soul's dilemma. As he heard the town crier call out midnight, he knew he must make a decision.

At last, lowering his head, he sighed, "If this be your will, I give it over. I desire my friend's life—nevertheless . . . your will be done."

The room was very still. John was not aware that the others had been watching him and listening to his conversation with the Lord. As he turned about, seeing their incredulous faces, he sat down quietly to await the Master's will.

Nearly an hour later a knock came at the courtyard door. Fear gripped the household. They waited apprehensively as a young servant girl went to answer the summons, fully expecting an enemy to enter the scene.

"Who is it?" the girl called. The distance across the court and the barrier of the door muffled the response, so they did not recognize the voice. But suddenly the maid was running excitedly back to the gathering, having left the door bolted in her haste. Her face radiant, her tone ecstatic, she cried, "It is Peter! Peter is outside!"

John's heart leaped to his throat. While unbelieving listeners insisted that the girl was mad, confused, or deluded, she continued to affirm her witness.

Now the knock came again—insistently, repeatedly. John went anxiously to the entry, his companions following, fearful but curious.

Without hesitation, John threw open the door and stood face to face with the big fisherman.

The onlookers, stunned, could scarcely believe what they saw.

"Peter," John stammered, his eyes welling with happy tears.

"Yes, I am here!"

The baffled crowd was loud with excited questions, and Peter, beckoning them to hold their peace, began to explain.

"I was asleep between two soldiers, and was bound with two chains. Guards were outside the door of my cell. Suddenly I was smitten on the side and rose to see an angel standing over me. His radiance filled the prison, but the soldiers did not see. He took me by the hand, and as I rose my chains fell off. 'Follow me,' the angel said, and so I did!" Peter was breathless. "Truly, I thought I was dreaming! He took me without interruption through the first and second ward. Watchmen did not even seem to see me, though I passed before their very faces! When we reached the gate to the street it opened of its own accord, and I followed the angel into the way. Suddenly he disappeared, and I was left to myself. When I recognized all that had happened, I knew that the Lord had surely delivered me out of the hand of Herod, and from all the expectation of the Jews!"

John studied Peter carefully. "At what time did the angel come for you?" he inquired.

Peter thought a moment. "It took me not quite an hour to get my bearings and find my way here. I would guess he came about midnight."

Chapter 19

John was not afforded the pleasure of Peter's company for long. It was expeditious that the great fisherman leave Jerusalem until Herod would withdraw his hand. That very night he fled with his wife, Deborah, to a secret place.

Though John was thankful for Peter's safety, his subsequent departure left the apostle more lonely than ever. As believers left John Mark's home, rejoicing in God's deliverance, and as the elders and their families went their separate ways, John and his followers walked silently back to the house of Zebedee. Exhaustion from the several-day vigil swept over the apostle, flooding him with fear that enemies of the church could lie in wait around any corner.

Responsibility crushed him. How was he to care for his conglomerate family and manage the church singly? Even the other apostles looked to him for leadership. There was no James, no Peter. For the first time, he must shoulder the chief apostleship entirely alone, thousands depending on him in this most difficult period.

Added to this was the fact that since the church had sustained the murder of James and the exile of Peter, John would be Herod's prime target.

At last the group reached the richly carved door of the old home. John ushered his people inside and bade them good night. When the household was dark and quiet, he went to his own room in the gallery.

The central view from John's quarters was of the courtyard below, but on the far side of his chamber, on the outer wall of the house, a narrow aperture gave him a glimpse of the city streets. Restless with anxiety, John could not think of sleep, but paced back and forth before the little window, stopping now and then to gaze upon the night lights. A passing cart sent a chill down his spine, and he straightened soberly. "Fool," he whispered to himself, "are you going to fear every footfall, every shadow? If the Lord protected Peter, will he not keep you, as well?"

But the horror of James' grisly death leaped vividly to mind, and John closed his eyes angrily. Even Peter's providential escape could not erase that memory. And, as so often happens, the depths of despair followed quickly on the heels of a miracle. John feared. There was no reasoning with his feelings. He simply feared—miserably, torturously.

"Master!" he pleaded. "Why did you let my brother die? What will become of Peter? What of the church? Why am I left alone?" Bitterness welled from his heart. "Curse this Herod! And overthrow him in his pride!" he demanded. "Bring me aid! Bring me an able assistant! For I cannot manage alone!"

John yearned for the physical presence of his Lord! Infinitely he desired his touch! Loneliness obsessed him. He could not endure his vacant room or the emptiness of his heart a moment longer.

The sound of footsteps in the court beneath brought him outside to the gallery rail. He would have been satisfied to see any human form, to observe the motions of any passing servant. But the dim light warmed his heart and stirred his blood as it identified the source of the sound. Mary of Bethany, apparently on some errand, passed from her chambers to the kitchen across the way.

Perhaps it was loneliness, perhaps it was the appropriate timing—John did not stop to analyze his motivation—but he called to her softly, anxiously, not to be held back again.

"Mary . . . "

The young woman turned quickly and stared in surprise at her master's beckoning hand.

"Come here a moment," he smiled, attempting to camouflage the desire the sight of her inspired. But the woman did not move, finding his request difficult to interpret. What could he want at this hour? If he wished her to run some errand he could merely say so. Why must she come to him on the gallery?

Her face grew warm and red, and she studied him with perplexity. "What is it, master? What may I bring you?"

John took a few steps toward the stairway and beckoned again. "You may bring me some companionship," he called gently. "I am feeling very lonely tonight."

Mary weighed his words. They appeared harmless enough. To obey them would be in keeping with her position as his servant, though out of keeping with tradition. To go to him, alone, in the night . . . it seemed out of the question—and yet, surely the great apostle of the church was innocent in his request.

As she studied him, however, more than fears for *his* intentions troubled her. Her own desires frightened and bewildered her. Often she had dreamed of such a moment, when the master, whom she had loved from afar these many years, might call her to his side. Secretly she had harbored thoughts of his embrace. And if she felt such things, was it not possible he felt them as well?

She often sensed his looks in her direction. She recalled the first day he had come with the Lord to Bethany. She had been unaware of his admiring gaze as she had sat at Jesus' feet. But Martha had noted John's attraction for her, and had told Mary of her observations.

Though the young woman had considered such things frivolous at the time, with the passing months John had come often to mind, and frequently when she had been in his company, she had felt a stubborn glow rise to her face, and a growing desire to turn his way.

Such feelings had been her own secret these passing years, but they could not remain so eternally. The bronzed, golden-haired fisherman of Galilee, the handsome son of Zebedee, had come to be more to Mary than one of the Lord's disciples, more than a great apostle, more even than the master of her new home. She loved him—deeply, fervently. She desired that he return that love. And tonight, when their eyes had met in John Mark's house, she had been unable to cover her longings.

Just now, when she had sat alone in her room, she had not truly needed to leave it and cross the courtyard, directly beneath his quarters, knowing he might hear. She could not, therefore, blame him for granting her desire—that he call out to her.

Still, she trembled with the impact of the moment. Dare she approach the stairway? What would be the consequences?

Through the pale glow of night, John's sea-blue eyes lured her. Making a hesitant move forward, she placed a foot lightly on the bottom step. The apostle's heart raced excitedly as she came to him slowly, uneasily up the flight. When she reached the top stair, she could not look him in the eye, but he reached for her hand and lifted her face to him. For a long moment they stood thus, gazing at one another, as they had done across the fire at John Mark's house.

Light conversation would have been hypocrisy. No preliminaries were necessary as their expressions confirmed the contents of their hearts.

John leaned over her, his breath coming heavily. "You feel as I do, Mary. Say you do!"

The girl's resolve to shelter her vulnerability waned with his touch. "I do, master," she whispered.

John's soul flamed with desire, and he drew her to the gallery railing, enfolding her in his arms. "You love me, Mary. Say you do!"

The young woman trembled, but submitted. "Yes, master, I do love you . . . "

The confession filling his ears with sweet thunder, he held her tightly and touched his lips to hers, kissing her hotly, lustily. He was no longer lonely, and he would not be again. The girl had charged his heart and soul with joy, and he kissed her again, and then again.

As he did so, his hands caressed her deep, dark hair, and moved down her slender arms until he held her two small hands in his. Suddenly, he was overcome with her nearness. Reason fled him and he could think of nothing—nothing but making her his own.

"Come, Mary," he whispered, leading her toward his chamber door.

The girl's heart pounded madly, but suddenly she struggled against him. Nearly overwhelmed by his passion, she would have yielded willingly, anxiously—but she dared not.

"Master," she stopped short, "I cannot enter your chamber!"

John grasped her to him rudely, and kissed her again, but she wrenched herself free.

"You are a man of God, my lord! Such a thing would not be right!"

The apostle stared at her wildly. His natural instincts cursed her rebellion, but his spirit knew she spoke the truth. Still, he cared not at the moment for the things of the spirit.

"I need you, Mary," he groaned. "You said you loved me! Can you leave me now?" His arms reached for her again, and she wavered as she read his longing and despair. Holding out one hand, she touched his cheek tenderly, and he enfolded her fingers in his own, holding onto them with a grip of triumph.

But then, Mary withdrew her hand resolutely, and turned from him, tears filling her eyes.

"Truly I love you, my lord," she replied. Then looking at his chamber door, she sighed, "But such a thing would not please your God and mine."

John stood in helpless silence as he watched her hurry down the stairs, and into the solitude of night.

Chapter 20

The interlude on the balcony would remain a secret between Mary and John, but in its wake a certain tension would be felt in the house of Zebedee. As the two fulfilled their duties in the home, they would not speak of it together, but it would be always in their thoughts.

Those were days of confusion and misery for the apostle. Had the times been different, had they met under freer circumstances, nothing would have prevented his asking Lazarus for the hand of his sister in marriage then and there. But these were not easy times. He could not know but what Herod would come against him any day, and to marry the woman of Bethany only to leave her a widow in her prime seemed unbearably cruel.

Days on end John was tormented with the dilemma—his consuming love for the woman, and his sense of practicality. True love demanded the best for the one loved. He could not think it good for Mary to commit herself to the tenuous relationship which such a marriage would entail.

Still, John longed for her. As day after day they lived in the same house, as he could not avoid seeing her, his need raged like a lion within.

Prayer was hindered by perpetual doubts that he must not be as spiritual, as free from worldly attachments as the Lord would have him. Otherwise, he reasoned, why would the girl be on his mind so constantly? Even as he performed his duties with the church, she was ever-present in his thoughts.

Autumn approached, evidenced by frequent changes in sky and wind. Today the apostle walked across town to oversee a meeting of elders at John Mark's home. To his right flowed the brook Kidron, past the environs of the Garden where Jesus had spent his last hours in prayer.

As John thought on the Master, a pang of guilt swept through him. Things had not been right between himself and his God these months since that night with Mary. Repeatedly he had asked the Lord's forgiveness for his hasty and impetuous actions. But somehow, he had not felt the Master's pardon.

Often the haunting words of Jesus had come to him concerning the place of marital love in the life of his followers: "There are some eunuchs which were born so from their mothers' wombs," Jesus had once taught, "and there are some which were made eunuchs by men. And there are eunuchs which have chosen to be so for the kingdom of heaven's sake. He that is able to receive it, let him receive it."

To this day John had considered those words to imply that the greater a man's spirituality, the less he would need or be drawn into a relationship with a woman. It was easy to think this was the Lord's meaning, and therefore, John continued in remorse for his incontinence. Though he wished to believe he had been pardoned, he still felt its effect, and could not deny his feelings for the girl.

He sat beside the brook for a moment, and tossed a pebble into the water. "Master," he whispered, "if only you were here! If only I might know your will! If I were able, I would divorce myself from all thoughts of this life. I would join you where you are. But I am not able! I cannot negate my love for Mary! Forgive me, Master!"

The cool rushing of the waters soothed his mind somewhat, and in their current the presence of his Lord was almost tangible.

"It is true that in yielding to your own control you were wrong," the Master counseled. "But once you have accepted my death as yours, you need not ask forgiveness again and again."

Tears of relief and joy came to John's eyes. A very heavy burden was lifted with that certitude. "What, then, of the girl?" he sighed. "What am I to do?"

It occurred to him that Jesus' first miracle had been to bless the marriage at Cana, and that he had taught it was honorable for two to become one if he ordained it. But somehow John did not feel free to assume much from this. Confused again, he awaited the Master's touch.

"Rest in me," the answer came. "Do not be concerned for the things of tomorrow. Take no thought for your life, but seek first the kingdom of God and his righteousness, and all these things will be added unto you."

Chapter 21

Trumpets blared in the stadium at Caesarea, on the Mediterranean. Herod Agrippa, who had come here to celebrate the games and to render honor to Caesar, was about to deliver an oration to visitors from the neighboring province of Phoenicia. Certain cities of that region, Tyre and Sidon, which had been assisted by Herod, had greatly displeased the monarch in the past, but today they had sent emissaries desiring peace.

Taking immense pleasure in the knowledge that they wished to placate him, Agrippa had determined to take advantage of the moment. He had spent days preparing a speech which would awe and humble them, and which would bring glory and credit to himself.

The audience awaited his entrance into the arena, which had been elaborately prepared for the event. Gaudy decor gleamed brilliantly beneath an autumn sun. A rainbow of banners and streamers covered the balconies. A fine retinue of soldiers lined the field, their steeds decked handsomely in scarlet and gold.

Herod's household, numbering in the hundreds, watched eagerly for his arrival, and the emissaries of Phoenicia feigned equal excitement, though they endured the pomp and display out of official duty only, and not out of affection for the man. Their country relied on Agrippa's financial assistance, and it was for this reason that they would tolerate the humiliation about to be heaped upon them.

At last, from the wings, Herod came forth, arrayed in the most spectacular apparel, and followed by a horde of attendants. His clothing, woven completely of silver thread, and of a rare and marvelous design, flashed blindingly in the sunlight. His appearance struck awe and fear in the hearts of those who looked on, friends or otherwise.

Trumpets rang again, and the great crowd cheered. Whether their applause was from honor or obligation, it mattered not to Agrippa. He reveled in it.

When the king had taken his seat upon the marble throne, his chamberlain motioned for silence, and the throng quieted.

"Loyal subjects," the king began, "the times and the seasons are often slow to bring justice, but when it comes, it is known to be just. At last," he eyed his previous enemies, "your country has seen its folly and returned to the bosom of its keeper . . . "

The emissaries chafed. How they loathed him! Agrippa's self-serving delivery continued for nearly half an hour, as he recounted his past generosities and their supposed slights of him. Always he was made out to be the offended, yet eternally patient, overseer of their rebellious and impious nation. And what could they say in retort? They dare not risk the loss of revenue, and the possibility of war.

Therefore, when the speech was completed a mighty shout ascended from the congregation, and the emissaries cried, "All hail, Herod! Yours is the voice of a god, and not of a man!"

Agrippa bowed his head in sham humility, the cheers continuing to ring from the court floor.

But his time had come. The True King of Israel would no longer endure his wicked pride. Suddenly, as by an unseen hand, Herod was smitten to the floor.

Women fainted, and children screamed. Soldiers swept over the platform, their horses whinnying in confusion and fear. The arena was a bedlam.

But no man could save Agrippa. He lay convulsant, purple, his body swollen with a nameless poison, his tongue bloated in his mouth—mute testimony to the ringing words with which he had displaced God.

Only days later, Herod's dead form lay in state at Jerusalem. Having lived fifty-four years, won the approval of Rome's highest, and gained a royal title, he had, nonetheless, died a most ignoble death. For, as his coroner reported, he had been "devoured by internal worms."

Chapter 22

The house of Zebedee was filled with laughter and excitement. The year of fear and persecution was ended. Master John need no longer be careful for his life.

Such liberty the death of Herod had brought! No Christian sorrowed for him. The victory of God was too evident to allow mourning over the tyrant's demise. The church breathed freely for the first time since James' death. Emerging from their underground, believers rejoiced together openly.

Tonight John watched from the gallery, as the servants and women of his domain happily prepared a banquet in Peter's honor. Word had it that the great apostle and his wife would be returning to Jerusalem late this evening.

The house which had been so long subdued was noisy with motion and joy. Salome, Martha, and Lazarus vied for the servants' attention, while the Lord's mother looked on in quiet pleasure, kneading dough for the dozen loaves which would be required.

John's heart was full. At long last, things were falling into proper place. His prayers had been graciously answered. Agrippa had fallen, and as soon as Peter returned, John would have the human aid for which he had pleaded.

But John's mind was filled with yet another anticipation. What would stand in the way, now, of his taking Mary for his wife? Since Herod's death, John had considered and reconsidered how to approach her with the matter.

He might have gone to Lazarus only. Such was the custom. But John could not bypass Mary's feelings.

Perhaps he had destroyed his prospects by his rash display that

373

long-ago evening. Perhaps he was a fool to think she would give him any chance at her affections. But whatever her inclinations, he must know them.

At last he knew what he would say to her, if ever he were given opportunity. Anxiously he watched the activities below, hoping Mary might enter the court. Martha's nervous orderliness kept the servants hopping, but the younger sister was nowhere to be seen.

"The kitchen!" John thought. Covertly he hastened down the back steps and through the work hall. Hearing women's voices, he peered around the corner and saw Mary with the servant girls, busily baking and cleaning. Her back was to him. Silently he motioned for the attendants to leave, as Mary continued to chatter happily about the best way to cater the event.

Finally each servant had departed, wondering at the master's strange command, but not questioning him.

John observed Mary with a smile, as she completed her dissertation to the now-departed helpers. "I couldn't agree with you more," he interrupted.

Mary wheeled about in surprise. Seeing that her master stood there, and that they were alone, she blushed, and, as she had done on a previous occasion, she quickly pulled her draped cloak over her long, sable tresses.

John drew near and shook his head. "Did I not tell you long ago, Mary, that I want your hair free and unfettered?" Raising a hand, he lowered her mantle and gazed into her dark eyes. The girl turned from him quietly. "What do you want, my lord?" she trembled.

Suddenly John's prepared speech was lost to him. He could think only of her beauty. Jacob could not have cared more for Rachel, nor Isaac for Rebekah. Often as a young boy, John had laughed at the stories of the patriarchs and their loves. How he had scoffed at Jacob, who labored fourteen years just to win Rachel's hand! But John had waited what seemed an eternity for this girl, and if need be would have labored a lifetime. However, he thought—praise God—there was no need to wait any longer.

Gently he reached for her, turning her to him. "Mary," he whispered, "have you forgiven me for that night when I . . . " Shame left him unable to complete the question.

The woman studied him incredulously. It was not like most men to concern themselves with the forgiveness of women. "Oh, master," she responded, "you were no more to blame than I . . . "

John looked at her wide-eyed, his courage spurred. "Then, you felt as I did! You wanted me, as I wanted you!"

Mary's face grew hot at the memory, and she turned nervously to her work. "Such things should not be spoken of," she replied.

"And why not?" he insisted, drawing her into his strong arms. "Such things, indeed, must be spoken of!"

Tears filled the girl's eyes and she cried bitterly, "Sir, you are cruel! What is it you want of me?"

"I want you for my wife!" he asserted. "I want you for my own!"

The young woman stared at him disbelievingly. "Truly, master?" she whispered.

"Did I not say it?" he sighed.

Mary pulled back, gazing at the floor. She weighed the moment carefully. Suddenly, reality was almost too beautiful. That her beloved master, the handsome and wealthy son of Zebedee, a chief of the church, her spiritual guide, could want to marry her! It seemed beyond possibility.

But suddenly her face clouded and she asked, "But sir, what of my sister?"

"What of her?" John asked in frustration.

"It is against tradition for the younger to marry before the elder! Martha has never married!"

"The girl can think of tradition at such a time!" he raved. "Mary—do you love me?"

"Oh—yes!"

"Then tradition be hanged! We will have our feet in our graves before Martha finds a man who can tolerate her!"

Mary hushed him quickly. "Someone will hear!" she warned, stifling the laughter which welled within her.

"Let the world hear!" John scoffed. "Say 'yes,' Mary!"

Radiant with joy, the girl of Bethany sighed, "Oh, yes, my lord, I will be yours!"

Overwhelmed, exuberant, John swept the girl from her feet, supporting her warm, tender body in his arms. The kiss they shared spoke of life itself.

Chapter 23

It was customary that betrothals, which were as binding as marriages in Israel, be of a year's duration. To John and Mary it seemed the movements of sun and moon had slowed to half-pace, time went so tediously. For the bride-to-be this interval was meant for preparing her trousseau. For the groom, it was a year of making his household financially secure.

Though the church still occupied nearly every waking moment, the apostle's activities served only to mollify a heart which yearned for the appointed time.

The sixth month of their betrothal, John was called away. A small church fellowship to the north of Jerusalem needed advice, so he and Peter answered the summons. A year before, John would have welcomed the chance to leave the city for a while. Now his only desire was to be near home, close to his intended bride. As soon as he could, he eagerly returned.

The last few blocks to the house of Zebedee, he ran more than he walked. Having sent word ahead, he knew Mary would be waiting in the court.

At last! Here was the gate. The latch felt good in his grasp. He lifted it and thrust the heavy door wide open. "Mary!" he called, "I am home!"

Expecting a flurry of response, he was greeted only by the sound of the court fountain. He walked quietly onto the patio, and a strange uneasiness overcame him. The house was terribly still. Not a voice could be heard. Something was very wrong.

Just as he was about to call out again, he perceived footfalls in a distant corridor. "Mary?" he asked softly.

Presently a form entered the archway leading from a wing of the house, and John turned expectantly.

"Master," a masculine voice met his ears.

The apostle was crestfallen.

"Lazarus?"

"Welcome home, sir."

John studied him carefully. Lazarus was not himself. He appeared very weary, and of barely concealed sorrow. "Where are the others?" John asked warily.

Mary's brother did not answer immediately, and that alone filled John with fear. "Speak, man!" the apostle demanded, grasping him by the shoulders.

"Things did not go well, sir, while you were away . . . "

"Mary . . . " John whispered, low and anxious. "Does it concern Mary?"

Lazarus nodded silently. "The women are with her now."

Without further word John raced through the archway from which Lazarus had entered and hastened toward Mary's quarters.

Salome was just emerging from the young woman's room when the apostle approached. "Son!" his mother greeted.

John quickly assayed Salome's heavy spirit and pushed past her militantly. "Where is Mary?" he demanded.

"In there," she pointed. "But you must not enter! It is not proper."

"Propriety may go to the devil!" he swore, and forcing the door aside, he stood face-to-face with the specter of his fears.

Mary lay, fevered and pale, upon her bed, the mother of the Lord sitting nearby where she had relieved Salome's watch. Four days and nights the women and their servants had bathed and soothed the girl in hopes the raging fever might break, but to no avail.

"Lord God!" John stammered, falling to his knees beside her bed.

"She will not hear you, son," Jesus' mother whispered. "She is in her own world, and has not heard us these many days."

The apostle fought reality. Clinging to the limp, hot hand which lay closest to him, he pressed it to his cheek and murmured bitterly, "The physicians . . . what of the physicians? Have they nothing to say?"

Salome had reentered the room, not wishing to desert her son in his torment. "They have tried, John," she answered, "but Mary is not the only one afflicted with the fever. There are many in Jerusalem . . . "

"There are not many Marys!" John interrupted. "She is the one I care about! Call the physicians! Now!"

"They have been here . . . often."

"And?" he retorted.

When both women looked away, unable to answer, he insisted again, "What do they say? Tell me!"

Salome hated herself for the message she must convey. "Many have died, John. More have died than not."

The apostle turned quickly to the dear one who lay before him. Tears, so familiar in his lifetime, did not this moment come forth. He felt too deeply. But burying his head in Mary's covers he pleaded silently, "My God, please, no! Jesus . . . Jesus . . . "

Chapter 24

All that day and night John stayed at Mary's side. Nothing would move him.

"How quiet she is . . . " he often thought. "If only she would wake and see me here. If only she would speak . . . " Even in this state the girl was beautiful to his eyes. Her lustrous, dark hair, with which she had once soothed the feet of Jesus, draped in waves over her pillow, was damp and ringletted where it met her hot forehead. Her eyes, closed in fitful sleep, accentuated her fevered skin with thick, heavy lashes, and her lips, usually so red with youth and vitality, still held beauty.

Midnight had come and gone painfully, slowly; then the darkest hours of night. Often he would whisper her name, never receiving a response. Periodically his tired gaze would travel to the wedding garment which hung splendidly in the corner of her room. Gloriously it reflected, now and then, the glimmer of moonlight off its jeweled bodice and gold-embroidered folds. Would it ever be worn? he wondered.

At last, however, just before dawn, as he rested his head upon her bed, he was jolted by the faint sound of speech. At first, he thought he had dreamed it, that he had fallen asleep and wished it. But then the hand he held seemed to tremble, and there was no doubt. Mary was awake.

Turning her head slowly, she opened her eyes for the first time since losing touch with the surrounding world. The apostle watched mutely as she studied him with seeming recognition. "John . . . " the word was barely audible, but it filled his ears with sweet music.

"Yes, I am here!" he answered brokenly.

For a long moment nothing more was said. John wiped her perspiring brow with a cool cloth, and waited while she looked dazedly about her. The morning sun was just peering in the window of the chamber. Tears of joy welled in his eyes. She must get better! She would get better! "Lord God, you will see to it!"

However, now she was speaking again, and he must listen. The words came with great difficulty, but it seemed she was compelled to say them. Gazing tenderly at her master, her lover, she whispered, "I was with him, John . . . I walked with Jesus. You must not fret or be sorrowful. It is good and happy there. There is no pain. The waters are cool and clear . . . "

John held her breathlessly. "Mary . . . " he shook his head, "enough now . . . "

Yet, she spoke again. "You must not be sad, my darling . . . " The syllables came laboriously, but full of peace and glory. "I only wish I might have died for my Lord . . . as others have . . . "

The dark eyes which had filled John's heart with enough love to last a lifetime turned toward the rising sun for the final time, and closed to see the sun of eternity.

Chapter 25

John stood alone at the foot of the mount behind the house where he had first met Mary. He often came out from Jerusalem to the little village of Bethany where so much of Christ's ministry had been performed. The town was just as it had been those many years before, snug and clean against the hillside. White and vine covered, the sepulcher which had once housed Lazarus now contained the one John loved as Jacob had loved Rachel.

Though the girl had been gone from him half a year, he still mourned her as though no time had passed. The mention of her name never failed to fill him with fresh sorrow.

The power of Jesus, which had supported John at his brother's passing, was upholding him once again. But he was not often aware of God's strength, for his soul and mind still raged much too loudly. Though James' martyrdom had been bitter to John, he could not question the circumstances of his brother's heroism.

Hundreds had been ushered into the church through his courage and example. With the deaths of the Baptist and the Master, good had triumphed.

But for what purpose had Mary died? What great value had such a death served? What kind of God could see good in such tragedy?

The apostle walked up the hill a way, and rested on a rock wall, staring blankly at the tomb. How desolate and hopeless it looked, an unfitting end for the finest life ever put in woman.

John had spent countless hours here since Mary's death, his duties with the church suffering drastically.

"Perhaps," John reasoned, "I did not submit as I should have. When I gave Peter over to God's control, he was released from prison. Did I cling to Mary too tightly? Have I been punished for loving her too much? Perhaps," he dragged up the past, "this was the consequence of my sinfulness that night on the gallery . . ." On and on his mind ranted.

The nectar of grief mixed with the dregs of guilt is a poisonous cup. Though John drank of it in great tormenting gulps, it could not bring Mary back.

For days after her death, John had been unable to look Lazarus in the face. The fact that Jesus had seen fit to raise him from the grave, and yet had taken his sweet sister, filled the apostle with bitter resentment.

"Where is the justice?" he cried. "Oh, Master, where is it?"

A still small voice within answered. "It is with me, John. I am the way, the truth, and the life . . . "

"But, Lord," he whispered, "did you take her to punish me for my sin?"

"Your sin was covered by my blood, John, not by hers . . . "

"Then you took her because I did not give her over freely. I did not give her up as I did Peter. And thus you took her!"

"John—it was my intention to release Peter. When you surrendered him, you did not change my will. You only brought yours into harmony with mine . . ."

But hadn't the Lord once promised, "Seek first the Kingdom of God and his righteousness, and all these things shall be added unto you"? How could John have a life of any kind without Mary? he longed to cry.

Somehow, however, the little faith which still inhabited him stifled such a question. His eyes were drawn to the tomb again, and he found himself reliving the day long ago when Jesus had come to the grieving family of Lazarus. At that time, the Master's words had challenged his listeners, and John could hear them again, just as he had heard them in his dream after the crucifixion.

"I am the resurrection, and the life," the Lord had said. "He that believes in me, though he were dead, yet shall he live . . . and whoever lives and believes in me shall never die."

John sighed with a shudder of relinquishment.

No longer would he desire to question. The certain fact that Mary's life had not truly ended, and that he would one day be with her again, denied all reason to question.

The Lord's words to Martha that long-ago day now challenged John. "Do you believe this?" Jesus had asked. Martha had failed the test. But John would not.

"Yes, Lord," he answered. "I do believe!"

Since Mary's death, Salome too had passed away. Peter had established a thriving church at Rome, and while other apostles traveled on far-flung missions, John spent countless months in isolation. It appeared permanent relationships were not meant for him. The apostle Jesus loved—the one who had learned, most painfully, how to love and accept others—seemed destined always to lose those he cared for.

One person only was left to share his days and weeks, to share the solitude of his soul: the woman who had come to be like his mother, Mary of Nazareth.

It was not until others had been stripped from him, however, that John came to realize Mary's personal riches. Though they had lived in the same house for many years, and though she had been his charge, John's preoccupation with church duties had prevented close attachment. He might have continued to overlook her, had the apostle Paul not returned to Jerusalem that year.

Surprisingly, a Gentile physician, Luke, was to be the catalyst of their relationship. One of Paul's most faithful co-laborers, Luke accompanied him to the Holy City on a special errand.

Matthew had, a few years previous, written an account of Christ's life. Geared mainly to the Jewish audience, it lacked appeal for Gentile readers. Luke wished to address the Roman world with another account, one which would record in more detail the events preceding Christ's birth and ministry. How better to glean the facts than from an interview with Jesus' mother?

It was winter when Luke arrived. As the evenings passed, the household gathered about the fire, and vivid pictures were woven from words and images spun by Mary's stories—some she had never before shared. As John studied her aging face, still sweet and peaceful despite time's touch, he wondered at the beautiful tales her heart had cherished so many years.

She spoke of her son's birth, and her face glowed with light and fervor. John remembered Jesus' reference to the strange events which had occurred at that time. Her cousin Elizabeth had given birth to John the Baptist when Mary yet carried the Messiah. Mary had visited her cousin, both babes being yet unborn, and the Baptist had leaped within his mother's womb at the nearness of his Lord. The Christmas story brought tears to Mary's eyes. And when she told of the child's being lost for three days upon a visit to Jerusalem, her hands trembled, so clear was the memory of her alarm. And then such pride she betrayed as she spoke of the boy's debate with the elders in the Temple.

Yet John felt it was more than Luke's clever inquiry which had brought forth the information at this time. John sensed Mary's growing need to relate her history, as if she sensed her time might be short for such things.

Painstakingly, Luke recorded all she told. Tonight, after the servants had departed and the room was darkened, Mary indicated she wished to remain beside the fire a while longer. John lingered too.

For the first time he realized how greatly she had been favored by God. And he recalled Jesus' voice as he had sung the closing hymn of his final Passover feast: "I am your servant," the Master had declared, "and the son of your handmaid. . . ."

Kneeling beside her chair, John took Mary's hand in his and whispered softly, "Mother, what are you thinking?"

"I am remembering the angel's message to me . . ." Gazing into the fire, she recited it. " 'Fear not, Mary, for you have found favor with God. And, behold, you shall conceive in your womb, and bring forth a son, and shall call his name Jesus.' " Here she trembled, taking a deep breath and closing her eyes. " 'He shall be great, and shall be called the Son of the Highest, and the Lord God shall give unto him the throne of his father David. And he shall reign over the house of Jacob forever . . . and of his kingdom there shall be no end.' "

With those last thoughts, ecstasy filled her voice. How hard it was, as the lonely years passed, to remember Jesus had promised to return and establish an earthly kingdom.

The fire showed time's lines on John's face as well, as he looked with her into the flames. The Master had been very gracious in granting him this woman's company till she, too, be taken.

Holding her hand gently, he smiled up at her and remembered the words she had quoted tonight for Luke—the song which the Spirit had given her when she yet carried her unborn child:

> My soul magnifies the Lord, and my spirit
> has rejoiced in God my Savior.
>
> For he has regarded the low estate of his
> handmaiden. For, behold, from henceforth
> all generations shall call me blessed.

Chapter 26

The Christian movement seemed always to run counter to the governing authorities of the day. From the outset, the Sanhedrin opposed the Baptist, then Jesus and his followers. In national leadership, Herod the Great had sought to circumvent the coming of the Messiah, fearing his lordship over him, and so had slaughtered numbers of male infants in the attempt. Herod Antipas had consented to the Baptist's death and the Nazarene's. Herod Agrippa had murdered James Bar Zebedee, and had imprisoned Peter. In imperial Roman government, Pontius Pilate had crucified Christ, and other procurators of Judea handled the Christian influence confusedly.

When Paul had come to Jerusalem with Luke, it was to be his last time there. Again he had met with the elders, and again he had answered accusations concerning his view of Moses' Law. This visit, however, had brought quite a stir among those Jews who opposed his "liberal" stand. He was bound, incarcerated, and finally brought before the procurator, Felix. Two years passed with no hearing, and no formal decision, while Paul was held in restraint.

Festus, successor to Felix, was just as indefinite in his dealings. Had Paul not appealed to Caesar, he might have gone free. Instead he had been sent to Rome, tried before the Emperor, and only then released. Presently, as John understood, he was again at work with the Gentile churches.

Because, during its first years, the church's influence was felt most strongly in Palestine, Caligula and Claudius Caesar did not take much notice. Even where it had become strong elsewhere, it had been considered nothing more than a branch of Judaism, and had thus been under the same legal protection. Though Claudius had begun to treat the gospel as a threat, going so far as to banish Christian Jews from his capital, he had not done much more.

The man now occupying the Imperial throne, however, could not ignore the church. As it had grown beyond Israel, the animosity of Jews throughout the Empire showed that this was not just a new form of Judaism.

Christians at Rome were particularly strong, Peter being their leader, and the big fisherman was a thorn in the present Emperor's side. It was not this alone, however, which eventually brought Caesar's wrath.

The ruler of the Empire was destined by his own infamous character to become the most notorious of the imperial line for insanity and unspeakable cruelty.

Nero, the man whose name would be carved with a bloody sword upon the pages of history, had reigned for ten years. Tracing his ancestry revealed a family full of capable but careless, noble but merciless individuals. Free spenders, they loved the arena and gladiatorial games. Nero's father was known for promiscuity, perverted sexual drives and brute treatment of those under him, as well as for traitorous conduct.

Surprisingly, Nero's first five years in office would be hailed the finest period in the saga of Roman administration. Taking the throne at only seventeen years of age, Nero had at the outset shown himself to be modest, beneficent, and merciful.

He made his first questionable judgment when he had his stepbrother, Brittanicus, the rightful heir to the throne, assassinated.

Though his reign continued for a time to be generally fair and praise-worthy, older leaders resented his interfering measures and attempted to divert him by encouraging his baser instincts. Gradually the youthful Emperor, tempted beyond ability or desire to resist, slipped into gluttony, wild spending, and all manner of crude and criminal behavior. Incognito, he began to frequent houses of ill repute, and, searching the streets in an ever-increasing desire for thrill, he fell into indiscriminate lust and crime.

Though rumors flew, few Romans believed Caesar capable of such atrocities. It was not until Nero made the mistake of assaulting a Senator on a lonely street, that he was threatened with total exposure.

Eventually, Nero's behavior became more overt. No longer afraid of public opinion, and considering himself above the law, he carried his sensuality into palace life. Though married to Claudius' daughter, Octavia, he became involved with the wife of a prominent Roman. Sensual Poppaea Sabina led him to seek a divorce, and when Nero's mother, Agrippina, objected, Poppaea persuaded Nero to destroy her. Attempts to poison and drown Agrippina failed, but finally assassins accomplished the deed, bludgeoning her to death.

Strangely, the same man loved poetry, the arts, and athletics. But not content to merely provide for others' talents, he began to inflict his own meager abilities upon the public, and became a laughingstock of the Empire.

Plots to overthrow the Emperor were laid, and Nero retaliated with a reign of terror. Any man whose death might advance him was a likely victim. Estates were confiscated. Nero divorced his wife and married Poppaea.

There was no stopping the mania. Nero, who considered himself a deity, would eventually erect a statue to himself, 120 feet tall. Hardly a god, however, he was, in his mid-twenties, a pot-bellied, drink-debauched lecher. Puny, wizened limbs, a bloated visage, and a mottled complexion made him a miserable sight to behold. Lifeless eyes peered from a colorless face, his kinky blond hair the only sign of youth remaining to him.

Thinking he had attained all life had to offer, he still regretted that one dream had not been fulfilled. Rome had always, to him, been an eyesore. Often he had envisioned it as it could be, splendid, golden, and orderly, with all tenements and hovels removed, with broad clean streets, and marble-columned porticos in line along them. If only he could have this, he would be happy, he thought. The old Rome would be the new Neropolis, shining and unblemished.

Chapter 27

Though local rule was difficult to bear, Palestine had suffered no particular ill at Nero's hands. Even the church in Rome, where Peter labored, was not yet directly troubled.

John was fifty-five years old. Not one day of his life had been spent outside Palestine. He was resigned to that lot. There was much to occupy him here.

But he relished news of the church in far-off regions, for there was not a province of the Empire exempt from the growing Christian movement.

There was increasing concern on the part of believers throughout the realm, however, as enemies accused them of aberrant and criminal activity. Christians met with mob violence and death, as public prejudice grew. Their religion of love and goodwill had become mistaken for a "dangerous superstition," and they who belonged to the Son of Love were accused of "sullen hatred of the whole human race."

Though the gospel had brought joy and peace to tens of thousands, it was becoming a virtual crime to bear the name "Christian." Because the presence of believers in a city sometimes gave rise to mass disturbance, Christians were increasingly the objects of government action. Locally, nationally, and imperially, authorities were confused.

In Jerusalem, as well as elsewhere, it was often imperative that the church meet in secret. John lived in perpetual fear that a new outbreak of hatred might expose his people to mob abuse. It had happened several times already, and when Christians had been murdered, the Roman procurator, instead of policing the streets for their protection, had sent his men against the victimized church.

Tonight John stayed close within the shadows as he left a meeting in a small, obscure shop. Church gatherings were held in various places and at odd intervals, so that authorities might not detect a schedule.

As he rounded a corner, he was met head-on by his fears. The sounds of a wild, shouting crowd greeted his ears from somewhere down the street. His impulse was to flee, until he realized the cries were not angry or hateful, but jubilant.

Curious, he made his way toward the uproar, until he could see the gathering. Jews, mostly poor and young, stood before the procurator's palace, chanting, singing, their fists raised in triumph. John listened carefully, but their joy was a mystery.

Finding a stranger on the edge of the crowd, he drew near and asked, "What is it, boy? What is the news?"

"You haven't heard?" The young fellow turned to him wide-eyed, his breath coming short, for excitement. "Rome is on fire!"

"On fire?" John was stunned. "But how? And how badly?"

The impatient youngster glared at him. "They say Nero started the fire! Nero, himself! First good move he's made in years! Half the city is in ashes! And thousands of the heathen with it!"

John stared mutely at the boy. He had heard of Nero's desire for a new capital. Was it possible he had ordered the destruction of the old city?

"Heathens are not Rome's only residents, boy! Is nothing being done to stop it?"

The young man looked at John strangely. "Anyone who lives in Rome is a heathen, to my way of thinking! As for the fire, Nero's putting up a good show, but rumors are he keeps sending his men to start it fresh! They say the old boy sits in his tower, at Maecenas, singing and playing his lyre, while he watches the flames!"

The crowd was backing away from the palace gates, and was heading for the streets where it would spread news of the conflagration with undisguised revelry.

John stood in numb wonder as the mob pushed past. "My Lord," he trembled, "is Peter safe?"

Chapter 28

The fire at Rome lasted nine full days and nights, leveling nearly the entire city. Besides thousands who had been burned alive, or crushed to death by falling timbers from countless multistoried complexes, hundreds of thousands now staggered through the debris and rubble of the streets, starving and terrorized.

John anxiously waited for word of the church and of Peter's condition. For days no message was forthcoming. Once again, as they had upon Peter's imprisonment under Agrippa, Jerusalem saints prayed ceaselessly for the great apostle, and for their brothers and sisters at Rome. Indeed, the church throughout the empire raised petition.

John and Jesus' mother sat tonight in the courtyard of the Zebedee house, frustrated by the lack of news.

Repeatedly, these days, John found himself remembering Jesus' words regarding Peter. "When you shall be old, you will stretch forth your hands, and another shall gird you, and carry you where you would not go."

That prophecy made it sound as though Peter would not die from an accidental cause, but would suffer a martyr's fate. Though John harbored the prophecy secretly, not wishing to inflict its foreboding sentiments on his brethren, it brought some relief for the moment. It did not seem likely, according to the Master's statement, that the great fisher of men would die in something like the conflagration which had struck Rome.

"Strange," John told himself, "that I should take comfort in Jesus' reference to Peter's death."

Mary had risen to tend the servants, when a knock was heard at the courtyard entry. "Perhaps it is news!" she said breathlessly.

Outside stood a young man, vaguely familiar to the apostle. As he stepped into the court light, John recognized him. "Sir," the young man began uneasily, "perhaps you remember me?"

"Yes, son. The other night, before the palace. You gave me word of the fire."

The boy shuffled nervously. "Sir, after having met you, I thought about you for days. I was certain I'd seen you somewhere before. It suddenly came to me yesterday that my great uncle pointed you out when I was but a lad."

"Your great uncle?" John shook his head bewilderedly.

"You may not recall the incident, but he and all my relations assure me of its truth, though it happened before I was born. They say that you and another man stopped one day at the Temple Gate Beautiful, and that by mentioning the name of one Jesus of Nazareth, you healed my uncle, and made him able to walk for the first time in his life!"

John remembered the incident very well, indeed—one of the first miracles of the apostolic church, a proof that Christ was with them in all his power. "Yes, boy, I do recall," he smiled. "I also remember being thrust into prison for that cause . . . but all to the glory of our Lord. Besides, you must understand that we were not the ones who healed your uncle, but that Christ, himself, did it."

The young man straightened and eyed John cautiously. "Well, sir, I don't know about that. But when I figured out who you were, I suddenly understood why you made that strange statement concerning the occupants of Rome."

"What statement?" John asked blankly.

"You said heathens weren't the only residents of that city. It struck me that no Palestine loyalist would consider any citizen of Rome, Jew or Gentile, more than a heathen. When I remembered where I had seen you before, I asked around and learned that you are the Apostle John, the one who leads the Jerusalem Christians."

John was wary now. Concerned lest he had allowed a spy or an informant under his roof, he demanded suspiciously, "Exactly why are you here?"

"I'm not sure," came the odd reply. "Understand that I don't believe as you do," he said determinedly, "but I'm not here to bring you before the authorities. The news I bear is trouble enough."

John was more perplexed than ever.

"I don't know what has brought me here," the boy reiterated, his face full of mystery. "But when I learned that you were the Christian leader, I felt compelled . . . yes that's the word . . . compelled to bring word of your people in Rome. And especially when I learned that your partner in the healing of my uncle is the leader of Christians there . . . Peter, I think, is his name . . . "

"Yes! Thank God!" John interrupted him. "What of Peter? What news do you have?"

"Out of respect for my uncle, I will consider your feelings, sir, and tell you that the news is not good, as you would see good. Recognize though, that only my uncle's experience gives me any inclination to be concerned for the state of your church."

Under other circumstances the apostle might have taken the boy to task for his insolence, but now he only spurred him impatiently. "The news, boy! That is all I care for!"

"I'm disappointed in Nero. I had given him credit for one smart move in setting fire to Rome," the boy began, "but I guess he's still the fool he always was. He's now claiming that the Christians put the place in ashes. I don't know why he won't take the glory for a job well done. I'm still convinced he did it himself. The rumors were too believable. But I guess he's either turned coward again, or sees a convenient way to call down judgment on a bunch of would-be insurrectionists. The stories are that your people are anarchists against Rome, for which I applaud them highly, though I don't see how that goes along with your talk of love and all . . . "

The boy continued to ramble, but John's mind had struck on the fact that Nero had leveled his finger at the Roman church. "How can he prove such a thing?" John interrupted once more.

"Prove that your people are anarchists?"

"Anarchists? No! My people do not concern themselves with the affairs of the Roman state. Our kingdom is not of this world, boy! How can Nero prove that they set fire to Rome?"

"Oh, that's been simple for him. He's found a group of no-accounts who've testified to the act."

"Christians?"

"So they say."

"So Nero has *paid* them to say!" John snapped.

Mary had sat silently by during this strange conversation. But now she rose anxiously. "Have we forgotten Peter?" she inquired. "Is there any word of him? And what are Nero's intentions against the church?"

The boy watched as John stepped up to the aging woman and

took her in his arms. Seeming, at this, to sense and sympathize with the gravity of their feelings, the young zealot answered carefully. "The news is vague. But it seems the testimonies of the wretches have implicated your friend, and that Nero has put him in prison. I'm sure the Emperor means no good for Peter or any of his followers."

Chapter 29

The sky above Rome would be smoky for weeks, and the stench of charred, rotting corpses, yet unburied, would permeate the air for months to come.

Any soul surviving the holocaust could be grateful; but for many thousands, existence in such a state was living hell. Only a third of Rome escaped the conflagration, and few remaining citizens were free from hunger and nightly cold.

Enough ground had been saved that Nero would have room to display his victims of accusation. And he would see to it that a remnant would be rescued from starvation to provide a good audience for his planned executions.

By the second day of the fire, Nero had found his paid confessors, and by the third day, after due publicity regarding the "infernal act of the Christians," while his own arsonists continued their rampage, he had begun the capture and incarceration of believers. He had waited until today, a week after the last smoldering embers had been quenched, to produce his prey for public mockery. He knew that by now the populace would be starving, not only for food, but for vengeance.

Peter slept agonizedly in a cold dungeon cell, his wife, Deborah, beside him. The great apostle, during his years in Rome, had symbolized a personal threat to the Emperor. Not only was the church considered "insurrectionist," but lately members of Caesar's own class and family had bowed the knee to Jesus, under Peter's preaching. And Nero could not stand for that.

Before one ray of morning sun had pierced the dungeon, wagons clattering on the cobbled streets and the shouts of soldiers wakened him. Listening carefully, he discerned that a great throng was gathering outside the prison. "Two loaves per family!" he heard a loud instruction. "Nero's generosity has provided for you! Two loaves per family!"

As the big fisherman tried to interpret the jostling noises outside, he concluded that the Emperor must have sent his men to feed the starving inhabitants of the ruins. The oppressed multitudes, in their desperation, were apparently converging from all quarters and clamoring around the wagon-loads of bread. From the sound of it, the entire surviving populace was gathering at the gates, though in reality the same scene was being repeated throughout the seven-hilled city.

Deborah awoke and raised questioning eyes to her husband. But he hushed her, and they listened in mutual silence as a new announcement was given to the crowds.

"The evil doers, the confessed destroyers of our beloved Rome, the despised race which call themselves 'Christians,' are to be brought forth for execution beginning tomorrow morning!"

At dawn, when a guard's keys worked the cell door, Peter stood ready for his moment of death. Deborah, ashen-faced, hid behind him, her cold hands gripping his cloak like small fists. Some of his courage had been imparted to her, but she did not face martyrdom as confidently as he. "Let it be over quickly," Peter prayed that morning. "At least let Deborah's hour be short, if not my own . . ."

Rough sentinels laid hold on him and his fragile wife, binding their hands before them and leading them, with thousands of others, down labyrinthine corridors and beyond the stony prison walls. The sun was not yet over the horizon, but already angry multitudes awaited their emergence from the fort. Roman soldiers restrained the crowds who spat and mocked the Christians.

Peter, Deborah, and the other unfortunates were loaded into carts lining the street. The apostle could scarcely look upon those for whom he had been shepherd all these years. That it was to end thus for *him* came as no surprise; the Lord had prepared Peter for this death long before. But why, he pleaded, must his people and his wife suffer an identical fate?

Praying for strength, he studied those nearest him. His cart, like all the rest, contained old, young, men, women, even children and infants. Jew and Gentile alike were represented among the faithful, and those who had once been wealthy, the educated and the wise, rode alongside the poor and ignorant.

Tears rose to Peter's eyes, but he begged courage to suppress them for the sake of his flock.

In one of the wagons a sweet young voice was lifted in song. At first barely audible above the roar of the throng, it was being joined by a dozen others, and then the chorus spread from cart to cart, until the music competed gloriously with the blasphemous tumult.

"The Lord is my shepherd . . ." the words swelled, "I shall not want. . . . He makes me lie down in green pastures; he leads me beside quiet waters. . . . He restores my soul; he guides me in the paths of righteousness for his name's sake. . . . Even though I walk through the valley of the shadow of death, I fear no evil; for you are with me; your rod and your staff, they comfort me. . . . You prepare a table before me in the presence of my enemies; you have anointed my head with oil; my cup overflows. . . . Surely goodness and lovingkindness will follow me all the days of my life, and I will dwell in the house of the Lord forever."

Deborah, who had, until now, sat in terrified silence in her husband's embrace, seemed to warm with the strains of that testimony. ". . . lovingkindness will follow me all the days of my life . . ." her voice rose to meet the refrain.

The carts began to slow as they approached the charred ruins of Circus Maximus. The stadium's great half-mile field, though black and heavy with debris, was the largest open area available for Nero's plan. As they approached the leveled walls, brutish soldiers ordered the Christians to vacate the wagons. Women cried out now and then. Here and there little ones clung to their mothers in abject terror. But for the most part the victims obeyed silently.

Scattered about the field were piles of clean, new timber. Nero could not have found such lumber in the ruins of Rome. Obviously it had been prepared in advance of the fire.

It all happened very quickly. Within moments great wooden crosses were being assembled. Though the believers were Roman citizens, they were not to be given the usual right to choose their mode of death. Crucifixion was the byword, and when it became apparent that even the mammoth Circus could not contain all the crosses, many were taken outside the arena.

Peter stood rigidly, knowing that at any moment he would be led to his appointed instrument of torture. Already, by the hundreds, Nero's victims were being ordered across the field, or beyond the walls.

The bloodthirsty crowd had found seats among the rubble of the collapsed stadium, perching on crags of blackened marble like vultures.

Suddenly, Peter and Deborah were grasped rudely by the arms. A sigh of fear and resignation escaped the woman's lips, but the apostle greeted his enemies without a sound.

Rather than being led forth, however, the couple was escorted toward the ruined walls, and high up onto a protruding granite ledge.

Noting Peter's bewildered expression, a guard snarled, "Did you think you would be treated like the rest? Nero is saving you for his dessert!"

"What do you mean to do with us here?" the apostle demanded.

"Caesar feels that since you have competed for his place in the affections of his people, you should welcome the chance to have his place in the stands. He wants you to enjoy to the fullest the spectacle he has prepared."

Husband and wife stood helplessly on the pinnacle where Nero's stadium box once rested. They would be forced to watch the murder of the people for whom they had lived and labored nearly a decade.

Only Christ's strength enabled them to endure the sights and sounds which rose about them. Only the power of Jesus saw them through the long day, until twilight when they were allowed retreat.

As Peter was ordered into the cart for return to prison, he cast a final glance toward the western sky. A blood-red sunset, above the city's jagged, black horizon, was interrupted by a thousand silhouettes—the crucifixes of his lost children.

Chapter 30

Nero's unrivaled genius for the sadistic and the macabre displayed itself unfettered for nine months. He was much too creative to settle long for such commonplace cruelty as crucifixion. Death by burning became a favorite with him. But even this, after a while, was too tame for his tastes. Adding a bit more sensation to the glow of the pyres, he had his victims appareled in fire-resistant clothing, mounting them upon trees to use as flaming torches at his garden parties. When this lost its appeal, he had helpless Christians bundled in wild animal pelts, and left them stranded at the mercy of hungry dog-packs.

Because Nero feared Peter might escape, he did not again let him out of prison, even to torment him with the sight of these horrors.

But Peter's own private nightmare was hellish enough. He was now in a separate prison from Deborah, the Tullian Keep, the most famed and fearsome dungeon of Rome. One day to be known as the Mamertine, the rock-bound pit had seen many a victim of the state die before his appointed day of execution. Men had gone mad here, they had starved here, they had strangled on the poisonous vapors of their own accumulated waste. No light ever entered the small fissure in the stone ceiling, for another chamber sat above.

And here Peter stood, chained to a wooden post, never allowed to recline. He could only spend the weeks crouched or slumped against the unsympathizing pillar.

Yet, even here his voice declared the story of Jesus, and after days of his undaunted witness, the guards themselves had joined in his faith.

Nero would gladly have seen him die there. But it seemed he lived on the strength of twenty men, and the Emperor feared to let him live longer, lest he convert the entire domain.

Eventually his death could no longer be postponed. The ruined Circus was filled to capacity. Even Nero had emerged from his palace to find a place in the black debris, where he sat in splendor, surrounded by his aides and parasitic admirers.

Peter stood on the field below. After weeks of torment, he was now barely recognizable as the mighty Rock of Christ. Pale and gaunt, his limbs emaciated and blue, his hair now streaked with white, his eyes set in deep sockets, he nevertheless stood boldly before his accuser. Nero had left him physically diminished, but his spirit was strong. And the Emperor was determined to crush it.

Caesar had one last torment for Peter before he would free him from this life. Deborah would be led forth first.

The apostle, flanked by two armed guards, his hands bound before him, endured and watched only in the power of his faith. One hundred, two hundred feet, Deborah was guided across the field, to the cadences of the jeering and applauding masses. Just once did she look back, and Peter called to her weakly but determinedly, "Remember the Lord!"

Forced to observe her demise, the apostle trembled and sickened. But at last the hand of death was laid upon him.

It seemed such a long way as he traveled those last steps of his life. The mob howled down upon him with the roar of a million devils, but all he heard were the words of Jesus: "When you shall be old, you will stretch forth your hands, and another shall gird you, and carry you where you would not go."

"But, my Lord," he returned silently, "though I would not come this way, still I would come, for I long to be with you . . ."

As Simon Peter stepped up to the prostrate cross, Nero glared down upon him in triumph, his usually lusterless gray eyes filled with hate. The apostle who had sworn he would die for Jesus lifted his gaze to his tormentor, but not in defeat or bitterness. For Nero had not conquered him. He was in fact *blessing* him. Unknowingly, Caesar was about to throw open the doors to eternity with Christ.

Dared the Galilean fisherman now speak openly to the Emperor of Rome? Yes, he dared. And his words told Nero, and the hundreds of thousands watching, that this fool monarch had not crushed him.

"If it be by means of the cross that I am to die," he called out, "let it not be with my head up, O Nero! My Master died that way! Crucify me head downward. I die for my Lord, but I am not worthy to die like him!"

Nero, incensed with humiliation, stared wildly at the man of God. Then, surveying the populace of his cremated city, he lifted his hand, and with one final gesture of blasphemy, set his seal to Peter's request. "So be it!" he ordered the guards.

And so it was.

Chapter 31

John would have preferred death in the Circus to his present vacuum of sorrow. In one way, he died daily. For he was now the only survivor of the twelve apostles of Jesus Christ.

About two years after Peter's death, the Apostle Paul had suffered a similar fate, beheaded under Nero's sword. Nor did the tyrant's craze stop with him. The persecution, which had only begun at Rome, had quickly spread throughout the realm, seeking out and destroying the greatest men who would ever bless humankind. James, the brother of Christ, and one of the pillars of the Jerusalem church; Philip; Matthew; John Mark; Matthias, who had taken the place of Judas Iscariot; Jude, the brother of Christ; Nathanael Bar Tholomew; Thomas; and even Luke, the physician—all had fallen under the curse of death. From Corinth, to Macedonia, to Ephesus, to Damascus, the mania had crawled across the map, crippling and bleeding the empire.

Though the church, instead of dying, had gone on to greater and greater growth, since the fire at Rome, John himself had often descended into the pit of despair. Life had become no more than prison, from which he desired release. It was true that he still had friends, that the Jerusalem church was healthier than ever. But Mary was fragile and aging, and his fellow Christians were no longer his peers, but mostly converts who looked to him for leadership.

John's face was surprisingly youthful, but it did betray the stress and disappointment of his history. And his golden hair was streaked with silver. He was not a very old man, but he often felt twice his age. Frequently the Master's words to Peter returned to haunt him. "If I choose that John tarry until I come, what is that to you?" Many nights that question drummed through his dreams, and he woke in a sweat of fear and torment.

"Lord," he would cry out, "will you come again? Will your Kingdom come?"

This evening, fitful with insomnia, he paced back and forth in the court moonlight. The sleeping house, oblivious to his misery, stared coldly down at him. All about the corners and crevices were a thousand memories, good and bad.

Over the months of persecution, he had come to understand the Lord's mercy in taking his beloved Mary when he did, sparing her the torture of the sword. Nonetheless, the very thought of her still filled him with desire and sorrow.

Sitting silent beside the fountain, he examined the fear of his soul. "Must it be, Lord, that I go on forever without kin or kindred fellowship? If my remaining years must be so, what purpose is in them? Can you not take me now?"

He remained without comfort a good while before, gently and patiently, Jesus responded. "You are not an old man, John."

"Master, I am as old as the others you have already taken!"

"But I am not finished with you, John."

"Lord," he bristled, "were the others so much more finished than I?"

Silence greeted him. But it clearly indicated, "That question does not deserve a response, for you already know the answer."

Of course the others had not been more spiritually complete.

They had been human, just like John, and just as lacking in perfect grace.

At last, however, the Master enlightened him. "Did I not once tell you that you would come to know me as no one else would ever know me?"

"Yes, Lord," John whispered, awed at the memory. But then, his humanity taking precedence again, he demanded sarcastically, "But why, Lord? Why am I so privileged, and why should such a gift bring such torment? I do not want such a privilege!"

At those words, he drew a sharp breath, scarcely believing he had said such a thing. But listening for a rebuke, he found only unutterable quiet and solitude. It was a fearsome emptiness which bespoke the absence of his Lord.

"Jesus!" he cried, "forgive me! I did not mean what I said!"

The Master had not really departed, but had granted John a taste of true destitution. "I am with you, John," he answered. "I am the way, the truth, and the life. Is it not enough to have that knowledge?"

The apostle sighed with relief and understanding. "It is enough, Master, to have you."

Chapter 32

Nero's insanity against all who would defy him had in no way dissuaded the desire of Zealot Jews to be free from Rome's dominion. It was now A.D. 68 and Jerusalem was at war.

Though it was a civil war, being fought among Jews themselves, and not yet leveled against imperial power, it was nonetheless the beginning of revolution. At last the incompetent and unjust rule of Judea's Roman procurators was being challenged by force.

Starting with Felix's incapable and inadequate administration, procuratorial government had grown from bad to worse. Albinus had plundered Judean cities, had levied merciless taxes, and had even gone so far as to free archcriminals for a fee. His successor, Florus, continued in the same form, but managed his post like a hangman, putting men to death by the score.

The ire of knife-wielding Sicarii, and of patriot rebel forces had flamed, now unquenchably. Vowing to crush any Jew loyal to Rome, they rioted in the streets, sought out and daggered their prey in the backs.

When Florus proceeded to confiscate a fortune in gold from the Temple storehouse, rebellion threatened. Jerusalem demanded that he be removed from office. He retaliated, in typical style, with force, entering homes by the hundreds, ransacking and destroying, murdering those inside. In a great display of victory, he took the rebel leaders beyond the walls of the city, beat them, and nailed them to crosses. In one gory afternoon, thirty-six hundred Jews were killed.

At last war-fever raged unchecked. Older and wealthier residents of Jerusalem, for the most part, advised against revolution. Young and poor rose in protest. With hardly a family remaining undivided, brother stood against brother, father against son. The Holy City was split, figuratively and literally, as each side claimed a sector of the metropolis. The civil strife would continue unless the present battle brought it to a bloody end.

Outside Jerusalem patriot troops had already laid siege to the old fortress of Herod the Great, called "Masada," which had been converted into a Roman camp. There Zealots had killed every one of Caesar's men. But on the same day, twenty thousand Jewish citizens had been slain by Gentiles in Caesarea, and multitudes had been marketed as slaves. Shortly thereafter a similar scene in Damascus had seen the demise of ten thousand Jewish residents.

Rebel Zealot forces reacted by leveling Gentile towns throughout Palestine, but they did not stop there. Syria had joined hands with Rome to crush the uprising, and so the Zealots laid waste their centers as well. So brutal, so vast were the massacres that whole cities were strewn with piles of corpses—the elderly, the babes, and women together.

As for John and his household, they wanted no part in the conflict. The Christian community, persecuted by both parties, held no affinity for either. Needless to say, most Christians held definitive opinions on the issues—most of them, without question, on the side of the patriots. But the world and its systems had become, for the church, only something to be endured as they awaited the Master's return and the hope of his coming Kingdom.

They could not, however, totally refrain from involvement. No Jerusalem citizen had that option. If one maintained an isolationist policy inwardly, he would nonetheless be pitched against the reality of violence which threatened his life, as it did the lives of any dwelling here.

John might have taken his family and escaped the war if he had tried earlier. He could have gone to some city outside Palestine. But the church had needed him, and so he had stayed.

The old Zebedee house was filled, these days, nearly to capacity. Numerous church elders and their dependents had taken up residence here since the civil revolt had begun. Their homes destroyed by Florus, they had been without shelter until John took them in. Those whose abodes had not happened to attract Florus' eye now offered the only lodging for many believers.

Recently, the residents of John's house had stayed behind locked doors, not venturing outside for fear of their lives.

The scene beyond the walls could be viewed from the roof. Not even that vantage point was safe from slings and arrows, but occasionally some brave soul would climb up to peer over the balustrade.

John himself did so tonight. He had heard a skirmish in the alleyway. Creeping to the roof's edge, he looked below. A band of conservatives was chasing a young Zealot through the dark passageway. The pursued man was obviously wounded already, and stumbled sadly in his efforts to escape. As his enemies came upon him, John sought to divert their attention. "Halt there!" he shouted.

Stunned at the unexpected command, the band stopped short, eyeing the darkness for the source of the order. In that moment, John descended the rear stairway and flew to the back hall. A servants' entry opened onto the alley. If his timing were right, he would be able to reach the young patriot and bring him to safety.

Just as he arrived at the door, however, he had second thoughts. Dared he risk the lives of his household? If he were to take a side in this fracas, his people might be called to the enemy's attention. Nevertheless, something spurred him on. He could not leave the young man to die when it was in his power to save him.

Throwing the door open, he saw the disabled soldier lying before him. Without a moment's hesitation he dragged him into the hallway, shut and barred the door. Just then, the pursuers' trampling feet were heard outside. Apparently the alley's acoustics had confused them as to the origin of John's command. Deciding it had not come from one of their leaders, they had returned to the chase, but too late. Their prey had somehow escaped.

The apostle breathed heavily. He slumped to the floor beside the boy, and held him in his arms. Looking tenderly at him, John was suddenly taken aback. This was the same fellow who had, four years before, given John news of the fire at Rome, the same lad who had brought him word of Peter.

"Boy," John whispered, "can you hear me?"

The young patriot lay in agony, but turned to him slowly, "Yes, sir . . ."

"It is I, John, the apostle."

A smile lit the boy's pained countenance. "Yes, sir, I know . . ."

The young rebel, whose name was Polycarp, quickly became a favorite with John. The lad, who had always been outspoken, had a keen and perceptive wit and an unquenchable desire for truth and justice.

The night of his rescue, it had been no accident that he had been near the Zebedee house. In the early weeks of the rebellion, his parents and entire family had been killed, and he, desperate for shelter and safety, had remembered the apostle. Seeking him out, he had been followed by the conservative band, but they had never suspected where he was going. And ever since, he had stayed close to the man of God, determined to do all he could to repay his bold, saving gesture.

At John's insistence, however, he had left his radical fever in the streets. If he desired to be a member of the apostle's family, he must spare them the trap of politics. Polycarp, full of the blood of dissent, had reacted sharply to John's command, but had consented nonetheless.

Meanwhile, since his entry into the home, he had watched the Christians skeptically, wondering at their absurd declaration that their loyalty lay beyond the present world, that they awaited a much greater kingdom than that of Rome or Israel.

What seemed to support Polycarp's doubts most strongly, was the fact that the more John's people attempted neutrality, the more their isolationism worked against them. Only a week before, vandals of the revolution party had smeared the outer walls of the fine old home with filthy epithets and lewd symbols. Daily since then, matters had grown worse, as both conservative and Zealot forces had shown disgust for the members of the house, establishing a common enemy.

Twice in two days, John and his people had battled the work of unnamed arsonists who had set fire to the building. Once, the men of the household had held at bay a pack of young rebels attempting to break through the sturdy bronze entry door. The graceful old retreat, the home of John's best memories, had become a meagerly armed fortress, a place of increasingly doubtful refuge.

Chapter 33

Once the revolution in Palestine had grown to such proportions that the imperial Roman government was forced to take action, the Zealot cause was doomed. Though the strongholds of Jerusalem—the guard stations, the gates, the walls, the palace of the procurator, the palace of the old Herodian line—had all been captured by patriot forces, and though the rebels had for a time conquered the Holy City and virtually the entire Palestinian region, they had not conquered Rome.

Already the mighty Roman general, Vespasian, had marched on Galilee, and had taken its key fortification, Jotopata. Now it was rumored that his son, Titus, was on his way to Jerusalem. Should the Judean capital be taken, the war would be ended.

There was talk in John's house of fleeing the city. Though the apostle left the decision to the individual families, he himself was confused as to what would be the right move. Daily, church members were vacating the metropolis; but there were still many Christians in Jerusalem. As their pastor, John felt he should stay. On the other hand, the Master had commissioned him to care for Mary, and he did not know what might befall her should they continue on.

Patriot fever in Jerusalem was so intense, its forces so numerous, that it was difficult to imagine how any enemy could overcome them. Already, in preparation for Titus, more than six hundred thousand were congregated to resist him. Male, female, no one was denied arms who had any strength to bear them. Day or night, John could look over the ramparts of his home to see throngs passing in the streets below, ready at a moment's notice to do battle for their homeland. Involuntarily his heart always thrilled at the sight. Though he had taken no side in the affair, he was still Jewish enough to feel a kindred spirit with them.

Intuitively, however, he knew their cause was not to triumph. He did not base his judgment on the size of Rome or the might of its forces. Time and again, in the history of his people, their tiny armies had overcome mighty foes, because Jehovah had been with them. But also, in their past, they had experienced severe chastisement, being so scourged that their culture had staggered beneath the blow. Somehow, John knew such would be the case this time, though he did not know exactly on what to base that belief.

It was not this premonition, however, which prevented him from joining the Zealot ranks. Had such been the case, he would have ceased to call himself a Christian, for the church, also, was experiencing great tribulation at the hands of its enemies. What prevented John from political involvement was the certainty that Christ's cause was paramount to all others. He was a Christian first, and a Jew second. If he must suffer as a Jew, let it be because Christ willed it, and not because he had taken a hand in the matter.

Still, John did not know if the Master would have him remain in the city or not.

It was spring, early A.D. 70. Life in the household was growing more and more tense, increasingly frustrating. Fuel was hard to come by. The men made desperate night scrambles outside to rummage for meager bits of kindling and dried animal waste.

Tempers flared easily. Sustenance was adequate, Zebedee having laid up a sizable store of dried and cured food. But all labored under the constant fear of Rome's intentions. Was it right that John should remain here with the Lord's mother?

If only he might find a quiet place to reflect upon this. The crowded house did not lend itself to such things anymore. He could not leave in freedom to wander beside the river as in the past. Perhaps if he spoke with someone . . .

Mary of Nazareth caught his eye as she sat across the court sewing a patch over a tear in John's last remaining cloak. Having given most of his better clothing to more needy members of the house, he had come to have but one well-worn outer garment.

John drew near and sat beside her, fingering the thread as it dipped up and down with the movements of the needle. No words were spoken for a time, but at length Mary ceased her handiwork and looked inquisitively at him.

"You are troubled, John. What is it?" she asked, her soft, aging eyes still full of warmth and love.

"I am confused, mother. For so many years my life has come in one neat package. I was destined to remain in Jerusalem when the others were sent on missions far from Palestine. So many times I longed to be with them, but I knew my place was here."

"With me?" she interjected.

Fearing he had hurt her, he explained quickly, "Yes, mother. But that has been one of the blessings of my life."

She smiled at him gratefully, and he went on.

"But now, when I have become used to the idea of remaining here, I suddenly find myself torn with doubts. I am to oversee the church, but daily it diminishes as my people flee the city. I am commissioned to protect you, but you are in danger here. I do not care if we stay or go. I only wish I knew what we should do."

Mary laid a hand on his shoulder. "Whatever you decide will be right with me," she counseled. "I am in your care, but you are in the care of God. He will not let you go the wrong way if you rely on him."

John sighed. "I know that is true," he smiled. "But still, though I have prayed and prayed, I have no leading whatever."

Mary straightened her skirts and took his hands in hers. "John, we all come to such forks in the road, times when the voice of heaven seems silent to our ears. At such moments, we have only to take a step in one direction or the other, and trust that he will close or open the door to our decision."

Chapter 34

John took Mary at her word, and found the door to departure from Jerusalem firmly shut for four long months. Titus had swept down upon the Holy City in merciless rage, cutting off all food supplies from beyond the walls. For two months the siege had stood at a near draw, as the enemies exchanged casualty for casualty, head for head. But when provisions began to dwindle behind the gates, the Zealots grew desperate.

John could not leave now. The option was not his, no matter how he longed for it. To set foot outside the walls was to commit suicide. Those who attempted escape were caught by the thousands and put to death by crucifixion. The massacre, which would go down in history as one of the most grisly, crowded the hills around Jerusalem with so many crosses that there was barely space to contain them.

Though John should have known Rome's capacity for inhumanity, he received word of the mass crucifixion with the unaccepting paralysis of fear. Such a thing, he told himself, could not happen here. It could happen in Italy, or in Damascus, or in Caesarea, but not here. God would not allow it.

After the third day, however, when breezes off the hills brought the stench of decayed flesh wafting over the city, he was forced to concede to reality. Indeed, it was happening here.

Life was a frenzy of noise and movement. Daily John's house grew more crowded, as its members rescued the wounded and starving in the street. With the warmer weather and the approach of summer, the problems of cold were exchanged for those of flies and pestilence. Close conditions made sanitation increasingly difficult, and the chance of infection among the wounded was an ever-present fear. Water had to be severely rationed, and robbers frequently broke in with the refugees to despoil what little might be found in the old retreat.

Polycarp watched incredulously from the sidelines as John and the others nursed the beggars who came near their door. Morning to evening, and through each night, a cook fire was kept burning, and the home's generous store of food was dipped into repeatedly until even it grew dangerously low. Without reference to class or political position, refugees found shelter here. At last the young Zealot could no longer hold his peace.

Retreating after days of ceaseless work, John, haggard and worn, had made his way to the roof where he hoped for a few moments' reprieve.

As he rested his head against the rampart, his vacant eyes gazed into the sky above. Was this the same blue heaven into which his Lord had departed so long before? And would he truly return? Of late, such hope had seemed almost laughable.

John was not laughing today, however. His weary hands lay motionless on his lap. How he needed this peace and solitude!

But the much-needed solitude was not to be his for long. On the roof were heard more youthful footsteps. Polycarp had sought him out and now addressed him directly. "Master," his words were pointed, "I have kept quiet for some time, but find I must speak my mind!"

John turned to him silently, offering a seat.

"Sir, I shall not sit. I cannot speak of such things while sitting."

"All right, boy. Speak then."

"I thought you rescued me because I was a Zealot. I learned quickly that such was not the case. I thought you might side with the Zealots in time. Now I do not expect that. I thought I might win some of your household to the defense of Jerusalem, but you refused me the attempt. All of this I have borne in silence. But now, you are harboring my enemies under your roof. I cannot stand for that!"

John lifted tired eyes to his young assailant. "We have spoken at length of my feelings on the war effort. You know that my interests lie with other things. I will take into my home whomsoever my Master brings to me."

The boy shuffled angrily. "Your Master! What has he to do with any of this?"

"He has everything to do with it, boy," John countered, suddenly charged with zeal, despite his great weariness. "He lives! His will is still at work in this world! He said all of this would come to pass, and that his Kingdom would one day reign over all the earth!"

Polycarp listened wide-eyed, not awed by John's words, but fearing for the elder's mind. Then he laughed aloud. "Preposterous!" he howled.

John took the mockery in stride, and then offered, "I know you don't understand, boy. I have often wondered about the reality of it myself. But as I see time pass, I remember more and more of the Master's words before he died, words which, when he spoke them, made no more sense to me than mine do, now, to you. He spoke of his followers being brought before synagogue councils, of their being tried and killed for his name. Do you remember Saul, the persecutor? He spoke of trials indescribable. Do you remember Nero's outrages? And he spoke of the destruction of Jerusalem. Do you not see Titus' plan? And how, if you do, can you deny that my Lord lives?"

Polycarp thought a moment, but still laughed doubtfully. "Why, it is easy to find fulfillment for any prophecy if one looks long enough!"

John stood, shaking his head, and stepped up to the ramparts. In the distance, toward the walls of the city, could be heard the sounds of war, terrible and bone-chilling. "I would have agreed, when I was your age," he answered. "I was just as much a skeptic as you, though I would have loathed the title. But let me tell you one more thing. For a long time I have felt that this war would be the near annihilation of our people. I did not know on what to base that assumption, but of late I have remembered what the Master said—words which must have stayed deep in my mind all these years. Before his death, after his entry into Jerusalem, he wept over the city. Looking at the Temple itself, he told us there would come a day when not one stone would be left standing upon another."

Polycarp stared at him blankly, and then seemed to tremble. Gazing at the Holy Mount silhouetted against a red-gray sky, he whispered, "Never! Such a thing will never be! The Temple is too great! It is the house of Jehovah!"

"No longer, my son!" John said soberly. "His temple is now in the hearts of men."

Chapter 35

The house of John had been spared the onslaught of Titus, but this did not mean the church had been untouched. Thousands of believers, along with Jews, had been killed. Fortunately, the majority of Christians had evacuated the Holy City before his coming, but still a vast number had remained, and the church had been sorely crippled.

Food was now all but gone from the Zebedee house. It was the Sabbath, and an orthodox Jew would not travel on the Sabbath. But John was not orthodox, and the apostle knew the time had come to attempt escape. The men of his domain, for the most part, would follow his example. He made it clear, however, that their decisions must be their own, that he did not speak to them for God. Surprisingly, a number decided to stay on.

Polycarp lingered near the door, watching as John filled a small satchel. A few crusts of bread and a small flagon of water were the only possessions the apostle would attempt to smuggle out. The young Zealot shook his head at what he considered the absurdity of John's decision, but the aging pastor did not respond. Taking Mary by the hand, John led her forth.

"Sir, do you really mean to go through with this?" Polycarp asked.

"The Lord willing," was his only answer.

Those of the household who would remain, and those who would make their own attempts to flee, stood together as their beloved master turned for one last look. "The Lord be with you, and keep you," he said gently. "The Lord make his face to shine upon you . . . and give you peace."

Tears were evident throughout the group, and as John spoke these words, grown men began to weep. "The Lord be with you . . . " they echoed.

John knew very well that he would not see a face among this flock ever again. He could say nothing more, but stepped back into the court a final moment. Lord God, he implored, why must it end thus?

As the believers gazed on their beloved leader, some considered that he had never looked so old, so time-worn. Was it truly God's will that he leave them? John opened his arms, and en masse they rushed to him, embracing and kissing him sadly.

"Little children, remember the Lord," John cried, his voice breaking with his feelings. Then, turning quickly, he took Mary by the hand and stepped through the door of the house of Zebedee for the last time.

The onslaught of Rome had been in progress for five months, though it could hardly be called an onslaught anymore. Titus and his forces had so devastated the population, it seemed all they did now was pick at their prey like vultures, occasionally swooping down upon the carrion as it rotted under their gaze.

In John's wildest imaginings he could never have envisioned what lay outside the house. He had glimpsed it from the roof on occasion, but being down on the street was a different matter. He and Mary could barely make their way through the corpse-laden corridors of town. Huge stacks of bloated flesh, black and festering, greeted their eyes and filled their nostrils with the stench of death.

Mary hid her face in her mantle, covering her nose and peering only at the street directly beneath her feet. Nevertheless, she could not avoid looking. The dead were too numerous, and she was obliged to walk directly over them from time to time. John held her close, but it took all his strength to contain his own stomach.

When rushing feet were heard behind them, they started fearfully. Wheeling about, however, the apostle sighed with relief. "Master," a young voice called, "if you must be a fool, let me be one with you!"

It was Polycarp. Seeing, now, no reason to remain behind, and belatedly realizing his need for John, he had decided to join him.

"Praise the Lord!" the apostle returned, reaching forth his hands. Polycarp grasped them ardently, and John suddenly recalled how it had felt to be a lonely, seeking boy. Embracing the Zealot warmly, he whispered, "How you remind me of myself when I was young!"

Chapter 36

Because there was no burial site within the Holy City, and because the Jews could not go beyond the gates to properly inter the dead, street crews disposed of the corpses in the most convenient way possible: they simply threw them over the walls. Already a hundred thousand had been removed in this manner.

It was an irony of the times that this macabre but necessary activity would facilitate John's exit from Jerusalem.

As he and his party came near one of the city gates, it was Polycarp who first spotted an opening. A small "needle's eye," a low passageway barely large enough for a single human being to use at one time, was situated alongside the great door. Created to allow entrance and exit when the gates were closed, but to disallow passage of large beasts and unwanted vehicles, it offered an attractive possibility for escape.

Until now, Titus had kept such places heavily guarded, but, for some reason, his forces had been drawn to another part of the metropolis. The only obstacle was a mammoth pile of cadavers, left from the desperate skirmishes played out upon these walls. Even now, however, self-appointed cleaning crews were busy dismantling the hill, passing body after body over the great stone divide.

Gradually the small doorway became more visible, until John, Mary, and Polycarp were able to draw near. "You are fools to try it!" a stranger called down from the mound of rotting flesh. "Others have tried, and they're in this pile!"

John lifted hesitant eyes to the onlooker, and then turned to

Mary. Encouraging him, she said, "At least out there we have a chance, however small. In here, there is none."

With this the apostle stepped forward, and bowing low, passed under the little arch, Mary and Polycarp close on his heels.

What met their eyes beyond the walls was even less palatable than what they had left behind. Another bank of carnage blocked their view to the Judean countryside, but in a sense they were grateful for this. If they kept well against the wall, it appeared they could travel halfway around the city behind the gruesome barricade, before they would have to make a run through more open spaces.

As they approached the corner of the wall toward which they had been traveling, it was with great trepidation. They knew their cover would now be gone, that they would be forced to take their chances across the Mount Olivet plain.

John listened carefully for sounds of the enemy. He did not question the fact that the fields were very quiet today, that Titus had taken his revenge to another sector of the city. Nevertheless, he was cautious, finding it difficult to believe the conqueror would have left any zone unoccupied.

Soon his intuition was confirmed. Rude, angry laughter ascended from the other side of the barrier. The sound of the voices was strange to his ears. The pronunciations were not purely Roman in character, though he could from time to time make out that distinct dialect.

Peering carefully around a grotesque slope of carrion, he caught his breath sharply. Several soldiers, Roman and Syrian, were hunched over the body of a dead Jew, no doubt freshly killed, for his flesh was still pink. Immediately John realized that this unfortunate had risked what he was attempting—escape.

Apparently having fled the city with coins in his mouth, upon capture, he had swallowed them rather than surrender them to the guards. Resenting his action, the pagan captors had nonetheless viewed it as no more than an inconvenience, and upon taking the man's life had proceeded to cut him open like a sack of grain. Now, before John's horrified gaze, they laughed together uproariously, extricating the gold pieces from the gullet of their prey.

Until this moment, John had contained himself admirably. But, though he tore his eyes from the hideous spectacle, it flooded him with waves of nausea.

"Lord, no . . ." he whispered faintly, the effect of months and years of war suddenly sweeping over him in sickening heaves.

Bending low, his stomach painfully constricted, he could only hope the feeling would pass.

At last, weak and shaking, he returned to his waiting charges.

"What is it?" they asked, seeing his whitened face.

"Nothing," he returned. "We will do well. The guards are busy."

John did not know how they accomplished it, but for the grace of God. Somehow they had attained the summit of the Mount of Olives. Mary, weak with fear and weariness, asked to rest, and the apostle felt they could now dare to do so. The three rag-clad refugees sat huddled together under the sunset sky.

John had often meditated here during his years of ministry in the city, but scarcely would he have believed that the site below was the same lovely valley he had known. Today it was scarred by the ravages of war, strewn foot by foot with the remnants of death and decay.

The crosses of Titus still stood as grim testimonies to the power of Rome. Their lifeless victims, having been left hanging for months, even now stared through empty sockets across the bloody fields, their mouths gaping idiotically.

John recalled another time when he had sat upon a mountain. The Master had given his first sermon to the apostles on a slope above the Galilee Sea, after naming the twelve. "Love your enemies," he had said. "Bless those who curse you, do good to those who hate you, and pray for those who use you despitefully, and persecute you."

John was not yet capable of such a thing. "You have brought me a long way," he spoke silently with his Lord, "but I have not yet come to that . . ."

As they watched the evening sun dip behind the horizon, a new light filled their eyes. Flames were leaping from the Holy Mount, the region of the mighty Temple of Jerusalem. Fresh cries of terror filled the sky above the city. Titus had struck the final blow to the culture and nation of Israel. The Temple was falling.

Polycarp drew near John and sat in silence. They watched for a long time together, saying nothing, tears streaming down their faces. At last the young Zealot turned to his aging friend. "This is what you spoke of, master."

"It is the fulfillment of my Lord's prophecy."

"But why must it be?" the young one trembled.

"Because they have rejected their Messiah," he returned.

Polycarp did not doubt any longer. Sorrowfully he observed the death throes of the city for which he would have given his life, and he asked, "Must it remain so forever?"

"I only know what my Lord said," John answered. And from rote he recited the words which had been burned upon the table of his memory.

" 'O Jerusalem, Jerusalem, you that kill the prophets, and stone those who are sent to you . . . how often would I have gathered your children together, even as a hen gathers her chickens under her wings . . . and you would not! Behold, your house is left desolate. For I say unto you, you will not see me again till you shall say, Blessed is he that comes in the name of the Lord.' "

VI

THE GLORY

*And the world passeth away, and
the lust thereof: but he that doeth the
will of God abideth for ever.*
1 JOHN 2:17

Chapter 1

The years since the fall of Jerusalem had been mercifully good to John. The apostles, who had gone to be with the Master before him, were being rewarded for their suffering with the riches of the Father's Kingdom. In other ways, John, who had endured years of loneliness and despair, was being recompensed for his pain.

Upon leaving Jerusalem, the problem of where to reside had been paramount. With the advent of Titus, no place in Palestine would be safe for Jew or Jewish Christian. So Nazareth, Mary's home, and Capernaum, John's native town, were closed to the three refugees. John had considered Antioch, where the church had thrived since Paul's ministry. But it lay in the Syrian province, which had allied with Rome in the destruction of Israel, and it would, therefore, be no safer than Palestine.

One more capital of the Christian movement lay in the northern province of Asia Minor. Fronting the Cayster River, Ephesus, chief city of the region, was a likely refuge for the only remaining apostle of Jesus Christ. Though the metropolis was one of the empire's politically strategic centers, the church there, which had also been founded by Paul, was one of the strongest in the realm. And John had heard often of the desire of its bishop, Timothy, that someone assist him in the ministry.

So it was that the apostle came to dwell in that distant port. He sat today in the doorway of the house which the church had generously provided him and Mary upon their arrival years before. Situated up the hill from the spacious harbor of Ephesus, it provided a good view of the streets and shops below.

This was a wealthy city, as evidenced by its cleanliness and perpetual activity. Its location brought continual trade from inland regions. The envy of many nations, it had been governed by a number of conquerors in its past.

When Paul had first arrived in the city about 26 years before, one of its principal sources of revenue lay in the sale of figures and shrines of the fertility goddess, Diana of Asia. Her Ephesian temple, four times the size of Athens' Parthenon, had been designated one of the world's seven wonders, and her priestesses performed as temple prostitutes.

It might have appeared a wonder in itself that the Christian movement had so thrived in such a setting. But credit for that lay primarily with the work of John's predecessor, Paul.

At the outset, most of his converts had been Jews, of whom there were many in Ephesus. But when his influence spread, persuading vast numbers of Gentiles to follow Christ, the city's economy suffered severely. The souvenir trade, relying as it did on the popularity of Diana, was now in jeopardy. When the idol-makers found that there were fewer and fewer Ephesians patronizing their shops, they rose in fury against the apostle and his followers. Paul's life had been spared, but the desire for his blood was not easily requited.

The idol-makers were not his only enemies. He had set himself at variance with Ephesian astrologers and gnostic philosophers. When members of those groups turned to Christianity, Paul had them publicly burn their books. One bonfire sent scrolls, valuing a total of 50,000 silver pieces, blazing into nonexistence.

By the time John arrived in Ephesus, he found a magnificent congregation awaiting him there, as well as up the coast at Smyrna and Pergamos, and inland at Thyatira, Sardis, Philadelphia, and Laodicea. His joy in serving these healthy, growing assemblies recalled the excitement and hope he had felt during the first years of the Jerusalem church—before Claudius and Nero had replaced hope with death and fear.

Worldwide, Christianity was now generally free of persecution. Vespasian and his son Titus, who had succeeded him to the throne, had been merciless in war, virtually destroying Judaism as John had known it. But they proved themselves compassionate and honorable emperors.

This, added to the blessing of new friends and followers, was a refreshment to John. Polycarp, persuaded by the constant witness of the apostle's life, had now come to belief in Christ, and now served as a key leader in the Asian church. With him, another young man had become especially close to John, a certain Papias. Of course, one of the apostle's staunchest comrades was the Ephesian bishop, Paul's convert and loyal disciple, Timothy.

One of John's lifelong desires—to travel—was also, at last, being granted. As adopted father of Paul's Asian churches, he was often called upon to minister throughout the province. And so his days were full, every bit as demanding as his years in Jerusalem. Only a few things marred these days with sorrier notes.

Often he thought of his homeland and its destruction. Never could he erase from his memory the sight of the Temple in flames, or the sound of the people's cries as Jerusalem was demolished. He had heard that the Zealots who remained when Titus assaulted the Holy Mount, had fought to the bitter end. Seeing the futility of their efforts, many had killed their fellow soldiers, and had then taken their own lives by the sword, or had leaped headlong into the incinerating building. It had been a matter of pride to expire on holy ground rather than at the hand of Rome.

One estimation said that nearly one million two hundred thousand Jews were massacred in Titus' siege of Jerusalem and in ensuing conflicts. Nearly one hundred thousand had been sold into slavery, and great numbers of these were subjected to death in gladiatorial arenas of the empire.

Indeed Judea could hardly be called a Jewish nation any longer, so few of that race survived in the region. Hunger was the lot of those who remained, and the dues once paid in worship to Jehovah, were now required for Caesar's heathen temple.

The priesthood was extinct, the Sanhedrin and the Sadducees nonexistent. With no Temple, no sacrifices, no land to call its own, Judaism would never regain itself. Countryless, helpless, the people were to content themselves with rabbis and scattered synagogues. Vast multitudes who had fled Palestine would be forced to endure the hatred and misunderstanding of Gentiles who had no appreciation for their way of life, their beliefs, their peculiar clothing, kosher foods, or circumcision.

Jews grew terribly poor, or due to their native drive, intellect, and instinct for financial affairs, often became fabulously wealthy. Either condition was scorned by their countless critics. And so, driven into their own exclusive society, they became even more despised and persecuted by the outside world. Their idolatrous neighbors may have traded with them, borrowed from them, and envied them, but they did not love them. The great nation of Israel, which had spread into every corner of the empire—Jehovah's chosen people—became the despised of humanity.

Since Titus had triumphantly entered Rome—displaying his Judean trophies, his multitude of captives and their displaced possessions, in a procession reminiscent of Alexander the Great—Israel had tried to rebuild itself. To a degree it had succeeded. Palestine was coming to its feet like the Phoenix which rose from its own ashes. But it would not be restored in John's lifetime. And the apostle, being a Jew from the beginning, ached for the well-being of his countrymen. They did have hope, but sadly it was the same hope they had nurtured for centuries, since the days of Abraham: hope for their Messiah—a Messiah who had already come and gone, and whom they themselves had driven blindly from them.

Another sorrow for John had occurred the third year of his Ephesian ministry. Mary, the Lord's mother, had slipped quietly from this life into her Son's Kingdom. John had found her lying still upon her bed late one morning. Since it was unlike the active woman to sleep past dawn, John began calling for her. Tiptoeing to her bed, he had bent to rouse her, but she had not responded. Her peaceful countenance and gentle smile told that her passing had been merciful, that Jesus, himself, had led her forth.

Perhaps because John had known such intimate kinship with his Lord, one of his greatest sorrows during these years had been the gnostic heresy, which Paul had never completely crushed, and which, in this capital of philosophy, was flourishing dangerously, even in Christian circles.

Gnosticism was not new to the world. Elements of it could be traced back to the Babylonians, Persians, Egyptians, Greeks, and even to certain sects of Judaism. Depending on the locale in which it grew, it could be generally mystical, occult, or intellectual.

Whatever their orientation, all gnostics held certain views in common: that the material universe was essentially evil, and the spiritual essentially good; that man has been imprisoned in the material world and seeks to return to the spiritual; that the creator-god of the material world was not the highest and best being, but that somewhere, in the spiritual realm, the Good God existed; that salvation for man lay in freedom from the material world and its hierarchy of authorities and the spirits which govern the planets. Salvation would come, they believed, when one grasped "knowledge," an ethereal wisdom which was available only to an enlightened few, and which would transport them into the kingdom of truth and spiritual reality.

Gnosticism would not have posed such problems for the church had it not seemed to be supported by certain elements in Christian doctrine. Gnostics were expert at borrowing what they could from others and amalgamating these facets into their own preconceived system. Christ became for them the revelation of the high, Good God. Since he was divine, however, they reasoned that he could not have come in human form, but had appeared as some sort of ghostlike apparition; or, at the very least, he had taken only a fleeting abode in the human body of Jesus, by what only appeared to be physical "birth." The God of the Jews was of course the creator of the material universe, and was therefore inferior to the real God, of whom Christ had spoken. And of course, Christ could not have died, since he had never had a physical body, nor would the resurrection have been necessary or real. Salvation, being reserved for the "knowledgeable," had not been given to those Christians who denied these teachings.

Gnosticism, to John's consternation, had infiltrated the thinking of some of the church's greatest intellects. How it would have grieved Mary of Nazareth had she lived to see the growth of the gnostic perversion! John marveled at God's mercy in taking her when he did.

Today, as John sat in the doorway, a breeze off the harbor ruffled a sheet of parchment which he had spread across his lap. Through the years he had found it necessary to debate with Christian leaders and with heretics concerning gnostic beliefs. But debate did not seem to settle the matter. Though Paul, in his own writings, had attempted to refute the perverted doctrines, the philosophers would often use that great apostle's words to support their own theories. Had he not spoken of the weakness of the flesh and the strength of the spirit? Had he not represented Christ as the overcomer of "the rulers of the darkness of this world," and of "spiritual wickedness in high places"?

It did no good for John to respond with Paul's teachings on the crucifixion and resurrection of the Lord, or with his words concerning the redemption and forgiveness of sins which was available, as Paul had said, "through his blood."

Daily the heresy was spreading through the church, destroying the very foundations of faith. Repeatedly, John's disciples and

Timothy had suggested he put his refutations into writing, so that the church would have tangible record of the truth.

John stared at the blank parchment as he had off and on for many days, not knowing where to begin, what to say. There was so much to relate. He had so many memories of his Lord, but when he sought to record them, he froze with the scope of it all.

"Did not Matthew, John Mark, and Luke already record such things?" he would argue when Polycarp or the others questioned him. "What need is there of yet another Gospel? And," he would sigh, "Jesus did so many things! If they were all written, I suppose that even the world itself could not contain the books!"

The young men would smile appreciatively, but would then answer, "Matthew, Mark, and Luke were not confronted with the gnostics as we have been. They did not deal with that problem."

"And besides," Timothy would spur him, "who will remain when you go from us, sir, to tell us what it was like to be with Jesus . . . to be the disciple Jesus loved?"

Chapter 2

Well toward evening John sat on the front steps of his home, contemplating what he would say in his book. He knew the young men were correct. A fourth Gospel must be written. The church must be healed, and if his story would help heal it, he would write.

All his protests against the venture had really arisen from a feeling of inadequacy. True, he was an apostle of Christ; perhaps, he conceded, even the most intimate of his followers. But he was still a Galilean, not educated in the more intellectual schools of Jerusalem or Judea. He had been a fisherman, unlike Luke—a physician; or Matthew—a trained revenuer. Though the son of a Pharisee, he could not claim great proficiency in theological studies, and though a capable student, his skills in exposition and logic had lain dormant too many years.

The aging friend of Jesus looked silently across the harbor waters to the coral sunset of the western sky. Memories of Capernaum and the Galilee Sea returned, and with them, memories of his times with the Master.

He smiled, yet doubts still hounded him. "You said and did so many wonderful things, Lord," he sighed. "How can I recall them all, and which should I relate?"

A sea bird flew up in an arc from the bay, toward the red ball of sun. John was filled with awe. "It is not your book, friend," his Lord whispered. "It will be my book. I will give you the words. I will refute the enemies of the church with my own wisdom, just as I refuted the Pharisees and the scribes."

Suddenly, John was liberated. Freedom swept through him and, as he raised his pen to begin, words spilled forth as though from the hand of Another, gloriously dispelling the lies and the myths:

"In the beginning was the Word, and the Word was with God, and the Word was God. The same was in the beginning with God. All things were made by him; and without him was not any thing made that was made. In him was life; and the life was the light of men; and the light shone in darkness; and the darkness comprehended it not. . . . That was the true Light, which lights every man that comes into the world. He was in the world, and the world was made by him, and the world knew him not. He came unto his own, and his own received him not. But as many as received him, to them he gave power to become the sons of God, even to those that believe on his name: which were born, not of blood, nor of the will of the flesh, nor of the will of man, but of God.

"And the Word was made *flesh*, and dwelt among us (and we beheld his glory, the glory as of the only begotten of the Father), full of grace and truth!"

Chapter 3

John's Gospel would not be completed in a creative flurry. It would be finished over a period of years, as he was led to deal with a multitude of issues that came to disrupt the church. Of course, his writings would effectively combat the gnostics.

John reminded his people that the Lord had called himself the "light" of the world, "the way, the truth, the life," and the "word" of the Father, and thus he used the heretics' favorite mystical terms to confound their own purposes. The apostle made it clear that Christ had come in the "flesh," that salvation was through belief in him, and not through the ethereal enlightenment so cherished by the gnostics.

With reference to their concept of the High God, John would emphasize, in a later writing, Jesus' supremacy, saying, "This is the true God, and eternal life." As such, he had, indeed, created the material world, John's Gospel proclaiming that "All things were made by him, and without him was not anything made that was made." Jesus, John insisted, had been crucified and had risen from the dead. The apostle declared that he himself was witness of these things.

But in Ephesus and elsewhere throughout the empire, wherever Christians gathered, a variety of problems would manifest themselves.

Just today John and Polycarp had arrived at Smyrna, about forty miles northwest of Ephesus, where a congregation was being torn by internal strife. John, though having a good many years behind him, still thrived on travel, and entered the meeting place surprisingly unwearied by the journey up the coast.

As he walked down the aisle of the assembly, he was greeted affectionately and enthusiastically by most of his flock, though antagonists were scattered among them. Polycarp, knowing better than to lead his master to a place of particular honor before a crowd, did as John would have insisted and found him a seat close to the people. The apostle would speak with them as with friends, or as though they were his children, in intimate, eye-to-eye conversation. He would not be elevated upon some platform before them.

The church body had been full of busy talk before John arrived, but as he took his place, even the dissenters and the rabble-rousers grew quiet out of respect for his position.

The aging gentleman sat silently for a while looking at his people. His sharp, clear eyes defied his years, though his hair, which seniority now allowed to grow to his shoulders, and his beard, which now reached patriarchally to his chest, were streaked more with silver than with gold.

He studied the faces before him a long time, reading a volume of need and confusion. Contentions had sprung up due to the varied backgrounds represented here. Jews were mixed with Gentiles, educated with uneducated, literate with illiterate. There were those dangerously close to heresy and idolatry, and those who remained loyal to the faith, but who considered themselves superior for so doing.

Due to conflicting teachings, there was confusion as to the way of salvation. And there were those who had carried gnosticism so far as to claim there was no material world, and therefore no evil or *sin*.

Carefully, John began to speak words which would eventually find their way into his Gospel and his letters to the churches. His time- and work-worn hands were full of motion when emphasis was necessary, but otherwise lay peacefully in his lap.

He began with the doctrine of salvation, telling the story of Nicodemus, and reminding them that, in Jesus' words, "God so loved the world, that he gave his only begotten Son, that whoever believes in him should not perish, but have everlasting life."

Confronting those who claimed there was no such thing as sin, he continued: "If we say that we have no sin, we deceive ourselves, and the truth is not in us. If we confess our sins, he is faithful and just to forgive us our sins, and to cleanse us from all unrighteousness."

Then with fatherly reassurance, he declared, "This is the record, that God has given to us eternal life, and this life is in his Son. He that has the Son has life, and he that has not the Son of God has not life. The blood of Jesus Christ, God's Son, cleanses us from all sin!"

For the Jews in the gathering, who had been persecuted by their own kin for belief in Christ, he related the story of Sister Rebecca at the Sychar well. "The woman said to Jesus, 'I know that the Messiah comes, which is called Christ: when he comes, he will tell us all things.' Jesus said to her, 'I, the one speaking to you, am he.'"

To those Jews who still depended upon old traditions for their righteousness, he firmly declared, ". . . the Law was given by Moses, but grace and truth came by Jesus Christ."

And for those of the flock who were tempted by the paganism of their day, he pleaded, "Little children, keep yourselves from idols."

Several hours he spoke with them, patiently answering their questions, reminding them of the hope of the coming Kingdom, and tenderly assuring their hearts concerning the faith. But he was still a Son of Thunder, as well as an apostle of peace. To those who challenged him with heresy and lies, he asserted, "Whoever transgresses, and does not abide in the doctrine of Christ, does not have God! Every spirit that does not confess that Jesus Christ has come in the flesh is not of God! If any one comes to you, and does not bring this doctrine, do not receive him into your house, or bid him Godspeed!"

As the evening drew on, the aging pastor grew weary. The assembly, having benefited from his teachings, watched sadly as he stood to leave. Gazing about the room, he questioned whether the truth had healed their wounds of discord and strife. "This is the message that you have heard from the beginning," he concluded, "that we should love one another, for love is of God, and every one that loves is born of God, and knows God. God is love."

Polycarp stood to go with the apostle from the meeting hall, the evening sky marking the end of day. But, as he always did upon leaving a congregation, John turned with one last admonition:

"Little children, love one another."

Chapter 4

In a society such as the Roman Empire, decent government could be guaranteed only as long as the Emperor remained decent.

For five years after the untimely death of Titus, his brother, Domitian, was a capable and generous ruler. But in 86 A.D., when a provincial governor set about to wrest the throne, all that changed.

Overnight Domitian became a tyrant, merciless and grasping. Winning the army to his cause, he quickly demoralized the Senate and established himself as dictator.

Proclaiming himself divine, he erected idols to his worship across the empire, and enforced a new priesthood to regulate such worship. As he sat enthroned within his receiving hall, those who entered were encouraged to embrace his knees, and to praise him as "Our Lord and God."

For those who refused to worship him, or who were reported by Domitian's numerous detectives to have crossed him in any way, dire were the consequences.

Many of the ruling class were exiled or put to death. The Cynics, the Stoics, and other scholars were banished from the capital.

But, of course, the most stubborn opposition to emperor worship came from Jews and Christians. And he would reserve for them his hottest revenge.

Fear once again gripped the church throughout the realm. For the first time in over twenty years, since the reign of Nero, Christians were under persecution for their faith.

When Domitian made it clear that no man, aristocrat, philosopher, senator, Christian, Jew, or Gentile was free to choose against the new state religion, emperor worship caught on quickly, the masses supporting it ignorantly but enthusiastically; the upper classes and the educated supporting it out of compulsion.

At last, Christians were among the only remaining dissenters. Accusing them of orgiastic meetings, treason, child sacrifices, and cannibalism, Domitian and his loyalists drew the empire into a mania of hatred against them. Every natural disaster, plague, earthquake, or famine was blamed on the church. And as the hatred grew, so did the multitude of paid spies.

If anyone retained the title of Christian, death was the sentence. They were thrust behind bars, they were stretched upon racks until their bones were pulled from their sockets, they were burned, scourged, broiled, stoned, seared, branded, and torn with scalding pincing irons; they were cast into the arena to be skewered by wild, horned bulls; or, if among the fortunate few, they were allowed to die quickly upon the gallows. Nor could they receive burial; their corpses were ordered left to rot on public display as a lesson to others who would neglect the Emperor's will.

John spent much of his time alone these days. He was gradually becoming weaker with age, a little more bent, his hands and limbs wizened with arthritis, his eyes not as clear as they once had been. It was increasingly difficult for him to travel, and his disciples now took on the task of managing the churches distant from Ephesus. Polycarp had gone to Smyrna as bishop, and Papias, 100 miles east, to Hierapolis. Timothy now lived with John, caring for the aging pastor like a son for a father. But even he was away from home today.

The apostle still had a great ministry, though mostly through his writings and letters to the children of his parishes. This afternoon he was in his quarters, seated with his parchments, working now and then on his Gospel, now and then drafting a note to a persecuted congregation. His greatest joy, if joy were possible under Domitian, lay in the memories he relived as he continually wove details from the Lord's ministry into the narrative of his book.

Such thoughts kept him close to the Master, whom he longed to be with once more. But often he would pass the hours interceding for his distressed people, praying that Rome's tyranny be lifted, and that Jesus would soon return to claim his own.

The heart of the patriarch nearly broke with the weight of it all, knowing that throughout Asia and the Mediterranean world those who looked to him as the elder of their faith were enduring unspeakable misery for the name of Christ. Christians were being torn apart individually and collectively by the pressure of the world. How tempting it was for them to recant, to blaspheme the name of Jesus! "Do not love the world or the things that are in the world," John would write to them. "The world passes away, and the lust of it: but he that does the will of God abides forever!"

Secretly he asked why the will of God must be so hard—why the church must be so sifted, so tried. "This is the victory," he would write, "that overcomes the world, even our faith." But inwardly he questioned if he, himself, had such faith as could endure Domitian's hand.

"Why, Jesus? Why am I left to bear this witness?" he implored. "If anyone must die for your name, why can I not be put to death? I am an old man, Lord, old and past my prime. Why must so many young men and women go before me?"

Already he had lived far beyond a normal span of life for his generation. Sometime, years before, he had made the mistake of relating the incident of Jesus' words to Peter concerning him: "If I choose that he tarry until I come, what is that to you?" And rumor had spread through the Christian world to the effect that John would never die.

How he longed to know such a thing was not true! How often he prayed, as Paul had prayed, that he might soon be "absent from the body" and "present with the Lord."

A soft breeze off the harbor found its way through the window of his apartment, and whispered through the feather quill in his hand. John could not find strength to go on with his writing, but sat sadly studying the page before him. Tears trickled down his face as he contemplated his lot, and the lot of the church. "Take me, Master," he pleaded. "I cannot bear it here without you."

"You have me, John," Jesus communed with him.

"But I long to see you face to face."

"You shall, John."

"But when? When?"

"Not many more days . . . "

"Months? Years? How long, my Lord?"

There would be no immediate answer to that question. "I have many things yet to teach you," was all the Lord would tell him.

"But, Master, what could be more important than being with you where you are?"

"My sheep. They are more important for the moment."

"But I have taught your sheep, my Lord. What more can I say to them?"

"You have spoken to them of love, John, for you have learned much about love."

"Yes, Lord. You have taught me much. I have learned much. I learned to love Matthew, to love the Samaritans, to love the woman at the well, to love Saul . . . I have taught your people love."

"But you have not perfected love in your heart."

John sat stunned, immobile. What more could he learn about love? Who was there he had not learned to accept, to thank Jesus for? And was it necessary that he embrace all of humanity in his heart? Had the other apostles done so perfectly? Of course not!

Frustrated, he stood up from his desk and walked to the window of his room. Passing below was a band of Roman guards, like those he had seen a thousand times in his life—haughty, young and strong, caring for no one but themselves and their empire. "Animals!" he breathed, gripping the windowsill angrily.

Suddenly, with that almost involuntary reaction, light dawned upon him, exposing his festering corner of pride. He had not changed, not really, not completely. Reliving a scene from his young manhood, he recalled a similar evening, when he had stood in the cloisters of the Jerusalem Temple, hurling the same epithet upon a band of troops who traversed beneath his gaze.

"Lord God!" he groaned. "That was a lifetime ago. Can it be I have learned nothing in all that time?"

Instinctively, he knew that anything short of complete commitment to Christ's control was really unworthy of praise or distinction. Yes—he had learned to love some of his enemies. But he had not learned to love the Romans, to love the persecutors of his faith, and his nation. As he had told the Master the night he watched Jerusalem in flames, "You have brought me a long way, but I have not yet come to that . . . "

Stumbling back to his chair, he slumped over his desk helplessly. "Jesus," he rationalized, "I cannot believe I am the only apostle who never mastered such love."

"Would it matter if you were not?"

John thought a moment. "Why do you try me so?" he hedged. "Who am I that you should care so for my development?"

"The mission I have for you requires an instrument fully yielded to my touch," came the answer.

John wiped the tears from his face and sighed deeply. "Lord, I do not know what you speak of. But I do not want to fail you. Master, I want whatever you have for me. I want to know you, as you promised, as no one else will ever know you. But," and again he sighed heavily, "I cannot love these men. I despise them. I have no ability to love them . . ."

With this admission, the room was instantly, marvelously full of peace and quiet, as though Jesus himself had found relief in the words. "Such is the confession I have longed for," he could feel the Master responding. And then, echoes of Jesus' teachings sounded from the past, when the Savior had walked the earth. "Ask, and it shall be given you; seek, and you shall find; knock, and it shall be opened unto you. Except you become as little children, helpless and dependent, you shall not enter the kingdom of heaven. Apart from me you can do nothing."

John thought hard on this. "But, Lord, Peter and James are in your Kingdom. When did they learn such dependency?"

"In the moment of their death."

"But I must learn it while I yet have days ahead?"

"Yes . . ."

"Why, Lord?"

"To receive what I have not given to anyone else. To receive what I have for the churches."

All things were still hazy to the apostle. But at last he submitted. "If such must be the case, I surrender. I will love whomsoever you wish me to love . . . if you will love them through me."

Chapter 5

The streets of Ephesus were wild tonight. It was the annual festival of Diana, the night when her image would be carted from the temple to the stadium. Up and down the thoroughfares, her devout, who had managed to mingle loyalty to the goddess with the new emperor-worship, chanted and sang, drank superfluously, and celebrated the sexual license which her cult inspired. As they ran uproariously through the city, they carried with them idols of Diana and the Emperor, as well as those of numerous other "divinities," but giving prime homage to those of Domitian, for the sake of safety.

John had withdrawn into the upper story of his home, with the disciples who had come to be with him during the affair. Silently the young Christians watched with him from his chamber window, as the mad throng danced behind colorful and hideous masks, swirling and shouting in revelry and abandon.

"When will Timothy join us?" they often questioned. Having gone across town to bear food to a poor family of the congregation, the bishop would have had to pass through the crowds on his way home. But he should have been there hours ago.

As the evening had worn on, and as the folly of the Diana worshipers had increased in the streets, numbers of them had stopped before the house of John, hurling blasphemies and insults at the Christians. "Swine! Traitors!" they would call. "We know you dwell here! Your time is short! Domitian will find you soon enough!"

And then, swearing and cursing exuberantly, they would cast stones against the face of the building and run maniacally away.

At length, John grew very weary. He stepped away from the bright street light and into the seclusion of his room. His friends, young and wakeful, continued the watch, but the apostle slept fitfully.

Rising after only minutes of rest, he implored the disciples to find what news they could regarding Timothy. The sun was about to ascend, and yet the bishop had not been heard from.

Willingly, a number volunteered and went down the steps to the front door—but not before another crew of rowdies had swarmed up to the entry, dragging some great weight behind them. John's aging eyes could not determine the nature of their actions, but he heard them call up to him, "Take a lesson, old man, from what you see!"

Before he could reach the young disciples, the idolaters had fled, and the front door had been opened. From the top of the stairs, John looked in horror at the gift they had brought. Timothy, beaten nearly beyond description, lay unconscious in the doorway, having received the vengeance of Diana and Domitian in return for his love of Christ.

Chapter 6

Two days later, Timothy breathed his last breath of this life and went to partake of life eternal. Broken and empty, John sat on the floor beside his bed. His mind a void of exhaustion and helplessness, he at last rose and faced the disciples who had stood vigil with him since the night of Diana's festival.

The room was very still. Women here and there mourned in whispered sorrow, but fear of the enemy prevented any greater display of emotion.

John said nothing, but walked to the desk where he had spent so many hours over the years. Though he moved slowly and with effort, his old body unused to the rude position of kneeling at Timothy's bedside, his face bore a determined expression. Reaching into the desk, he drew out the large rolled parchment of his Gospel, the labor of love he had done secretly and tenderly for the church. No one but he had ever been privileged to handle it, and, in fact, few of his disciples had even known of the precious manuscript.

Turning to his flock, he looked at Polycarp, who had come from Smyrna upon receiving word of Timothy's condition. "Child," John smiled through weary eyes, "this is the work you and our brother Timothy asked me to do, and which the Lord commissioned me to perform. Guard it and cherish it. Let its words be spread to all the church, for they are the words of Christ."

Polycarp took the priceless parcel gently into his hands, humbled by the great honor of handling such a gift. But another feeling also filled him, concern for why the apostle should be transferring the book to his people at this time.

"Will it not be safer if you are its keeper, master?" he asked.

"I shall not have the power to keep anything much longer," was the reply.

Even then, John knew they came for him. Before their footsteps were heard in the street, he knew. Though no one had told him, he realized that word had reached Domitian of his reputation as a leader of the church, and of his whereabouts. Before anyone else had heard of it, he had known of the command that he be found and taken by force.

Within moments, husky guards were beating upon the door, thrusting it open and ascending the stairs to his quarters.

"John, called the Apostle!" they demanded.

Frightened, speechless, the disciples fell back, Polycarp alone withstanding the soldiers to their faces and stepping defensively in front of his master.

"Son," John spoke quietly behind him, "it is all right. Let the will of Jesus be done." Then, walking forward, the man of God looked his enemies in the eye. "There will be no struggle here," he said. "I alone am Domitian's prey. Leave the children of my house to themselves."

The ruthless guards, for the moment dumbfounded, did not know how to respond to such gentility. But they quickly regained themselves, and grasped John by the shoulders, binding his hands behind his back. Then, looking at the disciples as if to say, "You were only lucky this time," they did not lay hold on them, but passed from the room with their solitary victim.

The disciples moved in terror to the window and watched their beloved pastor as he, bent and old, passed below. Turning only once to capture their faces in his memory, he called, "The love of Jesus keep you!"

Chapter 7

The small ship, which had departed from Ephesus carrying well over 100 prisoners of the Emperor, arrived at Patmos harbor July, 95 A.D. The political captives who stood on deck, linked to one another by heavy iron chains, were of diverse backgrounds, and had been arraigned on a multitude of offenses.

Some were accused of too free thinking, some were of astrological cults, some were the wealthy of Asia who had not willingly surrendered property to the king. John was the only Christian.

Had he been of less prominence in the church, he would have met with sudden death, or at the worst, torture and then release from life. But Domitian's plan for him was not quick extermination. The evil genius of the sovereign would reserve for the world's most famous Christian leader nothing but the keenest cruelty. He would be forced to labor in the marble mines of infamous Patmos Isle, a slow death by deprivation and exhaustion.

As Patmos had appeared on the horizon, John had reflected on its barrenness, its desolation. Jagged and gothic, it leaped from the sea in rocky pinnacles of gray and red, its arid, volcanic shoreline void of life. The tiny speck of earth as it interrupted the Icarian Sea, barely twenty-two square miles of ground, appeared hewn by the hand of a mad sculptor. Three great heaps of lava formed its highest summits, its irregular coastline strewn with white, toothlike spires.

As the ship dropped anchor in the harbor, it was met by the island's Roman officials. Quickly the prisoners were herded cattle-like down the gangplank, and through the registration gates. Strange, John thought, that we must be enrolled. How could any man be expected to escape?

"John, called the Apostle?" the registrar leered at him.

"Yes . . ."

Only a hollow laugh met his acknowledgment as the deputy stamped his papers. And then he was driven brutally forward by the guards.

Within moments, the company was being forced, again, to march on command of its keepers. For the most part the captives bore with their ordeal stoically, but as they reached their destination, John heard several at the head of the group murmur in fear. The company had been brought to the edge of a great chasm, and those toward the front who had viewed the site first, groaned in distress.

John could not immediately perceive the reason for the cries. But as those ahead were led down some great incline, and his turn came to behold the worrisome spectacle, he understood their fears. The prisoners, one and all, were being made to descend into a mammoth quarry, and, to their dismay, they found that they would be joining with hundreds of other captives brought here over the past years.

All the empire had heard of the Patmos slave mines, but no one could have imagined their true horror without firsthand witness. At the very bottom of the gorge, a small huddle of decrepit buildings marked the headquarters of the ancient Roman penal colony which had served the Caesars for generations. Ascending from that point, at various intervals, stood the overseers, most of them brutish and thick-browed by nature, hardened by years of duty on this unwelcome post, and, from their bearing and demeanor, apparently void of all mercy.

Then there were the chain gangs, captives of Rome—some true criminals in their own right, and many, like those with John, the innocent victims of political despotism. The stench of the pit nearly overwhelmed the new prisoners as they were forced to enter. Men who had not bathed in years—their skin hardened by ceaseless exposure, their limbs scarred and healed over countless times, or festering with open wounds where whip and rock had battered them—worked in the mire of their own excrement, never being allowed privacy for any reason.

As John observed all this, his stomach rose in protest. Some in line ahead could not contain their revulsion, but the apostle fought desperately to control himself. He felt as he had only one other time in his life, the day he had come upon the ghoulish soldiers who cut into the dead Jew, seeking his gold. But John, unlike most of his fellow captives, had been hardened to nausea as a lad upon the rocking sea. Turning, he pleaded, "Jesus, be with me . . ."

So this was the destiny Domitian had for him. To work despite his age and frailty, in the maw of Rome's devil island. Love his enemies? How could the Lord ask such a thing? "I am not able!" he would protest.

"But I am . . ." would be the Master's promise.

Chapter 8

The sun beat mercilessly into the rocky canyon, tormenting the men who labored there. This morning, no breeze from off the sea had found its way down the quarry walls to cool the bodies and ease the toil of the unfortunates in the pit. John shielded his eyes and peered above at the solar monarch which ruled the Mediterranean sky. Though winters on Patmos could be harsh, this moment he could scarcely remember a day in the year of his enslavement that the sun had ceased to assert its will, or that a cloud had dared to defy its power.

Twelve months of existence here might have been twelve years, for their pace. John had lost track of the days and weeks early into his imprisonment. The only events which divided time into segments were the rising and setting of the sun, both of which happened so abruptly each day, it seemed there was no dawn or twilight, only white-hot light or pitch-black night. Life had come to mean nothing more, it seemed, than extremes of heat, cold, light, dark, the void of sleep, and the pain of labor. Food, if it could be called such, was taken as one worked, and water was allowed only to *keep* one working. Could hell have been worse? John often wondered.

He had not been out of the pit since the day he had disembarked from the ship. He had almost forgotten there was any world above or beyond this hostile hole. The slaves slept only on crude wooden stretchers which ranged the lower levels of the canyon walls, and they were, at all times, chained together in great gangs about the quarry. Terrible sickness or death—these were the exceptional reasons a man's ankles were to be unfettered.

Of course, many days might pass before the overseers arrived to dismantle a dragging corpse from the iron rings, and an invalid might suffer with any kind of fever indefinitely before being sent to his cot. Even then, it was not for his sake that he was unleashed, but for the sake of the industry. The only other prisoners who might be given a measure of release were young boys and very old men who impeded progress. These were assigned the task of bearing water from the well below to the workers on the walls, or of sprinkling masses of straw along the ground to absorb the bondmen's waste matter.

Though John was the oldest one here, he had not been allowed such privilege. Domitian would rather see the marble trade suffer than allow him a sliver of benefit, and so orders had been sent, upon his capture, that the strictest regimentation must apply to him.

During John's initiation to the mine, he had frequently been assaulted by memories of the wealth of his youth. How was it that after nearly nine decades of life, the son of Zebedee, whose family had been so renowned in Palestine, so affluent and of such position that John had been allowed access to the very palace of the High

Priest—how was it that, now, bent and aged, he had come to nothing on this earth? His feet, which had once worn fine leather, now wallowed in stinking mud, swollen and calloused from iron ankle rings. His back, once accustomed to the finest materials, now bore only a tattered rag. And his body, once cradled nightly on linen sheets—whether in the hold of a ship or within the luxury of private quarters—was now obliged to find rest on a wooden plank. While others ate the food of gods, he was to be satisfied with crusts, and while others enjoyed the company of beauty and wealth, he was destined to suffer with the outcasts of earth.

When such thoughts overswept him, he found his only consolation lay in the realization, or the faith, that beyond himself and his present life lay the realm of the Father's Kingdom and that here and now, within him, that Kingdom existed.

Today John worked near one of the large earth ramps which descended from the island's face into the great pit. He and the young men to his right and left struck at the stony face before them with small iron picks, wrenching hunks of debris from the marble strata and tossing them into barrows which waited below. Some gangs concentrated their efforts against the quarry with massive rock-breaking tools; others hauled and carted huge chunks of the white stone up the sloping ramps. As always, overseeing each assigned task were ape-like wardens, looming with their whips to assure that no man rested.

John had suffered much ill at the hands of these overseers. They all seemed to have a personal vendetta against him, perhaps because he, more than the other slaves, had come to represent the spirit of freedom which their system wanted so to crush. John was weak, arthritic, old, but by the grace of Jesus, the apostle who had seen the reigns of eleven Roman emperors had not withered under Domitian's oppression. Though the guards could not have known the spiritual battle which often raged within John's heart, they did see the fruits of his surrendered life, and they were at a loss to deal with him.

Had such misery been his when he was young, he would have risen up in force against it. But today, when the whip drove itself into his back, when he was thrown face down upon the rocky embankment, his wizened, gnarled, and calloused hands grasping for a steady hold, he did not cry out.

Enraged, the tormentor hoisted his weapon afresh, and sent it crashing against the old man's spine. "Fool, damnable fool!" the accuser hailed him. "Will you live forever? And do you never say a word?"

John struggled to his knees. A fellow prisoner reached to help him, but received the strap for his efforts. When the apostle at last regained himself, the guard spat and demanded, "If your Jesus is truly God, why does he not free you from this life—and from my hand?"

John looked at his arrogant assailant compassionately, his dim, aging eyes gentle at the rebuke. "Friend," he responded, "my body will one day die, but I have life eternal. And, I have chains upon my feet, but my heart is free. Not all Domitian's legions can chain my heart."

Chapter 9

Over the months of his exile, the legend of John's strength of spirit became an example and a witness for Patmos' hundreds of beleaguered captives. In fact, the society of the oppressed within the pit came to look to the weak and bent old saint as a type of hero.

It had started with those closest to him on the chain. As his only strength had lain in communion with his Lord, the men who had worked near him had been the captive audience of his repeated prayers and songs of faith.

He had not intended to minister in this way. He had not thought of Patmos as a place of ministry at all. At first his prayers and his psalms had been spoken in the privacy of his own heart, but as the days had stretched into months, as the labor and torture had become more trying, he had not cared what others thought. He would call out to his Lord. He would pray to him aloud. In moments of joy, derived only from a hope beyond, he would even sing. It had been necessary to do so. It had been his sole salvation.

As a result, his fellow workers had taken keen notice of him. At first he had had his mockers, those who called him mad, who hounded him from the side. But gradually, as they had come to grips with their own hopelessness, they had begun to listen, to lay aside their scoffing long enough to examine his source of strength.

At last, dozens were seeking his counsel as they worked the pit, coming to understand and appreciate what he said of Jesus. Men who otherwise would have lived in physical ease and spiritual death, were coming to true life while in the jaws of bodily despair.

Once more, as under Nero, an attempt to crush the church had been turned to the glory of the Kingdom. For, even in the soil of Patmos, the seed of Christianity found root and grew.

It was about the fifteenth year of Domitian's rule, and John had been on Patmos fifteen months.

A near-winter storm was brewing out to sea this night, but the men would have no shelter. The apostle lay on his rack wrapped in a thin rag, the remnant of the cloak he had worn every day since leaving Ephesus. With each blast of cold air descending into the canyon, he shuddered miserably.

Only restlessly did he find sleep, but just as he attained it, rough hands were laid upon him.

"Shhh!" came a sharp, whispered command. "Say nothing."

John sat up with a jerk, but could not make out who stood over him.

"Old man, keep quiet!" the voice returned, as the hands reached for John's ankle irons. Someone was working the lock with a key! No one could have a key but a guard. The apostle shivered with fear, wondering at the meaning of this.

Suddenly, he was free! For the first time since leaving Ephesus, he was not bound by any cord or chain. But before he could let himself revel in the feeling, he stopped short. No Roman would unfetter him, unless . . . Only the very ill . . . or dead . . . were set free.

"My Lord," he whispered, "has my time come, at last?"

Quickly he was told to stand and follow the guard up the ramp of the pit. Since when does a Roman tell someone to follow? he wondered. Since when does he not drive his captives before him? John did not hesitate, but complied with the order.

The pungent scent of salt air greeted him as he stepped onto the rocky soil of the island's face. With intermittent glimpses of moonlight between quickly moving clouds above, John could see that the one he followed was indeed a guard, young and strong. Still he could not account for his odd behavior, commanding, but strangely gentle.

Straight across the field of stone the soldier marched, his bent subject following silently. They traveled some way up the island, and then cut over an expanse toward the shore. It was difficult for John to match the Roman's strangely hurried pace. At last, he stopped for breath, calling, "Soldier, what is the meaning of this?"

The guard, obviously anxious about the delay, turned and pulled John along. "Hurry, old man!" he muttered.

"I shall not!" John objected, standing his ground. "Not until you explain what lies ahead."

"They have asked me to remove you," the soldier answered impatiently. "You are a disruption to the camp and to the cause of Rome!"

"Because the prisoners have turned to Christ!"

"Yes."

"And what do you intend to do with me? Shall you put me to death at last?"

"Those are not Domitian's orders."

"And what are his orders?" John demanded.

"He has given no orders. I have decided this for myself."

Suddenly John recognized the guard's voice. He was chief of the overseers. Though young in years, he had already distinguished himself in service to Rome, and had therefore attained high rank for his age. He could be ruthless with the prisoners, but John realized it had been some time since this officer had shown inordinate cruelty. In fact, he had seemed occasionally to listen in on discussions with fellow prisoners concerning the things of Jesus.

John did not question him further, but followed quietly as the soldier trudged along the beach and then cut a path up a flanking hill. They came at last to a low cave buried in the side of the mountain, and the guard stopped.

Pointing John to the opening, he said, "Here." And then, almost apologetically, "It is the best I can do."

John, perplexed, bent down and peered into the hole. As his eyes adjusted to the darkness, he crept inside and sat against the wall. "Why have you done this?" he asked.

The guard sighed angrily. "I told you! You are a disruption to the camp. It is best you be removed . . . for the sake of Domitian!"

John was not convinced. Rummaging on the ground nearby he found a pile of clothing and food and a supply of water. "Is this for the sake of Domitian, as well?" he smiled, displaying a woolen robe.

"You ask too many questions!" the guard grumbled, and he turned quickly from him, disappearing into the night.

John crept from the cave and inhaled the fresh sea air. Tears of freedom welled in his eyes. The young man would hear him yet, if he called loudly enough. "The love of Jesus keep you!" he cried.

Chapter 10

Freedom had never tasted so sweet. For days John simply reveled in it. Having the liberty of the island, which, except for the region immediately surrounding the marble pit, was virtually void of inhabitants, he came to know his new home intimately. Under the misery of slavery, he had considered it the most unwelcome, pathetic site on the face of the earth. But with his newfound privileges, he came to marvel at its stark beauty, the openness of the blue-black sea which surrounded it, and the magnificence of its craggy landscape.

From its peaks he was granted the most awesome panoramas. Distantly north, the Samos and Mycales islands peered above the horizon, and southward, the Isle of Leros could be seen. Southwest across the Aegean lay Amorgas, and the volcano of Santorin. Many more specks of earth were gathered to the northwest.

It being now almost winter, storm clouds frequently tumbled toward the apostle's home from the region of the sea, bringing slashing Mediterranean winds and rain. Mighty waves often threatened his cave, but John was not troubled by the weather. So glad was he for the right of motion and decision, that he spent most of his time in the open air, challenging his old muscles with ever more distant hikes and steep inclines.

Often day's end would find him upon some great promontory, watching as the sun settled onto the horizon and was then quickly lost to sight. Never tiring of it, he thrived on the salt breeze, and the strong wind which perpetually battered his face and body. And his companion was the ceaseless rumble of the depths, the "voice as the sound of many waters," reverberating and ricocheting through the black canyons of the hills.

His only sorrow was his loneliness, the same condition which had been his lot so many years.

Countless times he thought on his children and what they might be suffering. He remembered the faces of those he had last glimpsed at Ephesus, and he wept.

With an aching heart he recalled the relationships he had enjoyed in his lifetime, and the inevitable questions haunted him: Why had he been denied permanency in such unions? Why had his friends been stripped from him, one by one?

He thought of James and his courage, of the Baptist's mighty beacon of faith. He remembered, painfully, the dearest friend of his youth, Peter . . . and so many more.

The women in his life came to mind like gentle songs—Salome, Mary the mother of Jesus . . . and Mary of Bethany. To this day, he had not shaken the memory of her face. Though he was old, he was not past feeling, and his heart grieved at the thought of her—longed for the day he would once again stand at her side.

Even more poignantly, though, he remembered the Master. If the stripping away of human ties had been meant to bring John more earnest yearning for his Lord, and more dependence on him, it had served its function well. The desire to see Jesus again, to touch him and hear his voice, had grown with each passing day. Somehow, the old saint sensed his time would not be long.

But still he questioned. "Lord," his old soul cried, "how long before I see the purpose in it all? How long before I understand your ways with me? Before I comprehend the sorrow of my life and the agony of my children?"

Sometimes the guard who had brought him from the pit came to see to his welfare, bringing him fresh food and water. "Is there anything you need, old man?" he would inquire.

Rarely did John have a request.

"I need nothing that my Master's presence would not supply . . ." he would answer.

But today when the soldier appeared, John responded with an unusual petition. "Yes, son, bring me some scrolls of papyrus, a jar of ink, and a quill."

"Papyrus, sir? But, why?"

"As yet the Master has not told me why."

It was the Lord's Day, Sunday, the first of the week, and according to church tradition, believers throughout the world would be gathering for fellowship and the commemoration of the Last Supper. Now that John had some cognizance of time, this, of all days in the week, was most painful. The old exile felt most alone when he remembered all of the good times he had had with his children.

But this dawn he had wakened without sorrow. A keen sense of anticipation gripped him, and he rose hastily. Girding himself with the woolen robe provided by the young guard, and gathering up the new scrolls, the ink, and quill, he left the cave and made his way to the mountain which gave the best view of the sea. This morning was reminiscent of his youth, when he had hiked freely above the Galilee waters. Exultant, he came at last to rest on the great height and stood motionless.

As certainly as a woman senses that the time is short for her to be delivered of child, John knew instinctively that the moment had come to receive what Christ had for the churches. Waiting in the cold haze of dawn, he had twinges of fear, but the Spirit assured him, "You are worthy, John. You are worthy."

As the sun came leaping over the horizon, his heart pounded madly. And in that instant his soul was suddenly charged with spiritual light.

Transported into the very Spirit of God, he heard a voice behind him, as of a trumpet, saying, "I am Alpha and Omega, the first and the last. What you see, write in a book!"

John turned quickly, in terrible fear, to ascertain the source of the unearthly call. And being turned, he saw seven golden candlesticks, and in the midst one "like the Son of Man, clothed with a garment down to the foot, and girt about the breast with a golden girdle."

John trembled. This was Jesus, but not as he had appeared after the resurrection. At the Transfiguration upon Mount Hermon the apostle had witnessed something of the Master's heavenly glory. But now the Lord's hair was like bleached wool, white as snow, and his eyes . . . they were as a flame of fire. His feet shone like fine brass, "as though they burned in a furnace," and his voice was as the sound of many waters, deep and awesome.

Overcome, John fell to the ground, as though dead. But the Master bent down to raise him, his gentle hands compassionate as always.

"Fear not," he spoke tenderly. "I am the first and the last . . . I am he that lives, and was dead; and behold, I am alive for evermore, Amen." Then, piercing John through with his omniscient eyes, he said, "I have the keys of hell and of death. Write the things which you have seen and the things which are and the things which shall be hereafter."

John could not speak. He longed to embrace his Lord, but felt suddenly unworthy, and so stood silent, head bowed, ready for whatever was to come.

As it was revealed, it would alternately fill John with heart-stopping dread, and mind-splitting ecstasy. It would flood his soul with great sorrow and with unspeakable joy. For it would be the story of man's future and God's eternity.

"Unto the angel of the church of Ephesus write," the Lord began, "Fear none of those things which you shall suffer. Behold, the devil shall cast some of you into prison, that you may be tried, and you shall have tribulation ten days. Be faithful unto death, and I will give you a crown of life." Speaking in turn, to each of the seven Asian churches, the Master chastised them for their inconstancy, warned them of retribution, and loved them till the end, saying, "He who overcomes will be clothed in white raiment; and I will not blot his name out of the book of life, but I will confess his name before my Father, and before his angels. He that has an ear, let him hear what the Spirit says unto the churches. As many as I love, I rebuke and chasten. Be zealous therefore, and repent. Behold, I stand at the door and knock. If any man hears my voice, and opens the door, I will come in to him, and will dine with him, and he with me."

John absorbed the voice and the words fearfully. What would his little ones suffer? Was Domitian's fury never to end? Or did the Lord refer to some future persecution?

Having no time to contemplate this, however, he was compelled to look high overhead. "And, behold," he would record, "a door was opened in heaven." "Come up here," a voice called trumpet-like, "and I will show you things which will be in the future."

Immediately, without explanation, John found himself in another realm. He did not even know whether he was in his own body. But whatever the circumstances, he knew he was in the Father's Kingdom, and saw a figure sitting upon a throne.

"And the one who sat appeared like a jasper and a sardius stone," he wrote, "and there was a rainbow around the throne, like an emerald. . . . And out of the throne proceeded lightnings and thunderings and voices. And before the throne was a sea of glass like crystal, and before and about the throne were four beasts full of eyes before and behind . . . and they did not rest day and night, saying, 'Holy, holy, holy, Lord God Almighty, which was, and is, and is to come,' . . . And I saw in the right hand of the one who sat on the throne a book written within and on the backside, sealed with seven seals. And I saw a strong angel proclaiming with a loud voice, 'Who is worthy to open the book, and to loose the seals of it?' And I wept, because no man was found worthy to open and to read the book, or to look on it. And one of the elders said to me, 'Do not weep. Behold, the Lion of the tribe of Judah, the Root of David, has prevailed to open the book, and to loose the seven seals of it'. . . .

"And I beheld, and I heard the voice of many angels around the throne and the beasts and the elders, and the number of them was ten thousand times ten thousand, and thousands of thousands, saying with a loud voice, 'Worthy is the Lamb who was slain to receive power, and riches, and wisdom, and strength, and honor, and glory, and blessing.' And every creature who is in heaven, and on the earth, and under the earth, and those in the sea, and all that are in them, I heard saying, 'Blessing, and honor, and glory, and power, be unto him that sits upon the throne, and unto the Lamb for ever and ever.' "

On the vision would continue, inexplicable and mysterious. As the Lord opened the seals of the book, John would witness further awesome wonders.

Passing before him would be the drama of humanity from his day until the end of time, all portrayed in the most beautiful and vivid allegories. Great armies, going forth "conquering and to conquer," terrible and awesome judgments upon the earth and all its inhabitants—earthquakes, famine and pestilence, thunderings, lightnings and hail, the sea turned to blood, the sun blackened and the moon red as blood. He would see the stars fall from heaven, and every mountain and island moved out of their places, and he would see locusts like mighty horses prepared for battle.

He would see war in heaven, and the infamous dragon, "that old serpent, called the Devil, and Satan," cast out into everlasting torment. And he would see war on earth, the battle of the great day of God Almighty. He would see the destruction of Rome—and ultimately of all who blasphemed the Lord—fire from heaven devouring the enemies of God, and the triumph of good over evil. "Behold," he would hear the Master cry, "I come as a thief. Blessed is he who watches and keeps his garments, lest he walk naked and reveal his shame."

And John saw heaven opened, and a white horse, and the one that sat upon him was called Faithful and True. In righteousness he would judge and make war. His eyes were as fiery flames, and on his head were many crowns. He wore a garment dipped in blood, and was called The Word of God. Armies followed him on white horses, clothed in fine linen, white and clean, and he had on his garment and on his thigh a name written, KING OF KINGS, AND LORD OF LORDS.

There were great voices in heaven, saying, "The kingdoms of this world are become the kingdoms of our Lord, and of his Christ. And he shall reign for ever and ever."

Then John saw a white throne, and the one who sat on it . . . "and I saw the dead, small and great, stand before God. And the books were opened, and another book was opened, which is the Book of Life, and the dead were judged out of those things which were written in the books, according to their works. And the sea gave up the dead who were in it; and death and hell delivered up the dead who were in them, and each was judged according to his work. And death and hell were cast into the lake of fire . . . And whoever was not found written in the Book of Life was cast into the lake of fire."

But along with the spectacle of destruction and vengeance John would see the ultimate glory reserved for God's faithful ones, and his old heart would be filled with joy unspeakable.

As he watched from his unearthly vantage point, he would see a magnificent numberless multitude of all nations, and kindreds, and people, and tongues, standing before the throne, and before the Lamb, clothed in white robes, and having palms in their hands. "Salvation to our God who sits upon the throne and unto the Lamb!" they would cry. And he would be told, "These are the ones who have come out of great tribulation, and have washed their robes, and made them white in the blood of the Lamb. They shall hunger and thirst no more, the sun shall not light on them, nor any heat. For the Lamb who is in the midst of the throne shall feed them, and shall lead them to living fountains of waters, and God shall wipe away all tears from their eyes."

John would see a new heaven and a new earth. "And there shall be no more death," he would write, "neither sorrow, nor crying, neither shall there be any more pain, for the former things are passed away."

"Behold I make all things new," Jesus would tell him. "It is done. I am Alpha and Omega, the beginning and the end. I will give to him that is thirsty, of the fountain of the water of life freely. He that overcomes shall inherit all things, and I will be his God, and he shall be my son."

At last John was taken into a high mountain, and shown a

glorious city, the holy Jerusalem, descending from God. And the city had no need of the sun, nor of the moon, to shine in it, for the glory of God, and of the Lamb, lightened it, and there was no night there. "And nothing shall enter into it," John would write, "that defiles or works abomination, or makes a lie, but those who are written in the Lamb's Book of life . . . and they shall reign for ever and ever!"

Jesus gazed at his servant tenderly, but urgently. "Behold, I come quickly," he said, "and my reward is with me, to give every man according as his work shall be. I am Alpha and Omega, the beginning and the end, the first and the last . . . I am the root and the offspring of David, and the bright and morning star."

Then turning from John, he walked away, into the clouds of glory, looking back but once, and hailing his beloved disciple. "The Spirit and the bride say, Come," he called. "And let him that hears say, Come. And let him that is thirsty come. And whoever will, let him take the water of life freely . . . Surely I come quickly. Amen."

It was the dark of night on Patmos when John again returned to himself. He sat where he had first come that morning, atop the great promontory of the mount. The man who, in his youth, had doubted the validity of visions, was limp with emotion, and remained silent for countless minutes.

Blinking age-dimmed eyes, he looked about him. This was real rock he sat upon; the wind and the sea were real and unchanged. His body, so youthful and vibrant during the revelation, was once again old and bent.

But the prophecy would not leave him. As he gazed at the parchment on which he had transcribed the entirety of the witness, the words stood out in sharp contrast to present life. He did not understand all that he had seen; nevertheless, he knew it was true—that the promised Kingdom would come, if not soon, then in God's good time.

Tears flowed from John's old eyes—eyes which throughout the apocalypse had seen with the clarity of an eagle's. And etched on his memory was the final cameo of Christ, as he had stepped from sight into the clouds of glory.

"Surely, I come quickly . . ." the promise echoed in John's heart.

And he, looking heavenward, whispered brokenly, "Even so, come, Lord Jesus."

Chapter 11

The young guard who had befriended him supported John carefully down the gangplank. So weak with years that he could now only walk with great difficulty, the elder apostle turned his head to glimpse one last time the ship which had first taken him from these shores. On board, masses of ex-prisoners, set free by the death of Domitian and the emergence of a kind and just Caesar, watched silently as their aged hero was returned to Ephesus, after eighteen months of exile.

Multitudes of men who had endured the torment of Patmos alongside him, men who had come to the peace of the Savior through his witness, wept unashamedly at the farewell. "The love of Jesus keep you!" they echoed his familiar phrase.

John raised a feeble hand to hail them Godspeed, as the ship hauled up anchor for other ports of home.

Polycarp ran joyfully to meet his master, enfolding him in the embrace of love fulfilled. Overcome with emotion, John and his dear son in Christ wept openly.

The young soldier turned hesitantly to catch the ship before it left the dock, his eyes also moist, but his were tears of parting. "Take care of him," he called brokenly to John's waiting friends.

"We shall, soldier," Polycarp returned. "God be with you."

The Lord had yet more years of service for his beloved disciple, years which John would spend joyfully, despite his physical limitations. In accordance with the Master's prophecy, John had truly come to know him as no one would ever know him. How much the aged apostle had to share with his children!

Tenderly, he looked at the hundreds who had come to greet him at the dock. Happiness filled his old eyes, and he turned to Polycarp lovingly. "You have done well, my son." He smiled.

"You left me more than a scroll to care for, didn't you, father?" Polycarp nodded.

The warmth of the reunion was too much to contain. "Indeed," John laughed. "But I have yet something else for your charge."

His wizened hands tremulous, he reached beneath his robe for a parcel. The awe he felt whenever he touched the scroll of the Revelation was evident upon his furrowed brow. "Here, son." He passed it carefully to his servant.

"Another Gospel, master?"

"The completion of the Gospel." John smiled.

Polycarp did not understand, but asked no more questions.

With the ensuing years, it became increasingly difficult for John to participate in church events. But his spirit was always with the believers as they met. His Gospel, his letters, and his Revelation had come to be the mainstay of the Christian community throughout the world, and his theme of love the measuring rod of all motive and decision. For the Son of Thunder had truly become the Apostle of Peace, and the Disciple of Love.

He had made it clear, however, that, despite his frailty, he must never miss a Lord's Day meeting. The great Eagle of the Church guarded his fledglings jealously, and he would attend the gatherings even if it meant, as it did eventually, that he must be carried to and fro upon a stretcher.

Because of their affection for the old pastor, the young deacons always allowed him to give a benediction at the close of each assembly.

"Little children, love one another," would be the repeated message.

At length, the young people began to tire of hearing the same words from his mouth. "Master, why do you always say this?" they began to question.

Raising dim eyes to them, eyes which had witnessed more in a lifetime than any man in history had been privileged to see, he answered compassionately, and with the hard-earned wisdom of his years: "Because, it is the Lord's command, and if this alone be done, it is enough . . . "

EPILOG

And many other signs truly did Jesus in the presence of his disciples, which are not written in this book: But these are written, that ye might believe that Jesus is the Christ, the Son of God; and that believing ye might have life through his name.

And there are also many other things which Jesus did, the which, if they should be written every one, I suppose that even the world itself could not contain the books that should be written. Amen.

John 20:30, 31; 21:25

LIVING BOOKS

*Inspirational bestsellers from the people
who brought you* The Living Bible.